# Autodrome

# Kim Lakin-Smith

# Thanks

Firstly, a huge thank you to my agent, Joe Monti, for cleaning off the rust spots and for keeping the faith, to my publisher, Emma Barnes at Snowbooks, for giving Autodrome a wonderful home, and to the talented Tatiana Galitskaya for such a beautiful cover design.

As much as I love a corroded rat rod or renovated woody, *Autodrome* owes its nuts and bolts to four people with a far greater degree of knowhow. Lee Whitmore, thanks for helping me with the detail and for inspiring me, you nutter! Marc Williams aka Walking Encyclopaedia – thanks for an answer to every question and for being a buddy. Ian Guy, artist and imaginer of all things cool – thanks for your amazing paintings which helped me to breathe life into Autodrome. And thanks to Del Lakin-Smith, for riding shotgun with me from start to finish, keeping me fired up even when the words threatened to run dry, and for helping me navigate through life even when the road is dark and the map's unclear.

Finally, to all the hoodlums and hot rodders out there - thanks for letting me gawk at your vehicles, bask in burnout, and dream up new worlds where the petrolhead is king.

Proudly published by Snowbooks
Copyright © 2013 Kim Lakin-Smith
Kim Lakin-Smith asserts the moral right to be identified as the author of this work. All rights reserved.
Snowbooks Ltd | email: emma@snowbooks.com | snowbooks.com.
British Library Cataloguing in Publication Data. A catalogue record for this book is available from the British Library.
ISBN13 9781909679047 paperback
9781907777837 hardback

First published 2013

For Del
My Speed Demon

# Chapter 1

7.30am, Showdown Saturday. One hour before the citizens of Autodrome got their streets back and were free to go about their lives again. The newly risen sun was already heating up the place.

Armed with bottled water and gas-flash cameras, fans crowded the sidewalk. Uniform officers prowled the far side of steel barriers temporarily erected to keep the hordes safe – or was it to keep them contained? One boy hooked a leg over the barrier and was in the process of clambering over to get a closer look at the finalists' vehicles when a baton lightly touched him. He cried out and fell back. An officer held up his weapon and visibly cranked up the juice in the glowing tip.

Before any crowd members could object, a roar of applause tied their minds back to the race. The finalists were crossing the tarmac, arms raised in salute. One was a girl with long brown hair in a high tail, wearing oiled overalls and tinted aviators that exaggerated the sensual angles of her face. The other was a boy in low slung jeans, belt chains, black t-shirt and a pair of red lensed goggles.

The boy had a swagger to him. He scrubbed a fist over his spiky black hair. The girl seemed less aware of the crowd and walked determinedly over to the first roadster, a two seater without a roof, or side or rear windows. Resting a hand on the rim of the car, she leapt nimbly into the driver seat. The boy slung open the door of his ride and slid in. He popped the headlights as was written into his contract; neon blue gels weakly projected the ANTRAM logo onto the floor. The girl followed suit. Her car's yellow gel headlights projected the MASTERCARD signia.

On cue, feedback emitted from a thin metal obelisk – one of several dotted about the city's road system and which pumped out the latest race stats and scores on an hourly basis. The onlookers cheered as the announcer's voice broke through.

"Welcome to Showdown Saturday on this glorious June morning! School's out, which means its time to see what Autodrome's teen racers are made of. First up, two bright young track talents fight it out for a spot as a Pro Leaguer. In a chopped 1931 Ford roadster that goes by the name of Grey Rat, we have Zar Punkstar, fifteen years old and already an established face at the Death Pit. And in pole position is Raina Jubilique. Also fifteen, Raina learnt from the best, her daddy, Pro Leaguer with wings, Johnny Law."

A reverential hush settled over the crowd. Out on the track, the girl bent her head and marked out the sign of the cross on her forehead and either shoulder.

"Raina drives Candy Stripe, a 1927 Ford roadster in raspberry and cream. Download details of these vehicles' make, model, rebuild and race history from our website, www.proleaguerqualifiers.com, in association with Tyre Universe – your one stop shop for tyres on the hop."

Moulding his spine into the bucket seat of his patched-together rat rod, Zar Punkstar was growing tired of the chit-chat. He pressed in the clutch and twisted the key. The engine spat dust from its throat and coughed out smoky revs. Raina set her roadster running. The engine turned over with a light spit-spit, more even than Grey Rat's which seemed continually on the point of cutting out. Zar knew his rod though. Every gasp of that engine was like an extension of his breath, his heartbeat.

The obelisk projected a holographic start line across the road. Raina trickled forward. Zar moved in to the left. He allowed himself a sideways glance, but Raina sensed his eyes on her. Before Zar could look away, she struck out her tongue and fixed her eyes back on the road.

There wasn't time to retaliate as a rippling green start flag projected into the air in front of the vehicles.

"Good luck kids!" cried the autonomous voice.

The start flag swished down. Zar curled his lip. Mashing the gas peddle, he fired up the rat rod's eight cylinders and shot forward in a scream of burnout, Raina matching him. He worked his way up through the gears in seconds.

With the advantage of a smaller, torpedo shaped body, Raina's roadster nosed out in front. Zar kept his cool. Raina had pole position, which meant she would enter the bends of Fabricator Flyover on the inside. But his rod had a wide wheel base, a roll bar for added safety in the wham-bam arena of the Death Pit, and an extra kilo or two of bodyweight, all of which had its own advantages. In fact, as they sped into the curve that took them over the flyover and down into the Maintenance District, they stayed neck and neck. Crossing over the giant highway called The Artery, Zar saw the factories spread out in front like a vast military base. On either side lay the two faces of the city – west and east, otherwise known as the winners and the losers in the game of Life.

As they hit the straight, Raina gained the advantage. Even when one of the city's huge car carriers pulled out from a factory's gates and took up most of the road, the girl kept her cool and slid neatly around. Zar was less fortunate. With the carrier cutting a wide arc to complete its turn out, he was forced to mount the curb, breathe in as he sped past the colossal vehicle, and steer back onto the road a metre short of a street lamp.

Dead ahead lay the gates to Black Stacks, the largest automobile manufacturer and home to Frank Oz, the city's chief investor. A tremendous iron colossus, like Hell's insides turned inside out, only Black Stacks could boast the power to physically part the seas of the road in Autodrome.

Lost to the dark side of the factory where its shadow swallowed up a half kilometre of its neighbourhood, Zar realised he had opted for the opposite track to Raina. He had no choice but to trust his instincts. *Don't push it*, he told himself, and stayed steady on the gas, his chest as tightly cramped as the warren of streets he was negotiating. With no space for a sidewalk, race fans craned out of the upper storey windows like lunatics out of a burning asylum.

He pulled onto a wider road at the exact instant that Raina's ride purred in alongside. For a couple of blocks, it was a drag race, both cars transformed into jets as blowout streamed off their exhausts. But as they approached an intersection, the lighting rig overhead flashed red.

The two roadsters skidded to a standstill. As if by magic, two pit crews gathered about the cars and set about changing tyres, cleaning windscreens and refuelling from gas pump packs strapped across their backs, hose trailed over a shoulder.

Zar risked a sideways glance again.

"Anyone would think you were following me, Raina Jubilique," he called.

Both engines idled begrudgingly.

Raina smiled. "Funny that. Could've sworn you've been my shadow the whole way so far. Who's following who, Zar Punkstar?"

He gave a begrudging half-smile. Noticing how pretty her hands looked on the steering wheel, he was beaten to the punch again as the lights went from amber to green, the pitch crew falling back to the sidewalk with lightning speed.

Raina crushed her loud pedal. Zar's reflex was out by a millisecond. The girl's roadster put a car's length between them.

They hammered it into Meat Market. Fans of the race circuit gave way to beggars, hawkers, painted ladies, snake charmers and pill pushers – the whole colourful bizarre which made up Autodrome's red light district. A billboard squatted on a rooftop, the same advertisement papered all across the city. 'Race Fast. Win Big!' it declared alongside the image of a grinning teenage boy with a Pro Leaguer trophy in one hand and fanned out dollar notes in the other.

Zar's ride rattled fiercely as he increased his speed. Raina's roadster was a restoration job boasting a neat paintjob. A steam-cleaned V8 engine hidden under the hood as well, he suspected. In contrast, he drove a rat rod with rusted panel-work, steel wheels and exposed engine guts taking up the front half of the chassis. He could fit right into Meat Market, what with his Frankenstein vehicle, his absentee father and his addict mother. But didn't Raina belong on the right side of the tracks?

Apparently not he realised with a jolt as the mayhem gave way to a quieter zipcode. These streets were crisscrossed with metal lanterns and home to a hotchpotch of housing pods painted in desert shades. The Hispanic quarter appeared to recognise Raina as a sister and breathe in to accommodate her. He clipped a curb, the cab of his rod ricocheting with the impact. A hubcap whirled off onto the sidewalk, a shiny new coin set spinning. Perhaps the token was payment enough. The road broadened, and they were on the fast tarmac strips of the test tracks and heading into the Maintenance District. Passing the lockup alleys, row on row of garages, and the steel and iron melting pot of the Scrap Yard, he felt a wave of hurt. This was his father's stomping ground.

The pain refocused him. He would not lose today, not to Raina Jubilique, not to anyone. Double-clutching, he drove the stick into a lower gear and shot a burst of gas through the engine. The added weight of his vehicle gave him the advantage and he powered ahead of Rain as they curved around the colossal Dixie Island.

"Come on!" he whooped.

With Raina at his heels, he levelled out and cut left onto the colossal 18 lane highway, the Artery. The highway was exceeded only in breadth by the strait called Lady Luck Lough on the far side of the city.

This was where the real games began. While the race fraternity could cordon off sections of downtown, the Artery was too significant a trade route with the world beyond the city to close down. Instead Zar and Raina played cat and mouse between the dense flow of traffic. Horns blasted and wheels shrieked as the two competitors zigzagged in-between.

Raking the steering wheel side-to-side, Zar slipped between juggernauts, trikes, buses, saloon cars, motorbikes, and every type of automobile imaginable – and Raina matched him. Zar glanced back to see her lose a wing mirror when a Dodge Ram truck attempted to shunt her. Raina was having none of that. A flick on the steering and she slotted her roadster into a micro gap behind Zar. In return, he opted to ride the hard shoulder.

It didn't take Raina long to cotton on. She settled in behind him for the next three kilometres, Zar finding a cruise rhythm at 180 on the dial.

Speeding along the fat vein of tarmac circumnavigating the city, Zar knew how wondrous the sight of Autodrome must be to newcomers – also how terrifying since it presented a clear fault line. To his left, the suburbs of the west were laid out on a clean grid system, the generously proportioned housing pods spit-shined and buffered by the power of money. To his right was the east and upper east-side, where the city seemed aged beyond its fifty year existence. The east was home to the city's poor, who also happened to be the good proportion of Autodrome's work force. Housing pods burgeoned like mushrooms. The frames of decrepit buildings fingered the sky like blacked bones. And somewhere out there, amongst the grime, was the street where he lived.

*Existed more like*, Zar thought sourly. He kept his hands steady on the wheel. It was up to him to break free of it. Up to him to earn more than the few bucks at the Death Pit that had enabled him to keep food on the table. Up to him to win.

'Black Stacks' declared a tourist sign to one side of the highway. Zar knew the hologram was his cue to exit. He took the next slip road and hooked a left onto Tourist Trap, Raina glued tight to his heels.

The shutters were going up on the stores. Windows advertised 'Tonka Toys', 'Signed Memorabilia', 'Monogrammed Overalls', 'Bumper Stickers' and every sort of tat. Here, the tourist's dollar extended to the city museum. Glass walls displayed its merchandise like any other auto dealership. Thundering down the strip, the g-force flattening his cheeks like tenderised meat, Zar wondered how many visitors would really want to step into his shoes. For most, a ride in the cars of the ChuckUp Ghost Train would prove wild enough.

But he and the girl at his back, they excelled in Autodrome's gasolined atmosphere. They'd been raised to it. In Autodrome, kids could learn to drive from the age of 10 in extracurricular lessons at school, just like kids outside of the city taking up soccer or cheerleading. Between the ages of 10 and 15, a kid could choose to enter the Underager racing competitions. After that, the most talented were eligible to enter the Qualifiers, risking life and limb for a short lived career as a Pro Leaguer. Money was the main attraction in a city where a teen racer could deliver their family from squalor into a life worth living. But broken limbs, concussions, crushed dreams – they all took their toll on the body. The majority of Pro Leaguer opted to retire in their mid twenties. Those who continued were destined to descend through the league ranks and end up as washed up soaks in the Death Pit. Pro League racing in Autodrome was a young person's game – quite literally.

Raina shunted the rat rod with the nose of her roadster. Lurching forward, Zar found his face millimetres from the steering wheel. Slamming back into his seat, he understood why the years took their toll on Pro Leaguers. Either side of him, the sidewalk was marked with dried-up flower bouquets in honour to racers with wings, namely those who had made the wrong call and lost their lives. At the same time, he understood better than ever before why young men and women sacrificed their safety for the thrill of competing. He'd wanted to go up against Raina Jubilique ever since she'd proven herself a force to be reckoned with out on the test tracks. Passing Black Stacks and the bleary-eyed tourists who turned to hoot and cheer, theirs felt less like a Pro League Qualifier and more like a death race.

A kilometre ahead, he saw the projection of a huge chequered flag indicate the finish line. Fans crowded either side of the street. Their roar was deafening.

Zar was aware of Raina pushing everything she'd got in an effort to overtake. And her roadster definitely had the speed. But every time she tried to hook out and around, he blocked her. With his gaze yo-yoing between the road ahead and the predator at his back, he zipped from one side of the road to the next, pre-guessing Raina's manoeuvres.

The road slipped beneath his wheel like black ribbon. *This is it*, he told himself. *My time to be somebody. My time to matter. My time to shine.* Seconds cracked by, mini explosions in his head. He was across the finish line suddenly, the swish of the chequered flag coming down between him and Raina like the blade of a guillotine.

§

"You did it!"

Zar smiled, tremendously happy to see a friendly face. "Hey Tripster."

A tank chair advanced on wide caterpillar treads. The tall black kid with nappy dreads and a face torn out of a comic book manipulated the sensors in one arm panel to steer. He flashed his pass to a Uniform officer who started in their direction.

"Management," he called as the officer returned his baton to a hip holster and turned away.

Glancing at Zar, Tripster broke out a grin. "That was phenomenal, Punkstar. The girl was on you 'til the last. Sheesh, did you drink your fill of Lady Luck Lough or what?" He pointed to a giant screen projecting onto the side of the nearest skyscraper. A terrestrial channel replayed a bird's eye view of the race, captured by the cameras aboard the station's dirigibles. Straight after, an ad flashed up advertising free test track runs for Underagers.

"Told you to keep it tight on Dixie Island, didn't I?" said Tripster, and he winked knowingly.

Zar nodded and crossed his arms. "You did. What would I do without you and your game plan?"

"You'd loose." Tripster kept up his smile. "But together we crushed it. A rider hasn't hugged that track the way you did since Danny O in 2090. Time of 3 minutes 44, bringing him in as the fourth fastest Underager to qualify Pro. Ahead is Lily Lush. Lily was a stickler for her 1941 Willys Coupe. Pro street tubs..."

Zar pretended to yawn.

"...bear claw latches...yeah, well, we did it," Tripster muttered as Zar was distracted by Raina making her way over to the presentation dais in a nearby square. She was accompanied by a Hispanic girl in heels and frills who fussed at her with a consolatory expression.

Raina's friend positively snarled as Zar and Tripster fell in behind.

"Think we're in there?" shot Tripster over the hum of revolving treads. Zar scrubbed at Tripster's hair, and the pair laughed conspiratorially. It felt good to laugh on such a beautiful golden day as this, to put aside the pain of his home life and just be the kid who won a race for a while.

As Zar approached the dais, the atmosphere seemed to suddenly shift and the crowd quietened. Many bowed their heads. Turning back towards the road, Zar saw a black hearse roll slowly by. Through the long rear window glass, he could see the coffin inside was decorated with graffiti and topped with a skateboard. After the hearse came the mourners' cars, windows blacked as if to seal the reality of loss away from the rest of the world.

Another day in Autodrome, another teen racer's funeral, thought Zar a little numbly since no one forced any kid to race yet they all longed to be the latest track star. To be first across the line. To be a household name. He was no different.

The funeral procession moved on. Zar became aware of the crowd straining at the steel barriers again and chanting his name. He felt his face flushing and tried a wave. It struck him as off kilter that the crowd had quietened in reverence to another of the city's dead only to cheer him on, their soon-to-be sacrifice, before the minute was out.

His hand melted back to his side.

"Don't tell me you're shy?" Tripster looked concerned.

"Nah, just soaking it all in," Zar lied. Waiting to hold his trophy, the noise of the crowd in his ears, he felt emptied out like an oil can. Was this all he was to the citizens of Autodrome – just the latest in a long line of disposable teen racers? Then again, wasn't fame and adoration precisely what he had been aiming for throughout his racing career to date?

He searched the crowd for a face he knew he would never find. Of course his father wasn't there. Sol Punkstar would be holed up in his workshop, tending to his inventions like saplings. There'd be no tearing himself away to witness Zar's greatest achievement on the race circuit to date. No time to indulge in pride, in sentimentality, in family. Tears threatened in Zar's eyes. He refused to give in to them.

But as Raina took her place on the lower pedestal and received her runner up medal, it occurred to Zar that he wasn't the only one with ghosts. Raina would also search the crowd for an absent father. And the girl didn't even have the consolation of victory. Instead, she would have to take the route he had done so many times before and lie in the darkness of her room that evening, evaluating every move she had made out on the track and asking herself which one had cost her the race.

As much as Zar sympathised, he also knew that he'd waited his whole life for that moment. Ever since he had turned ten and got his licence to race, he'd put in more hours on the test tracks than anyone else he knew.

It was his turn to mount the winner's pedestal. An adjudicator presented him with the Pro Leaguer trophy every Underager dreamt of holding – a sky-pointing albatross with gleaming brass wings and a staved oak body.

Raising the trophy, and with it the noise of the crowd, Zar felt his spirit soar. He'd done it! He'd raced a worthy opponent in Raina and still come out on top. In that instant, nothing hurt. There was only possibility and achievement and racing glory.

A length of ticker tape spooled off his Data Streamer watch. Zar heard the small tick-tick of the paper feed. Manoeuvring the trophy under an arm, he ripped off the tape and scanned it. The words printed there weighted him down like lead.

"You okay, Punkstar?" Parked in front of the dais, Tripster stared up at him in earnest.

Zar slipped down off the podium. "It's from my dad. He wants to see me," he said numbly.

Tripster had sense to stay silent.

"Had a eureka moment apparently." Zar dangled the albatross trophy by the neck and stared out at the crowd. All the hurt and all the disappointment came rushing back. "My one day in the sun and the bastard still manages to eclipse me."

§

# Chapter 2

"Red or green soda?"

Condensation flowed over the rim of a large chest cooler.

"Red's fine," said Zar. He heard the tension in his voice and tried desperately to keep his emotions in check.

His father appeared from behind the lid. At 48, Sol Punkstar was worn and preserved by equal measures. He had wild protruding eyes, dusty black hair tied back in a ponytail and a generously proportioned nose that had taken the best part of his life to grow into. Zar owed his height to his father, likewise his love of automobiles. Except while Zar chose to race the machines, Sol was obsessed with their assembly. There had been a time when Sol Punkstar was one of the city's finest architectural engineers, responsible for a good part of Autodrome's unique retro-futuristic skyline. But it was his love for mechanical invention which had consumed him in recent years – like a virus, Zar often thought.

Resting a soda and a beer on the lid of the cooler, Sol took a flat spanner from the utility belt around his waist and cracked both. He kept a grip on the soda bottle as Zar went to take it.

"Are the powerbrokers still out there in the dark?"

Zar couldn't contain his frustration. "Thanks for coming, Zar. Gee, Dad, it's only been six months. I was happy to drop everything the instant you got in touch. Even if it did ruin my crowning moment as a Pro Leaguer.' He rested his trophy on the lid of the cooler. "And no, I didn't notice anything in the dark because it's broad daylight outside."

Sol shrugged off the fact. "It's the light that enables them to watch." Eyes glazing, he tore a hand through his hair and launched into a frantic monologue. "Stupid man. Played your cards too soon. Should've taken up the offer of protection when it was offered. But who to trust even among the Uniform? No matter, what's done is done and there's no access to the blueprint anyway!" His gaze fell on Zar's trophy. "Got yourself one of those beauties at last."

Zar felt the sting of the 'at last' and gritted his teeth. He was used to his father ranting in third person, the result of too much time spent alone in the workshop with only the whir of gears and glug of oil for conversation. But the intonation that he should have been raking in trophies long ago was just too much to bear.

"It's not just about trophies is it, Dad? It's about bringing in money since mum's too high to hold down a job while you..." Zar flapped a hand in his dad's direction. He let it fall and shook his head. There were so many accusations to lay at his father's doorstep, to do with lack of care in every way imaginable. The worse of them stayed unspoken though, leaving him to mutter, "Well, you never have got around to paying maintenance all that often."

Sol tutted. "Money doesn't grow on trees, Zar. One day you'll learn that."

The injustice of his father's assessment of him wounded Zar deeply. Tears pricked at his eyes. "I risk my life every weekend in the Death Pit to keep mum and me afloat."

"And love every minute of it, I've no doubt." Sol shook his head, impatient. "But I don't want to hear childish tales of the Death Pit. You have a Pro Leaguer trophy at last. Just as well. The powerbrokers are more vigilant by the hour and what is the point in putting these mechanisms in place if you aren't going to do your part? But now you have an albatross. It is essential you snap off the beak and..."

"Hang it from the rear view mirror of my hotrod," Zar said, forcing his hurt back beneath his ribs. "I know the tradition."

"Forget track superstitions. Keep it on you. That is paramount...How's your mum?" shot Sol unexpectedly. Perching on a stool, he put out his eclectic blue shoes and rolled back on the metal casters so he could lean against a workbench.

The subject switch left Zar nauseous. He pictured his mother, how she had shone for him in his childhood. She had shone for his father once too, before a handful of pretty pills became Mindy Punkstar's drug of choice. Over the years, Razzledazzle had left its stain on her. Zar too.

He swallowed against the knot in his throat. "She's peachy king," he lied.

"And school?"

"School's out, Dad. It's the summer vacation. Why else would I be racing? We practice term time. We race out of term time. But you don't want to hear about that, I'm sure. The truth of it is that you've invited me here to admire whatever piece of junk you've invented now, then you'll shoo me away for another six months."

His father took a swig of his beer and dragged a hand across his mouth. He sat forward, suddenly intense. "I had to protect the blueprint. I worked on the design over many years and each time I found a new piece, I stored it away." The lucidity did not last. Sol's eyes grew wide. "That way I keep the jigsaw broken – safe from prying eyes. I thank the stars it isn't it in my power to give it to them even if it saved my throat from being slit."

"Dad, you going to show me this latest invention or shall I leave you to get on?" Zar gestured in all directions of the garage. "Looks like you have a lot on your plate without me adding to the clutter."

Sol slammed up out of his seat, the stool shooting back on its casters. "You insist on being flippant when I'm talking about a design of global significance! See beyond yourself, Zar. When the gas stocks ran low, did we all sit around and feel sorry for ourselves? No, we found ways to cross-engineer gas and steam technologies, and one day soon we'll break free of those constraints. Can you even start to comprehend what the powerbrokers are willing to sacrifice for the technology? And they are always there, Zar, no matter how blind you may be to their existence."

Zar stayed silent, aware of the same sense of dripping away he always felt when his father made him feel stupid, or pointless. It had always been the same. Everyone in the city knew that Sol Punkstar had a brilliant mind. Less well known was his inability to cope with the heartbreak of real life over the years, or his abandonment of a young son and a drug addict of a wife. Not that the fact stopped Zar from longing for his father's approval, or being desperately hurt by his inability to earn it.

"The powerbrokers?" he said at last. The weariness he'd seen in his father infected him. He wondered whether to just walk out.

"Representatives of the Rupine Group. There's no point asking if you've heard of them, even if they are one of the world's largest private equity investment firms. Aerospace and defence, energy and power, automotive advances and transportation – they've got their sticky little fingers into everything. Promise me, Zar. If they leave the shadows and come for me, you'll keep that albatross beak safe?"

Sol's intensity made Zar push against the natural cynicism he felt at all this talk of global investment firms, conspiracy, and blueprints. "I promise, dad," he said softly. He jangled the chains at his belt, a comfort mechanism.

"Good lad." Sol drained his beer. Enthusiasm blazed across his face. "I have an invention to show you. A prototype. I'll fetch it." Striding off to the far side of the workshop, he disappeared into the backroom he used as living quarters.

Zar ran the belt chains between his fingers and gazed at the dismembered mechanisms and boxes of scrap, the weathered benches, ceiling mounted pulleys and mechanic's pit in the concrete floor. He had loved the workshop as a child. Nothing had compared to the time he'd spent perched alongside his father on some rickety stool, cleaning engine parts together. Occasionally his father had asked him about school. Mostly though, their conversation had been confined to race anecdotes, or tales about Sol's involvement in Autodrome's architectural construction. Back then, Zar listened with the same enthusiasm as any other kid enjoying a little one-on-one time with a parent, and it had never occurred to him to savour those moments. Then his father left home. After that, the few times Zar did visit the workshop, it struck him as a dump of broken parts.

Sol came hurrying back into the workshop, a cardboard box under an arm. He skirted the pit and eased the box onto a bench. Diving his arms inside, he lifted out a clockwork mechanism that reminded Zar of a smaller version of a gutter bot – hulking cages on revolving treads that sucked up the city's dirt and dust. Once, twice, Sol fumbled with a wind mechanism at the base of the thing. By the third attempt, Zar lost patience, livid that his father was incapable of showing interest in his achievements, even more furious with himself for desiring it.

"I could be out there celebrating my win today! You know, dad, I'd hoped you might congratulate me. But I guess a man who abandons his family takes no pride in his son's achievements." He hated the words on his lips. They had a stinging quality, as if he'd spit up poison.

Sol eyed him from beneath his heavy brow. "You always were a boy who needed praise. But at fifteen? Well, we can indulge that once we're finished here." He beamed. "See this as my gift in honour of your victory."

Zar grimaced. "Does it have a returns policy?" He picked his trophy up off the cooler. "I'll give you and your clockwork wonder time to get reacquainted and call back later."

Reaching the door, he paused.

"You know, Dad, once upon a time, you invented me too."

He glanced back. His father's nose was already buried in the internal workings of the device.

Zar closed the door behind him.

§

# Chapter 3

It was midday. Commuters infested the network of sky rails known as the Ziplines that arched over Autodrome's downtown districts. Most people travelled in the city's cabs – fat bluebottles of processed plant fibres and tinted glass with buzzing rears. Some relied on personal transport: a steam trike with a gleaming saffron-coloured engine; bugs with aluminium bodies and tall dungcake burners mounted up back like ovipositors; tremendous iron spiders – great craning things that wheezed out silken threads of steam – and even a skinless mechanical lion ridden bareback. Huge iron snapdragons called Scoopers hid in the shadows, ready to crane out and catch any falling traffic in their jaws. High above, freight and passenger dirigibles hung like elliptical planets in the burnished desert sky. Far below, Cherry Street was crowded.

Zar kicked off his skateboard and wove in and out the busy hoards. Several passersby broke into applause when they caught sight of the trophy he carried. Zar hurried on. Wounded by his father's treatment of him, he couldn't shake the fear that folk were indulging his immature achievements. His discomfort increased as he passed a roadside shrine to a dead racer. A cross of baby pink carnations marked the spot. Zar hugged his trophy, hoping to hide it inside his arms, or take strength from it.

Distracted, he hooked a right into the Hispanic district. The temperature seemed to rise. Brightly painted housing pods thrust skyward like giant concrete flowers. Fabric hung at the slits of windows and low doorways. Garlands of pierced-metal lanterns crisscrossed the thoroughfare, which was home to pedestrians on mopeds and goods' laden donkeys.

'Come to rub it in?' said a girl's voice.

Zar turned to see Raina in a doorway. He was taken aback by her appearance. He was used to admiring her in greasy overalls since she was usually to be found under the bonnet of a vehicle at the school garage. But now he was looking at a girl whose hair fell in waves at her shoulders. She was wearing a cropped red gypsy top, dark denim Capri pants and red pumps. If Zar had thought her beautiful coated in engine oil, now he was blown away. He was also furious that life had dealt him a second blow that afternoon. Not only had he stumbled into Raina's territory, victor's trophy in hand, but now he felt vulnerable after his run-in with his father. He tried to formulate a comeback but only managed to mumble that he wasn't thinking.

"Funny that. You were on the ball earlier." Raina's eyes blazed. The fire died back, as if reflecting her disappointment in her own abilities.

Zar smiled weakly. "It was a good race." He felt obliged to tease, "But I guess it was inevitable I'd win in the end, you being a girl."

Raina bunched back her hair between her hands. "One great thing about being a girl is how protective your family can be. Have you met my nine older cousins, all welders at Black Stacks and built like steel rhinos?"

Zar was primed for a fight. But Raina's talk of family made him think of his mother wilted on the sofa and his father having already forgotten he was even at the workshop that morning.

"Look, Raina. You may think life is about winning some stupid race but sometimes bigger issues are at stake," he snapped. "Sometimes life is wack and no amount of trophies is going to make it better. Not that I'd expect you or your nine cousins to understand that."

He started to walk away but Raina called out after him.

"I got jars of fresh-made agua de tamarindo. You want?"

Zar stopped walking. Away from his father, he felt the lighter side of his personality start to resurface. "If you want me to stick around, you've only got to say." He couldn't suppress a grin as he turned around.

"Oh, please." Raina held out a jar which Zar accepted. Keeping her in view, he sank a good draft of the tangy liquid.

"I don't know much about you, Zar Punkstar, except you do pretty well in the Death Pit, which is an aptly named hole that no parent in their right mind would let their kids near." Raina rested her head on the doorframe. "Yeah, there's more to life than winning out on the circuit, but in your case, I'm not convinced. I think you live and breathe the race. Appeared that way this morning. So for you to sit there and tell me there are bigger issues at stake, I guess I've got to believe you."

Zar was unnerved by Raina's perceptiveness. He'd found himself sneaking a glance at her more times that he liked to remember in the past. She was one of those girls at school who was so intensely into the race circuit that it was difficult to see the personality beneath. But now it seemed she'd noticed him back, and enough to form an all too accurate opinion of him.

He was equally surprised when she ushered him into a courtyard to one side of the building. Taking a seat on a semi-circular bench besides a Joshua tree, the jar cradled between his palms, Zar became aware of tinny folk music coming from a radio at an open window and the gentle pour of water from the fountain in the centre of the courtyard. Feeling his cares start to fade, he leant forward and stared at the fountain. It was crowned by a metal albatross.

"My father wanted to commemorate his win," said Raina by his ear.

Zar sat back, unnerved by her closeness. He waved casually at the fountain. "The beak is still in place."

"My father didn't go in for stupid traditions. To him, the trophy symbolised perfection – the perfect rider, the perfect race. He saw no reason to desecrate his winnings."

"Funny that. I'd have guessed a Pro Leaguer like Johnny Law would've been the first to follow track traditions. But I guess the person in public can be very different from the person in private."

Raina shrugged. "I was nine years old when my dad died, too old to escape grief, too young to know what he was like as a man. As a father, he was good when he was here."

Zar noticed a small frown appear between Raina's eyes. He felt an inkling of common sentiment. "Your father was married to the race circuit, huh?"

Raina shot him a quizzical look. "Of course. Isn't everyone in Autodrome? But if you mean, did he neglect us, no, Zar, that's not my story. Is it yours?"

Zar was taken off guard again. He wasn't ready for this conversation. Before that day, Raina had barely acknowledged his existence. But here she was, plying him with agua de tamarindo and probing words. It was all too girlfriend'ish for his taste, and he needed to concentrate on his racing career. *Didn't he?* He squinted across at her. She was so very pretty. But the instant he considered pursuing the attraction, he was reminded of his father's assessment of him. Someone as talented as Raina didn't need to be weighed down.

"No offence but I really don't want to get into that with you...with anyone." He drained his jar and passed it over.

Raina decanted some of her drink into his jar and handed it back. She kept her arm outstretched, a smile at her lips, until Zar accepted the fresh measure.

"So your dad deserted you in the past. Reckon you'll turn out any different?"

Zar visibly bristled and Raina gave a musical laugh. "For you, it's all about the race."

"It's not as black and white as that. *I'm* not as black and white as that."

"Course not. Like me, you're a shade in-between," she snapped with heat. It didn't take her long to cool down again though – and Zar couldn't help thinking they shared that in common.

She stared at him, fiercely intense. Yet he had a sense of cogs turning inside her mind, of patient evaluation. She spoke slowly, as if considerate of the effect of her words upon him.

"Thing is, Zar, you have talent and with that comes the obsession to get to the top. Plus, that last stretch in the race today, how you guessed my moves even before I knew them myself? Gotta say you're one Lucky 13."

Zar snorted at the colloquialism while secretly flattered. A Lucky 13 was seen as being in league with the devil and attracting all of the earthly rewards that entailed. And he certainly was in the best place he had ever been in his life. Yet he had been dwelling on his father's neglect and paranoia alongside his mother's half-life of Razzledazzle addiction, and those things hurt. But here was this amazingly talented girl telling him that she'd lost that day because his skills outweighed her own. Just to be sitting here on this bench alongside Raina Jubilique was an achievement in itself. Girls like her didn't need boys like him. But apparently, and for reasons he didn't even want to begin to pick apart, Raina was giving him kudos as a racer, and possibly as a friend. She saw the good stuff over the bad.

He nodded and basked in Raina's perception of him. It occurred to him that there might be a way to impress her even further. "Your dad held the record for the youngest Pro Leaguer to win every race in Autodrome, right?"

Raina nodded. "He was twenty one."

"Then I'm going to win every race before I hit twenty. Including the Ramrod Rally." Zar jutted his chin. "Sooner or later, Frank Oz has got to reinstate that race. This last year, it's like the Pro League has had its heart removed. Frank Oz treats Autodrome like his personal universe, with him as the parent and us his kids."

Raina shook her head. "That's *exactly* how it is."

"Well, I'm tired of being patronised. I want to breathe free of that iron lung, Black Stacks, and the tyrant who lives inside."

There was something quizzical about the way Raina looked at him. He had an idea that he had impressed her, but wasn't sure how or why. Either way, she resorted to her musical laugh.

"Breathe free of Frank Oz and Black Stacks? You're in the wrong city for that. Frank Oz just about owns this joint and every racer in the place."

They were interrupted by a cry of "Raina! Where are you, girl?"

Raina retrieved the newly drained jar from Zar. She looked tired suddenly. Zar thought he caught a trace of disappointment in her voice as she said, "My friend, Katiana, is very protective. She'll be far from happy to see you."

There wasn't time to debate the point. Raina's flashy friend appeared around the corner, hips penduluming. The instant she spied Zar, the girl started yawping.

"What you doing here, crowing at my best girl like a rooster?"

Despite his irritation at the interruption, Zar found the glitzy Katiana amusing. He grinned, a red rag to a bull. Raina gave him a whispered tut-tut and was forced to restrain Katiana who took swing after swing at him, more for show than intent to injure. Then Katiana started with the names.

"Jarini! Rafael! Ruben! Felix!..."

Zar glanced at Raina. "The cousins?" he mouthed.

"Cruz! Eru!..."

Raina mouthed back, "I'd start running."

Zar tucked his trophy under an arm.

"You watch, Raina Jubilique. The day they bring back the Ramrod, I'll be on the winning team. Get you a spot too, if you play your cards right."

In spite of the wriggling fish in her arms, Raina managed an indulgent smile.

On the street, Zar glanced in either direction then took to his skateboard.

§

# Chapter 4

Zar found himself back at the workshop sooner than he would have expected. He was still locked between rage at his father and hurt, but he would take an interest in this latest invention – if only to prove in his head to Raina that he was different to his parents.

Finding the door unlocked, he stepped over the threshold and was struck by the smell of the place. It bought back memories of all those happier times. The sweet scent of oil, the smoky, rust smell of worked metal. Yes, he had loved the way the place smelled once. Even now, it reminded him of how, as a little boy, he'd explored the numerous crates and heavy wooden drawers while his father tinkered nearby.

His throat tightened. Those memories were as dusty as his surroundings. Now the crates had toppled over, their contents spread over the floor like blood and guts. There was a profound silence to the room; it unnerved Zar. How unlike his father it was to have gone out and left the door to the workshop unbolted! Fear speckled his skin like flecks of ice water.

"Dad?"

No answer. Again, the immensity of the silence inside the workshop struck home. For a moment, it was as if the walls of the place rose up around him, or as if he was the one who had swallowed down a pill and was shrinking down, down, to a state of nothingness. The child in him didn't want to go any further into that cave of a room where shadows slept. But it was the premature adult in him who won out – the one who dealt with his mother's seizures, who fought out on the race track to pay their way, and who refused to abandon his father now, even if the favour would not have been returned.

Gripping the makeshift weapon of his trophy, Zar inched forward. Dusty sunlight filtered in at narrow windows near the ceiling. Below, the workshop was bathed in gloom.

Each heartbeat was a tiny sharp punch inside his chest. Spotting the cardboard box which had housed his father's invention lying empty on the floor, Zar scanned the benches for the apparatus he had refused to take an interest in. There was no sign, but he did notice a wrench tipped with a dark glossy substance. His gut twisted doubly as he saw a thin wet trail leading to the pit. Barely breathing, the roar of blood like the rub of a million insects' wings in his head, he approached the edge and peered down.

His father lay below, one leg hooked underneath him, the other outstretched. His arms hung by his sides, his hands open as if in welcome. His head was slumped against his chest.

Zar instinctively knew his father was dead. His stomach cramped and he collapsed down onto one knee. *Can you even start to comprehend what the powerbrokers are willing to sacrifice for the technology?* A dirty swirl of emotions tore through him. He wanted to sob and scream, roar with pure rage like a wild thing, and punch the body repeatedly until he forced the breath back in. It wasn't meant to end like this, so broken between the two of them, so utterly cut off from one another. Yes, he'd been unable to shake the blistering anger – something his father had always delighted in picking at, like a scab that was never left alone to heal. But deep down, Zar had wanted his father, needed him, and even the few painful moments they'd spent together over recent years had been like gold dust to him. Gold dust that slipped between his fingers and sifted away.

Dropping the trophy, Zar sat on the edge of the pit and awkwardly lowered himself down. For an instant all he could was stare into his father's eyes – so very still and distanced. The mouth was slack while the gaunt cheeks appeared sunken further. Zar could have stayed there, let the anguish overwhelm him, starting from the base of his feet, rising through his trembling legs, and continuing all the way up.

Instead, he forced himself into action and manoeuvred his father away from the wall. He dug his hands up under his dad's armpits, half expecting brittle bones to break, the chest to cave in. He was reassured by the warmth and flexibility of the body so soon after death. Sweat broke out at his forehead as he struggled to lever his father up the side of the pit. The physical contact cut at him like a scalpel attacking his inner organs. So this was the feel of his father's arms, thin as a boy's yet wiry. This, the feel of his father's hand with its toughened skin and fibrous knuckles. This, the press of his father's cheek to his. An intimate, easy touch between most fathers and sons. In his case, a last crass reminder of how utterly alien it felt to ease his father over the side of the pit. Balancing on the toes of his sneakers, Zar rolled the body away.

Dropping back down onto his heels, he was overwhelmed by both the strain of the physical task and waves of inner agony. The pit walls threatened to seal him in. As his sight telescoped, he was struck by the horrid realisation that he was going to faint and take his father's place in the pit.

*I'm stronger than this*, he demanded of himself. *I am not my father's vision of me. I'm stronger.* Sheer will alone dragged him back from the abyss. He sucked in great lungfuls of air, and blinked away the slip of red across his eyes. It was a small, sour victory. Zar quietened his breath.

Stretching up his arms, he was about to climb out of the pit when he noticed an object jutting from the wall against which his father's body had been slumped. The act of observation gave him focus and he knelt down.

The object was slightly longer than his thumb and tapered. Zar ran his fingers along it – metal with a shallow indentation either side. The light was too poor to make out any further detail.

Zar levered himself out of the pit. Aware that he needed to bottle up his emotion for the time being, he took care to avoid looking at his father's body and went straight to the workbenches, where he began to rifle through the drawers. Locating a torch, he eased back down into the pit and began to animatedly wind the handle, the beam flickering into life and slowly strengthening with each turn. He knelt, shone the beam onto the object, and felt an immediate throb of recognition. A beak from an Albatross trophy!

He ran his damp palms down the sides of his board shorts and tried to dislodge the beak. It would only twist counter-clockwise. Closer inspection revealed the base was locked into a cog. A second cog was located alongside. It had a similar central slot...to accommodate a second Albatross beak?

A second Albatross beak? His mind squirreled round on itself – did his father have a spare? No, he didn't think so. But there was definitely need for a second. So where in the world had his father expected to find another? His father's words from earlier that afternoon came into sharp focus suddenly. "Got yourself one of those beauties at last." Zar stared down at the cog with its vacant slot. His stomach somersaulted. *He* had the second Albatross beak.

Zar was out of the pit again. This time he couldn't fight the urge to meet his father's veiled gaze. He swallowed against the crush of emotions that threatened to turn him into the child he longed to be in that moment and snatched up his trophy instead.

At the workbench, he grabbed a pair of pliers from the wall rack and fitted them around the base of the Albatross's beak. The welding was tight. He wiped his palms down his board shorts again, tried to get a solid grip and wrenched the pliers around the beak. Sweat blistered at his forehead. He tried again, and again, teeth bared against the effort.

With a sudden, small crack of welding matter, the beak separated from the rest of the trophy. Zar didn't give himself time to catch his breath but slid down into the pit again. He re-directed the torch's beam and tried the beak against the slot of the second cog. Rage broke over him like scalding water. It didn't fit! No, he wouldn't have that. He frantically retried the beak at every angle.

Collapsing back on his heels, he breathed heavily and took a moment to direct the torch's beam at the base of the beak. He noticed what appeared to be a scrap of welding material embedded in a tiny indentation. Retrieving the pliers, he prised the bead free then retried the beak against the second cog. This time it slid into place.

Steadying himself, he cranked both beaks anticlockwise – and became aware of a dreadful grinding noise. All moisture left his mouth as a panel of phosphorescent green light opened in the floor.

He knelt down and retrieved a slim silver canister from inside the compartment. *I should have believed you, Dad,* he thought as a great wave of guilt mingled with the loss to overwhelm him. *You said they'd come. What's the chances they were looking for this?*

Cradling the canister to his breastbone, he slumped back against the side of the pit and slid to the floor. Tears raced down his cheeks. He clutched at his sides and drew his legs in close, tucking himself up against the world.

§

# Chapter 5

Sooty Black was a suit with creases in all the wrong places. He had egg yolk on his conspicuous yellow tie. Zar noticed because a tie encrusted with egg was indicative of the level of personal care he had come to expect from Sooty. A detective in the Homicide branch of the Uniform, Sooty wore his suspenders, off-the-peg pants and jacket, and a faded striped shirt with the authority of a man who was admired by those ranked under him and considered capable if unconventional by those above. He was exceptionally gaunt, with watery blue eyes and thin hair dyed the same insipid brown as his boots. Sooty had been his mother's on/off boyfriend for four years now. Too jittery to have attempted to feature as a dad substitute, he had been a good solid dependable guy over the years, and Zar was glad to see him that afternoon. Egg down his tie. Frown between his eyes.

Sooty patted Zar's shoulder. The momentum petered out and he let his hand drop. His gaze moved to Sol's body.

"You moved him." A statement not a question.

"He looked wrong." Zar's instinct had been to get his father the hell out of that hole and back into the light, and because it was Sooty questioning him, he couldn't be bothered to lie.

Zar considered confiding in Sooty about the secret compartment in the pit and its contents. Strangely, he felt the need to protect the mild-mannered detective, but from what? Watching the Homicide team pour over the room, Zar wished there was some way to protect himself. Sooty was right to suspect him of further activity in the room.

A rookie Uniform shouldered the door to the workshop open, stacked coffees in hand.

"Detective."

"Thanks, Lazarus." Sooty took two coffees off the top. He handed one to Zar.

Sipping the steaming fluid, Sooty eyed his team. "You didn't kill your dad, Zar. May be a moody toad at times, a nasty opponent at the Death Pit...yeah, I know about that, even if Mindy thinks you work weekends at a fast-food joint." His stare was weighted with all he left unsaid, about his not having betrayed Zar to his mother and his dislike of Zar dicing with death at the Death Pit. Mostly though, the weak blue eyes acknowledged that life was a balance between responsibility and risk.

"But you're not a killer." Sooty took a fresh gulp of coffee. "For one thing, whoever slugged your dad wore a signet ring the size of a small moon."

"A signet ring?" Zar felt a flutter of hope. The thrill faded to a numb realisation. No amount of evidence would resurrect his father.

Sooty gestured to the body. "Circle of discoloration on one cheek. We'll get an impression."

Zar felt immensely frail all of a sudden. He had been so busy worrying that he hadn't had time to absorb the fact that someone had murdered his father. He had seen dead bodies before, loss of life being one of the accepted dangers of the Death Pit. But this was the first time he had lost someone who had mattered to him. The sight of his father's cold dead eyes haunted him and a sob threatened to burst free of his throat. He forced it back below. Boys who needed their mother cried, and he hadn't the luxury of acting his age.

Sooty leant in by his shoulder. "So what's if there's a time delay between you finding the body and your call. Way I figure it, you were a kid in shock."

Zar bristled despite his grief. He hated being patronised. Then again, if he would let anyone off calling him a kid it was Sooty. The man was one of the good guys, in a city where the term 'good' only ever equated to 'race-worthy'.

Sooty slurped his coffee. "This." He indicated his surroundings with the cup. "It's what I do. And I'll do right by your dad. For yours and Mindy's sake."

Staring into those weak blue eyes, it struck Zar as profoundly sad that his mum was incapable of loving Sooty more than a bunch of pills. Had either of his parents ever been truly capable of love? Had he inherited that hang up? While he acted the player at school, it had only ever been a game to him. With his life wholly dedicated to the race track and caring for his mother, there hadn't been time to nurture any stable relationships. But that didn't mean he was as hollow as the two who had made him, did it?

Zar discarded his coffee on the workbench and dug his hands into the pockets of his low slung jeans.

"Come over sometime, Sooty. I'll get mum a new dress, help you drag her out the door." He hated the desperation in his voice.

Sooty tried a smile. He drained his coffee before gesturing to the open door. "Talking of Mindy, get on home and break this to her gently. Anything comes up, I'll keep you in the loop. Otherwise, you got my digits."

Zar nodded. He heard the zip close on the body bag.

The detective moved in by his shoulder. "Stay out of the fast lane, Zar. At least until I get some answers."

§

# Chapter 6

Razzledazzle. One hit and you were buried in a velvet goldmine. Darkness so rich and encompassing you bathed in it. Other times you slept cradled. And there were always stars, pinpricks of honeyed light. A Bliss drug, Razzledazzle tucked you up for as long as the drug was in your blood stream. But once it dissipated, then came the moment all addicts dreaded, when you were pulled from the glitter pit and thrust back into blistering reality.

When Zar was seven years old, he wanted to go to the place mummy spent her evenings and took a pill. But while his mother bathed in the euphoria of psychotropic mindlessness, Zar's young mind had expanded far beyond the comfort zone of a small boy's understanding. While Mindy went to her nirvana, Zar went tumbling down a rabbit hole of not-quite-faces, coffin-heat and slithering dark. For two hours, he writhed and tore at his own skin and cried out. There was no one to hear him.

Even at such a young age, Zar recognised the agonising need for another hit just as soon as the trip began to fade and he found himself back out in the cold, his mother still comatose on the sofa. Only those terrible visions formed out of his mind's own dark, and fear of his mother missing some of her precious pills, kept him sober.

How times had changed. These days it was he who tried to monitor Mindy's intake. But not that evening. Having broken the news of his father's murder, he did not have the heart to deprive Mindy of her hit. He had even gone so far as to peel the sugared pink jacket off the pill. *Pink for girls, blue for boys, green for everyone in-between.* It was all marketing with no chemical difference in the makeup of the drug. The sugar coating was metabolic padding designed to gradually introduce the drug to the user's biological system. Mindy had no time for easing in. She grabbed the pill from Zar and swallowed it, smiling at him with tear-reddened eyes.

She started to sink. Oscillating between relief and despair, Zar carefully laid her head on the bed. A blanket was slung over a bottom bedpost; he thought about it and draped it over Mindy's lower body.

He paused at the bedroom door to glance back. No more crying for now. He closed the door behind him.

Entering the living room, Zar caught Tripster's eye. His friend nodded blankly. Having come over straight away at Zar's request, Tripster had examined the canister and agreed it had to hold a Paranascope scroll before fixating on brewing tea and fading into the background.

At that moment, Zar was so incredibly glad of his friend, of the history between them and of all that was unsaid.

He crossed to the far end of the room and the glass bay designed to give out onto a view. Over the years, pods had stacked on top of the one he and his mother shared, blocking out the sun. The park opposite had been replaced by pressure filtration tanks and the tumour-like drainage of a water treatment plant, the chimneys of Black Stacks sprouting beyond. He felt the fresh well of tears and looked away. Time had rotted everything, the east of the city, his family. The only way to survive this latest wound was to stay focused on the legacy his father had left him.

Unhooking a latch to one side of the bay, Zar pulled a concertinaed blackout screen across the view. He reached up to a wall-mounted hurricane lamp and turned up the flame.

The large leather box sat on the dining table, coated with a layer of dust from so many years stored under his bed.

"Present from my dad when I was a kid." He ran a finger through the dust and opened the lid. "Safe to say I didn't get around to using a Paranascope that often."

Keeping his chair in a low gear, presumably in an effort not to disturb Mindy, Tripster moved alongside.

The projector consisted of twin anamorphic lenses mounted on a telescopic limb alongside a mirrored spool which was rotated via a small crank and winding key. A scroll fed in, allowing the mechanism to project blueprints, landscapes and three dimensional models — just the sort of thing to amuse his father.

"I'll start it up." Zar twisted the seal off the cylinder and shook out a scroll that glowed eerily in the room's softened light. He guided it into the Paranascope's feed slot and worked the brass crank on the left side of the box. The scroll drew in around the central spool. An ornate brass key was attached to the mechanism via a tatty piece of string. Zar inserted the key into a lock on the right side of the box. Turning it, he heard the tinny wind of clockwork. Parabolic mirrors unfolded either side like wing flaps. The bottom mirror was concave; it soaked up images from the scroll as the cylinder started to revolve. He watched a blurred image originate at the second lens then broaden out to project a convex hologram.

"It's a cityscape," breathed Tripster.

"Its Autodrome," Zar clarified. Heart on fire, he walked into the hologram and stood waist-deep amongst the roads and buildings. The first thing he noticed were tiny oily bubbles drifting around the cityscape. The second was a spectral glow emitting from certain locations. He was struck by how organised the bleed seemed. Then he saw the truth. The scroll was dip-dyed to project a pattern.

"A trail," he murmured, tracing the glow with a finger. "Cherry Street." He followed the route to the enormous Dixie Island, from where it curved right onto The Artery. Halfway across the city, it plunged under the sky rails called the Ziplines before holing up north where it solidified into two symbols. The first was a green eight ball, except the number was a zero. The second looked like an empty test-tube.

He reached out. The icons projected onto the back of his hand.

"What's with the symbols?" asked Tripster.

Zar bounced a bubble into the tube where it settled like an abacus bead. "It's interactive," he breathed. Laying his head on one side, he squinted at the vista. "My dad died to protect this map. It's up to me to work out what it means I guess."

He didn't have time to dwell on the fact as an authoritative thump sounded on the front door at the far end of the room.

*Uniform?* Zar's natural instinct was to bolt. But he reminded himself that he had done nothing wrong and instead worked the small brass crank in reverse until the hologram dissolved and, in one neat action, the mechanism's distended limbs wound in. He closed the lid and fastened its metal clasp.

Running around to the opposite side of the table, he pushed a depression pad on the wall. A panel slid open to reveal a closet stuffed with coats and random brick-a-brac. He pulled out a paint-stained sheet and tossed it to Tripster.

"Cover the machine."

Striding over to the door, he manipulated the revolving spy plate with a finger – and found himself eyeball to eyeball with whoever stood outside.

"I spy with my little eye," said a man.

Zar tried to place the voice but couldn't. Snapping the spy plate shut, he pulled a copper funnel out on its drag hose from a hook and put his mouth to it.

"What do you want?"

Sound filtered in from an audio-grid alongside the funnel.

"To pay my respects to Sol Punkstar's widow and his son."

Zar was instantly put on edge. Given the circumstances of his father's death, he was wary of newcomers to the door who possessed too much knowledge. Then again, he wasn't entirely sure of the etiquette when it came to folk calling on a deceased's next of kin.

"You covered the Paranascope?" he shot back over a shoulder.

Tripster was seemingly engrossed in one of Mindy's trashy romances. He waved casually at the sheeted Paranascope.

Zar spun a wheel in the heart of the oval door. Pistons shunted. Steam oozed. Two fat titanium rods slid in towards the centre. Taking a deep breath, he punched the gel pad in the centre of the wheel. The front door opened on pneumatic slow release.

§

One hand tucked in a jacket pocket like a handkerchief, the other free to gesticulate, Zar found himself face to face with a promoter of the tailored breed. The man's suit was green, his tie and shirt a paler, complementary shade. He was in his late forties, Zar guessed. Tall and tanned, with clear blue eyes.

From the moment the man stepped in, he infected the room with his air of a salesman. Zar also detected an undertone. He caught the man staring at him as if his body housed a thing that had momentarily clawed to the surface.

The newcomer handed out business cards. Etched on thick creamy paper, the ornate script read: 'Braxton Earl. Race Promoter. Specialist in Pink Slips, Stock Car, Dragster, Drifting, Single-Seater, Touring, Rallying and Off-Roading.'

Zar scanned the card with distaste and professional fascination. He had been right in his assumption; the man was a promoter with an address way out west.

He cut the visitor off mid-flow. "If you knew my dad, how come we've never met?"

"We have met." The man showed too many teeth. "Okay, so you were five years old at most, but Sol did introduce us at the Death Pit – which I understand you're now a fan of," he shot from behind a hand as if Mindy was capable of listening in from next door. He flashed Zar that sabre smile. "I bought you an ice-lolly."

Zar felt a tug of recollection – a man had blotted out the beam from a spotlight overhead as he leant down to pass him an ice-lolly. His mother had reminded him to say thank you.

"I don't remember, Mister Earl," he lied, noting how his words redoubled the intensity of the clear blue eyes opposite.

"Call me Braxton. No point us acting strangers, not when I'm here at Sol's say so. Hell, wasn't like I could let it rest until I've done right by him. See, you might've been a little kid last time we met, Zar, but I know enough about you to fix me a nice little extortion racket. You know what I'm alluding to, I'm sure,' the man added with a wink.

"You've seen me in the Death Pit and want to blackmail me with the threat you'll pass that info onto my mother." Zar snorted. "Time for you to take the quick-booted route out of here."

He was already striding in the direction of the door when Braxton called,

"Wouldn't bring in much of a return now, would it? Time I've squealed about you and the Death Pit, Mindy'll have re-dosed and skipped back off to La La Land."

Zar spun around, his whole body trembling with rage. "You know too much about my family for my liking, arriving here on the same day my father was killed."

He was unnerved when Braxton sank down on the sofa, put his forehead in his palms and sighed.

"It was a joke about my having the skinny on you. I ain't the type to chastise a kid for his love of the race. In this city? You kidding me? I was just trying to ease in to more important conversation. But I've gone about it wrong and now you want to jack me out on my ear." He stared up at Zar with moist eyes. "Sol and I were buddies. We grew apart only in circumstance, never in what lies here." He smacked a fist off his ribs, a corny gesture vindicated by his apparent sincerity. "Gonna give me a second run to explain what I'm doing here, kid?"

Calming down, Zar still felt the hairs stand up on the back of his neck. "Going to stop calling me kid?"

"Don't like that? Yeah, you're definitely Sol's son." The shark smile re-emerged. "So, I've got a secret to share. Wanna ask your friend here to give us five?" Braxton jerked his head at Tripster, who twitched his lip while keeping his gaze on the pulp fiction.

"Tripster stays." Zar had no intention of telling his only true friend to leave him alone with this wily stranger. Plus, he was tired of dramatics. The day's events weighed on his eyelids like coins.

"Whatever's good for you, kid...I mean Zar." Braxton abandoned the sofa and flexed back his shoulders. He thrust a finger in the direction of the paint stained sheet on the table.

"You got inside the projection I take it. Guy with your street smarts is bound to have tried looking at the thing from all angles."

Zar swallowed awkwardly. This Braxton Earl knew about the scroll? How was that even possible...unless the man had some genuine connection with his father?

"Listen up, kid. Your dad and I worked together a few years back. He brought along the engineering principles, I brought along the cash and the wherewithal to push an idea. Anyway, I guess you could say I got the best out of the deal and, Sol, well he didn't seem to mind, at least until six months ago when he turns up on my doorstep. 'Braxton', he says, 'If ever they reinstate the race, you get my kid onto a team. He has to compete in order to know where to go next. Promise me that.' And I did promise, figured it was the least I owed him. Which was why I got here quick smart, soon as I heard the news." Braxton flipped back his jacket and stuck his hands on his hips. His face hardened. "Your dad wanted me to get you to race."

"I already race," Zar hissed. "Perhaps my dad didn't notice, what with all his efforts to be the saviour of our time. Shame he didn't stop to ask if anyone needed saving. Except my mum and me. We'd have liked to have had him home with us instead of holed up in his workshop with his latest crap machine."

"But he'd had a breakthrough.' Braxton appeared to rein himself in. "Which isn't important right now. What is important is for you to come meet your team."

Zar was barely listening. Anger, hurt, shame, so many contradictory emotions were racing through him like poison at that instant.

"Same day I go Pro, a promoter claims to have been bosom pals with my dead dad. I reckon a sly old coot like you thought you'd sign me up quick while the other promoters were keeping a respectful distance."

Braxton shook his head. "I had to come, whether you thought it disrespectful or not. Ask me its fate that the same day Sol Punkstar passes away, the Ramrod lives again."

"The Ramrod Rally's reinstated?" Tripster stared at Braxton. Despite himself, his eyes grew wide and his face flushed with youthful hope. "Frank Oz relented?"

"It's breaking news, but, yeah, the great man is letting us out to play again."

Zar felt his whole world seesaw. Alongside the ache of grief came a rush of excitement. He'd always said he'd give anything to race the Ramrod, but he had never expected to see it reinstated while Frank Oz was still alive. It seemed so astonishingly unlikely.

"How come you know so much?" he asked, deeply suspicious.

"Same way I knew Sol'd turn his life's work into a treasure map." Braxton gestured to the covered Paranascope. "I'm no code breaker, Zar, but I'm guessing you got a scroll in there that projects the start to a race route, and that race route is the..."

"Ramrod Rally!" Tripster was a rubber ball of excitement. "So the only way to activate the rest of the trail is to take part?"

"Exactamondo." Braxton rubbed his hands together gleefully as if he'd struck a deal. "Sol always was the secretive type. Which is why the race fraternity of Autodrome trusted him to map their most challenging races. He had the mechanical and architectural know-how necessary to create the most challenging of obstacle courses. Guess he had an inkling they'd reinstate the Ramrod sometime soon and built a whole other secret route into the course this time around."

"My dad plotted the Ramrod Rally courses?" Zar scrubbed at the back of his head, astonished.

Braxton raised an eyebrow. "My thinking is he created a trail based on clues only you'd know the answers to."

Tripster looked impressed. "Wow, Zar. Any idea where the trail will lead?"

The promoter hooked back his lips. "To paradise."

Zar didn't like those words one bit, not with his mother passed out in the next room and his father's blood still tucked beneath his fingernails. Striding over to the door, he slammed the gel button and stood aside as the metal slab hissed open.

"I don't know what you hope to gain by telling me all this but I suggest you leave now. I'm not racing until my father's buried and I know who the hell killed him. Plus, there's my mother. She needs me right now."

"Needs the Razzledazzle more like," jibed Braxton, but he wore a look of resignation.

He paused at the door. "I promised Sol I'd get you to race the Ramrod if it ran again. Right now, I know that means diddly squat to you. Right now you want to put your dad in the ground and your mum in rehab. But if there was one thing you could do to prove yourself to Sol, it would be to take part in this race and solve his conundrum. It'd be worth far more to him than tears at his funeral." He tapped his Data Streamer watch, a hunk of platinum and black glass 15 years younger and about fifty times more expensive than Zar's legacy version. "I gotta get going anyway. You got my card. The team is meeting at mine at ten am. Be swell if you could drop by." The promoter disappeared off down the corridor whistling an old fashioned tune.

Zar heard Tripster arrive at his elbow.

"Who was that? How'd he know about the map? How'd he know the Ramrod was being reinstated? You going to enter?" Apparently sensing Zar's exhaustion, Tripster stopped with the questions. "You've had one hell of a day. I'm gonna head home." He sucked his lips. "I'll call you tomorrow. Take it easy."

Tripster left, the treads of his chair scuffing over the remaining threads of the communal hallway carpet.

Zar punched the gel pad and sealed out the world.

§

Three am the shouting started, like the cries of the dead through the thin wall separating his bedroom from his mother's. Zar woke in a shock of recognition and scrambled out from his sweat-dampened sheets, already processing what he needed to do. *Get her cool. Keep her safe. Phone the Uniform.* Adrenaline cut through his fatigue like a vitamin shot. He ran out into the hall and swung around to burst open his mother's bedroom door. Fumbling for a switch, he flooded the room in piercing electric light that brought tears to his eyes even before he saw her.

She was kneeling up in the centre of the bed, arms outstretched as if opening herself to the world – or beseeching it to absorb her. Her skin was grey and glistening while an intricate network of capillaries and veins had risen to the surface. Shivering all over, she looked like a marble angel brought to life.

"Mum."

Mindy's eyelids fluttered.

"Shit, mum. No!"

Years of caring for his mother through the temporary highs and all-too-common lows of her addiction had exposed Zar to the signs of an overdose. He launched himself at the bed just as she fell off to one side. In the act of supporting her, one of his fingernails scratched a sickle shape in her arm. He hated adding his own wound to her already damaged flesh.

"What the hell did you do, Mum?" he cried, a sob catching in his throat.

He braced her lolling head between the crook of one arm and his chest. Her lips were blue, her eyes rolling, the pupils reduced to pinpricks. Foam bubbled up at the corners of her mouth.

"What did you do?" he repeated in an anguished whisper.

Suddenly her limbs began to jitter. Zar held her close, playing the role of the father to the child and feeling a stranger in his own skin. This was false affection. A violent hug under the only circumstances he would ever perch on his mother's bed, holding her and hating her and hurt by her all at the same time.

*Why was she whiting out?*

His gaze fell on the split capsule of another Razzledazzle pill on the bedside cabinet, like the remains of a bug carcass. The stupid woman had taken another hit on top of the dose he had already given her. He wanted to scream in her face. Or wrap his arms tighter around her, and squeeze and squeeze until he forced the sickness out.

"I gave you enough," he demanded, rocking her in his arms and burying his face against her shoulder, utterly ashamed of his part in her predicament. *I'm exhausted too,* he wanted to cry out. *Everything is going up in flames.*

Deep down inside, he knew he had to keep on fighting. His mother's breath came in sharp, shallow bursts. He felt the bird-like flutter of her heartbeat where her back pressed against his chest. Death might be his ultimate gift to her, but Zar had no intention of going down a route as dark as that. He shifted awkwardly out, eased her twitching body down and snatched up the phone from beside the bed.

It took five minutes for Uniform to respond to his call and send an ambulance. During that time, he ran out into the hall and punched the gel pad of the front door to hasten the crew's entry. Coming back into the bedroom, he yanked open the bedside drawer, scattered the floor with the debris of hose and underclothes, and located a sealed foil package. He tore it open to retrieve the syringe pre-loaded with a narcotic antagonist. Kneeling beside the bed, he prised his mother's right arm away from where she held it tight against her body, exposed her inner elbow and delivered the shot.

"I'm here, mum. Can you hear me? You just need to calm down." He put the syringe back down on the bedside cabinet and laid a hand on her arm. Seconds passed painfully slowly as he waited for the medicine to kick in. Sweat burnt beneath his armpits. His throat felt sandpapered.

When she went limp on the bed, Zar had the briefest respite of relief. Except, she wasn't stabilising he realised with desperate clarity. She had stopped breathing. Panic kept him momentarily paralysed. *Was this it? The*

*breakdown of his childhood via twenty four hours that*
*saw both his parents die in hideous circumstances?*

*That was not going to be the way of it!*

Zar dived forward, bringing his face close to his
mother's. Clamping her nostrils shut with one hand, he
forced his mind to focus on the act of resuscitation and
not the reality of pressing his open mouth to hers. He
exhaled for five long seconds, like he'd seen actors do in
movies, drew away a while, then repeated the breath. The
taste of her was sour, the crust of froth at the edges of her
mouth making him baulk at the effort. The strap of her
nightdress had slipped, exposing her breast. He tried not
to process the image, just tugged the strap back up in-
between breathing for her. Every part of him wanted to
break free, run to the shower and soap himself and scrub
and scrub until the mess of what his mother had become
washed down the drain. Instead he stayed and fought to
keep her with him.

On arrival at the hospital, medics whisked Mindy
away on a stretcher. He was left to crawl into himself on
a steel bench in the waiting room. A nurse brought him a
hot drink, said "Look like you could use one," and passed
it over the steely kindness required for her profession.
He tucked the cup in close, pressing it to the dip at the
base of his throat to feel its warmth. His head throbbed

horribly. Numbness set in as he concentrated on a small fleck of dirt on the tiled floor. He sipped from the cup until the drink went cold. Then he slept fitfully, neck cricked, legs folded in close.

Seven hours later came the news that Mindy was stable. Zar tried to process the information while struggling to ease out his stiff, blood-starved limbs. He sat forward and put his aching head in his hands. The pain lessened slightly. His mother had hauled herself back from the brink, just like every other time she had overdosed. The tragedy was she would more than likely put herself back there again before the year was out.

The knowledge cut at Zar like a fistful of razors. No matter how you shaped it – death or drug-addiction – his parents' neglect of him was a scar on his life. The thought dug up under his ribs and made his heart hurt. There would be no fairy godmother to save him, no benevolent uncle to step in, no happily ever afters. His only option was to save himself, and in order to do that he needed to stop with the heartache and get angry.

His father had left him one thing – the legacy of the Paranascope scroll. It had been his dying hope that Zar would find it, suggesting a tangible connection between the scroll's contents and his father's murder. Moreover, while Braxton's arrival had seemed a mighty coincidence,

Zar could not deny that taking part in a Ramrod Rally was one of his greatest ambitions as a racer. And why shouldn't he grasp his moment in the sun with both hands? He had been concentrating on grieving, but the truth of the matter was that his father had abandoned him to the role of his mother's caretaker long before. Dying was just another way for his dad to shirk his responsibilities.

Zar raised his head from his hands. Wasn't it his time at last? Wasn't this when he got to say '*Screw you, I'm going track down a killer, earn enough money to get mum clean, and win the race of my life in the process!*' And if he was going to travel that path alone, he needed to take the first step to breathing free of his parents. To independence.

As dawn spilt the sky into a million red jewels, Zar put pen to paper at the warden's desk, signing off Mindy's care to those who could scrub her down on the inside. He walked out of the hospital without a tie to family or the world, and with one ambition. To race.

§

# Chapter 7

In his last television interview before his stroke, Frank Oz maintained there was only one way to build and sustain an empire, and that was to dominate trade routes.

"Look to my Turkish forefathers," he said, his large black eyes flashing. "The Ottoman empire was the heart of the eastern and western world for six centuries, and why? Because my forefathers controlled the trade routes. This is why Autodrome needs to outstrip production and delivery across the world's autotrade. We're the only suckers with the passion for it," he'd added wryly.

"But what makes you think Autodrome has any chance against global conglomerates such as Toyota, General Motors, Volkswagen, Ford? The city can't even sustain a decent standard of living for the eastern portion of its population."

The great man had sat forward with the bulked up look he always got when a meeting went off point and he wanted to get back on track.

"Thirty years ago, the Red Depression threatened to destroy every trace of creative vision. But even with the countries of the world amalgamating into five new states, I was the money spinner. New Europe, Africonia,

Underland, the Terraformed States, R'asia...the rest of the world was in meltdown but I was a grease monkey in a place where nothing mattered but the race."

"This was Dubai's MotorCity?"

Frank closed his eyelids. "MotorCity was a state-of-the-art theme park. But it outgrew itself." His dark eyes flicked open, sharper than ever. "When plans to revive their country's Grand Prix fell through, I persuaded the old Russia race fraternity to solidify R'asia's state of interdependence by investing in a new proposal. While cash-rich but food-poor countries such as the United Arab Emirates often leased fertile land from other countries, I could see no reason why we shouldn't turn the tables. We'd be slap bang in the terrain of one of the few remaining oil suppliers in the world, allowing us to fuse gas usage with new steam technologies. A water source and broadly flat terrain attracted us to this desert strip. Here we set about transforming MotorCity into a living breathing metropolis. Into Autodrome."

"But beautiful as our history is, there's no getting away from the fact that the dream has fractured. This is a city where some have and some have not. Many teens have their youth, and even their young lives, stolen because they feel the pressure to bring in an essential wage from the race circuit. What do you say to the folk who are sitting at home wondering why they work night and day to sustain the trade routes you mentioned, but see so little in the way of a return?"

Frank Oz stiffened. "I repeat that, just as my ancestors found a way to prosper via trade, so we will find a way to dominate the automobile industry."

"But didn't the Ottoman Empire fall?"

A year later and, entering the clean streets of the west on his skateboard, Zar couldn't remember how Frank had answered the question. He just remembered how the man had looked older suddenly, aged by heartbreak and shattered dreams. It was a look which translated into the downward spiral of the city's east. In contrast, the west had continued to prosper.

He'd visited the area once as a child. Sol needed to deliver some architectural plans to a client and the four year old Zar had been allowed to tag along. Nose pressed to the car window, Zar had gawped at the wide roads, the luxurious housing pods and acreage of lawn – home to the retired royalty of Autodrome's racing circuits – and thought himself in wonderland.

*This is a city where some have and some have not.* The interviewer's phrase resonated anew as Zar got his first glimpse of 249, Easy Street.

Encircled by formal gardens, the pod resembled a black bauble afloat on a neon ice rink. Walking up the transparent path, Zar felt as if he was floating too. He arrived at a tall front door. Tugging the pull-knob, he heard a distant tinkling from somewhere inside.

Minutes passed before a girl answered the door. Zar initially put her at twelve, maybe thirteen. But while her face resembled a china doll's, he soon realised that she was closer to seventeen.

"You're late." She managed to look down her nose at him while standing short of his shoulders. Her coldness was reinforced by her appearance. Black satin knee-length dress with a high lace collar, black lace gloves, black riding boots, and black hair scalped into a bun.

The girl stood back. When he didn't react immediately, she sighed, "If you're waiting for me to roll out the red carpet…"

Zar held up a hand. He hoped he matched her for abruptness. Striding over the threshold, he entered a circular hallway. A transparent staircase spiralled up the inner wall. Overhead, a light-spike chandelier extended and ebbed like a sea anemone.

"This way." The girl led him left along a corridor lit with sunken spotlights.

"I'm not late because I'm not expected," Zar grunted in answer to her first statement.

She fixed him with eyes as black as her outfit in the gloom of the corridor. "You're one of my father's business assets and, as of five minutes ago, you're holding up proceedings."

After the night he had just had, Zar was on his last nerve. "I can see it was a mistake to come. So how's about you run off and explain to daddy why his asset just turned heel and got the hell out?"

"No need. We're here." The girl thrust open a set of double doors.

Daylight flooded the corridor. Zar pinched up his eyes – for a few seconds, it was as if he was back at the hospital, chasing after medics as they rammed the trolley through flopping acetate doors. Then Braxton Earl blocked out the light.

"Good to see you, Zar!" He slapped an arm about Zar's shoulders and told the girl, "Isha, fix a drink for our young friend." His attention returned to Zar. "My mistake. Less of the young, hey?" Releasing his stranglehold, he swept out an arm. "Whatcha make to my personal oasis?"

Zar's eyes flittered about the room like butterflies uncertain where to settle. They were in a huge tropical greenhouse. Overhead was a roof of vaulted smoked glass. Underfoot were shimmering green tiles. A banqueting table was laden with fruit bowls, juice packs and seafood on ice. Mismatched chaise longes and bamboo armchairs stood at the far end of the room. Everywhere else was given over to lush forestation: desert succulents, banana trees, large fleshy flowers. A waterfall streaked the inside of the glass.

"Impressive," said Zar, adding, "But it does make me wonder how a pad like this belongs to a promoter I've never heard of? All this, it costs."

"A freakin' fortune," cut in a male voice from overhead.

Zar glanced up. A figure with unnaturally long limbs was spread-eagled across a ceiling panel. The figure flick-flacked down the glass.

The Fly – yeah, Zar knew enough to recognise a gang member from Era 5.0 when he saw one – plopped down onto the ground. With a hiss of steam, the Fly concertinaed the long metal poles he used for suction into a sheath at his back.

Braxton flashed his razor smile. "Eight Ball, let me introduce…"

"Thanks big guy, but I got a tongue." The Fly strode over, his cocksure expression backed up by the tilt of his biker's cap. Zar put him at seventeen. He wore jeans that were cuffed at the ankles, a t-shirt in mother's best shade of white, and a weathered leather with the collar tugged high at his throat.

Zar stared at the Fly in awe. He knew Era folk clung to their stereotypes. That didn't mean he was any less thrown to meet a gang member in the flesh. Not that he was going to show his naivety.

"I'm Eight Ball. You got a name?" The Fly masticated a matchstick.

"Birth certificate says so."

Eyeballing him a moment, the Fly bent back at the spine and snorted. "That's a helluva chip on your shoulder. What's your cause, rebel?"

"One that is justified, I have no doubt," said a voice with a taste to it, like dark rum and cream. A girl stood up from an armchair. Of Africonian heritage and similar in age to the Fly, she cut an impressive figure. Her neck was long and sinewy. Snake tattoos curved either side her throat. Her nose was broad and misshapen, her top lip freshly split. In basketball boots and a black and gold kaftan, she reminded Zar of a desert warrior.

Zar inclined his head. "Hello. My name is Zar Punkstar."

"Justice Hunter." The girl stared back over a shoulder. "He has manners."

"Which will make him a fine addition to the team," said a new voice. A pair of legs was slung over the arm of a chair which faced away. Zar noticed the shoes first. Navy wing-tip brogues punched out of croc and shined like alloys.

The shoes climbed down. A guy a little older than the rest, nineteen even twenty, emerged, wearing top dollar cut and cloth. He wore a canary yellow silk shirt and a navy trilby. One cheek was marred by a zigzagging scar. Rather than detract from the guy's looks, the scar added to them.

The mobster from Era 3.0 stuck out a hand. "Valentine Heart."

Zar returned the handshake. "Thanks."

Something about Valentine Heart appealed. The same couldn't be said for the grease monkey in stained overalls and a chequered shirt who emerged from behind a giant saguaro cactus, still zipping his fly.

Braxton plumped up like a rooster. "Jesse James! You don't urinate in a man's garden if he's got bathrooms a piece for each of ya."

"Chill, grandpa. A guy's gotta let loose if the notion takes him. Know what I mean, cherry bean?" shot the grease monkey at Isha.

Picking at a fruit bowl, the girl froze, a grape halfway to her mouth. Zar noticed a trace of a smile at her lips. It backed up his instant dislike for both of them.

Wiping his palms down the bib of his overalls, Jesse strode over. Up close, he was older than Zar had first thought, sixteen maybe, with punked red hair, a dangling skull-and-cross-bone earring, and urchin freckles. He offered Zar a 45 degree hand lock.

Zar dragged the back of a hand across his nostrils then accepted the grip, pleased with the snarl that muddied Jesse's cocksure expression.

"So you're the upstart Braxton wants us to race alongside." Jesse crossed his arms. "What makes you so freakin' special?"

Zar emptied his face. Nothing made him special. He was just trying to swim against a tide of circumstances that threatened to pull him under. But he wasn't going to say that to a jerk like Jesse.

"What makes me special? I have a brain, scarecrow."

"That so? Me, I'm all about the brawn," Jesse snarled, pushing up his sleeves.

"Ease off." Valentine's hand went across the mechanic's chest. "Zar's dad was murdered yesterday. Braxton filled me in," he offered when Zar froze, eyes cold with suspicion.

"Your old man was diced?" Eight Ball slowed his churning jaw.

Zar nodded. It felt unreal to tell strangers his father had died let alone been murdered, especially when he was struggling to admit the fact to himself.

Justice's soft brown eyes settled on Zar. "Braxton says we're to graft you onto our team." Her gaze sharpened. "You'll pardon my directness, but why should we?"

*Why indeed?* Zar felt the weight of his circumstances. His father's murder, his mother's overdose, his newly qualified Pro Leaguer status next to these more experienced racers, all of whom were staring at him now, waiting for some logical explanation as to why he should join their pack. He wanted to say '*Because I deserve a break after the last twenty four hours. And because I'm a hell of a racer.*' But the effort of holding his own among a roomful of strangers was weighing heavily. He didn't know where to begin.

"I can give you some reasons," said a girl.

Zar felt a burst of utter, beautiful relief. He recognised that voice. Lit up on the inside, he saw Raina rise from the last of the chairs with its back to him.

Braxton leant in. "Girl caught my professional eye a year back. Plus I thought it'd be nice for you to have your girlfriend along."

"She's not my..." Zar left off there. Raina was an excellent choice either way.

She walked towards him with her usual air of quiet confidence. "Zar qualified as a Pro Leaguer yesterday with the fastest race time in fifteen years. He's achieved top credits at school in Track, Vehicle Maintenance, Rudimentary Mechanics and Race Law. And it is my experience that Zar has some of the quickest responses on the race circuit. Unfortunately," she added with a shrug.

"Why'd we listen to you?" sniffed Jesse.

"Because I have the second fastest race time in fifteen years. And because I'm right."

"Whoopee do." The mechanic hooked up his lip. He backed off though and was soon whispering into Isha's ear. The girl stared at Zar then Raina and laughed nastily.

"What about the rest of you? Why are you taking part?" Zar demanded. If they were going to analyse him, he was happy to turn the tables.

Valentine narrowed his eyes. "Some of us got a score to settle."

"Revenge, Valentine? That's wasted motive. What about the opportunity to make a better life for our families? My share of the prize money from a Ramrod win would help me set up my folks and my kid sister in a nicer neighbourhood. One that doesn't see Razzledazzle as the strongest form of currency." Justice looked vulnerable suddenly. "Plus, I've need to exorcise my ghosts."

Zar sensed a new tension in the room, to which Jesse proved as sensitive as a two year old with a jack hammer.

"Me, I'm all about the kudos. Every girl loves a winner." Jesse winked at Raina, who looked away in disgust.

Zar was secretly pleased at Raina's brush off. He noticed Justice eye the younger girl appraisingly.

"And what about you, Raina?" she asked softly. "What's your story?"

§

Growing up, Raina had always been aware that her father was quite something, both at home and out on the track. It was inevitable perhaps that she should follow in his footsteps, developing a love for the mechanics of automobiles alongside a passion for driving them. Thanks to her dad, she'd learnt Math via trays of nuts and bolts, Geography via the maps of grand prix routes lining the walls, and Physics via his explanations of the workings of the internal combustion engine.

But it was out on the track that she had seen her father really come alive. His passion was drag racing and he'd become an instantly recognisable celebrity in his souped up Triumph Stag. Johnny Law they'd called him, because he was a law unto himself, taking on meatier machines – Hudson Hornets, Ford Thunderbolts, Chrysler 300Cs – and nearly always winning.

Even so, Raina had never appreciated just how much of a celebrity her father was until his funeral. Then she had seen countless strangers weep for a man they knew by sight and reputation alone. The service had been held out on one of the test tracks in The Maintenance District, a home from home for a man like Johnny Law. Holding her mother's hand and all cried out, Raina had been surprised to feel a renewed sense of kinship with the racing fraternity. The smallest details had affected her. One man had worn a pair of Nomex grip gloves in red and black, the very same style as her father's. Whether the racer had worn the gloves incidentally or in deliberate homage to her father had been irrelevant. It was the reminder which gave her comfort. Likewise, the rub of oil under another man's fingernails which she'd noticed when he'd come over to shake hands and offer his condolences – and in that instant she might have been shaking her hands with her father again. Staring out across the track that afternoon, Raina had felt her grief bed down a little. Her father lived on in the suits, goggles, gloves, and head gear, and in the oil-stained lifestyle of the racers. That afternoon she had realised there was one way to truly stay close to her father and that was to quite literally step into his shoes. Join the race circuit, be her father's daughter and take up winning in his place.

"My father was Johnny Jubilique," she said. "Better known as Johnny Law."

"Yowser!" cut in Jesse, ever the wise guy.

She ignored him.

"My dad taught me that you're only as great as your next challenge."

The Africonian girl, Justice, nodded, as if that was explanation enough as to why anyone would race.

Raina felt a twist of shame in her gut as she clarified, "I lost out on becoming Pro Leaguer today. I've plenty to prove and the Ramrod's going to give me that opportunity."

"Yes, the Ramrod gives plenty. It also takes plenty away." There was a break in Justice's voice as she spoke. A sad glance passed between her and Eight Ball, Valentine also.

Raina didn't doubt that Justice was right. She had attended enough teen racer funerals to understand the very real dangers of professional rallying. Having lost the Pro Leaguer title to Zar though, she needed to distract herself with the kind of challenge which would have appealed to her father – and they didn't come much bigger than the Ramrod.

She stared at the boy who had beaten her in the Pro Leaguer Qualifier. Her pride was bruised but Zar looked exhausted. His eyes were dark circles while his skin had a grey tone. Despite his lack of thanks when she'd stuck up for him earlier, she couldn't help feeling he was being forced to cover up the agony of his circumstances with a paper-thin veneer of bravado. Rumour was Zar's mother was a Razzledazzle addict. And now his father had been murdered. She couldn't help feeling there was more to him than a mouthy kid with a lucky streak. What that 'more' might be, she'd no idea. But she was in the right place to find out.

"Look, I don't know how much Braxton has filled you all in, but the Ramrod is a way for me to get answers," Zar announced to the group, his voice brittle. "So while it's great the Ramrod will help you settle old scores or scare off spooks," – his gaze shifted from Justice to Raina – "or prove you're as good a racer as your old man was, I'm all about working out which sick bastard murdered my dad and what the hell kind of secrets he died to protect!"

Raina felt a tinge of resentment; was her cause any less worthy? Likewise, it appeared that Zar hadn't won his team mates over just yet.

The Fly slung his hands onto his hips and chewed the matchstick between his lips. "Thing is, while it'd be a blast to carve up the city in the Ramrod, find us all a little peace of mind and pocket a nice earner in the way of prize money alongside, why should any of us goofs put our necks on the line for you? I'm no square but see it from my side of the tracks. You might just have a killer on your tail and maybe I got enough heat on me already."

"You've always got heat on you, Eight Ball." Justice winked. Eight Ball flipped her the bird. "As far as I'm concerned, if Braxton says we need Zar onboard, we need Zar onboard," she continued evenly. "What do you say, Valentine, Eight Ball, Raina? Jesse, I'm discounting you, since you've decided it's your job to aggravate Zar every which way you know how."

"That's out of order!" spat the mechanic, but Justice brushed him off, a tigress batting away a gnat.

Valentine swept out his arms. "Life's worth nada if a fella can't race, hey, Zar. Anything else is your own business."

Eight Ball exhaled noisily. He nodded.

"And you, Raina? What do you say?"

Raina lifted her chin. *Time to provoke a little more fight in her potential team mate.* "I say Zar got lucky on the track today and any fool could outrace him. I'm sure Zar would rather die than prove me right."

"Nicely put," interjected Braxton. The promoter crossed his arms. "I want Zar on the team. He'll be back up for Valentine if needs be." He stared hard around the room at the weird collective of racers, as if daring them to disagree.

Apparently his say so was reason enough. The team lapsed into silence.

"We're agreed then?" Braxton turned to Zar. "As for this motley crew, Zar, they might look rough around the edges, but they're hand picked for the job. Trust me on that, as Sol trusted me to get you bruising in the Ramrod."

§

The way Zar had always understood it, the Ramrod Rally was about toughing it out against a bunch of competitors who had no more mind for rules than a pack of rabid dogs. Now it emerged that there was method to the madness, including a carefully assembled team to cover all bases: a captain to shape the team's choices over the course of the rally, a mechanic to fix and botch vehicles in-between bouts, a navigator to concentrate on spying the marker projections and guiding the team along the quickest route between them, a bodyguard to help ward off unwelcome intrusion, and a number of drivers to take part in the racing challenges.

Braxton rubbed his hands together. "Start flag waves tomorrow at noon. This is the flow of things. The Rally lasts twenty fours hours. The route is marked by sky projections. Teams consist of between five and ten drivers. Experience tells me to stick to six, seven max – less bodies to get across the finish line. All team members must finish, regardless of their physical condition or which vehicle they end up in. All clear so far?" He rocked back on his heels. "There are five bouts. The first and fifth are races to and from the Era ferries. The bouts in-between...Well, no one can really guess what'll go on once you reach the Eras."

Zar's stomach somersaulted with this last reminder. Accessed only by the iron sharks of the commuter ferries, the Eras were similar to Raina's father – a law unto themselves. On the far side of Lady Luck Lough across a stretch of salt flats called the Wastelands, the Eras were not for the faint hearted. So he'd heard. The good folk of Autodrome steered clear of those outlands.

Braxton swiped his nose as if scenting victory. "So here's the set up. Jesse, mechanic. Raina, navigator. Valentine, Justice and Eight Ball, you guys will be eligible for the fight zones, you too Zar. Then there's the role of team captain. Valentine, you up for the job?"

The mobster shook his head, begrudgingly Zar thought. "I got enough going on just playing my part in the Ramrod, you know. But thanks for the offer."

"Yeah, you're right. Best to separate the roles of captain and fight zone competitor. I'm thinking we need a strategist, someone with enough bite to keep you crazy kids in line. And we need a bodyguard. You don't wanna be bothered by Riflers, not when they can literally snatch out a win from under you."

"Why not roll the two into one and get Persia Gold." Valentine let out a belly laugh. His laughter faded. "I'm kidding, Braxton. Braxton..!"

It appeared the promoter had missed the joke. Rubbing a hand around his chin, Braxton nodded. "You're gonna need a bodyguard for the Wastelands. Persia's got experience in that field, plus she's the nerve and the wherewithal to captain the team."

"Hot damn, Braxton!" Valentine looked flustered for the first time. He chased an itch up under the brim of his hat. "Whaddya say Eight Ball, Justice?"

Eight Ball shrugged.

Justice looked icy. "Hell'll freeze over before Persia agrees."

Braxton threw out his hands in delight. "Zar'll convince her. Way I've heard it, he's got a rep not only as a speed demon but also as a ladies man."

Raina couldn't suppress a burst of laughter.

Zar shot her an acid look. "I've no issue getting this Persia Gold to sign on, but..." He indicated Braxton aside.

Massaging the back of his neck, he said softly, "This mechanic's spot. I don't get the Jesse James thing. Ask me, he's a hustler."

"Jesse comes recommended on the highest authority." Braxton eyed Zar with resolve.

"Okay. Well, I have a recommendation too. Including this Persia Gold character, the team will number seven but you said we can stretch to ten. I think my friend, Tripster would be a real asset. He's a brain."

"Same kid I met at your pad yesterday?"

"Yeah, that's the one. Good on road knowledge, race stats..."

"No can do on that score, I'm afraid, Zar."

"What?" Zar felt the same rent inside he had felt whenever his dad undermined him in the past.

"This ain't a joyride. I brought Raina onto the team because she's a talented driver, but there's no room for hangers on." Braxton held up his hand. "Yeah, I hear you, this kid is a brain, and maybe he'd be an asset, but he's also a young offender. Theft remember? That act was never going to garner him sympathy from the racing fraternity given how much the Riflers like to plague us. Plus the kid can't race again 'til he's done his time. Simple as. So I don't mean to undermine you..." He stroked his chin and gave a snort of laughter. "Hell, who am I kidding? Yeah I do." The laughter faded away and the promoter got a savage look back in his eyes. "Around here my word is law. Your friend is a young offender and a liability. Jesse meanwhile? He's simply a jerk. So my advice to you would be keep your head down, concentrate on the matter in hand – namely the race and your daddy's treasure map – and let a grown up decide on the best team to aid you."

Zar felt a great charge of heat bubble up from inside. He flushed, hating everything about Braxton in that instant. Not only was the man deeply patronising, but he kept demonstrating an uncanny knowledge about those closest to Zar. Hearing his friends' and family's secrets spilt from the man's lips was eerie and disorientating. It made him want to lash out at Braxton, dislodge a couple of those dangerous looking teeth in his shark's smile. At the same time, he knew his fate lay wholly in Braxton's hands. He was at the mercy of a man who wore sincerity like a mask which kept slipping.

The promoter folded his arms. "I'm telling you as a true friend, as a father would a son, be careful who you trust in this game, Zar. There's wannabes and sour losers aplenty out there. You and Tripster – you got history as I understand it. Maybe your friend Tripster isn't all that happy he earned his nickname in a more literal way than most. Maybe he'd like a way to trip you up in return?"

Just when Zar thought he couldn't be pushed any further, Braxton surprised him. "Don't you dare talk trash about Tripster! He's been a true friend when all you other slimeballs were only ever interested in how much cash I could make for you before I got taken out on the track. He's worth a million of you and your boy wonder there." He spoke in a loud whisper and threw out an arm to Jesse James, who might not have heard him but had definitely cottoned on that he was the subject of their dispute. The kid crossed his arms and sneered all too happily.

"Look, Zar. I don't mean to offend you. We just can't take a risk by including your buddy on the team."

"But you'll vouch for Jesse James instead?"

"He'll toe the line." Braxton unfolded his arms and smoothed the creases from his shirt. "Meantime, don't know if this will ease the pain any but here's a piece of info for you. There ain't no method of communication allowed once you strike out on the Ramrod circuit. Data Streamer watches that are pre-hologram, they're permissible." He indicted Zar's outmoded Data Streamer watch and the state-of-the-art model he wore on his own wrist. "Mine won't pass, but your timepiece is ancient, less a watch as a toy. Way I hear it though, some hacker sorts have the ways and means to expand the gadget's uses." Braxton got back his predatory smile and winked.

Zar gave nothing away. He knew Tripster had the brain power to reengineer all manner of legacy technology, even if the firewalls of the city's conglomerates resisted his and others' efforts. Who these 'others' were, that was information he'd never considered asking for and Tripster had certainly never volunteered. Only thing he knew was that his friend often found the means to retrieve and redistribute information without needing to leave his own four walls or the confines of his tank chair. But how did *Braxton* know about such things, and how deep did his knowledge really go? Was it really Tripster who was untrustworthy, or Braxton?

Regardless, Zar couldn't see a way through to getting Tripster on board. He switched subject. "And this bodyguard. Any ideas where I'll find her?"

"Ah!" Braxton got the look of an excited Doberman. "Persia likes to frequent your neck of the woods. The Death Pit," he clarified with a flash of his dangerous smile.

§

# Chapter 8

Zar tried to distinguish the faces of individuals on the teeming terraces of the Death Pit.

"It's pointless me searching. I've never met this Persia Gold."

"You'd remember if you had." Valentine didn't take his eyes off the crowd.

"Talking of folk who run out on a friend, where's Eight Ball?" said Justice, draped in colourful Kente cloth and a scowl.

Valentine frowned. "Didn't expect you to play judge and jury, Justice."

"I didn't expect you to name-drop Persia to Braxton like that," Justice retaliated. "And don't look all coy about it. We all know you were secretly hoping we'd end up here chasing after her."

"Whatever you say, Justice." Valentine kept his gaze steady. "As for Eight Ball, try the concession stand."

Justice nodded. "That guy always did think with his stomach." She narrowed her gaze. "As for Persia, she lynched herself."

Zar gave up trying to understand the politics of his team mates. He stared about him, feeling frustrated and oddly isolated. Again, the niggling pressure of keeping it together in front of these older, wiser racers hit home. They might be just a couple of years older him, but boy did they exude confidence and experience! The loneliness wasn't helped by Raina's desertion of him. While delighted that Jesse chose to hang back at Braxton's with the repugnant Isha, he'd been sorely disappointed when Raina bowed out of a visit to the Death Pit. "My dad didn't approve of the place. A demolition derby without honour, he used to call it," she'd explained. Zar had taken it as a personal slight.

"I'm going to take a look around," he announced to Valentine and Justice, both of whom proved too self-involved to offer more than a grunt and a backwards wave.

Weaving in and out of the crowd, Zar felt his shoulders physically relax. For the first time in forty eight hours, he felt he didn't have to perform or live up to an impossible ideal. He was back in the dive where he earnt his crust. Even the stench of the Death Pit was soothing: fast food, sweat, stale beer, and closer to the dust arena, an oily farmyard odour.

Descending to the first terrace, he stared past the barrier into the arena. It was between bouts. Interim entertainment was provided by a monster truck, the wings of which were each graffitied with a fist. Built to entertain rather than race, the 20,000 pound truck was demonstrating its brawn, bouncing off gas shocks to slam-dunk the hood of a motor home.

"Didn't expect to see you here. Heard about your dad on the news. Sorry dude."

Zar recognised the guy as one of the few faces to stick around at the Death Pit. Most kids were out of there inside a month. It was good to see him.

He reciprocated the handlock the kid offered.

"Thanks, Davey." His gaze returned to the arena where the monster truck ran over the top of the motor home, partially crushing it. He chose not to dwell on thoughts of his dad and asked instead, "Have you seen any bodyguards around here, Davey? Protecting a truck maybe, or keeping tabs on a rich kid wants to kick it with us dirt bags?"

"Considering your future career, Punkstar? Death of a loved one'll do that to you. I understand why you'd turn your back on this gig." Davey slung a thumb over his shoulder at the parts' strewn arena. "But a bodyguard's gonna meet more trouble, the likes of which neither you nor me could handle. We're road hogs, Punkstar. We ain't fighters."

Zar nodded. "Which is why I'm looking to hire a bodyguard. Goes by the name of Persia Gold."

Davey gave a knowing grunt. "Yeah, I noticed her. She's been patrolling the pit last couple of days. You got it bang on, Punkstar. She's minding a rich kid sent to get his Death Pit spurs by his rich daddy. You got your pit pass?"

Zar produced a small plastic coated card from his pants' pocket.

Davey jerked his head towards the far side of the arena.

"Go say hi to the pretty girl."

§

Backstage of the Death Pit, Zar was numb to all but the machines. Each vehicle was a master class in re-engineering: reptilian body plates, slick spray jobs, fat tyres and integrated weaponry. Zar wrapped his arms around his chest. Life in the pit left him breathless, always had, ever since he first signed up at age thirteen to earn a buck in its rule-free arena. It had also given him a chance to really get to grips with his driving skills, given that it was illegal to drive on the open road in Autodrome until the age of 15, the Pro Leaguer race championships being the exception to the rule.

One vehicle stirred him more than all the others. Parked in a roped off section labelled 'Out of Action' was a 1931 Ford roadster, his Grey Rat. He'd taken a job pumping gas the previous summer just so he could save up for that ride, and it had served him well, both in the pit and in the more glamorous qualifiers. Right then, he knew it was idiotic but he couldn't help feeling a flood of warmth to the pit of his stomach. His ride was the closest thing he'd got to something he was proud of. Not only that but Grey Rat was nothing to do with any other soul; living or dead.

"I gave her the once over," said Davey, arriving alongside.

"He."

"Sorry?"

"That vehicle is one mean son of a gun."

"Ah, okay then." Davey scratched his head. "No damage to write home about anyway. So next time you want to kick it out in the pit, *he's* good to go."

The two smirked at each other. Their good humour didn't last."Magnificent, aren't they? Shame your pile of junk is a blot on the landscape," interrupted a boy's voice seesawing on that awkward cusp between bass and falsetto.

*Just when things were looking up.* Zar's irritation reflected in the steam billowing off various straining boilers. He turned around slowly. "Evening, Sputnik."

The kid had a face like an Arabian toad – skin goose-bumped with acne, eyes too wide apart and a sour mouth. "My name is Bogdashha," he corrected petulantly.

Zar stared at the kid. "Our name's kinder."

"Think you're better than me, Punkstar?"

"In terms of results, I am better than you, Sputnik. You're not still upset about that wipe out a couple of weeks back? It's never good to hold a grudge."

"You call it a wipe out. I call it sabotage."

Zar had a vague recollection of the incident, how he had waved the kid in front of his revving ride only to release the brake at the maximum collision point. Did he feel bad? Not for a second. There was no room for niceties in the Death Pit, which was how he had taken out the right wing of Sputnik's ride and secured victory. Admittedly, most drivers tended to give the kid a wide berth, given that his father was Nikolay Obshina, one of Autodrome's elite ex-Super Leaguers. Zar, however, didn't believe in a free ride. No matter who his father was, Sputnik was still a spiteful runt.

The kid rocked on his toes as if preparing to launch. "I'm not upset, Punkstar. I'm vengeful. Next time you hit the Death Pit, I'm guaranteeing my win." He gestured past Zar with a nasty smile. "Thanks to my older brother."

Zar glimpsed a mass out the corner of an eye and turned towards it. The newcomer appeared birthed from the concrete floor. His neck was a solid shaft, his shoulders packed with muscle. There was a blockishness to the kid's head, as if it had been deliberately squared off. The eye sockets were small and sunken, the hair cropped, the nose pan-caked like a boxer's. A bruise stained one giant chop of a cheek.

"Zamochit." A single utterance in a rumble of bass.

Sputnik snorted. His tongue slopped over his lips. "Vladimir's not much for talking. But the words he does use, he chooses well. Zamochit. *The breaking of bones.*"

Too right the brute chose well, Zar thought with faint sting of panic. He had had curses aplenty thrown at him in the past and all refused to stick. But Davey had been right in his earlier observation. Zar was a racer not a fighter. Vladimir, meanwhile, might be only a year or so older, but he appeared constructed for the sole purpose of carrying out murderous acts.

Not that Zar was about to let the brute smell fear. "Let me ask you something, Vlad," he embarked, forcing back his shoulders. "Where's the honour in you taking me out on Sputnik's behalf? If it's the family name that's at stake, shouldn't the kid wrestle the bear himself?"

Vladimir stared down without blinking.

Davey attempted a feeble intervention. "Come on, lads. Let's save it for the pit."

Zar was about to diffuse the situation or aggravate it – he hadn't decided which – when a husky voice interrupted.

"Getting big bro to molest the newcomer, honey? Makes a change from beating on my client. All the same, I'm going to have to ask, no, insist you stop. And before you try it, I don't give a crap who your daddy is."

Green cowboy boots. Denim jumpsuit sprayed onto seemingly endless limbs. Long blonde hair. A heart-shaped face. Hazel eyes. Tanned skin. Zar didn't need an introduction. Persia Gold in the flesh was introduction enough.

Not that that prevented him from colouring up at her intervention. Or shooting his mouth off.

"Thanks but I can handle junior and his pet gorilla here."

"Ah, you speak Stupid too." Persia broke out a smile that could sustain life. She presented her hand – a formal gesture that suggested she was used to dealing with clients and difficult situations in spite of being seventeen at most – and Zar shook it in spite of himself. "I'm Persia Gold," she said extraneously.

"This is nothing to do with you, bodyguard," weaselled Sputnik.

A quick arm movement and Persia floored him, much to Zar's amazement and not inconsiderably delight. While Davey made his excuses and scarpered, Vladimir didn't flinch. Instead he seemed to eat Persia up, beady eyes aglow.

Sputnik scuttled back on his heels in crab-like retreat. His mouth was bleeding. "We've all got a soft spot, bodyguard. Yours will be found," he snarled.

"I give you A for dramatics but I'm predicting D-minus on the delivery. As for mountain boy here, dude, you gotta have better ways to spend your time than playing nursemaid. How's about you scat?" She cocked her head at Sputnik while feeding a strip of gum between her lips. "Take the cheese weasel with you."

Much to Zar's surprise, rather than power forward and annihilate them both, Vladimir inclined his head towards Persia with a flash of teeth. Steering the dazed Sputnik ahead with the plates of his palms, he strode away.

Zar wanted to say thank you. Pride prevented him and instead he turned on his saviour. "I'd have dealt with those losers just fine without your interference."

"But Persia makes fights so much prettier to watch."

Valentine stood a few feet away, pinstripe jacket tucked back where he thrust his hands in his pants' pockets. Justice glowered to his right. To his left, Eight Ball chewed on a fresh matchstick, a scar of ketchup at his chin.

"Valentine Heart." The bodyguard crinkled her nose.

"Persia Gold. You're looking swell." Valentine tried out a grin. "Do I get a squeeze from my best girl?"

"Try it and I'll lay you out, chump."

Valentine's smile flickered. "A rain check then."

"Justice, Eight Ball." Persia nodded. "So all the gang's together again."

"Not all the gang." Justice's face was a web of strained muscle.

Persia shook her head. "That was doggish of me." She squinted at Justice as if sizing her up and saddened by what she saw. "How you been?"

Justice stared back. "I quit school. It got in the way of real life. I train in the week, cage-fight on the weekends. Taken down every opponent put in my way to date. Think you'll be any exception?"

Persia appeared taken aback by the other girl's anger. "Justice…" Her words petered out and there was an awkward pause, broken only when Valentine gestured lightly in Zar's direction.

"Persia, this is Zar Punkstar. Son of Sol Punkstar." He exhaled heavily. "Was the son of Sol Punkstar, I should say. Sol was diced a couple of days back."

"Sol Punkstar, the architect dude?" Persia turned to Zar. "Sorry to hear that, man." She stayed serious. "So what's the lowdown? Are the gods just smiling on me tonight or could you gearheads want something?"

Zar couldn't join in the uncomfortable reunion. Instead he cut to the chase. "The Ramrod Rally has been reinstated."

"Uh-huh. I heard. Kicks off at noon tomorrow."

He kept with the straight talking. "Braxton Earl has put together a team. We're short of a bodyguard. Plus, your name has been put forward for team captain. We need someone with knowledge of the Eras and the smarts to steer us to victory."

"Ah!" Persia looked as if she had stepped out of the dark. "Braxton Earl – the shark with a heart. Except he left me adrift with piranhas on my heinie."

Valentine stroked his scarred cheek. "Braxton should've stepped up to the plate to defend you, but he was no more of a schlepper than the rest of us."

"No duh, Valentine." Persia turned her hazel eyes on Valentine. "If there's one real operator here, I'm looking at him."

The mobster remained unflappable. "This ain't about me, doll. It's about the lotta us proving something."

"Thing is, I've spent the past year proving something – that life goes on. I've learnt to fit in school in-between carving myself a new niche as a sometime bodyguard. So while the rest of you be sure to enjoy this little get-together, I don't need no backwards."

Zar didn't want to give in that easily. "Persia. We need a team captain and Braxton says you're the best. I don't know what happened a year ago..."

"You're right. You don't know what happened and I suggest you don't go yanking my chain trying to find out. Look, Zar. Nothin' personal, but I wouldn't spit on some of your team mates if they were on fire, and they sure didn't care to help me out in the past. So while it's been cool-o-roonie to catch up, I'm kinda busy and kinda outta here." Pressing two fingers to pursed lips, Persia saluted them and strode away, hips swinging.

Eight Ball gave a low whistle. "I hate to see her go..."

Valentine nodded, "...but I love to watch her leave."

§

Persia wasn't a gal to fall for a sob story or a handsome face. That was Valentine's take on the matter. Want his advice? Zar should forget Persia's smart mind and mouth. Forget Persia.

Judging by the emotion on Valentine's face, it was difficult for the gangster to take his own advice. Nonetheless, he tore himself away, tossing back over a shoulder, "You know this joint better than anyone, Zar. I'm guessing it won't be hard for you to hire us a different bodyguard. We'll work out the team captain thing amongst ourselves."

Justice spared no energy on crocodile tears. "Persia's right. We don't need no backwards. We especially don't need someone who'll evaporate when the going gets tough." But Zar detected a level of deeper feeling, saw its flicker in her soft brown eyes. Justice left the pit with Eight Ball in tow.

Zar squeezed his fists into his eyes. Why was everything such an uphill battle? Not only did he have to deal with his own demons but now he had to cope with those of his team mates as well.

He let his hands drop. His view was smeary. No way was he was going to let Persia get away from him!

Five minutes later and it was becoming clear that nothing about the Ramrod or his part in it was going to come easy. For all of Persia's magnetism, she continued to elude him. Zar found the bay where she supposedly holed up, a ventilated tin can cut in half and bolted over a pit in the concrete. While the backstage area lit him up like a flame to gasoline, the mechanics' pits were decidedly less welcome. His mind whirled with images of his dad's cramped body in a hole. Again, he resisted the tremendous weight of grief which threatened to pull him under.

"Persia Gold!" he called forcefully. No reply. He exhaled through his nose and was about to exit the bay when he heard his name whispered.

"Zar...Zar Punkstar." Gone the backchat. Persia's voice was thin and pained.

Heart punching, Zar traced the sound to the far side of a huge staved water butt where he found Persia struggling to stand, an angry red welt at her forehead.

"Rug rat slugged me out cold." Taking in the empty bay, she pressed the heel of a hand to an eye and groaned. "He took the Ford Escort."

Relieved to see that her injury was minor, Zar hitched up an eyebrow. "You gave him a Ford Escort?"

Persia grimaced. "Safest bet for a kid like Eugene. Except he wasn't meant to get out there yet, not when his daddy has enemies. I got wind of a tag team sent in to bust the kid up. And now he's loose on the field, which means I gotta get out there." She tried to stand but her eyes rolled back to show the whites and she staggered.

Zar held her by an elbow. "If the kid's determined enough to chance it in the Death Pit that he'll take a swipe at you, why not let him take a turn out there? Way I hear it, his old man wants him to experience life on the tough side of the tracks."

"Except it ain't peachy like that, Punkstar." Persia made a hammock of her fingers to rest her forehead in. She inhaled and forced her eyes up. "Eugene's a type one diabetic. He's also prone to chronic epilepsy. It's illegal for him to drive on the open road ever. How bogus is that for a kid in Autodrome? Which is why his daddy sent him here. Let the kid taste what it's like to beat the drag where it's okay to collide with oncoming traffic. Except now Eugene's truckin' it alone with a pair of jive turkeys' on his tail, and I need to get my ass in gear before he gets tattered."

Before he could build a mental wall to keep the memory out, Zar relived his mother ODing in his mind, how she'd struggled against him while he'd tried to stop her body from failing, how he had held her close when all he wanted to do was run and keep on running. Mindy had brought the episode on herself. All the same, no one should have to suffer like that, let alone a kid with no choice in the matter.

He narrowed his eyes. "More than your job's worth to let the kid get slammed, right?"

"Hit the road, Punkstar. I gotta stand and I might blow chunks." Persia tried to get up but fell back again, cursing.

"I've forty heats in that dust bowl under my belt," said Zar, forcing authority into his voice. "I'll bring back your boy, Eugene. In exchange, you'll agree to captain me and the rest of the team in the Ramrod."

The beautiful eyes frosted. Zar didn't wait for an answer.

He was about to exit the bay when Persia hollered after him, "Number 9, sky-blue Ford Escort. Eugene starts to wipe out, load him up with this baby." She sent a small white object scooting over the concrete.

Zar picked up the adrenaline pen.

"You need to find a muscle..." Persia began.

"I know what to do with it," Zar interrupted. He went to leave when another thought occurred to him. "And Persia. If my ride gets mangled out there, I'm going to need to borrow yours for the Ramrod tomorrow."

Before the girl could object, he charged off in the direction of his Grey Rat roadster.

§

The tractor moved forward, trawling the studded roller gate in its wake. Zar eased the nose of his ride into the wet dust, straining against the seat belt to make out the cluster of action at the opposite end of the arena. Air bled from his lips. He hit the gas, slamming into first gear to gain traction on the watered ground before ripping back to second as his speed increased. Steering between the chicanes of fatally wounded vehicles, he powered towards the main root mass.

The hit came from behind, a cramming jolt that had Zar whip forward, his face a centimetre from the steering wheel, then flip back into his seat. It didn't pay to take the attack personally. Most of the time anyway.

His vehicle stalled. Zar restarted the engine, re-rooted the stick and swung hard left to circumnavigate the arena, avoiding a three car slam that saw doors concave and a hood crumple. Two vehicles locked horns across his route, a white pearl Lexus and a pale blue Ford...a Ford. His gaze flew to the number on the driver door. 9.

Zar decided to say hi the best way he knew how. Pumping the revs, he hauled on the handbrake and threw his roadster into a wide arc, colliding with both vehicles.

All three machines ricocheted back in the dust. Someone cursed at volume – the kid, Eugene. Face stippled with mud. Lips tumbling over themselves.

He had found him. But what to do next? Zar didn't want to humiliate Eugene by battering the Ford into submission, plus it wouldn't go down well with Persia if he did any accidental damage to her charge. His only real options were to keep the Ford safe from attack or mangle the opposition in as short a time as possible. Sparky with adrenaline, Zar decided to attempt both.

"Eugene! You got a couple of bogies on your tail," he called against the roar of the Death Pit.

Either Eugene couldn't hear or he was in no mood to listen. Instead, the kid mangled the gears and reversed around the rim of the pit. Belching steam from a squat boiler on its roof, a reengineered Subaru yanked right as Eugene drove past. It skinned the Ford's left wing in a cascade of sparks.

So intent was Zar on the collision that he momentarily lost track of the rest of the field. When it came, the fresh hit was a twisting iron fist in his driver side door – a strike seen as bad form in most competitions but which garnered hoots and applause from the Death Pit's bloodthirsty audience.

Zar had instinctually scooted over onto one side of his seat, leaning away from the impact as his door blistered. Righting himself, he glanced sideways. The thrill of the pit drained from him as if his throat had been cut. Engorging the driver seat of a red and gold Chrysler sedan was Vladimir.

The thug tore back his lips and grinned – a ghoulish expression. Zar shrugged off the horror of it. Vlad might be a heavyweight in terms of physical size, but here in the pit, he was just another set of wheels.

Floodlights blazed overhead like hovering UFOs. Beyond the pit, the stands were lost to starless dark. Zar guided the roadster in and out the twelve or so active vehicles, two of which collided head-on in his wake, their radiators erupting in great churning geysers of lemony fluid. The crowd hollered. Vehicles aquaplaned. Wheels revolved in ruts, throwing up manure-like clods or showering spectators in filth.

Tucking in alongside a graffitied Pontiac minivan, Zar surveyed the field. Vlad was backed up behind a glut of vehicles, some of which were hacking out a few last sticky revs and smoking under the hood. Given their unwavering pursuit of the Ford, he pinpointed the tag team as the pearl white Lexus and the steam-fed Subaru.

Any respite was short. Breaking free of the snarl-up, Vlad steered the sedan hard at him. Zar slid between the tag team as they rumbled past and glued himself to Eugene's bumper. The hand signals the kid peeled off showed he was anything but happy...Except no, that wasn't it, Zar realised with a jolt. He recognised a seizure when he saw one thanks to his mother and her Razzledazzle addiction. Difference was Mindy was always stowed in the safety of her bedroom whereas this Eugene kid was behind the wheel of a moving vehicle. His best bet was to get the kid hauled up at the barrier. But how to shrug off the tag team before they attacked from either side? Zar felt a wave of nausea mixed with elation. He needed to take out all three vehicles in one run.

A wham on the brake pedal and the roadster ground to a halt, spitting sawdust. Zar caressed the accelerator, keeping his foot on the brake. All around, cars wrecked themselves on the hard skulls of others. Bonnets crumpled. Water slopped. Steam hissed between broken rivets.

Zar let loose the break and floored the accelerator. Careering over the damp surface, he scraped along the driver door of the Lexus before hooking hard left to place that same cruel kiss on the Subaru. The tag team ricocheted out – just as the Pontiac minivan skidded into the Subaru. Zar caught the impact out the corner of an eye as the skin of both vehicles buckled. Easing off the gas, he twisted round in his seat. The Subaru's boiler had cracked like an egg. A quarter of the arena was misty with steam.

Turning back around, he saw the Ford slow as it headed for the barrier. He was relieved; Eugene must have jerked his foot off the gas.

Then he saw the last few moving vehicles steer around the bend and charge as a pack. The Ford was directly in their path. At the same time, the Lexus flew out of the mist, an angel of death intent on the Ford. As for Vlad, the Chrysler appeared caught on the mangled bonnet of a fellow competitor. The two machines were waltzing, the sight of which gave Zar a game plan.

...If his rat rod could hold out. There was grit in its engine noise. The vehicle also listed; he suspected the front left wheel arch had been misshapen after his earlier side-on with Vlad's meaty sedan. He pumped the gas and propelled the roadster at the Ford.

There were a few seconds of white noise before he hit the rear of the Ford and threw himself sideways, forcing the roadster into a side wheelie. G-force whiplashed his neck. Blood screamed in his ears. He slammed back down into his seat, steering into the left hand wing of the Ford, splintering off a thin skin of patch plates and hooking his ride onto the driver door. The cars were bonded. Zar glanced left and right. He and Eugene were about to get grand-slammed by every other vehicle on the field.

"Hold on for me," he urged his rat rod. Zigzagging the stick into reverse, he put the peddle to the floor and tried to have eyes everywhere. The conjoined vehicles bucked. Eugene looked like a zombie in his driver seat. Misfiring neurological impulses put pressure on his stiff limbs.

"You hold on too, Eugene," Zar muttered. He spun the revs and shot back. The Ford was a parasitic twin he carried with him, and in so doing, he opened up the field at the precise moment of collision between the Lexus and the stampede opposite. The noise at impact was a buckling cacophony. Flames shot up in great rips of ambers. Drivers tumbled from glassless windows and already fire extinguishers were set on them and their vehicles, safety officers appearing magically on the scene. As the flames were smothered, the reverence of the crowd was replaced with animalistic elation.

Zar felt like a gladiator blooded from his kill. He unhooked his seatbelt and leant across and in at the window of the Ford. Eugene was lathered in sweat, his face contorted. Zar fumbled for the insulin pen. He flipped off the lid and was grabbing for the kid's arm when he became aware of a strip of dark to his left. A car sped towards them. Vlad grinned in the driver seat.

There wasn't time to fasten himself back in. Time vacuumed as Zar relived his mother's sad smile as he had placed the sleeveless Razzledazzle pill on her tongue, his father's last embrace as he had lifted him from the pit. Plunging the insulin pen down onto Eugene's arm, he waited for the switch to pain at the Chrysler's impact.

A tremendous roar woke him from his stupor. He saw the hulk of 66 inch tyres pass in front, forcing Vlad to steer off course. The sudden wrench to the Chrysler's steering wheel seemed to be the final straw. It bunny-hopped three times and stalled, leaving Vlad to escape through the empty window frame in a hot-faced scrabble just as the monster truck mounted the roof of the Chrysler and crushed it. Passing over the top, the truck tipped down onto the ground and powered back around in an earthquake of noise. It came to a halt in front of Zar. The engine idled, the door opened and long legs encased in skin-tight denim emerged. Persia jumped down. She nodded as if in acknowledgement of her debt to him, then raised her hands and clapped.

The crowd were on their feet now, whopping and hollering for Lucky 13, the number daubed across what remained of Zar's driver door.

Eugene stirred an instant then slept. Zar fell back into his seat. He'd survived, which was more than could be said for the steaming hulk of his rat roadster. Right that instant though, he was too annihilated to take it in. He closed his eyes and let the noise and relief seep into his bones.

§

# Chapter 9

Friday 13th. Two minutes to noon. Zar was in
the driver's seat of Persia's Road Runner, a 1970's
muscle car in classic Sublime Green with a thick black
stripe down the hood. This was his kind of vehicle, a
gas guzzler without any fancy reengineering. It had
the pared back interior he craved in a ride alongside
elemental mechanics; the steering wheel was a generous
metal hoop, the peddles chunky enough to mash if
circumstances called for it. Aside from his decimated rat
rod, there was no other vehicle Zar would rather trust his
life to. The fact that Persia Gold was riding shotgun made
the experience even better.

"Get a scratch on her and you won't be grinning,"
murmured Persia.

Zar nodded, but nothing could wipe the smile off his
face. Yes, there might be an argument that he and the rest
of Autodrome's young racers were just pawns to be played
and sacrificed by the likes of Frank Oz. But the race
circuit offered Autodrome's poorest teens a swift footed
route to fame and fortune – the stuff a kid's dreams were
made of. Zar felt as if he might explode with excitement.

He was taking part in the Ramrod Rally and his ride was a Road Runner!

The vehicles belonging to the rest of his crew were just as wild.

To the right was Eight Ball in his 'borrowed' ride – so he had informed Braxton when they convened earlier, a smug set to his jaw. The Ford Skyliner was a confectionary in desert island blue with sterile white wings. Silver trim and alloys soaked up the sun's brilliance. A low windshield hugged the front seats. The hardtop was retracted under the rear deck lid. Hand on the dished steering wheel, matchstick between his lips, Eight Ball was the perfect match to the Skyliner's weighty cool.

To the left, Justice grew out from the saddle of her Dodge Tomahawk like a dragon rider. The quadricyle was breathtaking – a polished chrome engine set between dual front and rear wheels. Zar had seen an early example of the concept vehicle in the city museum, an impractical bullish machine. But this new model was small, light, and thanks to a counterweighted exoskeleton, very manoeuvrable.

The same could not be said for the vehicle in front – a gleaming fire truck with a staved boiler at the rear and a giant fly wheel revolving over its left wing. Procured by Braxton to give the team added muscle, the vehicle boasted extinguishing facilities, hybrid steam/gas engineering, and, underpinning the wheelbase, a sealed gas reservoir and periscopic hose to refuel vehicles on the move. The truck was manned by Jesse James. Since the vehicle had the best view both inside the cab and out on the roof, Persia had decided it made sense for Raina, the team's navigator, to ride alongside Jesse. Not that Persia's decision sat lightly with Zar. But he did trust a girl like Raina to handle a buckshot like Jesse.

To the rear, Valentine's steam car struck Zar as one of the coolest pieces of kit he had ever seen. Reengineered from a Cadillac V16, it was a golden calf of a vehicle. Bubbled hood, wings, and headlights. Sharkish grill.

A siren sounded and a voice laden with reverb announced, "Ladies and gentlemen, welcome to the Ramrod Rally!" All around the car park, giant video screens showed a man in a sharp black suit and ornate waistcoat. The crowd went wild behind the barriers.

"I am Nikolay Obshina, ex Super Leaguer," said the man extraneously, and a tremendous cheer went up. In Autodrome, there was no higher accolade. All the same, Zar would have been nonplussed usually, his logic being that in order to have produced Sputnik and Vladimir as offspring, Nikolay Obshina had to have a dark side. That day though, he cheered along with the rest.

"A year ago, the team I was managing came in at a track time of 22 hours 20 minutes 7.40 seconds with four out of five trial victories under our belt." Nikolay held out open palms. His audience responded with fists banged on the roofs of vehicles and cries of support. Zar felt a new, wonderful lightness within.

"Today you, the new blood, are here to race. The Ramrod Rally is comprised of trials across the city. First trial is speed. Follow the skull projections, waste time if you want attacking your enemy, but remember only the first three teams to reach the docks will continue. The qualifiers will then sail across Lady Luck Lough and the wastelands to enter the Eras, where the second trial will be revealed." Nikolay lifted his face to the spotlight. "Ladies and gentlemen, start your engines!"

Keys twisted. Cranks revolved. Peddles were caressed.

Zar felt on fire with anticipation. This was it. The Ramrod Rally. The moment he'd dreamt of since he was old enough to understand what it meant to rise to a challenge and to win.

The air horn sounded. With a great swell of noise and gaseous stench, the rows of vehicles started moving.

Circumnavigating Dixie Island, they fed right as one conjoined mass to hit the eight lane highway, the Artery. The more experienced teams stayed tight, leaving the flakier contingent to zip in and out of the crowd.

Eye on the rear view, Zar saw his first glimpse of dirty road tactics. A hover bug jostled a rider in a one-man riot wheel. With the fat wheel that powered the vehicle at his back, the rider leant left then right in an effort to elude the bug. It wasn't enough. The bug accelerated suddenly to pull in ahead of the riot wheel, its twin engines smoking the flesh off the rider's bones. Zar winced as the riot wheel tipped over. Oncoming vehicles shunted it about the track like a hockey puck.

A second hover bug decelerated to fall in alongside its twin. Zar felt his insides twist as Persia leant over and yanked on the steering to throw the Road Runner into a tight spot between Eight Ball's Skyliner and Valentine's Cadillac.

"Sorry, man. That second bug was giving us the hairy eyeball." Before he could complain, she twisted hard around in her seat and gestured over a shoulder with a thumb. "Hotdog! That's a helluva formation. You diggin' this?"

Zar felt his breath catch. The convoy of vehicles overtaking them was one slick organism. At the head was a Kettenkrad, a cross between a motorbike and a miniature tank. A gold and turquoise monster truck served as the thorax while the hover bugs positioned themselves as wing cases. A Mazda RX-7 sports car was glued to the tail of a Toyota Supra Mark Eight in abdominal formation. The drivers wore spray-on navy jumpsuits and magnifying brass goggles, confirming Zar's suspicions that they were an elite band of Pro Leaguers.

The Kettenkrad eased off the gas, allowing the rest of the crew to speed by then zipped back in. Now the monster truck headed up the pack. In the moments it took for a new skull projection to direct the pack off the highway, the truck decimated a motorised tandem and a smaller sand buggy, scattering remains in its wake.

Persia gave a low whistle. "Notice their racing credo?"

"Pro Leaguers." Zar kept his gaze on the Kettenkrad's tail as the crew pulled ahead. "We're not capable of outstripping them?"

"Eight Ball'd have a shot. Reckon you'd give the gearheads a run for their money too. But while Jesse's coolio at handling the fire truck, the weight of it'd pull us down. Best hope we have is chill 'n' be cool. As long as we can shake the Frankensteins on our tail."

Zar adjusted his rear view. While the Pro Leaguers had resembled a gorgeous steel butterfly, the latest team to muscle in were a darker strain. They spread out behind Valentine's Cadillac, taking up the width of the highway. The lead vehicle was a steam coach – a great craning glass and steel pumpkin with giant cartwheels and a rear-mounted chimney stack. Squatting alongside like an overzealous bodyguard was a colossal landship with spiralled copper funnels, a revolving turret and what looked like a snowplough mounted up front. Foot soldiers included a blacked out caddy hearse, an armoured sand buggy, a raked Harley V-rod, and a cyborg on skates supported by two aerodynamic, wheel-tipped wings.

A skull appeared right of a fork in the road just as the coach drew out in front and straddled two lanes, leaving the Road Runner in danger of being forced left. Zar hooked an arm around the back of the bench seat, twisted at the waist to see better, and eased the vehicle in centimetres from one colossal iron cartwheel. They scraped in by the skin of their teeth – just as the steam coach shunted sideways, forcing Zar to take the muscle car onto the sidewalk.

"Watch how you treat her, dude," hissed Persia, teeth jarring.

Zar grinned and floored the gas. They streaked past the coach, flopping back down onto the roadway just short of a fire hydrant.

"Betcha there's a bitch steering that princess coach," spat Persia. "Rich bitch, too," she added.

Zar threw the Road Runner wide as they entered a hairpin, forcing Persia to grip the bench seat in order to stay upright.

"The newcomers are snaking us while our team's trapped behind," she barked.

Zar sharpened his focus. They were climbing the terraces of upper eastside. The road beneath became pitted. Flimsy iron railings hemmed them in and while Zar had no fear of heights, he did fear defective engineering.

The road forked again. The right lane was resurfaced with cats' eyes running down the central strip. The left lane was a disused trail leading to the defunct Black Rods railroad bridge. A skull projected a few metres up the marled track.

Persia nodded at the road ahead. "My advice, man. You need to peel off for a while, get your skateboard and scoot. We're about to go off-roading."

A skin-pricking tide of nerves washed over Zar. *Time to go it alone.* Which was exactly what he had been wanting all along. Except, now that the moment had come he couldn't help feeling as if he wanted to shrink down inside of himself, be young and vulnerable instead of the hardnosed brat everyone expected.

Begrudgingly, he swung over to the side of the road. He grabbed his skateboard from the back seat. Taking a deep breath, he cranked the door open and slid out, Persia scooting over and belting up.

He peered in the open window. "I'll catch you up."

"Get a wriggle on, honey."

Persia pulled away, spitting grit from beneath her wheels. Left behind, Zar felt a new emotion – regret to be missing out. But he guided his skateboard underfoot and pushed off back down the hill.

His route was immediately intercepted by the churning iron and steam motion of the steam coach. Curving around the side of the coach, Zar saw the driver staring down – a R'asian princess with olive skin and huge black eyes. She cupped a hand to her lips and blew him a kiss. He almost lost his footing on the board.

The cataclysmic grind of the landship forced him to carve wide. As he skated past, the turret cranked in his direction. Zar's flesh prickled under that all-seeing eye and he forgot the uneven road surface. Snagging the nose of his board on a jag of concrete, he careered forward and flew through the air. He landed, tucking into a skin-shredding ball.

A quick mental check. All bones intact. He forced his trembling limbs to support his weight and raised his eyes. The cyborg skidded past, showering him with grit. Zar blinked in time to see Justice materialise on her Tomahawk and give chase.

Eight Ball cruised by in the Skyliner. But now he noticed the Harley from the Frankenstein team heading in his direction. Zar stared desperately about him for his board – just as Eight Ball hit reverse. The back fender of the Skyliner struck the Harley as its rider attempted to angle away. Only its hefty fairings kept the bike righted. Seconds later, Valentine rumbled up in his Cadillac and bull-horned the sand buggy. He tipped his trilby as he passed.

The fire truck skidded on to the soft verge at the side of the road. Raina leant out the passenger door.

"You okay? That looked like it hurt."

*Why did she have to witness his wipe-out?* Cheeks blazing, Zar raked a hand through his hair, threw back his shoulders and gave Raina the thumbs up. He recovered his board from a pothole and lifted it up onto one shoulder. The fire truck pulled off with a clinkered engine grind and a thick belch of smoke. Raina put her head out the open window, looking back until Jesse steered the truck off onto the dirt track.

Zar ran to the opposite side of the road. He watched Persia's supercharger strike out onto the old railroad bridge. The steam coach was hot on Persia's heels, closely followed by the landship. Spores of rust danced in the air below the bridge like spray off a tarnished waterfall.

A new convoy drove past, but the skull projection had disappeared. The slower vehicles opted wrongly for the resurfaced road. Zar looked back out to the oxidised bridge and the machines crossing it. The bravery his team required for that act alone was awe-inspiring. But there was nothing to be gained from standing there – he had to trust in his team to make it to the other side.

He dropped his board and kicked off.

§

# Chapter 10

Vladimir exited the groaning bridge and crossed the stretch of scrubland to where east met west. The landscape beyond was dominated by super homes resembling mirror balls, folded paper with a car park under a wing, shining cubes and huge blocks gorged out like black cheese to reveal balconies and staircases.

A skull appeared up ahead. Vlad took his foot off the gas and let his fellow competitors streak past. He hooked the Hearse around. The west was a playground but he was wanted to go hunt rats, and for that, he needed to back up to the city's east end. Not that he wanted to tear himself away from the blood sport of the race, but he had his orders.

He felt his swollen cheek with large, clumsy fingers. Yeah, he'd messed up, but that didn't take the sting out of the punch.

He thought back to events of two nights previously and the sight of the mechanism smashed on the concrete below the balcony. Clockwork, rubber tubes, gears and chains. It had turned out to be a pile of junk. But it had seemed his best shot, given the inventor's refusal to hand over the device no matter how hard he was pressed.

"Did you expect it to be just lying there in a cardboard box on a bench?" the voice had hissed, leaving him feeling partly ashamed and partly determined to justify any further trust in him. Not that he'd expressed either emotion, but just stayed quiet while the abuse flowed.

"So he may or may not be dead? May or may not be beaten to a pulp?" The eyes had burnt into his. "At no time did you think to engage brain and back off? I wanted you to persuade him to part with the device, not destroy our sole link to it. Without Sol Punkstar, all we have is an idea that could assure our entry to the Rupine Group at last but also the knowledge that we'll never get close to it without his say so. And I presume you managed to dust the entire area with your prints?" The voice had grown nasty. "I could line the pockets of the necessary Uniform. But that's hardly the point. You were given instructions yet went in heavy handed, and we need that blueprint. You do understand that it has the potential to send this business global – and I mean the real business." A sweep of the hand had taken in the white-tiled lab below the balcony, the glass vats filled with pink, blue or green merchandise. "Increased speed of shipments, the tightening of existing distribution networks, and the muscle of the Rupine group at our back. We're looking at a different league. And you jeopardise it all for the rush of inflicting violence!" The fist had connected and Vlad had reeled from the force of it.

Now, as he took up the trail of the mouthy kid on a skateboard, Vlad accepted that he enjoyed conquering minds via the weakness of the human body. But he'd also sense enough to know he'd pushed it too far. In the future, he'd stay in the shadows where he belonged and watch. At least until the time came to sink the knife in.

§

Zar was back where it had all started, in the Maintenance District of lockups, car washes and garages. His dad's workshop was a couple of blocks across. The scroll had indicated the area as his initial destination, but that was where the specifics stopped and the guessing games started. What exactly was he looking for?

He thought back to when he had activated the scroll and triggered the first section of the trail. There was a green eight ball, its traditional figure eight replaced with a zero, and there was an empty tube. Random symbols... except that would never be the case when his father was involved. Sol might have struggled to communicate verbally, but he could be relied on to create a systematic treasure hunt.

A green ball marked with a zero, the Artery, Black Rod Bridge...Zar's frustration threatened to hem him in. Kicking off, he brought his foot back up onto the deck of his skateboard and wove along the sidewalk. The numerous garages were open, each unit a furnace. Voices echoed. Hydraulics wheezed.

Near his father's workshop, the price of real estate bottomed out. This was the blot on the Maintenance District's landscape. Shutters were dilapidated and half-hung, brickwork scrawled with tags, alleys littered with shredded tyres, old oil cans and dog faeces. These streets led to the rag-and-bone hills of the Scrap Yard, like carrion birds circling a carcass. The area had never struck Zar as quite as filthy as it did at that moment. Here the city seemed less about the thrill of the race than the stench of death.

Zar dipped into the next alley. It was deserted. He lifted his wrist and tapped out the number using the tiny crank. Retrieving a strip from a pocket, he discarded the wrapper, worked the constituent between his palms to soften it and spread the warmed Goo over the watch face. He tapped the lever once with an index finger. A small electric charge liquefied the Goo. It gave off a faint synthetic scent.

He heard five pulses. The Goo puffed up. It settled into a three dimensional scan of Tripster's face.

"How's it going?" The Goo face grinned. "I've seen the coverage on the box."

Zar felt a sense of childish wonder. The watch had been his father's once upon a time and he still remembered Sol showing him how to use the Goo aspect of these older models. He still couldn't quite get his head around the idea that Tripster and his fellow hackers had simply tapped into the technology as a way of communicating below the city's radar.

"Nasty route," he confided. Were ears listening in to their conversation? He reminded himself that Tripster had assured him the line was secure. "Took the team over Black Rod Railroad Bridge at the terraces. I slipped back east to try to find the first puzzle piece."

"So what we got – the ball image from the Parana...?"

"You got it fired up?"

"Naturally."

Zar saw a flicker of contempt on Tripster's face. He swallowed, wishing he could take back his interruption. But Tripster carried on talking and the best thing seemed to be to let the moment slide.

"...we got the green ball symbol and the locale pinpointed to within a street or two. What else?"

"There's the railroad bridge. Competitors have got to risk their lives on that bone shaker."

"Very Ramrod." The Goo face grimaced. "So, the Maintenance District, a condemned railroad bridge, the green ball icon. Seems we're talking a game of chance here. Black Rod Bridge straddles east and west. It was part of the desert railroad until decommissioned when the west decided to sever that particular tie with the east. Built by the same guy who designed Black Stacks. What was that dude's name? Mikhail something. Mikhail..." The gum eyes widened. "Mikhail Vasiliev."

"I've heard of him. Dad lost out on the design bid to him. Mister Frank wanted a darker style. The guy build anything around here?" Zar froze. He thought he heard the scrape of a boot sole. His eyes snapped left. The alley was deserted. He forced himself to concentrate on what Tripster was saying.

"Calling up his details on the VDU Mat." There was a tinny whirring. "Okay. Mikhail Vasiliev. Son of a naval officer. Childhood obsession with steam-powered submarines...always struck me as an underrated application. You're dropped into an ocean full of what? Water. Water makes steam. Granted there's the storage issue with dung cakes. But there's got to be a way to dredge the mid-Tertiary beds of solid faecal matter.

Happy days for marine life as it'd decrease the carbon dioxide levels arising from an ocean bed lined with shi…"

"Tripster, I've got to get back to my teammates," Zar ventured.

There was a brief pause. Tripster continued, "Vasiliev studied architecture, urbanism, landscape and building technologies at Princeton. Died of interstitial nephritis, aged 78. Here's the skinny on his designs: Black Stacks, Black Rod Bridge, Fabricator Flyover, Skullduggery Mansion Block on Easy Street…didn't know he did that one…" The Goo mouth puckered. "Nothing listed in your part of the east."

"Check the footnotes."

"Yes, Sir." The ghost eyes flicked side to side then widened. "We may have something. *Artist Roy Sam erected a monument in memory of Mikhail Vasiliev.*"

"Roy Sam?"

"Hold on. The green ball has a zero on it, right? Listen up, man. 'A pastiche of the formalist aesthetic of postminimalism and Catalan modernism, the sculpture is reconstituted stone and consists of a roundel divided into thirteen segments circumnavigated by a brass ball set in constant clockwork revolution. Hence the monument's nickname: the Roulette Wheel.'"

"Roulette. The green zero. Game of chance. That's it!" cried Zar. But his stomach sank. "No way they'd stick something like that in this dive."

"You'd think, except Roy Sam was a socialist. Wanted to give art back to the people. So he erected the monument on the one site where we are all made equal?"

"A cemetery?" Zar floundered. Where was the nearest spot they buried the city's dead?

"In Autodrome?" The Goo face smiled sardonically. "No, man. In this city, the one place we all come undone is the Scrap Yard."

§

# Chapter 11

Zar wasn't shocked by the flicker of resentment which had crossed Tripster's Goo mask. It had to be hell for the guy to be stuck indoors and away from the heat of the race, even more so to be assigned the role of a brain in a wheelchair.

The previous night, Tripster had listened to Zar's talk of the Ramrod, enrapt.

"So Braxton's hooked you up with some major players." The kid had nibbled the quick of a little finger. "Justice Hunter. She was a phenomenal rider...I say was because she's been absent from the track for a while now. But Eight Ball. He's a prime speed racer...aside from the gambling." There was a moment of silence before he thrust a finger at Zar. "Valentine Heart. There's a racer still showing us the money...except Valentine's into drag strip and the Ramrod's long distance. But aside from those blips, your team's smoking." Tripster showed his teeth.

Zar had got to his feet and started to pace.

"Braxton got Raina in as navigator. She's got crazy skills out on the tracks and knows the meat and bones of an engine."

"Easy on the eye too." Tripster kept up the grin. "You need familiar faces around you when the pressure sets in," he added, his large brown eyes hopeful.

Zar swallowed. The guilt of Tripster's exclusion from the team was killing him. He tried a different tack. "Braxton made decisions based on skill sets."

Tripster nodded sagely.

"No time for indulgence," Zar clarified.

When Tripster shook his head, Zar lost all hope at breaking the news gently. He threw up his hands and went for it straight up.

"You're not on the team, Tripster. I tried to persuade Braxton, but he says we've got a full house. I can't take the risk of going against him. Not when I could lose my place on the team and jeopardise finding out who killed my dad."

Tripster's smile faded – the pain in his eyes cutting Zar to pieces on the inside. "Understandable. We both know the rules of my probation mean I can't actually get behind the wheel." His brow cleared. "Not everything that's thrown at you in a Ramrod can be solved with wheels or muscle. I could be a tactician."

Zar ran the chains at his belt through his hands. "We got a full quota."

"What about this punk mechanic Jesse? Said yourself he struck you as a deadweight. Between Raina and me, we can fix pretty much any engine."

It was difficult for Zar to maintain eye contact. He'd gone up against Braxton as much as he dare on the point of Tripster versus Jesse. But at the end of the day, it was Braxton's team – and he needed the in more than the promoter needed him.

"I've got to listen to Braxton. We've got to have the best possible team. You know I'm doing this to solve my dad's puzzle. You also know how much I want to win this."

"But we're a team. You ride, I research the opposition, pre-guess their manoeuvres. And you can persuade anyone to do anything. Look how things turned out with that bodyguard at the Death Pit."

*Look how things turned out with me and this stupid wheelchair*, Zar suspected Tripster wanted to add. Instead his friend just twisted a fist into his knotty dreads and exclaimed, "Give me one good reason why I'm not your right-hand man this time around!"

It was all too much for Zar. He'd relieved himself of the burden of his mother's care – something which ate away at him incessantly – only to find a new dependant in Tripster. His frustration flash-fired. "Because this is the single most important race of my life. Because this is just the way it is!"

The words fell between them like poisonous rain.

"Now I see your true colours, Zar Punkstar." Tripster's malleable face was less comical now, the manipulation of flesh and muscle hard. "Guess I was an idiot to think you were really okay with my arrest last year. I thought you were an ally. I thought you were a friend."

"I am a friend, Tripster. Who came and bailed you out?"

"I didn't ask you to."

"Didn't matter. I did it. Who made sure everyone knew it was an Underagers' Board race log you hacked into, not the freakin' book of the dead? Who told you to ease up on cramming the race stats? Who said it was borderline obsession?"

Tripster clenched a cushion in each fist, but Zar couldn't let up. He had to make his friend see that he would move heaven and hell to help him, but he couldn't risk his spot on the Ramrod team.

"Tripster, you were there for me in the past and there isn't a single day I don't think about it and how grateful I am to you. That night on the Ziplines when we were kids? You followed me because you were trying to talk me

144

down and you're the one who gets injured. I wish to hell I could've taken the fall for you."

"Seems the scooper decided I wasn't the one worth saving," Tripster muttered.

"You've always had my back. Yeah, I may not understand what possessed you to steal a race log last year..."

"I was trying to get you insider knowledge, you know that. Didn't really think about it beyond that. Especially didn't think about the log actually being worth something. Guess even us geniuses have our off days." Tripster pulled a cushion onto his knee and played with a tassel. His anger visibly melted.

"I do want you to be a part of this race," Zar said quietly. "As my man on the ground. I need you to keep the Paranascope scroll safe and interact with it as per my feedback from what I uncover during the rally. Also..." He breathed in deeply. Was he asking too much of his friend? "The Ramrod rules ban the use of communication devices. But I was wondering about Goo."

Zar made the suggestion tentatively. He knew some bits and pieces about Tripster's involvement with the teen hacker community, including how they had learnt to adapt the technology of outmoded Data Streamer watches to their own end. There was even rumour of a central hub used to reroute secret messages between the hacker community using the photomesh technology known as Vitreous Goo. But as Zar knew, if you wanted a hacker to let you use a mode of communication unique to their community, you had to tread lightly. Even if that hacker was a friend.

"Goo? You mean those putty strips? Practical joke slime from Korea."

"It may be imported from Korea as joke slime, but rumour is Goo is put to a different use here."

Tripster stared at Zar. "Says who?"

"You know, just street gossip." Zar shifted his eyes about the room.

"Street gossip?"

"Okay, it was Braxton!" Zar threw up his hands in exasperation. He dropped them and resorted to running the chains at his waist through his fingers. "I just really need your help," he sighed, staring over at his friend. He knew he was asking Tripster to keep to the benches but still help out in the most exposing way.

Tripster seemed to sink into himself, deciding whether to risk the secrets of an underground community, or analysing the technical role he'd been ascribed. His lips had formed a fragile smile.

"Gotta say yes, haven't I? As you say, I've always had your back."

A day later and it pained Zar beyond belief to think of his friend stuck at home, watching the fun go by on a television screen or VDU Mat. Arriving at the huge iron gates of the Scrap Yard, he wished even more that Tripster was with him. Infesting ten square kilometres of the city, the Scrap Yard was home to crushers, jack hammers, cranes, ballers, cable strippers, pulleys, winders, and shredders, and was the hole into which every machine crawled to die.

He found a Scrapey at the entrance and asked for directions.

"Art student, hey? Most folk don't even know the thing's here, which is a shame because, as lumps of stone go, it's quite something."

The man had pulled at his nose as if to distract from his admission. Rounding a scrap hill and coming face-to-face with Roy Sam's masterpiece, Zar was forced to agree. A large structure, ten metres in diameter, its reconstituted stone had turned a moss green shade in that rusty environment. Symbols ran around the edge. Zar cocked his head to examine them. He had picked up enough Old Russian from the Death Pit to understand he was looking at numbers. Один, два, три...1, 2, 3 and so on. There were abstract sketches below each which Zar took to represent Vasiliev's life's works.

There the logic ended. The spindle at the centre was a wilting stalk, the wheel sloped at an angle so as to distort perspective. One moment Zar felt as if he overlooked the sculpture, the next it appeared to rise before him in a wave, the illusion aided by a brass ball revolving on its rod in a ceaseless clockwork grind.

A Peregrine Falcon circled in the vivid blue overhead. Zar watched the falcon tuck in its wings and dive. It would take agile prey to escape the stab and tear of that raptor's beak...With a burst of clarity, he remembered the beak off his trophy which he now wore on a string around his neck. He had used it to spring the compartment in his father's workshop pit and release the Paranascope scroll. Was there a similar keyhole in the sculpture?

The sun razored down. The brass ball continued to carve a shallow trough in the surface. Zar felt about the underside of the stone rim. His fingers located a notch and he pulled the beak pendant out from his shirt and over his head. Contorting his spine, he climbed under the rim, relocated the notch, and was in the process of fitting the beak to it when his attention was drawn to movement nearby.

A pair of commando boots halted a few feet away. Zar froze. For the first time since the race had begun he felt a thick knot of fear inside. His gaze flew to his board, lying to one side of the monument. He breathed shallowly. It could be a Scrapey with a sudden interest in the sculpture, but his sixth sense told him to stay incognito. His father had died to protect certain information. It made common sense that his assailants would try to access that information via him.

The footsteps receded. Zar waited, allowed his heart rate to settle some then let his arm drop. His shoulder burned. Easing out the muscles, he refitted the bead to the notch and twisted it. As a coarse rattling broke out overhead, he quickly retrieved the beak and slid out into the light.

He watched in awe as the spindle rose up, the action unscrewing a reservoir of sand which tricked from freshly exposed slots in the centre. Something was happening to the stone wheel, a matter of distorted perspective again or were the segments taking it in turns to seesaw? The revolutions of the brass ball also sped up.

Glancing back over a shoulder, Zar was sure the noise of the thing would bring the Scrapeys running. But suddenly all fell quiet. The sand bled back beneath the joins. The numbered segments resettled. Only the brass ball continued to circumnavigate the rim. Zar heard a click as if its motion activated some new trigger. He caught movement at the base of the spindle.

There was no other way to investigate than to climb up onto the wheel, taking care to step over the rod of the brass ball as it passed. He knelt down and slid a hand inside the panel that had opened up. His fingers located a small ball and a second rough object. He drew both out into the light. The sand brick had no special markings, but there was a suggestion that the brick had been hacked by a human hand, chipped rather than broken. The ball was a small green bead engraved with the number zero and small coloured dots running around the edge of the white ellipse.

Stepping over the rod again, he jumped down and deposited the brick in the rucksack at his back. He checked the series of coloured dots on the bead again. Two green, three pink, one blue. Zar had a mental image of depositing a coloured bubble inside the empty tube. Tapping a ticker tape message into his phone, he cranked the tiny dial to send then put the bead into his rucksack.

With a last glance at the Roulette Wheel, now emptied of its secrets, Zar retrieved his board and kicked off. There was another puzzle piece to find before he crossed

paths with his team mates. Time was tricking from his
hands.

§

# Chapter 12

If his visit to the Scrap Yard had afforded Zar any respite, the Meat Market was a full-on furore. The exotics, toothless madams and jack-knife pimps were greatly reduced in number by daylight. Nonetheless, Autodrome's red light district still crawled with hawkers, hustlers, dealers, professional beggars and every other type of street rat.

Zar skated between the human obstacles. Two women in frayed hot pants blew kisses as he passed.

"Shawarma!" called a street vendor, lifting his cutter to a trunk of spiced meat.

"Salchipapas!" cried another.

The atmosphere was risky and exhilarating. Zar dodged the cup of fries and dark red hot dogs thrust under his nose. Seconds later, he was forced to duck again as a walking rag pile lunged at him. The beggar stared after him, a bloody bandage knotted about an outstretched hand.

Zar forced his eyes front and tugged on the straps of his rucksack, reassured by its weight. It was hard to know if he was safer amongst the hoards or whether he was making it easier for his pursuer to slip the knife in then dissolve back into the crowd.

There was a vibration at his wrist. Zipping in-between a couple of the stalls selling knock-off shades and trainers, he abandoned the chaos for a doorway. A bag of belongings was stowed in one corner, a filthy blanket crumpled alongside.

He detached the strip of ticker tape from his watch. Keeping half an eye on his surroundings, he scanned Tripster's message: *Cool beans! We got another empty tube and a pin-up girl icon. New route also activated. Meat Market, around Binders Boulevard. Watch out for Riflers.*

Relief flooded through Zar. He might actually be capable of solving this thing! Yet along with his elation at the newly triggered section of route, Tripster's parting sentiment left him with a nasty taste in his mouth. Parts pirates – Riflers as they were commonly known – were the lowest of the low as far as Zar was concerned. To his way of thinking, if you wanted a ride, you worked for it – in the pits, the dealerships, the car wash, even the Death Pit. Except Riflers didn't think like that. Riflers thought life owed them something. Like someone else's motor.

The idea of encountering those parasites filled his chest with tight black rage. But he reminded himself that anger was only useful if channelled towards the true enemy – in his case, the bastard who murdered his father. Plus, the combination of crowds and daylight would persuade the Riflers to lay low.

However, the instant he hooked right onto Binders Boulevard, the din of Meat Market was replaced with an unsettling hush. The road was a strip of parched concrete ulcered with weeds, the buildings burnt out, boarded up or locked behind steel grids. A deserted truck stop was a basking ground for lizards.

Zar stepped off his board and listened. Binders Boulevard was a ghost town.

He walked along the sidewalk, board under his arm, until his eye was drawn to a weathered billboard. 'Welcome gamblers, swindlers, thieves and crooks' declared a presumably tongue-in-cheek slogan. But it was the accompanying image of a winking pin-up girl that caught his attention.

Behind the billboard was a dilapidated building, part water tower, part Grecian temple. Arches were interspersed between slim columns, the upper arcade topped with a gangrened copper dome. 'Grand Dame Casino' declared the sign above the door. Zar shivered despite the sun.

"You'd better be right about this, Tripster," he muttered, and, slotting his board into the straps of his skate rucksack, eased through a gap in the boarded doorway.

He emerged into a large foyer. The room was mistily lit where sunbeams filtered in at the dirty upper windows. Dust and plaster littered the tiled floor. Ceiling coving dangled off its glue threads. A light spike chandelier several times larger than the one he had seen at Braxton's pad glowed overhead, the illusion spoiled where some spikes crackled on and off. But its motion did tell him he was not alone in that rotting hull.

A broad staircase led to a balcony and, presumably, the main casino. Zar gripped the mottled brass banister and started up the stairs, taking in the carpet underfoot, polka-dotted with bird droppings, and the wall recesses either side. Tucked into each was a marble figure. To his right was a muscular Adonis, a fat woman squeezing a halved orange over her mouth, a screaming Medusa with flowing snakes for hair, and a wistful looking man brandishing a fist. To his left was the figure of a sleeping man, another preening in a hand mirror, and the winking pin-up.

Lust, gluttony, greed...Zar couldn't remember the rest, but he knew enough to recognise the theme as the seven deadly sins. It was the sort of joke his father would have played, installing the ultimate sinners to preside over a hedonist's paradise.

A bird squawked up in the rafters of the place. Zar caught a flash of motion out the corner of an eye. His stomach somersaulted as he glanced up at the balcony then down to the foyer. Dust motes whirled in the hazy sunlight.

He forced himself to concentrate. The winking pin-up appeared to represent pride. Peering into the recess behind the statue, he saw nothing but rat pellets and cobwebs. He tried to manoeuvre the limbs then lift the statue. The thing was welded solid to its base. He ran a hand over the marble surface. As he skimmed one side of the neck, he found a notch similar to the one he'd located on the underside of the roulette wheel sculpture.

Retrieving the beak pendant from inside his t-shirt, he leant in to the statue and slid the beak into the notch. He gave it a sharp turn. His heart cramped as he heard a faint metallic click. He gave the beak another quarter turn. There was a clunk as something heavy dropped. Whatever it was must have activated a pressure pad. With a faint grinding noise, the pin-up started to rotate and unscrew from her bolt plate.

The statue revolved twice more then halted. Zar knelt down. He slid a hand between the figure and the bolt plate, recognised the rough surface of a second sand brick and retrieved it. Remembering the ball he had found with the first sand brick, he checked for a new object. This one was a brass pin-up in profile and wearing a necklace of tiny coloured beads.

Slinging down his rucksack, he deposited the brick and trinket inside. He eased the pack across his shoulders and was about to exit when he sensed the new arrivals.

"Raw! Maw! Jack 'en Dore! We got a rat here a'nibblin'."

A Rifler stood at the top of the stairs. Fists on skinny hips, tattooed bare chest, graffitied board shorts and mullet. Two more stepped in alongside the first. Zar risked a glance down to the foyer. The foot of the stairs was similarly guarded.

*We're road hogs, Punkstar. We ain't fighters.* Davey's words from the Death Pit. Drawing on the fight spirit he always adopted in the Death Pit, Zar centred his nerves and counted off the Riflers. Three at the head, two at the rear.

"Nibble nibble little mouse, who's that nibbling at my house." The leader sat down on the top step. He pulled back his lips. Zar put him at fifteen.

"String him up by his gizzard, Lothaniel!" called a mohawked punk from below.

"Slit his throat and drip him dry," cried his partner, a club kid in waist-length green dreads and cyber goggles.

"Sorry for intruding on your patch, guys. I'm just a tourist's lost his way."

Zar regretted the words the moment they left his lips. What an idiotic thing to say! How did his being a tourist make him any less the target?

"Hear that lads?" The apparent leader, Lothaniel unfolded his arms and stood up. He descended a couple of steps, eyes fizzing every sort of wrong. "I see that skateboard on your back. Queer tourist who invests in an Alien Workshop deck, Spitfire wheels and Grind King trucks. Gonna tell me that's a fake Pro Leaguer beak you got slung around your neck bone as well?"

Zar's gaze whipped down. The makeshift pendant must have slipped out of his shirt as he was retrieving the sand brick. He squirreled it away – and immediately regretted his response again. Now the Riflers knew it was worth something.

"Sell for a pretty packet, those do." Lothaniel eyed the gape in Zar's shirt.

"Piece of tat my mum gave me." As he spoke, Zar did a slow 360, taking in the banisters either side of the stairs, the wall recesses, the ornate rails at the balconied second floor. What lay beyond was a big fat unknown. Overhead, the light spike chandelier crackled and ebbed.

"Your momma got good taste." Lothaniel glanced left and right. "Whaddya reckon, Jack 'en Dore?"

A teen warrior, bald but for a plaited ponytail at the centre of his skull, nodded without expression. Alongside him, a teen vampire sneered, 'Yessir.' The kid wore yellow contacts. Long black hair greased his thin shoulders.

"You're not getting this pendant," said Zar quietly. He noticed a rent in the right hand wall a couple of metres up.

"Raw! Maw!" Lothaniel jutted his chin towards the Riflers at the foot of the stairs. "Acquire that piece of glitter, will ya?"

As the mohawk and club kid powered up the stairs, Zar ran at the banister and jumped. Driving hard off it, he stretched to tuck one hand into the rent in the wall and grab a hangnail of plaster wire mesh with the other. He climbed up to the flaking rail of the balcony, and he predicated company. First came the vampire, lips retracted to expose teeth that were all the better to eat him with. A quick turn vault and Zar hit the ground in a semi-crouch, one leg extended to take the vampire's feet out from under him.

The Riflers hollered at one another as Zar charged into the casino. The main room was dimly lit, the dome overhead algaed and fractured. No matter, thought Zar. If he couldn't see perfectly then neither could his pursuers – which was just as well since he was facing an assault course.

The dark was colonised by slots machines, each a metre and a half tall and topped with an outsized silver dial. Most had spilt their guts. The floor was littered with intestinal wiring, number strips and glass fragments. Zar used the carnage to his advantage. While the Riflers kept to the pathway of carpet, he was free to hurdle up and over the slots. The beak pendant knocked against his chest as he ran.

Leaping into the centre of the first of several roulette tables, he felt the breath snatched from his lungs. The warrior had tracked him, presumably running down one side of the room to avoid all obstacles then moving in to take a swing. Zar caught the punch in his side. He skidded onto one knee, face close to the table's baize which smelt of things gone off. Powering his arms, he clambered to his feet again and leapt between the gaming tables. The Rifler matched him turn for turn on the ground.

As he ran, Zar unclipped the board from the holster at his back, bounced it underfoot and planted both feet on the deck. He ollied off the table onto a long bar, flipping the board 180 degrees with a toe midflight. The deck struck the Rifler's forehead, a minor hit but enough to leave the kid reeling and win Zar back a bit of distance.

Weaving his board along the bar, he saw a second set of railings and a second light spike chandelier up ahead. In theory, what lay below was a mirror image of the foyer he'd just left...in theory. As the bar ran out, he stamped on the nose of his board and caught it. Biting back fear, he took a blind jump off the edge.

§

# Chapter 13

Jesse gave a generous tug on the fire truck's steering. "Backatcha!"

The hover bug dogged left. It had been on them all the way from Easy Street.

"We need to lose that bug!" Raina called out.

"You think?" Jesse shot her a glance – sort which made her want to scratch, it was such an irritant.

They crash-dived around one corner and the next, spectators hanging out the doorways and windows of the pods either side. The skull projections flashed up in rapid succession.

"You see the bug take out that trike back there?" Jesse glanced at his wing mirror and looked nervous. "Nasty little suckers," he muttered under his breath.

Was Jesse losing his nerve? Raina was having none of that, not when she was out of the driver seat and thereby out of control of the vehicle. "We got two factors on our side," she told him evenly. "One – physics. Bugs are classed as land vehicles. Got a maximum altitude of eight metres. So, yeah, while the thing's capable of clearing this beast, the extra thrust would exhaust its already fuel-heavy engines. Two – sadism." In the wing mirror on her side, she saw the bug swing out wide to the right. Her eyes bored into the cockpit. The driver's goggles seemed as much a part of the bug as its alloy engines, as if the driver was some bioengineered bolt-on.

Raina hated the thought. She loved to race, loved it so much it often felt as if oil ran through her veins instead of blood. But it was control over her emotions which kept her grounded. She only had to look at Zar to know how damaging it could be to need to win over every other life experience. And she was more realistic than that. Wasn't she? Except, here she was riding shotgun alongside a guy she barely liked let alone trusted her life to, and all in the effort to prove she was a winner after all. Why did that matter so much anyway? Her father was long gone. Who was she trying to impress?

The road widened, the chaos of pods giving way to a large intersection banked by four garages. A skull flickered into view last second.

"There!"

"I see it. Don't get your panties in a twist." Jesse hooked a right and over-steered, drifting the huge fire truck in a controlled arc.

They straightened up. The bug was nowhere in sight.

"And that's how you shake off a tic," Jesse sneered. He shook his head and, taking one hand off the steering, gave himself a physical pat on the back.

Raina wasn't so sure and leant out the window in time to see the bug tuck in behind. She grimaced and fell back into her seat.

"You're going to have to scratch that itch harder."

"You gotta be kidding?"

"Nope." Raina brushed a hand over her forehead. Jesse was a better driver than she would ever have given him credit for being. All the same, it made her soul hurt to have to sit this one out. Plus he proved himself an aggravating jerk every time he opened his mouth to speak. For not the first time, Raina got a sinking feeling inside that she hadn't got to race the Ramrod alongside Zar. He aggravated her too, but in a very different way to Jesse.

But this was no time for regretting facts she could not change. Right that moment, she needed to take the lead and shake the bugs off the fire truck's tail, before her dreams of Ramrod victory went up in the flames.

The thought gave her an idea.

"Okay, you gave the double-bluff back there a shot. But we're never going to outdo a hover bug with drifting manoeuvres. It's their natural flight pattern. If we really want to get rid, we need to irritate the irritant." She unhooked the latch on a small door to the rear of the cab. "Back soon."

"Where're you going, sugar lips?" Jesse looked panicked then angry. He dabbed at his sweating top lip with the back of a hand. "Do me a favour and sit pretty. Let the big boys handle the opposition."

Raina didn't give him the pleasure of a reply. She squeezed through the doorframe on her knees and out onto the narrow steel platform that ran between the coke troughs. The boiler was a great staved buttress towards the rear. A series of greased chains fed alongside either coke trough in narrow channels, linking up in two fat knots over the feed plates. Attempting to keep steady against the tide of motion, she hauled on two leather loops suspended off the framework above her. The chainlink revolved through its greased channels, the feed plates lifted and a fresh quantity of coke spilt through.

What to burn? Something that would produce enough smoke to force the bug to back off, but not enough to envelop the truck itself. She'd liked to have started by burning Jesse's brain. He certainly didn't seem to have use for it. Second choice was a spare coil of rubber hose pipe. She slung it down into one trough and yanked hard on the corresponding leather loop. Coke spilt into the belly of the fire alongside the hose, which slivered in like spaghetti. She released the loop and the feed plate slid back down.

Back inside the cab, she closed the small door, thumbed the latch into place and collapsed back down onto her seat.

"What the hell did you stoke this baby with? She's giving off some serious smoke back there."

*Indeed she was.* In the passenger side wing mirror, Raina could see a cloud of dense black smoke polluting the atmosphere behind them.

"Now haul on the brake."

"Excuse me?" Jesse's freckled face looked ready to rebel.

"Hit the brake while the bug's blinded, moron!" Raina hissed. Time was ticking, and the trick was a good one but a temporary one.

At last Jesse did as he told, and the tremendous vehicle decelerated in a great squealing of steel. Raina braced herself for the impact of being rear-ended by the bug. But the Pro Leaguer in that metal gnat was too skilled to be caught out; he scooped around to the front of the braking fire truck and accelerated away, twin exhausts blazing. The truck's sharp deceleration meant they avoided the blowback.

Jesse brought the truck to a standstill as the smoke cleared. He stared Raina hard in the eye.

"Here come the cavalry. Now, do I have your permission to go again?"

Glancing in the wing mirror, Raina caught a glint of silvered motion at the receding intersection. Vehicles poured around the corner like rainwater sluiced out a drain. Heading up the pack was Eight Ball's Skyliner, flagged by the Pro Leaguer Kettenkrad and Justice astride her Tomahawk. Valentine bought up the rear, shouldering one of the Pro Leaguer sports cars.

"Uh huh."

Jesse snorted. He pulled off from the curb.

Inside the minute, the warehouses came into view. Beyond lay the docks. Time for the team to bag themselves a ferry ride.

Raina kept her eyes peeled for a pedestrian. Things were getting near the wire. Zar needed to catch up pronto.

§

Meat Market's clamour was soon replaced with the asthmatic purr of the motor. Zar shifted position in the back of the truck and winced. Blood leaked from a gash to his left shoulder. He'd cut himself on broken glass when exiting the casino. Yet for all their hot pursuit of him, the Riflers had not attempted to step outside. Like vampires confined to the dark, they had clamoured at the threshold, defiant he would surrender the beak sooner or later, even if they had to prise it from his cold dead fingers.

Zar put the threats behind him. The pick-up was heading in the right direction and the traffic flow was good. Before long though, road users would be directed away from the Ramrod course and he'd have to go it alone again.

That moment came all too soon. The truck slowed and Zar leant over the side to see that the road ahead was closed. A Uniform officer redirected traffic with a Paragun. Tiny fly wheels rotated the metal lozenge that housed the lens. Holographic ticker taping arrows sprayed from the tip.

Zar leapt over the side of the pick-up and offered the driver a thumbs up. He was distracted by the noise originating from a nearby overpass. A skull projected over one end of the overpass like an eerie jack-in-the-box, Ramrod competitors ricocheting off side rails which bowed with the force. When a car came crushing down on top of the rail, bodywork folding, he heard the rest of the competitors screech to a halt. Zar's pulse accelerated as, in the aftermath, he heard the sound of an idling muscle car.

Yes! There was Persia, standing on the rim of the Road Runner's open driver door as if she balanced on stunt pegs. He couldn't make out her expression but her hand signals more than conveyed her annoyance at the hold up.

Zar thought quickly. He was on 59th Street. If he cut through Devil's Cove, a dank rib of an alley, he'd come out at Coddington Dock half a kilometre from the ferry bay. He threw down his board and turned into the lightless alley. Daring the bad stuff to leap out, he raked up speed. Determined to reach the far end before the rally drivers, he nearly overshot. The sidewalk was under him suddenly and he was forced to powerslide to a halt. A huge cartwheel revolved centimetres from his face. The steam coach churned away in a whirl of dust.

He glared left then right. The road was greasy with fumes and smoke. Vehicles slopped into one another, punch-drunk on the knowledge they were so close to their destination. Tyres shredded. Metal sparked. And he realised it was freakishly dangerous amongst the carnage, his body so soft next to the iron monsters gnashing all around.

His gaze went to the overpass. The cyborg with the wheel-tipped wings swept down, a germ next to the monster truck and black reaper of a hearse bringing up the rear. Was it paranoia or did the caddy hearse set its course arrow-straight for him, Zar wondered in blind panic? His choices were to run or let the driver add his vitals to the slush pile.

A newcomer provided a third option. Cresting the overpass, the Road Runner opened its throat and plunged. While there was a path of destruction in its wake, the muscle car steered around each wrecked vehicle and moved in tight behind the hearse. Roaring sideways, it aimed for a smoking mound of metal – or, as it turned out, a makeshift half pipe. Zar held his breath as the Road Runner struck the mound, rose up and soared over the flaming helllands to land out front of the hearse in a ripple of shocks.

The muscle car roared up, Persia simultaneously leaning sideways to pop the passenger door. Zar barely touched down in the seat before the team captain floored the gas again. Grappling for the door handle, he sealed them in.

Persia yanked the wheel to avoid a crush of Harley Davidsons competing as one hybrid organism.

"Where's the rest of the team?" Zar yelled, fighting to right himself.

Persia threw him a glance. Her eyes were luminous. "What a ride, man! Our crew are smokin'. Clock the rear view."

Zar shifted around in his seat. The hearse was hot on their heels but so too was Eight Ball's Skyliner, Valentine's reengineered Cadillac, Justice's glossy quadricycle and the brutish fire truck...He remembered Raina perched up in the cab, breathing the same air as Jesse, and his insides squirmed. At the same time, he noticed Persia scout out Valentine in her rear view. He looked back to see the mobster steer wide then crush back in to send the hearse into a tail spin.

As their team powered up, Zar turned to see a bend in the road give way to the final straight. Spectators lined the sidewalk, clapping and hollering as the surviving drivers careered towards the shimmering Lough.

The Road Runner sped over the finish line. Zar braced his arms on the dash.

"How'd we stop?"

Before Persia could answer, the car shuddered and slowed dramatically. There was a faint flopping noise as they coasted forward.

"Air stunner," said Persia. "Siphons enough air outta the tyres to slow us but without spoiling them. It makes us gearheads pay attention to the fuzz."

She pointed up. Uniform hovered over the vehicles in pods suspended from small blips. Team details were stickered onto each vehicle's roof and Zar watched the officers punch the details into their handhelds with metal nibs. Most competitors were directed into a cornered off area where vehicles steamed and fell apart. The three ferry bays lay directly ahead. One ferry had already set sail, its great iron lung expanding and collapsing.

"The Pro Leaguers," said Persia. "Guess we didn't bag first place." She blew a bubble with her gum. It popped, coating her full lips in pink rubber before she tucked it into her mouth and kept on chewing.

Zar heard the whir of a Uniform blip overhead and his stomach flipped. The wave guard of the second ferry lowered to the fixed ramp and docked in a whistling release of steam while the Uniform swept down to appear at Persia's open window.

"Congratulations. You qualify to continue on to the next stage of the Ramrod. Your team may board."

The officer steered his pod back up again.

Persia glanced sideways and broke out her glorious smile. "Groovy."

Overcome with delight, Zar leant out the passenger window and punched a fist into the air. Eight Ball and Jesse James hammered their horns. Valentine's steam car root-n-tooted. Justice gave a sharp salute.

He craned his head back in. It felt amazing to qualify to continue. So good and such a phenomenal relief.

The good times didn't last.

"Looks like your boyfriend's along for the ride too." When Zar looked blank, Persia grabbed his chin and turned his face towards the third ferry, now lowering its wave guard. His elation turned to mud. The hearse was boarding. Vladimir's face ghosted the driver side window.

Persia guided the Road Runner down the ferry ramp. Zar pulled his rucksack close as the iron walls caged him in.

§

# Chapter 14

"How'd you get cut?"

Persia pointed a talon at his shoulder. With the adrenaline of the race fading, Zar was aware of the wound again. It ached in a way that should have been distracting but was, oddly perhaps, a useful outlet for his internal pain.

"Ran into some trouble."

"Get what you were after?"

Zar started to undo the rucksack, but Persia interrupted him.

"Hot dang, you're too trusting, dude! You know nada about us hustlers. Want my advice? Keep whatever you got there to yourself."

Zar hugged the rucksack. Strangely, those words hurt him. He'd wanted to believe he was among friends. But Persia was right. What did he really know about his team mates bar Persia and Valentine's love/hate obsession with one another, Eight Ball's suspicious acquisition of the Skyliner, Jesse's lousy attitude, and Justice's air of heartbreak hotelness? Perhaps it wasn't the obvious enemies like Vladimir he had to worry about. Perhaps he would be wiser to watch his back around his own team.

He said nothing. Just nodded.

"All right!"

Persia flashed her dazzling smile. Zar couldn't help noticing how beautiful the girl was. Something told him he wasn't the first or the last to admire Persia Gold.

"Quit crushin' on me. I'm outta your league," shot Persia in a tone that said she was not to be messed with. "Just," she appended slyly.

"Hello Punkstar."

Zar whipped his head aside to find Raina leaning in at the open passenger window. He felt a rush of blood to the face as her eyes flicked to Persia then back to him.

"Spare a moment to say hi to the rest of the team?"

"Er, yeah, sure." Shouldering his rucksack, which housed his skateboard in a harness, Zar thumbed the door catch. He glanced back at Persia.

"Catch you in thirty?"

The team captain was applying lip gloss. She pressed her lips together and released them with a pop.

"Later, sugar-pie. And Zar?" She looked serious. "Wanna get that arm patched or take a leak, do it now. I ain't stopping for no mother once we hit the wastelands."

§

Raina led the way through the creaking hull. Zar heard the deep thrum of the iron lung bolted up top – a concertinaed membrane that sent air to the rooftop furnace which, in turn, heated a crater of boiling sea water. The engine was located to the rear of the craft. Zar imagined it as a nervous heart spilling steam from its arteries.

His team's vehicles were parked haphazardly around the car port. Valentine's steam car was in the shadows, hood cranked, goddess icon ascending like a silver tilde. Set back-to-back in a single crank case, the twin straight 8 engines chittered. Slanted across the centre of the car park was Eight Ball's Skyliner. Somewhere along the route, the Fly had activated the crank to raise the hardtop. Zar marvelled at the Fly's good fortune in doing so. The roof and a wing were gouged in places, as if the vehicle had been attacked by a giant predator.

A pair of legs stuck out from the Skyliner's hood.

Raina peered in at the engine and tutted. "Head gasket?"

Jesse emerged from the cranked hood. He drew out the dip stick and swiped a rag over it, cleaning off a layer of mayonnaise-like sludge.

"What's the tale, Nightingale?" Eight Ball strode over, a soda in hand.

Jesse leant back against the wing. He cocked his head. "You said this wasn't your ride. Ask me, you were stitched up by whichever buddy lent it to you."

Eight Ball squinted at the mechanic and chewed his ever-present matchstick. "We're talking hours to change a head gasket."

"Only option is to botch it." Raina kept her eyes on the engine. "Use sealant. Re-torque the head bolts."

Jesse scuffed his spiky red hair with a fist. "Worth a try."

"Do it." Eight Ball bared his teeth around the matchstick. "Shafted by a Rocketeer. Of course those runts wouldn't risk Pink Slips on a decent ride."

Jesse patted the Fly's shoulder. "Don't sweat it, bro. We haven't all got the skills to outsmart the competition, but I'll get you up and running."

In seconds, Eight Ball flicked out a telescopic metal baton from the sheath at his back and thrust it up under the mechanic's chin. "Rattlin' my cage, nosebleed?" he snarled.

"Well, you've clearly got the situation in hand, Jesse. I'll leave you to it." Raina arched her eyebrows at Zar and together they walked away.

"I'm going to grab a soda. You want one?" Zar asked.

Five minutes later, he found her leaning against a riveted pillar at the rear of the boat, staring at the oblong of sky above the waveguard. He put the first aid box on the floor and handed over one of the sodas he'd collected from an icebox on board the fire truck.

"Here." He breathed in. The hull smelt of gasoline and brine. But near the waveguard, the air was cleaner.

Raina jutted her chin towards the interior. "In there smells like death. You think it's a portent for what's to come in the Eras?"

"Could be." Zar grimaced. With its bleak hull and unseen workforce, the ferry seemed an appropriate conveyance over the Styx-like Lough.

Raina hooked her thumbs in the belt loops of her frayed denim shorts. "You ever visited the Eras?" She oozed confidence. Zar suspected she felt anything but.

"Nope." He stared at the panel of sky. "I've enough drama in my life."

Raina frowned. She changed tack.

"My friend, Katiana, says you're bad news."

"She's right."

"My momma says nice boys don't earn an extra buck at the Death Pit."

Zar swallowed a mouthful of soda, forcing it past the lump that rose up in his throat. "She's right too."

"My cousins say they could wipe the floor with you out on the track."

Amused suddenly, Zar tipped back his head and chucked in his throat. "There I've got to disagree. Tell your cousins, when it comes to Pro League, its quality that counts not quantity."

"That true?" Raina's mouth had a pretty slant.

Zar dropped his chin. "Are you flirting with me, Raina?" He squinted up, but her face hardened. He had said the wrong thing.

"You annoy me so much when you do that," she said coldly.

Zar sighed and played his part. "When I do what?"

"Act like you're lesser than you are."

She surprised him again. How come the girl always managed to obliterate his expectations of her?

"Does it make you feel better, safer, to treat me the same?" she spat. "Sure, I can flirt with you, Punkstar, but only because I think there may be someone worth getting to know beneath the bravado. Yeah, you might've got yourself a chequered past, but it takes some guts to enter a Ramrod."

"This isn't about guts. It's about obligation." Zar couldn't get used to Raina. She had an uncanny ability to dig beneath his ribs and get at the truth of him.

Raina eyed him. She picked up the first aid kit and unfastened it. Zar felt bio-shocked as she laid cool fingers on his arm, just below the glass cut.

"If you mean you're doing this for your dad, the dead aren't grateful for our efforts. We can't impress them or amend wrongs," she said softly, applying antiseptic.

"Who are you trying to convince of the fact, you or me?"

Hurt came into her eyes. Zar didn't like the idea he had caused it, but pride prevented him from apologising.

Fortunately Raina's look became quizzical. "When we were talking the other day, you asked if my dad had been married to the race circuit too – suggesting your dad had. That true?"

Zar flinched on the inside. Why was the girl so determined to delve into the sticky heart of him? Wasn't that what girls did though, tried to prove they knew you better than anyone else in some sort of battle for his Pink Slips?

He cocked his head and considered Raina. She was impossibly pretty. More than that, she was someone he liked to talk to, even when they were travelling to the ends of the earth it seemed. Would it be so bad to confide in this girl who would drop him like a stone just as soon as the race was over?

"My dad left when I was seven. My mum, she's not always well. She's got an addiction, a bad one." His voice caught. He hated his weakness, wanted to ball back into himself just as he had done back at the hospital when waiting on news of his mum's condition.

As if registering his difficulty, Raina broke in, "When I was little, I had a favourite uncle called Raul. One of those men who looked like he'd been fried in palm nut oil, but who'd a way about him that would make you feel happy and safe all in one." She swallowed. "He didn't seem the sort. But Razzledazzle doesn't have sorts, does it? It just lures folk in with its candy packaging. And before they know it, living out here in the real world is too difficult. Uncle Raul overdosed one night. Suicide maybe." Her mouth trembled, and she looked like a lost little girl suddenly. "All this flesh, it weighs heavy, you know."

Zar stared at her. How was it possible for Raina to shape words in such a way? It was seeing things exactly as they were, without frills, without excuses.

"My dad left and there was nothing I could say to get him to come back. One thing I've always known though. It wasn't my fault he left." Zar narrowed his eyes at the strip of sky, allowing the truth to eek out. "Some kids blame themselves when their parents split up. I don't. My parents messed up their own lives."

"You know, Zar, I feel for you, and, yes, I know you hate that. Thing is, all this bitterness, it eats away at you. Damage like that, it can get so bad it's impossible to repair. So if you really don't feel responsible for the break up – and there's no reason you should – how come you act so defensive? Parents might have a few years on us but they're just as flawed. Some are just better at hiding the fact than others."

"I'd like to see things as black and white as that, Raina, but you're a better person than me." Zar couldn't tear his eyes away from her. He could feel her breath near his lips. Her eyes were oceans.

"Again with the black and white. You've used that same phrase before. And again I'll say, you and me, we're a shade in-between. We may be a blend of our parents, but we're separate from them. We can forgive them for leaving us. We can choose to move on."

The ferry rocked violently and Zar clutched Raina on instinct. He wanted to hold her, keep holding her until her skin left an imprint on his. Maybe then he would know her half as well as she appeared to know him.

He pushed her gently away.

Raina flushed. "Just the caterpillar tracks locking in around the wheels," she muttered, referring to the amphibious ferry.

"Time to suit up and boot up! Five minutes 'til we doc," called Persia, who had materialised a few metres away. "Ferry'll take us a kilometre in. Then it drops us."

"We cross the wastelands alone?" Raina asked calmly. Zar saw how her bravado hid a more delicate girl beneath.

"Which is why Braxton got me to sign on as team captain and also bodyguard. I've some experience with the wastelands. It's my gig to get you to the other side. So give your honey a lick of sugar and get ready to peel out."

Persia strode back down the hold. Everyone watched her pass – Jesse lowering the hood of the Skyliner and cleaning his hands with a rag, Justice wiping the sweat from her forehead with the back of a hand, Eight Ball manipulating the matchstick between his lips, Valentine leaning against his Cadillac, hat low over his eyes.

The interruption brought home the reality of their situation. Part of Zar desperately wanted to stay tucked up in the corner of the ship with Raina. The other part knew it was time to race again, and that his commitment lay with finding his father's killer and doing the best he could to help his team win.

He started to walk away when Raina called after him, "This other stuff you've got going on during the rally. Let me know if I can help."

More than anything, Zar wanted to stop, turn around and say 'Yes, help. I'm on my own, I've no idea how to act or feel anymore, and I think you may be the only person here I can trust.' But the words stayed lodged in his throat. Instead, he gave a backwards wave and kept on walking.

§

# Chapter 15

The sky was a wash of azure blue that faded like denim at the horizon. Ahead lay the five kilometres of salt flats known as the wastelands. To the naked eye, the soft noodled sand was a driver's paradise. But Zar knew the Sabkha was not to be trusted; a broad sheet of salt-encrusted desert, it was prone to flash flooding and sudden subsidence. Yet it was precisely these dangers which had attracted the desert racers to the area in the first place.

As a child, Zar had watched their tournaments on terrestrial television. Before the existence of the deadly Pro League, the city's youth had dreamt of taking part in the Desert Races. Teams were required to assemble their vehicles from a water barge piled high with scrap metal and parts, then pitched against one another across a vast obstacle course. It was not enough to be the fastest; racers had to solve conundrums to access each new section of the race. Some puzzles were physical, others mental. All required competitors to think and act on their feet and still entertain the masses.

Until its ban alongside the Ramrod, the Desert Races had owed its origins to the rebels who opted to turn the salt flats into a steeplechase arena thirty years earlier. The area was useless in realtor terms, and while the rest of Autodrome set up home on the opposite side of the Lough, the original racers had built on a substantial ridge of bedrock five kilometres in from the salt flats. Quite how they evolved into the retrograde inhabitants of the Eras was a matter of folklore. Some said the township was haunted by the ghosts of motorists past and present. Add in gang warfare, Uniform corruption, self-policing and death races, and the Eras became the ulcer on Autodrome's fantastical skin and bone.

Crossing the desert strip on route to the Eras, Zar's emotions oscillated between fascination and blind fear. He clung to the steering wheel and stared across the white-gold miles. It was just possible to make out the graffitied wall that enclosed the district. How far did the wall stretch? His eye skimmed the length of the horizon.

"Wild, ain't it?" Persia rested an arm along the back of the bench seat. Her eyes danced every which way. "Once we're through the pearly gates, you'll see the Eras are even sicker on the inside. Once we're through," she repeated with grit.

"So this is the old race track? Not exactly smooth running," said Zar, steering around a large sink hole in the road.

"Never could beat the drag for long out here without the salt cooking up the concrete. Season or two at best. After a while, the track became just one more obstacle to negotiate."

"You were a desert racer?" His admiration for Persia skyrocketed.

The girl flashed him a look that said his kudos was premature. "Not a racer. I was a Uniform cadet."

Zar let out a silent whistle. "You sure?" he said stupidly, incredulous that a girl like Persia could have ever been taken seriously in the Uniform. Not only that. She was putting in extracurricular hours as a bodyguard. He'd met a couple during his time at the Death Pit, both ex-cons, as was clear from their strike-now-ask-questions-later approach to the protection racket not to mention the prison barcode tattoo on an inner wrist. Both times, he found himself questioning whether the folk who employed the muscle might not just have let the wolf in the door.

"I got first dibs on my own history. What? You think just because I'm a girl, I can't be taken seriously?"

"No, I think because you're a hot girl, you'd get hit on instead of taken seriously." Zar couldn't see any point avoiding the obvious. But his cheeks coloured all the same.

"Got me down as a blonde airhead, huh, Zar? That's bogus, man. I was acing cadet school while you were still soiling your pants at 13 with a first taste of the Death Pit. So, yeah, I might look like a bunny, but that's half the trick of it. Get a dufus drooling and he ain't nowhere near as dangerous. But don't go confusing the way I use this shape of mine with the real me. I play, but I don't *play*, ya dig?"

"I dig." Zar glanced at the older girl and understood how easy it would be for Persia to use her allure to her advantage. He could also see the spike of intelligence in her gorgeous eyes. Persia Gold knew how to use her looks, but never abuse them.

"Quit hairy eyeballing me." The girl glanced aside and winked. She pointed ahead. "Now pull out, will you? I want to see how Jesse's doing up front."

Zar eased the Road Runner off the main strip onto the salt skim. Drawing wide, they were able to check Jesse's progress at the head of the caravan.

There was no denying the team mechanic was gutsy. Watching Jesse slam the fire truck in and out the various folds and crevices in the road, Zar could've sworn the guy had driven the route before. Certainly no one could accuse Jesse of treading lightly in the Riflers' territory. Meanwhile, he was in the company of an ex Uniform cadet. What was the story there? If Persia really had aced her cadet exams, how come she was slumming it back at high school and part-timing as a bodyguard?

Zar remembered Persia's warning about how little he knew about his fellow team mates. He checked the rear view; his rucksack was safely stored on the back seat.

"So, as a cadet you used to help keep the desert racers in tow?" He nodded at what was left of the arena – a halfpipe protruding from the salt scales like a hunk of fuselage, tarnished iron rails, the coiled ammonite of a concrete launch ramp. "Why'd the Uniform close this playground down?"

"I turned in my badge just before the Desert Races were shut down," said Persia crisply. "Which had zip to do with the desert racers themselves. Frank Oz called time on many things after events a year ago." She kept her eyes glued to the convoy.

Zar wasn't in the mood for niceties, not when the fate of the team lay in the hands of a girl who seemed to specialise in secrets. He was about to ask how come she had turned in her badge – no small deal for any cadet, let alone one with the steel of Persia Gold – when he noticed a streak of movement off to the left.

"Riflers!" he cried out. He fought to suffocate his alarm at the fact.

Persia's gaze didn't budge. "Only if you count the fact they've stolen a minute of our lead time. Team Pro Leaguers," she clarified as he tucked back in behind the others. "There's the other pack of jokers northeast."

Zar stared out of the driver window. A third caravan moved across the filmily middle-distance. The elaborate silhouette of the steam coach was unmistakable, as was the black obelisk of Vladimir's hearse.

"There's more than one race track?" Zar's stomach plunged. He'd been so focused on the Riflers that it hadn't occurred to him to worry about the other teams.

"It's a head trip out here, man. Track was re-rooted so often it's spaghettied to the max. Good thing our man up front has his groove on."

"Raina, you mean. She's the navigator."

"Dynamite!" interrupted Persia, checking her side mirror. "The hacks are catching up. That'll keep the Riflers below."

Zar checked his own side mirror to see the sky dotted with the airships of the terrestrial TV networks.

"Keep the Riflers below?"

"Riflers go to ground, airhead. Look what's out there. Then look harder."

Zar alternated his gaze between the road and the landscape either side. He focused on a grid of wooden pallets laid almost parallel with floor level. Almost...From the underside, he caught the emerald glow of lightspeed Bi-Oculars.

"I see them," he gasped.

"And the suckers see you, but don't sweat it. With this welcoming committee, ain't no way they're crawling out. Time comes we gotta split and leave the Eras, it'll be a whole different ball game."

"Meaning?"

"For now, we keep on truckin' and soak up the sunshine."

Persia retrieved something from the glove box, a cassette – as alien as every other bit of that weird ride to Zar. She punched it into the player slot and cranked the volume. Guitars seesawed, drums ratta-rolled, horses whinnied, and a human tomcat screeched, "I'm baaaaaack! I'm back in the saddle again!"

Persia settled back in her seat.

"Don't you just dig Aerosmith?"

§

# Chapter 16

The street hung about itself like a suit jacket on a wire hanger. Red brick buildings gave out onto narrow alleyways littered with fire escapes and the pages of broadsheets. Cars rumbled up and down the unmarked strip. To Zar, the vehicles epitomised everything he knew about 1930s' design – streamlined mudguards, chrome headlamps, radiator grilles. Except, there was something dangerously offbeat about these modified vehicles. Bodywork hunkered low to the ground. Windows were reduced to tinted slits. Water tanks sat up back like gleaming egg sacks, lines feeding off in geometric patterns along either wing.

Zar eased the Road Runner through the street, regretting the loud throb of its engine. He felt an inexplicable desire to blend in with the queer theatre of Era 3.0. It was hard to pinpoint what unnerved him – the sinister vehicles or the way the inhabitants dressed, accurate to the smallest detail, he guessed, yet so at odds with their true place in time. The women wore hose, heels, cinched jackets and tight, knee-length skirts. Their hair was pressed into sleek waves or curls. The men wore double-breasted suits and long, generously cut pants. In rolled shirt sleeves and braces, the younger men stood in groups to smoke or clutter the steps of an apartment building.

Quite literally entering another era, Zar couldn't fault the authenticity of his surroundings. *Delaney Street* was papered with advertisements including a banner for 'Radio City Music Hall' stretching the length of a building and tin plaques for 'Diner: $1.50', 'Virginia Gold Flake' and 'News and Mail Sold Here.' There were billboards for movies, cigarettes, motor dealerships and the latest cure-all in garish Technicolor. Tucked in alongside were family-run stores – Rudley's Doughnuts, R W Hogg and Son General Store, Better Tires Sales Co, Dr. Finkelstein ('Extraction $9.00 by lady attendants'), Gately & Fitzgerald Furniture Co, Stilman's Butchers, and Pinnager's Millinery.

Zar put his nose to the windshield, utterly in awe. Every detail was perfect and, at the same time, peculiar in that perfection, from the ragamuffins leading a pony along the tram tracks to the red and chrome lozenge of a streetcar.

"Era 3.0. It's far out, for sure," said Persia. She folded a fresh stick of bubblegum between her luscious lips.

"And folk live like this, everyday? It's so...weird," Zar blurted. He quickly realised he'd chosen the wrong person to appeal to. "How many Eras are there?" he appended.

"1900, 3.0, 5.0 and 7.0 are the biggies, but there are smaller districts dedicated to other time periods."

"So we're driving through this 1930's movie set in a 1970's muscle car, and behind us is Eight Ball in his 1950's rod. That's got to disrupt the status quo?"

Persia tucked her gum into a cheek. "Often as not, we don't infringe on other Eras. But ain't no rule about driving through a place. Parking up, that's a different ball game. Outsiders gotta get a permit to park an Outtastep vehicle in a different Era. But, as I said, most prefer to stick to their own pad."

"What about currency? Does the Uniform have jurisdiction here?" Zar nodded to indicate their surroundings. "Where'd all this stuff come from?"

"Whoa there, eager beaver. We use the same mullah as every other district of Autodrome. Uniform still get up in our faces – in fact, watch your back because they use a much harder line here. As for all this *stuff*, where'd any other retro fancier go for a ride and threads, or to kit out their crib? Stores that deal in the necessary or online from anywhere in the world. Or folk whip up a replica." Persia frowned. "But enough jiving. We've got to stay sharp for our next rendezvous point."

Just then, Zar spotted something incongruous with his surroundings. "What the...?" He twisted around in his seat for a second look. "I'm pulling over."

"Didn't we just cover that, dodo? You need a licence to..."

Zar wasn't listening. He slung the muscle car in alongside a United Dairies horse and cart at the roadside and thumbed the door. The rest of the team parked up as he strode back down the sidewalk. Shielding his eyes from the sun with the flat of a hand, he stared up at the billboard.

The advertisement showed two women in flying suits astride a pair of Harley Davidsons with exposed glass guts. Between them stood a heavily tanned man, hands on hips, shark teeth bared.

"Admiring the boss?"

"Apparently," Zar said to the mobster, arrived by his side. "Why is there a billboard ad featuring Braxton in the middle of Era 3.0?" The very fact seemed to confirm he was right to be suspicious about the all too showy promoter.

Valentine held onto his trilby and stared up at the billboard. "'Braxton Earl's Hybrid Automobiles. A name you can trust,'" he read in amusement.

"I don't get it. Braxton's got that swanky pod on Easy Street. Plus I thought he was a promoter. Since when did he run a motor dealership?"

"Since he became the Eras' top dog in the field of hybrid vehicles. Before that, Braxton was a biggie in desert racing promotion. I should know. I signed on as a juvie with him. Eight Ball and Justice too. We lost touch when the Desert Races were canned, at least until he came striding back into my life last week flashing that big old smile."

"But if he made it big here, why's he holed up with the richies on Easy Street?"

"Maybe he appreciates the breather outside these honeyed walls. That, or he's been writing orphan papers."

"Huh?"

"Bad cheques." Valentine winked. Zar was clearly in no mood for jokes and the mobster changed tack. "How ya doin' anyways? First time in the Eras, I bet. Quite the ride."

"You're telling me." Zar squinted sideways. Valentine was an ex-desert racer and a straight talker; both were traits he admired. The guy's scarred cheek made him appear older than his years. Or was it the way Valentine behaved – as if he'd never had parents let alone a childhood, but had just materialised behind the wheel one day.

Staring past Zar, Valentine lifted his hat a fraction. "Thanks for watching our backs in the wastelands, Persia."

"It's all about the mullah, Valentine. Else I'd beat the drag the opposite way and let a cheese weasel like you rot." Persia hooked a thumb over a shoulder. "How's about we concentrate on the gig we got going on? Starting with our next destination."

"Sure thing." Valentine shrugged at Zar, who started to walk away when he heard the gangster shoot under his breath, "Gal, we gotta jaw sometime."

"Close the shades, Valentine. I ain't jiving with you no way no how," he heard Persia spit back. Seconds later, she was by his side again.

They strode back to find a Uniform officer taking an interest in their weird array of vehicles. The man wore a lightweight taupe jacket with a high collar, taupe shorts and a matching peaked cap. Zar expected him to produce a notebook and write them up a ticket. It shocked him to the core when the officer yanked a handgun out of a hip holster and aimed it at the Road Runner's front right tyre.

"No permit displayed, which means you folks have got exactly ten seconds to haul out before I start with the tyre.

After that, if you're still inside my jurisdiction, things'll get a whole heap nastier."

"Let's ship out folks!" Persia called out to her team. Zar noticed that she kept the officer's firearm in view at all times, even as she sidled into the driver seat.

Zar couldn't help feeling that none of this made sense. A Uniform threatening them with a firearm because they had parked illegally?

"We're participating in the Ramrod Rally," he shot back in exasperation. "We aren't here to disrupt things. We're just passing through."

His heart skipped a beat when the officer switched aim from the tyre to his head. There was an instant of utter blind fear when the sky itself seemed to darken down and every bit of him wanted to run.

"Answering me back, kid?"

The next moment Zar felt a heavy hand cuff him about the ear. Deeply shocked, he realised the blow had come from Valentine.

"You're outta line, little brother. It would hurt Momma's heart to hear you speak to a man of the law like that. Say sorry to the officer. Now!" bawled the mobster, flecks of spit lodging in Zar's eye. He eased in close to add in a harsh whisper, "You don't know what you're messing with. Now do as I say else the game'll be over. For good."

Zar glared at Valentine. It was all too familiar, this undermining his decisions, this making him feel like a twist of worthless flesh. But the gun was real, he understood that much. As was the officer's motivation to fire it.

"Sorry, officer." The words clung heavily to his lips like gum.

For a few seconds, the man stared at him blankly. Zar's breath stayed packed inside his lungs.

At last the officer lowered his gun.

"Scat."

"Do as the officer says." Valentine eyed the Road Runner with meaning.

Burning up with rage and humiliation, Zar got back into the vehicle.

"Way to go, Einstein."

Mercifully, Persia kept her eyes front. Otherwise she would have caught Zar delivering her the same annihilating glare he had directed at Valentine.

He slunk low in the passenger seat. Persia torched the engine.

The convoy pulled away under the pointed gaze of the armed officer.

§

What would it take to make his father notice him, Zar had often wondered? To be acknowledged as a viable human being and not just a kid anymore? Deep down inside, he'd always known that when it came to Sol Punkstar, he might as well have asked for a piece of the moon. His father had no interest in a fifteen year old boy who was shifting inside his own skin or struggling to reconcile a mind of his own with the demands of those who'd always told him what to do. Teachers, Uniform officers, absent fathers – they all knew best apparently, and he was meant to just go along with it. Except, that didn't sit so well anymore, not now he'd learnt to cope with a Razzledazzle addict for a mother and earn a buck amongst the savages at the Death Pit. Yet here he was relegated to the Road Runner's passenger seat. Face burning. Reduced to a child again.

Persia broke the silence.

"You'd think they'd give us a clue where to swing by next."

Zar stared intently at the road.

"Ah, come on dude. We didn't mean to get heavy back there, but these streets, they're a whole shade darker than the ones you got back home."

"You think so?" Zar rounded on the team captain. What the hell did Persia know about his life or the darkness which had crept inside his own home? "There may have been a time when where I live was a decent zipcode, but that was before that bit of the city got lost in the shadows. So maybe I didn't expect a Uniform to pull a gun on me because I parked illegally, but don't any of you goofs dare treat me like I'm stupid. I've played enough hard ball in my life and I can get myself out of sticky situations."

Persia held his gaze. "Sorry but I'm handing it to Valentine this time. He prised you out of that hole you dug for yourself and with enough smarts to keep us all supping air still."

"I'd have managed just fine. I'm not a little kid!" Zar blurted, furious at the whine in his voice, even more furious at the way he had been treated.

"Then man up!" Persia tore the foil off a strip of gum and folded it between her lips. "We ain't got time or motive to be jiving like this."

Zar ran a palm back over his head, exhaling heavily. Persia was right. There was no point demanding respect from his team mates only to act like a kid when he messed up.

He forced himself to take deep breaths and then swallowed. "Okay then."

"Okay then." Persia glanced over and flicked the switch on her megavolt smile. Twisting in her seat, she stared out the back window, where Justice was riding close to the rear of the Road Runner. She jabbed a finger forwards. The Tomahawk roared and Justice pulled alongside the car.

"Wanna pull ahead and see if you can track down the next skull maker?" called Persia out of her open window.

Justice didn't reply, just opened up the throttle of the Tomahawk and roared away.

Zar sunk down in his seat and sighed. "I just want to get out of here."

Persia clucked in her throat. "Amen, brother."

§

# Chapter 17

'Science Fair: World of Tomorrow' declared the arched sign overhead. Zar and his team passed below it and out onto a promenade with immaculate lawns stretching either side. In the distance was a giant white tower, topped with the skull projection which Justice had located earlier.

At the end of the promenade, they were ushered into an underground car park where they were greeted by another member of the Uniform kited out in taupe and a peak cap. The officer made his way down the row of vehicles until he reached the Road Runner and stared in.

"You are the team captain?" the man asked with the same air of military efficiency as the previous officer they had encountered.

Persia played it straight. "Yes officer," she replied curtly.

The man gestured to a concrete pedestrian ramp. "Park up and then take the elevator to the courtyard. You compete in half an hour. Do not leave the courtyard for any reason. You are to be contained."

Zar didn't like that phrase. The stiff yet violent attitude of Era 3.0's Uniform reminded him of a darker period in the history of the world. It aggravated him, this make believe but with real guns and Uniform acting as dictators. But his recent humiliation was far too raw. He stayed silent as Persia dribbled the Road Runner forward.

§

Everywhere was spectacularly clean and ordered. Chrome waste scuttles were located every couple of metres like sentinel robots. Neem trees fountained in the corners of the courtyard, their trunks ringed with metal benches.

Zar consumed his fill of hot dogs and cream soda from a concessions' stand then slipped off to the bench furthest away from the others. He fired up a stick of Goo on his watch's face plate and cranked the dial.

Tripster's face bubbled up.

"You sly dog, Zar! I saw the live coverage of you crossing the wastelands. The cameras got close ups and, mate, who is the babe you're sharing that gas guzzler with?" The Gooey hologram leered.

"She's an ex Uniform cadet who'd soon as snap your spine as hand the hugs out." Zar glanced back at his team. They were busy refuelling their empty stomachs. "Let's speed things up," he said. "How'd we trigger the next section of route?"

The Goo solidified into a mask of concentration. "What happened at Binders Boulevard?"

"Aside from a run-in with Riflers in the Grand Dame Casino, it was a success. I found a statue acting as a safety deposit box for a second sand brick and a brass pin-up with a necklace of coloured beads. I figure the necklace relates to the next number sequence. Here's the order. Six green, three pink, one blue. Put bubbles in the empty test tube in that order."

"Yes sir." The jelly eyes rolled. They focused on a spot beyond Zar's shoulder. "Six green...three pink...come here, you slippery little sucker...one blue."

The gooey lips pursed.

"What happened?" asked Zar, on a knife's edge.

"...Nothing."

"Nothing?"

"No change, mate."

"You coming, Zar?"

It was Raina, stood far enough away not to intrude.

"Keep trying." Zar thumbed the dial crank, flattening the Goo. Still smarting from the way Valentine had treated him in front of the Uniform officer and the team, he was not in the mood for niceties.

"You my mother now?" Breaking off the constituent, he tossed the chips into a nearby waste scuttle.

Raina went from light to dark. "Hell, no! I get your crap for the length of this race. Your mother's had fifteen years worth."

"Sure she has." Again, Zar was struck Raina's uncanny ability to reach inside him and find the sore spots. He was haunted by thoughts of his mother suddenly. He'd persuaded himself to leave her in the safety of drug rehabilitation. Yet hadn't he really abandoned her to Razzledazzle withdrawal?

The reminder must have left its shadow on his face. Raina's look turned to sympathy. Zar felt it burn.

"Let's get back to the others." He grabbed her wrist, but she pulled back.

"I'm not out to get you, Zar. I know you suspect everyone, and don't get me wrong, I'd still want to beat you out on the tracks. But I've no secret motive. You can trust me. Or is that the problem? Worried I'll get too close for comfort? If so, let me remind you..."

"Yeah, yeah. You're one trophy I'm never gonna win. Good job I've got my eyes on a greater prize," Zar fired back nastily and he strode off in the direction of the bodacious Persia and the rest of the team, fed and watered and kicking up their heels.

He got to Valentine first, who stared past him and grinned.

"Broads. They're designed to keep a fella dangling."

"I'm no one's meat puppet!" Zar snapped. He wasn't over Valentine's undermining tactics.

"Zar, I'm sorry about earlier." The mobster took off his hat. He looked so sincere suddenly that Zar was taken aback. "I was just tryin' to look out for you and the team. I'd sure appreciate it if what happened didn't gum the works between us?"

Zar felt the edge taken off his anger. Valentine had a smooth way about him, and an intensity which let you know he spoke his words with care and meant every one of them. It seemed petulant to hold a grudge and he cleared his throat. "They got us shepherded in. What's next?"

"That's where a gal like Persia comes in handy." Valentine dipped his head towards the team captain.

The subtle dig was not lost on Persia, who approached the two of them but made Zar her sole focus.

"I smiled nice at that Uniform." She cupped a hand over her mouth and threw out a kiss to a baby-faced officer waiting on the concrete ramp that led away from the courtyard. The officer looked weak-kneed and Valentine lowered his hat over his eyes, shoulders shaking.

"Word is all three teams are here. Uniform directed each to a separate holding area. In a few minutes, us lucky critters are gonna be reunited. We're walking up that concrete ramp, or Helicline as they call it here. Heading for those." She pointed past the treetops to the giant skull projecting over the giant white spike. The upper third of a white sphere was visible below, the surface tessellated like a golf ball.

She gestured towards the ramp.

"After you, honey bee."

§

# Chapter 18

The white spike called the Trylon was rigged with ropes, weights and gears to lift an iron elevator above the fairground. But it was the huge golf ball of the Perisphere into which Zar and his team were shepherded.

Usherettes stood either side of a high-ceilinged vestibule – trolley dollies in red suits, stiff ringlets and odd little peak caps with satin top knots.

"Swing-a-ding-ding." Eight Ball grinned around his matchstick.

"Swing indeed." Justice raised her eyebrows at the Fly. The pair knocked elbows in shared intent.

"Sweet heaven!" Jesse brought up the rear. "Howdy ladies. Gonna take us bad boys in hand?"

The usherettes smiled as one and gestured inside like maniacal air stewardesses.

Jesse blew air between his lips. "Okaley-dokaley. That's not creepy." He skulked off in the direction the usherettes pointed.

"Ladies." Valentine raised his hat as he passed – and Zar noticed even those ice maidens melt as the gangster fired up the charm. When Persia breezed through, a dream made flesh, the usherettes were suddenly wooden again.

Zar, meanwhile, was distracted by Raina. He couldn't help brooding over the way he had treated her earlier, snapping back just because the pressure of juggling the race and his father's quest map were getting to him.

As they entered a second antechamber, he grabbed her wrist and pulled her back.

"Raina, just now, I didn't mean to be a freak." His gaze flicked ahead. No one was listening. "I've got a lot going..." His words petered out as she stared at him. *She thinks I'm an ass*, he told himself, turning his anger inward.

"Now you want to apologise? Aren't you the emotional yo-yo?" Raina pulled her wrist free and humphed. "But shouldn't we be concentrating less on games and more on the Ramrod, especially now we got more than our own company to worry about?"

She cocked her head towards the room. Zar followed her gaze to several jump-suited clones taking up sofas to their left. The Pro Leaguer team, he realised with a rush of intimidation and awe. Raina was right. His sole focus should be the next bout in the Ramrod. Their oscillating relationship could wait.

Zar followed his team to a second seating bay. He sat down astride the arm of a leather sofa and took in the antechamber. A pair of floor-to-ceiling double doors were decorated with a blue and gold sunburst. Glass and chrome sconces bathed the room in a soft glow. The walls were tiled with geometric mosaics of skyscrapers, airships, ocean liners, and cars with monstrous grills like Megalodons. Zar was reminded of the predatorial way in which they'd been herded inside the Perisphere. He ran his belt chains through his hands, taking comfort from the solid metal links.

The final team marched in, headed up by the R'asian princess with the wet-sand skin and smouldering black eyes. Zar remembered the steam coach thundering past him back at Black Rod Bridge and how the girl had stuck her tongue out like a first crush in the playground. This time she met his gaze without expression, but it was enough to set his pulse racing.

He was less enthusiastic about Vladimir's arrival. The brute flopped onto a sofa in a third seating bay and sprawled its length, oversized commando boots dangling off the edge. His thick lips twisted as he caught Zar staring. Before Zar could look away, he snapped his eyes shut and appeared to enjoy the sleep of the dead.

"This should be an interesting family reunion."

Justice poured herself onto the sofa besides Zar. She dipped her head towards the princess, who had deserted her team at the same time one of the Pro Leaguers stepped apart from his. The Pro unhooked his brass goggles, revealing a common lineage of lustrous hair, black eyes and soft brown skin.

"Who are they?" Zar felt a sting of envy as the two embraced.

"Fa and Fabrienne Oz."

"Frank Oz's kids?" said Zar, incredulous.

"The twins, yeah."

"Didn't even know they were still in Autodrome."

"Frank Oz kept the pair stowed in the belly of Black Stacks after Franklin's death, and who can blame him? If I could've salvaged some scrap to remind me of my Ruby, I'd have kept it locked away from the world too."

Justice's voice had dropped to a whisper. Zar read it as emotion. He wanted to ask who Ruby was and why she had mattered so much to Justice. But he realised they weren't the only ones to zone in on the twins. A hush had descended over the room.

"Good looking crew you've assembled for yourself." Fa Oz put his hands on his hips and looked every part the sultan.

"Your boys may be Pro League, but where's the advantage in all that spit and polish?" Fabrienne Oz smiled beatifically. "You've got to know how to play the game," she added, and, turning to her team, announced, "My brother thinks you are the devil's rejects."

Drowned out by the motley crew's objections, Fa mouthed, "I didn't say that," while his sister grinned, a djinn mixing mischief. Zar was equally impressed and repulsed by her slyness.

Fa waited for the hullabaloo to die down then addressed his fellow Pros. "The opposition claim they stand some chance of winning the Ramrod. Need I remind them who made it first to the ferries at Coddington Dock?"

Stood to attention in their navy blue jumpsuits, brass goggles worn at the forehead like an extra set of eyes, the young Pro Leaguers allowed themselves a smile but remained ultimately professional. In contrast, Fabrienne had opted for a darker breed of racer. Older and uglier than either Fa's team or Zar's, the team Fabrienne had assembled looked like they'd murder their own mothers as soon as race cleanly out on the track. Not that the fact stopped Zar from butting in.

"If you two could lay off preening then you might notice there are three teams in this race!"

Fabrienne glared at him. She burst into beautiful, terrible laughter.

"Aren't you the spitfire, Zar Punkstar?"

*She knew who he was.* Zar got a rush of blood to the head.

"Any relation of Sol Punkstar?" Fa eyed him with lazy amusement.

"Son of," Fabrienne provided. "Zar qualified Pro League this week."

"How'd you know that?" shot Zar, hot in the face.

"I keep abreast of events." Fabrienne circled him appraisingly. "Which is how I know to offer my condolences on your father's passing. Sol Punkstar was pivotal in the design of Autodrome's skyline."

"If you say so."

"I don't. Father does."

The mention of the great Frank Oz brought a reverential seriousness to the room's atmosphere. Fabrienne walked back in the direction of her team mates.

"You're wrong by the way, Zar Punkstar," she cast out, tilting her head and smiling prettily, a sprite with teeth. "I do know there are three teams in this race. I'm just waiting for your team of has-beens to pose any sort of threat."

*What the hell?* Zar was about to retaliate when the double doors opened, the sun motif splitting in two like a seal being broken.

A woman entered the room. Dressed in a tailored jacket and fishtail skirt, she had about her an air of the ring master. Two usherettes moved in to stand either side of her.

"Ladies and gentlemen! Welcome to the Perisphere."

The trio struck a pose before breaking into close vocal harmonies.

"Got to boogie, got to boogie, got to go oh oh,
To the Perisphere, put on a show oh oh,
Gotta pick your maaan, soon as you can can can,
Team one, two, three, heebie gee-bie-bie
Gotta pick a man, fast as you can can can
Or get the dah dah Ramrod bluuues..."

The women held their poses, grinning garishly in anticipation of applause.

"Say what?" said Eight Ball.

§

# Chapter 19

Valentine trickled his steam car up to the start line and waited, hands gripping the polished ebony steering wheel. He trusted that ride, knew it was hitting on all sixteen cylinders. Didn't mean he took a damn cent of it for granted. Not when the landship basked to his right, smoke seeping from its twin copper funnels, and the Mazda RX-7 with its wedged hood and flip-up lights purred to his left.

Persia had chosen him to take on the challenge despite Zar's best efforts to persuade her to pick him instead. Under different circumstances, Valentine would have stepped down to give the younger guy a chance. He owed Zar after humiliating him back on the street – even if the motivation had been all about preserving their team and not destroying Zar's confidence. But Valentine knew in his heart that this was his race. Zar's would come in time.

He checked the bank of gauges on the Cadillac's dash. Its rebuild had seen features from a Doble E20 steam-powered roadster introduced. Now he sat on a full head of steam about to make a 1000 lbs per foot of torque from a standstill with little vibration or sound. He twisted the radio dial. Billie Holiday's *Summertime* crackled over the airwaves. Time slowed. He breathed quietly.

When the chequered flag tripped in its wall slot, the crush of adrenaline was almost painful. The sports car accelerated with a waspish shriek while the landship lurched forward, gears grinding. Clutching the steering, Valentine used his other hand to twist a small throttle wheel mounted on top. The Cadillac leapt into motion with a swish-swishing sound as the flash boiler powered and the Sirocco blower kicked in, heating water into steam. Eyes on the straight, the gangster gave an extra tug on the throttle wheel – and was thrust back into his seat by the punch.

The road skipped by, its surface buffed to a sheen. Scoping out the opposition, Valentine realised the Pro had appliquéd the sports car to his left wing. Walls arose. The straight became an s-bend of brushed silver. A bobsleigh run, Valentine thought with a thrill as the steam car skated up the curved track at a 180 degree angle.

The track levelled again. Valentine's mind tick-tocked. The Mazda had a lightweight Wankel engine, a 50:50 front-rear weight distribution ratio and a low centre of gravity. It should be tripping over that slick surface, not hugging the steam car's shoulder. Valentine couldn't shift the feeling he was being flimflammed. But how and why?

He entered a new bend. Chrome banked either side. The iron throat of the landship was suddenly audible; Valentine saw the vehicle in his rear view, sledging in on several tens of tonne.

His gaze cut back to the road which branched in two a hundred metres or so ahead. Not a speed race then, Valentine realised. He'd have to call on the hoodoo of Lady Luck herself and choose a lane to take. He got a sense of his insides leathering, same as he always did when a contest hotted up. Gone the intestines, stomach and other inner organs. Now he was a desiccated strip.

The Cadillac shook as a great milling sound started up. Where the track split, a huge plinth revolved up from the floor to reveal a metal figure, head squared off like a diver's helmet. The breastplate was silky with reflections, the limbs segmented and glistening like a scorpion's. When the robotic arms winched up, revealing twin plasma cutting torches instead of hands, Valentine suddenly understood why the Mazda was clingy. Sparks were about to fly and his steam car provided a shield.

He cut right. The Mazda re-glued itself to his wing in seconds. He glimpsed the driver. In brass goggles and aviator cap, the kid looked no more human than the iron colossus attempting to fill them with daylight.

Something about the Pro's impassive attempt at sabotage turned up the flame in Valentine. Shunting left, he tore sparks off the sports car...except, when he prised their vehicles apart, he noticed the Mazda was unblemished. Its paint was diamond-impregnated, which took some serious folding green, he realised. It also meant that the sparks had to have flown off an alternative metal surface. His vehicle's own. Sweat creased in at Valentine's eyelids. He brushed it off with the back of a hand.

The robot's twin torches fired, throwing out two arcs of plasma. One cut steaming grooves in the metal road. The other scorched the golden epidermis of the Cadillac.

"Cook it up while you can, tin man. Cook it up while you can," Valentine murmured. For the time being, he had his parasitic twin to manhandle aside.

He dove right, taking the whale of the steam car into the upper groove of the track. *Keep in step with me, pug.* The Pro did exactly that. Valentine slammed a heel to the kickplate and braked. The steam car shuddered in rapid deceleration while the Mazda went flying out in front like a glider released from its aerotow. A dribble of plasma hit home. The metal bodywork rent apart. Steam spilt out behind the Pro's vehicle, colouring up the air.

Valentine lost sight of the sports car, distracted by the churning motion of the landship just centimetres from the Cadillac's bumper. He lowered a stiff lever near his left hip, cooked up a fresh head of steam and released it at the same instant that he raked a pair of flip switches amid the gauges. The sixteen cylinder engine ate up a pint of fuel in less than two seconds, sending a burst of power to the chassis. Alloys spun. Billie Holiday sirened. The steam car ate up the road.

Cruising clear of the landship, the gangster had no time to play the fool. Plasma arced either side of his streamlined machine. He adjusted his steering minutely, keeping the Cadillac between the molten beams. The fork in the road was on him suddenly. He aimed left, rocketed around the bend and was out of firing range.

Immediately, he faced another fork in the road. He opted left again but, after a short strip of track, found himself in a u-bend being directed back around. Easing off the throttle, he was wary of his choices, and justifiably so as a panel opened in the road surface and a second metal giant corkscrewed out of the floor.

The robot activated its torches in a wheeze of pneumatics. Valentine pumped the lever on his left, leant forward and revolved the winding clip of a large brass cog on the dash. A rectangular section of the Cadillac's left wing concertinaed, exposing a hidden mechanised gut under the seats. Air screamed in alongside the metallic churn of the wheels and engine.

Valentine worked the winding clip to crane out a metre-long scythe. A punch to the eye of the cog and the scythe was pulled taut against the side of the car via a rubber noose. A burst of plasma skimmed the bonnet as he did a fly-by past the robot. At the last second, he hit the eye of the cog again, slackening the noose and sending the scythe ricocheting out.

In the rear view, he saw the robot's sheared torso tumble off its main stalk. Winding the cog the opposite way, he re-secured the scythe inside the Cadillac's belly. The exterior noise cut off as the wing panel closed.

Seconds later, the landship powered into view, apparently having also taken the wrong lane at the second fork. Valentine raised his hat in mock greeting as he swung wide and around the iron brute.

Back at the fork, he opted right this time to enter a shining snakepass. And he understood then. Part two of the Ramrod was a deadly maze. His mission was to make it out first and in one piece.

"Son of a gun!"

Jesse pumped the iron crank. Steam billowed. They set off on a tramline at a forty five degree angle to that along which they had been previously travelling.

"Valentine's good at thinking on his feet," said Justice, crouched up on the bench to get a better view. "But I don't envy him trying to keep a grip down there," she added on cue as the Cadillac ricocheted from one side of the track to the other.

"Ask me, the landship's got the uppers in this game," sneered Jesse. He worked the crank. The spectator pod lurched sideways on track that seemed to belong to a metal rollercoaster left to rust in the rain.

"Cruisin' for a bruisin', nosebleed," muttered Eight Ball, his matchstick shaken from his lips.

"Soz, buddy. Just the way this gearstick grinds. But seriously, look at that sled." Jesse pointed down at the landship, coasting smoothly along, its reinforced steel oblivious to the plasma fire from the surfacing robots. "Got the weight to stick to the surface. Body armour too."

"But does the driver have brains to remember where he's been and crack the maze? Apparently not," Justice concluded dryly as the landship turned into a side road it had already explored twice. In contrast, Valentine appeared to have a grip on the layout. Bypassing the red herrings of numerous side roads, he headed for a fresh section of the maze.

Justice sat back down alongside Zar on the bench seat. He sensed her eying him intently.

"Didn't think I was your type, Justice?" he said sourly. He'd failed to persuade Persia to let him take part in the trial instead of Valentine and it had left a shadow on his mood.

Justice didn't need the fact explaining to her and said gently, "Don't stay mad at Persia. She may not be my favourite person, but she is an excellent choice as team captain. No chance in hell I'd race with her otherwise. And Valentine is the perfect choice for this heat. He's a drag-race aficionado, used to out-sprinting his opponents – or attackers in this case. Plus, his ride is reengineered to give him a fighting chance. You, meanwhile? It's less about exclusion than giving *you* a fighting chance to solve this quest you've got going on."

Zar jolted hard against her shoulder as Jesse switched directions. "Sorry." He rubbed a hand around the back of his neck, and sighed.

"So why are you perched up here with us instead of making the most of this break to go off exploring?"

Justice smiled, her boxer's nose spreading and exaggerating her off-beat beauty.

Zar tried to overcome his wounded pride. Justice was right. While it hurt his sensibilities as a racer to be overlooked in favour of Valentine, Persia had rejected him for the right reasons. No matter how much it cut away at him, he needed to solve his father's conundrum above all else. Which meant he had to be free to pursue the clues. Plus, as he stared down into the arena, he realised that Valentine really was proving himself the right guy for the job.

He squinted over at Justice. She struck him as genuine. Her fighting spirit went far deeper than the lean body; she was a survivor, like him.

"I hit a dead end," he confided, needing to trust in someone at that moment. He hoped Justice was the right choice.

"I doubt that. You always seem to find a way to get what you want." Justice cocked her head towards Raina, in danger of toppling out the pod as she craned her neck to get a better fix on events below.

Zar harrumphed. He gazed off into the middle distance. "Just don't know where I'm going wrong," he said softly.

They were propelled off each other's shoulders again. This time, Eight Ball mustered in and physically removed Jesse from navigation duties. Justice smirked while Zar wrapped his arms about his chest and narrowed his eyes thoughtfully.

"My dad left me a legacy. Colour-coded number strings set off new clues. But we've tried entering the latest set of digits and narda."

"We?"

*Was he right to trust her?* Too late to hold back now.

Meeting Justice's warm brown eyes, he said, "Friend's babysitting the scroll. Tripster. A brain."

"In which case, the fault must lie with the one feeding him the information."

Zar retrieved the pinup trinket from his backpack.

"Six green, three pink, one blue."

Justice studied him a moment. "My hunch is you're the type to rush in, guns blazing," she said shrewdly. "Chances are you just needed to slow a little. Give your mind room to work out the kinks."

Zar stared down at the trinket. He turned it over in his palm, and then back over again. Justice said the fault lay with the information he was feeding Tripster. *Six green, three pink, one blue… Six green, three pink, one blue…*

And then he saw his mistake with blinding clarity. "She's wearing an earring!" he exclaimed, his face radiant with relief. "A freakin' pink earring."

His fingers got busy typing into his Data Streamer watch. But then he stopped and glanced at Justice.

"Thank you."

She smiled broadly. "Guess you're back on the scent."

§

# Chapter 20

Ticker tape spooled from Zar's watch. He tore off the strip and scanned it.

'Good save! New route leads to Science Fair. Also triggered a skull icon and another empty tube.'

So Tripster had unlocked the third section of the route. Zar let out a long, jittery sigh, so overwhelmed was he by relief. There wasn't time for celebration. Instead, he tried to get his head around the latest information. A skull icon – another symbol linked to Autodrome's hotrodder culture. As for the empty tube, it would be another case of uncovering a colour coded sequence.

He scrunched up the ticker tape and was in the process of pocketing it when Justice said, "Can I help?" Her eyes were alive with sharp intelligence. Concern too, and while the idea of anyone worrying about him niggled, Zar was starting to doubt if he could, or should, try to solve Sol's quest alone.

"I just don't know, Justice."

"What you looking for?"

Zar took a risk, confiding in her further, "Something here involving a skull."

She nodded. "Only one building to match that brief. The Trylon."

"The Trylon?" Zar frowned. "But there have been skull markers used throughout the race. What would make that particular projection so special?"

"Maybe its lit up rather than projected." Justice shrugged. "Worth checking out."

"But the ride doesn't go all the way to the top."

"No, it doesn't." Justice clucked in her throat – and Zar got the impression of intelligent analysis again.

She turned to him, long neck decorated with ropes of muscle, nose misshapen from boxing bouts in the practice ring. "I was 13 when I met Ruby. I'd known I was gay for the longest time, but my sexuality wasn't the problem, more my lifestyle as a racer. I was already in love – with the race track. Plus, I'd got what many called a death wish. Me? I called it guts. Before I met Ruby, no other girl had come close to understanding what it meant to me to race. She was my lifeline. And because she understood my ambitions as a racer, she also taught me to exist off the track."

Justice wrapped her hands over one another. "Here's the rub though. Ruby cheated before she died. Might've been once, might've been multiple times. All I knew was the lipstick on her collar wasn't mine." Her brown eyes glazed. "We never got to talk about it. Tension was already running high with the Ramrod the next day. So I slotted the pain away, figured we'd clean up the mess after the race."

Zar heard breath slip between her lips – sigh of the wounded.

"Listen, Justice. I'm a lousy listener..."

Justice shot him a look to lily-liver the toughest opponent. "Have the respect to hear me out." She twisted a promise ring on her left index finger. "Ruby cheated and it hurt. But there isn't a day goes by when I wouldn't share her with a hundred others just to have her back. My point is this, Zar. I've never told anyone about the cheating before. Why'd I tell you now? I think you need something on me and now I've given it to you. In return, you're going to take my advice and believe I won't screw you over. Okay?"

Zar stared at the girl. Like Valentine, she seemed to have experienced life in a way which made her act older than others her age. But beneath the surface he caught glimpses of a hurt young woman.

"Okay," he said softly.

She nodded. "I'm going to get you help. Help that won't ask no questions, won't tell you no lies. But it will mean trusting someone other than me. Someone I trust."

Justice jerked her head at the Fly and called out, "Eight Ball. Pull over, will you?"

§

# Chapter 21

They exited the Perisphere to find it was early evening. Zar was relieved to be out in the open. The arena was architecturally impressive, but it was just a cleaner version of the Death Pit – and while it was the competitors who tore shreds off one another in that dust bowl, the Perisphere's ability to trigger a robot army brought it too close to a sentient organism for his liking. It also added to his distrust of his surroundings. Suits, fake smiles, false advertisements – everything pointed to a time of superficial properness. But behind the façade, he glimpsed a subterranean of authoritarianism, strained reserve and weird science. Era 3.0 creeped him out.

"What's buzzin'?" Eight Ball squinted over, matchstick bobbing at his lips.

Zar eyed the Fly. Was he really about to pour out his secrets to yet another person he barely knew, especially about something as crucial as a clue left by his dead father? What he was about to share with the Fly could make or break him.

As if sensing his reticence, Eight Ball flopped off his leather cap and scratched his head. "Justice might come across badass but she's got the jets to get you and me out here and it ain't to pucker up."

Zar nodded, but ran his belt chains through his fingers Justice had put her faith in him. More than that, she had given him hope thanks to the bionic steeplejack standing opposite. The least he could do was take the help when it was offered.

"I'm on a puzzle trail. Solved a couple of my dad's riddles so far. His latest is out of reach though. Literally." His gaze went to the Trylon.

Eight Ball's eyes followed his. Replacing his cap and remoulding it, the Fly gave a low whistle. "As in 700 foot out of reach?"

"And the ride only goes up 600." Zar pointed to a billboard showing an apple pie family gazing admiringly at the Trylon alongside the slogan, 'Experience a brave new world 600 feet above the city.'

"Not my style to piggyback a sky lift, but clock's ticking. Means you get to come summa the way too." Eight Ball put a thumb and forefinger between his lips and blew. The whistle did the trick. A Uniform appeared on the Helicline.

"Lads." The man raised his peak cap.

Eight Ball rested a hand on the officer's shoulder. "My buddy and me ain't never been to Era 3.0 before. What do we find when we get a minute's grace from the Ramrod, but the Trylon ride shut." Eight Ball leant in to the officer. "Squeeze us in?"

"The Trylon ride closed at 5.00pm. As you can see for yourself, the park has emptied of general public," said the officer, eyes pinched behind round spectacles. "It would be best if you lads waited inside the Perisphere," he added insistently.

Zar was all too aware of the man's handgun holster. But Eight Ball just slung his hands on his hips and kept on chewing.

"No sweat, officer."

The Uniform didn't move, clearly unwilling to trust the greaser to keep his word. With no evidence to the contrary, the man eventually stalked off in the direction of the underground car park.

Eight Ball continued to stare until the man was out of sight. "Let's split," he said without inflection.

A minute later, and a sharp click told Zar that Eight Ball had successfully picked the lock securing the gate of the iron egg elevator. No surprise the Fly listed apprentice locksmith among his talents!

Eight Ball concertinaed the gate aside.

"Peddle to the metal. Got our heels on fire here."

Zar stepped inside. The Fly rammed the gate shut in a peel of reverberating metal. A brushed chrome panel was inscribed with 'Up' and 'Down' alongside two push buttons. Eight Ball punched the top button and set the wheezing hydraulics into action. Ropes tensed. Cogs bit in. The elevator started to rise with a shudder.

Science World unfolded before them like a miniature town stored in an attic. For the first time in years, Zar appreciated the very real squalor of his own part of town. In contrast, Era 3.0 struck him as bleached and scrubbed down. Sanatorium-like in its essence.

He shook his head. "I don't get this place. Its living history, but from a time when life was so uptight, not to mention a breeding ground for fascists."

"Gives you the willies, huh? But trust me, these guys, they're having a blast. Sure it's full of squares who appreciate a tighter world, but this era's got a slick side too. The chicks for one thing." Eight Ball rested a boot sole against the ornate railing and grinned. "Then there's the speakeasies, poker dens, the big band music hall. Did I mention the chicks?"

The ground kept falling away. Eight Ball got tight-eyed.

"It'll seem kooky to an everyday Joe like you, but life in the Eras is about living on that hot tin roof between what was and what is. Take a look out there." The Fly pointed past Science World and the time-warped streets, out to the silver waters of Lady Luck Lough and the main trunk of Autodrome. "The city's swell. But some of us want our lives chrome-plated, especially if we were born the wrong side of the tracks. My folks brought me up in Era 5.0, their idea of wonderland."

Zar scowled. "But if it's as simple as people wanting to escape their present to live in the past, how come I was raised to know you didn't set foot in the Eras without inviting trouble?"

Eight Ball shook his head and grunted. "Could be this joint's fat city and we don't want cubes gettin' a look in, especially the rich cats on Autodrome's west side. But truth is we got a way of dealing with our own. Sure, we got a harsher branch of Uniform but most times folk get out of line in the Eras, well, they're just a wet rag for the rest of us. Best to send them to Nowhereville."

"Which is where?" Zar asked in spite of himself.

Eight Ball pointed down just as the elevator halted in a fresh sweep of steam. He switched to pointing up. "I'd better goose it if we're gonna find your daddy's puzzle. Any illuminations why he'd hang it where a normal guy can't reach?"

*Why indeed?* Zar could just imagine his father huddled over a pile of sketches at one of his workbenches, taking pains to make his treasure hunt as difficult as possible to solve.

"Another attempt to show up how stupid he thought I was," he said sullenly.

"Or a way of saying ask for help." Eight Ball tugged aside the gate. He retrieved the suction poles from the sheath at his back and snapped them out. Concentric metal rings clipped in at the wrist and elbow. Gripper mouths spasmed at the tips of the suction poles. Steam flooded from the compressed-air ejector pump stored in the back sheath.

"Here. You might need this." Zar took the string from around his neck and handed over the beak on its piece of string. He felt a sense of peculiar anxiety to be without it.

Eight Ball pocketed the pendant.

"It's cool to play the odd ball, Zar. But you gotta have the jets to know when folk are friends, and when those friends are rooting for you," he advised with a wink.

Before Zar could answer, the Fly had swung out of the open door and around to the outside of the elevator. Climbing onto the roof, he started to ascend, a creature returned to its natural habitat.

Encrusted with tiny red glitter tiles, the skull was a burning ruby in the failing sunlight. Eight Ball reached the base. He squeezed his brake levers, suckering the coruscated surface.

"What're we eyeballing here?" he called down.

"You're looking for a release mechanism which is triggered by the beak," came the shout from the iron cage suspended below.

Eight Ball adjusted his foothold so the microfiber barbs coating his shoes secured a better grip. Examining his surroundings, he was distracted by the view. The setting sun was intense tangerine, the sky a charcoal rub. Wasn't it just the most up there! The ground was fine for land lovers but a Fly needed to live in the air. Everything was dampened here. Except the sense of space and freedom.

"Find anything?" he heard Zar shout up.

"Not yet!" Eight Ball sucked in a lungful of clean sweet air. It refocused him. What was he looking for? Some kind of mechanism and a key slot to activate it. He worked the brake levers to open the throat of the compressor pump. Steam bled up from his shoulders.

Dilating the gripper mouths at the tips of his batons, he skated up on top of the skull.

The Eras spread out below like a beaded sari, the black underskirt of the desert beyond. Anchoring his feet, Eight Ball returned his suction poles to the sheath at his back, crouched and ran his hands over the glossy tiles.

"Anything?" Zar's voice carried a tight urgency.

"Still looking." Eight Ball ran his fingertips back the way he'd come. Yeah, there was something disrupting the surface. He peered closely at the area and located a series of nodules.

"Okay, eager beaver! I got something." He squinted at the nodules. "A word. *Gottlieb*."

"What does that mean?"

"Gottlieb." Eight Ball rolled the word around on his tongue. At the same instant, he realised he was kneeling dead centre of a large circular boss.

Unsheathing his suction poles, he clambered down the face of the skull – and felt a tremendous rush of anticipation when he saw the nose cavity bridged by a narrow metal bench. Prodding at it to assess if it would take his weight, he lowered himself onto the bench, legs dangling over the 700 foot drop, and ran his hands over the skull face.

"Bingo!" he whispered. There was a notch between the eye sockets. He slotted the beak in, gave it a twist and heard a grinding noise. A mechanism tunnelled away inside both eye sockets. Re-pocketing the beak, Eight Ball slid his arms inside and felt around until he located a plunger in each socket.

"Gottlieb's the name of a pinball machine manufacturer. One of the US originals from way back." he shouted down. He'd spent enough idle hours on the Humpty Dumpty, Knock Out, and Sluggin' Champ to recall the company stamp. "Lucky for you, I'm the pinball wizard," he muttered, and leaning back, tugged and released the sprung mechanisms in tandem.

The narrow bench rattled with vibrations. Eight Ball dislodged himself, shook out his suction poles and skated back up top. Things were happening beneath his feet, a tunnelling down of the spiral pattern to reveal preformed grooves. Seconds later, seven red balls charged out of side shoots.

He watched in fascination as the balls charged around the spiral, ricocheting off metal pins. Three balls swirled around and down into secret pockets, accompanied by fresh mechanical rumblings. Four...five....six. Something was burrowing up. Eight Ball moved to the outer edge of the spiral. As the last ball rolled into its pocket, a large electrified coil, the sort he'd seen in sci-fi movies, corkscrewed up from the centre of the spiral.

His voice coloured by panic, Zar shouted up, "The lift's going down! What's going on?"

Eight Ball had a good idea. Sooner or later, a Uniform patrol had been bound to spot the Trylon ride in action and take steps to bring the perpetrators back to earth.

"I'll meet you at the bottom," he shouted, and as an afterthought, "Don't get frosted down there. Keep your nose clean with the fuzz."

He fixated on the coil of blue lightning. What was he meant to do with that thing? Apparently he'd done enough. A synthesised voice began to play from unseen speakers, inflections matched by the zigzagging lightning.

"Pink, green, blue, Xanadu. Pink, green, blue..."

The message looped for a good minute. Then the voice suddenly stopped, and the coil flickered and snuffed out.

Eight Ball peered inside. On a glass shelf in the heart of the dead coil was a sand brick and a brass ornament.

The Fly put in his hand and retrieved both.

§

Valentine steered left. There had been no sign of the landship since the dead end. Meanwhile, the Mazda had latched on to his side a half kilometre back and was proving a tough critter to shake. Not that there was anywhere to hide. The route was lined with a squadron of iron men. His only hope was to outrun their guns.

With the Mazda at his shoulder, he opened up the Cadillac down the straight. The plasma torches weren't activated yet. Even so, he had an idea they'd be socking it to them any moment. Yet something didn't seem right. Why did the robots hold off?

Shooting back his hat with a fingertip, Valentine got a glimpse of...what was it? Some disruption in the reflective road surface. Pumping the brake to stop the whale of a Cadillac from skidding, he slowed while the Mazda shot away. There was every chance he'd blown it since no amount of sweat and steam would bring him back alongside that sledge. But if there was ever a time to trust his instincts...

He reversed back to the fault line in the road and, hot dang, it was a rabbit hole! A freakin' rabbit hole that tunnelled off the main branch and led to Hellsville, no doubt.

Valentine stared at the distant shape of the Mazda. Would you know it, the Pro had got a sniff of his discovery and was performing an impromptu u-turn. Except, at that moment, the robot legion decided to open fire. Streams of plasma arced in from either side, burning through the Mazda's bodywork.

Valentine drove hard at the rabbit hole. Silver slipstreamed around him. Time folded. His internal compass whirled. And then he was out, the track widening and the net of tramlines overhead.

With a filthy roar, the landship crested the bank to his right and sledged back down into the competition. At the same time, robots corkscrewed up from the ground, positioned like pinball targets. Valentine repositioned his hat above his eyes; he had a hunch that he was the ball.

The landship rumbled down onto the straight. Thick black clots squeezed from the smokestack. Tread groaned. The fat engine burbled. Watching the plasma make little impact on the landship's shield, Valentine understood there'd be no sacrificing his opponent to those white-hot streams a second time. Now he was the vulnerable one, which meant he needed to think fast if he was to stand a chance.

He tucked in his chin and turned up the radio. Billie Holiday crooned a soft, sour lullaby. *Go through fire, and I'll go through fire*...He needed a way to pass those sentries....*Sure, I'm crazy*...He had to be certain it would work...*Crazy in love, you see*....Well, roast him on a stick, if it wasn't as well to embrace the pinball analogy!

Cranking the throttle, Valentine mimicked the Pro's earlier tactic to wedge in behind the landship, using its bulk as a shield. They passed the first robot, which had engaged its firearms moments before. The iron man revolved to keep the landship in sight and, at the last second, Valentine broke away. Unable to keep both vehicles in its line of fire, the robot whirled in confusion.

The gangster repeated the same tactic for the second and third target. By the fourth, the landship had got wind of his parasitic piggybacking. Slamming sideways, it drove up a bank, forcing the Cadillac to climb an ever steeper gradient. Valentine gripped the wheel but even he couldn't fight the physics of weight displacement. As they flew past a fourth and fifth robot on the track below, the Cadillac's upper set of wheels lifted briefly off the ground – and Valentine got to thinking fast.

He needed to take the landship out and with something more effective than plasma streams. He needed to do so soon, given that the Cadillac was going to tip any moment. And he needed to find a way to navigate the final robot without getting shot up and limping to the finishing post. If he was lucky.

The answer came to him like a bullet. Valentine yanked on the throttle to unleash a fresh head of steam.

At the same time, he swiped the bank of switches on the dash, firing up the 16 cylinders under the bonnet.

It was a double whammy. Thrust back in his seat by the g-force, he just managed to keep a grip on the steering as the Cadillac roared out from the landship's shadow. He yanked the steering sideways. His vehicle was temporarily airborne. A tug on a second lever by his hip and the Cadillac touched down, its landing softened by the marshmallow wheeze of triggered hydraulics.

"Come on, gal! Let's dust!"

He sped across the track on the diagonal, facing down the sentry dead ahead. A glance over a shoulder told him everything he needed to know; the landship was on his tail. Plasma fire bubbled the Cadillac's hood. Valentine took it on the nose. Just as long as the landship kept on coming.

The robot was six metres away, three metres, one... Valentine pressed a button on the hip level lever. With a gush of funnelled gas, the entire cab craned up on metal stilts. The sensation was tidal, a bouncing off the suspension alongside a sudden lift. He steered the Cadillac over the head of the robot. The landship had no such trick up its sleeve. Valentine checked the rear view to see the machine try to change course last moment only to strike the iron man at a side angle. The robot's colossal

244

arms raised in attack mode to hook the vehicle's front spoiler. With a noise like androidal pack animals skinned alive, the landship veered over onto its side.

Valentine didn't have time to gloat. He disengaged the hydraulics. The cab jittered down on dumping cylinders. Ahead, two last robots were positioned opposite one another. In the seconds it took for them to realise he had put their brethren out of commission and engage their firearms, the gangster had pulled on the first lever again, wound the brass cog on the dash to crank up the side panel and worked like a dog to revolve the winding clip, craning out the scythe. Lactic acid burnt his shoulder as he punched the centre of the cog, pulled the scythe taut on its slingshot, and headed dead centre between the robots. Plasma arced in from either side. Valentine slammed a fist into the eye of the cog and dragged on the steering to pull a tight 360.

He flew out of the manoeuvre to drive hard down the straight. In his mirror, he saw the robots sit pretty a moment before their sliced torsos slid off and crashed onto the ground.

Valentine drove across the finish line. Whoops and cheers rained down from overhead. Bringing the Cadillac to a crawl, he let his head rest back. A face flooded his mind like water colours. Sensual hazel eyes. Soft mouth.

Baby blonde hair. Would Persia even care he was still alive?

§

Zar watched the Fly descend the Trylon in slow looping flight, a human lacewing against the red dusk. Landing a couple of metres away, Eight Ball concertinaed the small papery wings into the folds of his leather.

He nodded. "Officers."

One gun was trained on Eight Ball, the other needling Zar's neck. Zar swallowed, and felt the pressure of the barrel increase.

"How you doin' there, Zar?" Eight Ball had lost his joker side.

'How's it look?' Zar wanted to shout out, burning up with the same savage rage that overtook him whenever he was made to feel powerless. Instead, he forced himself to say evenly, "I was just explaining that climbing the Trylon was a prank – a dare."

"Yeah." Eight Ball popped a match into his mouth. "No disrespect intended, gents."

"Except for the fact I told you the ride was closed," said the officer they'd encountered earlier and who was now moulding his gun into Zar's spine.

"Sure thing, you got us there. But you fellas have gotta remember what its like to take a dare on. We got our reps to protect."

"Hmmm, trouble is, your reps don't mean squat to me or Officer Martinelli here. We're gonna bring you in because this isn't the kind of joint where kids go crawling about the place like untrained monkeys. Here we expect you to know your place, else we fill ya full of lead."

"Officer..?"

"Ciccone." The man spat out his surname like a curse word.

"Officer Ciccone. I gotta tell you and Officer Martinelli here, you got us good and you're right. Could be us two kids need to smarten our act up." Eight Ball started to reach into a back pocket of his jeans, and Officer Martinelli cocked his gun clip.

"Whooah there. I'm gonna show you gents the prize I won by clambering up there." Eight Ball's eyes scooted up to the skull aloft the Trylon.

"Don't you dare," muttered Zar. His muscles tensed, ready to fight to retain what was rightfully his. He was reined in by the blunt pressure of the gun. Then he saw Eight Ball offer over a roll of dollar bills.

"It'd be boss if you officers would look after this for me. That much green is only gonna get a pair of kids like us in trouble."

Zar felt the gun slacken at his spine. Officer Ciccone strode past him. He stopped alongside Eight Ball, eyed him, and closed his fists around the money roll.

"You boys keep your feet on the ground from now on," he muttered, pocketing the cash.

"Sure thing." Eight Ball nipped the peak of his cap.

"Come on, Martinelli. Let's leave these dum-dums to run home to their mommas." Officer Ciccone stabbed a finger towards the path. The two men re-holstered their weapons and walked away.

While Zar battled to bring his heart rate back to normal, Eight Ball rolled his match between his teeth.

"We win the Ramrod, you owe me those dollars plus interest on top of my cut of the prize fund." He glanced sideways at Zar, and cracked a smile. "These what you were after?" Reaching inside his leather, he handed over the sand brick and latest trinket.

Zar examined both, his heart rate quickening again – this time with excitement. The trinket was a brass skull with blue beads for eyes. He deposited it in his backpack along with the sand brick.

"Yours too."

Eight Ball held out the beak pendant.

"Thanks." Zar eased the string back around his neck and slid the beak inside his T-shirt. "And thanks for helping out."

"No sweat."

"So what happened up there?" Zar had hated not knowing what the hell was going on above his head. But he had put his trust in the greaser, in Justice.

"Pinball, like I told ya. *Gottlieb* was the clue. Maker of pinball machines the world over. I found a pair of flippers. Pinged them to release balls that scored off a set of targets. A pillar grew up outta that skull like a knock from a hammer to a cartoon bonce. Inside were the items I gave you."

"That's it."

"Yeah." The Fly masticated his matchstick, eye steady. "That's it."

"Thanks, Eight Ball, and thanks for handling those officers." Zar scratched the back of his head. "I guess I've just got accept that the rules are a little different out here."

"Like I said, no sweat. Guy with your smarts'll get the hang of this candy land in no time." Adjusting the collar of his leather, the Fly thrust a finger back in the direction of the Perisphere. "Now let's split and find the others."

# Chapter 22

There was a subtle blurring of the boundaries between the Eras. Zar had been too busy applying himself to the study of the track in the past to know whether this building was 1920s styled or that building 1960s influenced. But when a red skull projected a couple of kilometres south west and he slung the Road Runner in that direction, Zar found his surroundings unmistakable.

To his right was a high school with a fenced baseball court where stragglers still played ball while to his left were neat little houses with picket fences enclosing aspic green lawns...he guessed at this last detail since dusk had left a sepia layer on the place. At the end of the road, he turned onto what he took to be the Main Street. While the packed stores of Era 3.0 had exuded a need-to-sell-any-which-way-how, these premises were thinned out, as if they had yawned, stretched and stayed that way. This was a world of electrical goods' stores selling Bakelit appliances and mahogany surround TVs, of ice cream parlours with igloo frontages, of men in flannel suits and open-neck shirts, and women in sundresses and bobby-pinned hair. It appeared much more wholesome than the military vibe of their previous stop. Yet Zar still couldn't quite shake the sense of something contrived and therefore prone to corruption.

"Era 5.0," said Persia, eying her surroundings. "Looks pretty as a cupcake on the outside, but it's got the same gang law as the other eras, so do me a solid. Stay on the ball. Shame to act the doofus this far in. All this talk of trouble may seem fooey, but, trust me, man, in the Eras it's only ever a shot away."

The skull projection lit the sky above a parking lot.

"Reckon they got us on another race bout or a rest stop?" said Persia.

"This rally, who can tell?" Zar replied, pulling in.

Floodlights loomed overhead like the war machines of invading Martians. A stainless steel railcar occupied the rear of the lot, the name, Sunstrip Diner, scrawled in winking neon across the roof. Out front were fifty or so customised hotrods.

"We've got ourselves a welcoming committee though."

Persia dragged her eyes over. She showed no reaction, just said, "Like I said, do me a solid. Be on the ball."

Inside five minutes, the Road Runner and the rest of the teams' vehicles were parked up in a conspicuous row.

"Ain't this the most!" Leaning out the window of his beaten-up Skyliner, Eight Ball held up his hamburger while chowing down on a mouthful.

Persia kept her gaze on the gang members outside the diner. Zar couldn't help thinking she seemed suspiciously on edge.

"You know those guys?"

"Jived with a few. Woody Carrera, leader of the Snarks." She nodded at a young suit who was resting a loafer on the nerf bar of his Chevy Bel Air. "Rick Slick, wannabe hard guy with the Ninetyniners." The greaser was perched on the hood of a Ford Zephyr convertible, his strawberry blonde hair slicked into a giant quiff. "Susie Q." Persia shifted her attention to a thin girl in a beret and wearing all black. "Heads up the Beat Generation in a ladybug red Jowett Jupiter racing car."

Zar's heart sank. "Are they trouble?"

"What we've got here, sugar, are Snarks, Ninetyniners, and Beat Gen – gangs that cater to the gearhead, which is how I know they ain't here to brawl. They're here to witness a Ramrod first hand. They might act falaupoo when they've got somethin' to prove. Outside that though, they're kids waiting for us to put on a show." Persia crooked a thumb at a waitress on roller skates. Struck blind, the girl kept on skating.

"Something's up with the vibe though," said Persia, nose to the windshield.

On thing Zar was beginning to accept was that life in the eras was always unpredictable and there was no point sitting around waiting for the bad stuff to find you. He cranked his door. "I'm going to the rest room. Want anything from the diner?"

"Glue your hienie to the seat." Persia kept her eyes on the sky. Zar felt a fresh burst of irritation at being told what to do – or, as in the case of the previous trial when Persia had elected Valentine to race, what not to do.

Before he could argue back, he became aware of a low insectile hum. The noise was gradually increasing in volume. Black mist appeared over the surrounding buildings. The air swelled with the roar of jet power.

Zar felt a tight thrill of fear sweep over him. "What's that noise?"

Persia glanced across at Eight Ball, who shook his head, popped the lever on the Skyliner door and stepped out.

The team captain stretched her neck side to side.

"That, honey, is the sound of trouble."

§

The first Rocketeer touched down, filmy gas spurting from the twin exhausts of his jet pack. Two more alighted

253

either side, followed by four to the rear and eight behind as the gang stayed true to their flight formation. The noise off the jetpacks was a flaming roar. The smell was bleach and vinegar.

Over by the diner, the rival gangs were agitated. Lips curled. Shades lowered. Combs were slicked through greased hair. However, it didn't take long for them to realise the swarm was only interested one solitary gang member. A Fly who had left the company of his Ramrod team to stand centre stage.

"Well, ain't you just on cloud nine to see us, Eight Ball?" The first Rocketeer, a guy in his late teens, swaggered forward. His suit was silver grey and slim fitting, his tie a darker shade. A crisply ironed red handkerchief was visible at his breast pocket.

"Vinnie." Eight Ball stared over, matchstick in mouth, thumbs hooked in his belt.

The Rocketeer flashed a smile. "Surprised to see us?"

"Your timing always was crappy." Eight Ball jerked his head at the rest of the Ramrod competitors. "Kinda in the middle of someit right now. But if you swing back around, say same time tomorrow, I'll split a chocolate sundae with ya." Now it was Eight Ball's turn to smile.

"Drop dead twice, Fly. Think you got the jets to outsmart me?" The Rocketeer moved closer. "You've been living on the soft side of Autodrome too long." He cocked a finger at his chest. "Vinnie has ways of keeping track no matter where you hide. And know what I heard recently? Only that you'd gone and signed up to ride the Ramrod in a Skyliner." Vinnie shrugged. "Fancy? So me and the boys figure why chase after you when we can just sit back and wait for you to deliver the stolen goods here?" The Rocketeer stared past Eight Ball. "Although, I gotta say, judging by the state of the bodywork, you've done a lousy job taking care of her."

Eight Ball smirked. "Ain't my fault Rocketeers are sore losers." He removed the match from his mouth and used it to indicate the Skyliner. "'cept for a botched head gasket and a few chunks outta her, she's a helluva chariot."

Vinnie's mouth tightened. "She's peachy king. Which is why I got the pink slips in the first place."

"Pink slips. Funny you got around to them." Eight Ball raised his voice to share the discussion with the gang members and Ramrod competitors watching with interest. "Day I got to grips with that vehicle, I was made in the shade. Know why? Because Vinnie and me, we had ourselves a bet couple of months back. A pink slips race from 49th to Alan Street. So I spider over to the start at Rebel's Hour. But where's Vinnie? Not a peep. Instead,

I gotta take a shot against some kid with the snot still running offa him. Helluva mouth though. Shooting off about how we Flies should be grateful to Rocketeers for showing us how to really fly." Eight Ball shrugged. "What's a fella to do? I creamed that clown."

Flipping back his suit jacket, Vinnie put his hands on his hips. "'Cept my boys told you I couldn't race that night in plenty of time to set a new date. But Flies ain't about code and honour, are they? They're about taking what they can get. So you got the engines sweating with my second." Vinnie held out his hands in appeal. "Word is the rod you were pluggin' had black smoke pouring off its rear. Fancy that, hey? A Fly with a dirty ride."

The crowd stirred. Enough insults. Time to settle it. Eight Ball chewed his matchstick and tucked up his t-shirt sleeves. Vinnie cranked a valve at his jetpack, let out a snort of gas, and hovered just clear of the ground.

Before they could duke it out, the air filled with the hiss of hydraulics and the crackle of gliders. Flies spilled over a nearby building like insects from a disturbed nest. They descended in a half-running motion, driving their suction batons along the vertical wall. Some leapt from the roof, snapping out glider wings after a brief instant of free fall. Each one wore the same uniform: greased hair, black leather, and bovver boots.

Vinnie used the distraction to zip in and drive a Chelsey boot under Eight Ball's chin. Reeling back, the Fly quickly recovered and tucked himself into a hard ball of muscle. His suction batons concertinaed out. He rammed a pole onto the ground and vaulted forward to slam both feet into the Rocketeer's ribs.

Flies tumbled in from one side, Rocketeers from the other. Jetpacks greased the atmosphere. Suction batons cracked off bone. Exhausts burnt flesh. Fists clunked in from unexpected angles.

§

Raina had to admit it. Life in downtown Autodrome could get wild on the tracks but it was positively sheltered next to the free-for-all of the Eras.

"Permission to save my boy from getting his ass whipped out there."

Justice slung the request Persia's way. Something told Raina that, no matter what, a girl like Justice wasn't about to spectate from the sidelines. Persia was still in the process of nodding as Justice light-footed it over to the Flies and Rocketeers battling nearby.

Raina gasped as Justice took out a Fly with a backfist before swerving at the hips to floor a Rocketeer with an uppercut. A large Hispanic Fly powered in; Justice tucked her foot into his ribs with a straight kick. Two more Flies slashed their suction batons millimetres from her face. The poles collided in a high peel as Justice shot to the floor, taking out a Rocketeer to her right with a foot thrust. Blurring into a 360 degree turn, she knocked out the Hispanic Fly with a heel kick.

"She's incredible," Raina whispered. She glanced at Zar and saw the same sense of wonder reflected in his wide eyes. It hurt her that they couldn't stand alongside and share the experience, taking comfort in the fact that the other was also experiencing the eras for the first time. But she was used to standing on her own.

Focusing back on the action, she saw the two Flies come at Justice again. The girl curved a knee strike into the soft flesh above one Fly's hip, swivelled in a semi-circle and struck the second Fly in the chest then head with a double roundhouse kick. Three more Rocketeers flew into the fray.

Raina flinched as a jetpack scorched Justice's shoulder. What exactly was the deal here, she wondered frantically? Was she meant to stand idly by – like Persia, who watched from the sidelines, eyes quick as fireflies as they took in Justice's every jab and dodge. Or Zar, humiliated by Valentine earlier and loathe to risk his neck?

Then again, didn't the rest of the team just see the truth of the situation, namely that Justice was killer out on the field. The heel of the girl's palm connected with an assailant's collar bone; something snapped and the Rocketeer shot skyward in a whoosh of fuel and agony. Inside seconds, there was another Fly on her back, a girl in leather pants and a tight white T, tenderising Justice's kidneys with her fists. Justice had the advantage. She launched her head back to connect it with softer tissue; the girl lost her grip and zigzagged away, cupping her bloody nose.

Justice turned her attention to the Rocketeer recruits either side. She leapt up into box splits and took out the fuel feeds to their backpacks. They fell to earth like fallen angels. And now the field was cleared, she stood and waited, as if deactivated.

With no external distractions, it appeared that Eight Ball and Vinnie were free to settle things with an old fashioned slug out. But as Eight Ball struck his opponent a fresh hook to the jaw, Raina caught a flash of silver at the Rocketeer's palm.

Cheats, swindlers, riflers, they were all parasites on the warm wholesome body of the race circuit as far as Johnny

Law was concerned. One thing Raina had absorbed completely from her father was the belief that any race in life should be fair.

Running hard at the pair, she saw the knife slice in the Fly's shoulder twice in quick succession. The third strike never made it. She gritted her teeth to concentrate her strength and snapped back Vinnie's hand at the wrist. A muscular arm reached past her and wrenched, dislocating Vinnie's shoulder.

"Fighting's one thing. Murder's another, Vinnie. No car's worth that," she heard Justice hiss over her shoulder.

The hard bud of Raina's anger softened very slightly and she stepped aside. Something told her Justice was better qualified to deal with these two guys at each other's throats.

"Ain't about pink slips, bitch," Vinnie choked. "It's about my girl, Rosanne, getting hauled off to St Vincent hospital with a clot on the brain the day I was due to ride. It's about me staying true to the gang code and making sure that lowlife Fly got told I needed to reschedule. It's about my little brother stepping into my shoes in a worn-out Road Runner 'cause he didn't want no Fly saying I'd wimped out."

"What happened to Rosanne?" said Justice darkly. Raina thought the older girl looked like she'd been punched in the heart.

"In Tombtown Cemetery."

A tug to the shoulder made the Rocketeer cry out. The bone was back in its socket. Justice pushed the Rocketeer aside. She turned her attention to Eight Ball.

"You fix the race?" she whispered, voice gone cold.

"I'm bleeding here." The Fly kept his head down.

"Is that why you left Era 5.0? Your fellow Flies take exception to your cheap tactics? Maybe the only thing got them here now was the fun of a Fly and Rocketeer mash up?" Justice was no longer a gentle giant. Now she was bruised and battered, a warrior capable of scalping any who challenged her. "There's only one honourable thing to do here. Return the pink slips."

"That bastard cut me!"

Justice dug a thumb in at Eight Ball's wounded shoulder. Raina winced at the thought of the pain being inflicted.

"You're the one chose to play dirty in the first place."

A new noise faded in, the whir of sirens growing louder by the second. In their pristine blue and white, a squad of Era 5.0 Uniform arrived on the scene. Rocketeers and Flies scattered.

"Raina, you're witness to this," Justice shot sideways. She stared at Eight Ball. "Keys."

Gritting his teeth against the pain where he had been stabbed, Eight Ball rooted around in a jeans' pocket. He slung the keys over to Vinnie.

The Rocketeer caught the key ring on a finger.

"Let me know when you're fixed to race again." Strangely earnest, Vinnie pointed at the Skyliner. "Once we've fixed her up, it'd be hip to see if a Fly can win that baby's pink slips the right way." The Rocketeer rotated his shoulder a couple of times and sashayed off in the direction of his reclaimed rod.

Eight Ball glanced over at Raina, who was utterly bemused by the Rocketeer's changeable behaviour.

"Thanks girl."

Raina nodded slowly. She was beginning to understand that the rules her daddy had laid out needed to be flexible in the eras. Likewise, who were the good guys and who were the bad guys struck her as remarkably interchangeable.

Justice patted Eight Ball's arm, more softly this time.

"Let's get you patched up."

§

# Chapter 23

Zar stepped past a gun-toting life-size plaster cowboy at the top of the steps and entered the diner. The interior of the railcar was compact. Red upholstered booths ran along one side, the chef's grill and food stations along the other. Turquoise and silver barstools underpinned a counter that was littered with flyers, sugar pourers, napkin dispensers, a revolving drinking straw drum and a gumball machine. Tin signs, licence plates, miniature flags, maps and band photos decorated the walls. The air smelt of cotton-candy. Elvis was on the jukebox.

The rest rooms were off to the left, a bolt-on to the main trailer. Zar stepped into the gents and entered one of the two stalls. He mashed a Goo strip, applied it to his watch and manipulated the tiny crank.

Tripster's profile bubbled up.

"Zar, mate. What was with that street brawl? I caught it on terrestrial, well, the shots they got of it from the airship."

"Gang politics." Zar rested his head back against the stall wall. He'd thought about joining in the fray but held back. He'd already been burned in the Eras thanks to his tendency to act first think later. Plus he hadn't the physical skills to win in a fight. Not that that had stopped Raina putting herself in the way of a blade, he mused while burning up on the inside with admiration and self-loathing.

Tripster interrupted his thoughts. "You find another sand brick?"

"Yeah, I..." Zar cut off as he heard the door from the diner swing in. The newcomer opted for the Ladies. He lowered his voice. "I got three now. Just wish I knew what they were for."

"Data-map the pieces you got and I'll have a gander."

"You mean Gooey them?" Zar had heard of the technique but never put it into practice.

"Yeah, just mould it roughly around each piece. The Goo'll find the contours."

Zar squashed the Goo hologram like a fly. Slinging his rucksack off his shoulder, he dug a hand in and laid out the sand bricks on the cistern. Moulding the Goo over the first brick, he watched the constituent drip down, around and into every contour. He undid his watch and pulled on a tiny blip of metal, extending a pair of fine copper feelers which he probed the Goo'ed brick with.

"You got it?"

A pause.

"Got it."

Zar repeated the process with the other bricks then hid them away again. He reapplied the Goo to his watch. Tripster's features appeared in the malleable fluid.

"Three of them, right? I'll open up the models on my VDU Mat and see what's what. Now, about the last bit of the Paranascope route. What's the bubble order?"

"Two blue."

"That it?"

"Yeah, and let's hope I'm right this time."

The door to the gents opened. Footsteps approached the urinals.

Zar didn't want to risk continuing the conversation. "I've gotta go," he whispered.

Back in the diner, he made for the exit. He was distracted by the sight of Vladamir sneering across the length of the room, milkshake in one outsized hand, hotdog in the other. By his side stood Jesse James. The combination made Zar double-take.

"We'll see who's the real gimp on the cold side of the finish line!" Jesse snatched his burger off the plate and stomped up the walkway. "That grunt's got it coming," he shot at Zar before disappearing outside.

Zar secretly prayed both Vladimir and Jesse had it coming. He shrugged off the fact and walked out of the diner, intending to head back to the car park, maybe hunt out Raina before the Ramrod officials got around to kicking things off again. But then he heard his name, spoken in hushed tones to the side of the steps. Zar recognised the voices.

Moving behind the cowboy statue, he pretended to look inside his backpack and glanced over the rail. His suspicions were confirmed – Eight Ball and Justice were talking below and he was the topic of conversation.

"...kinda lightning box," said Eight Ball.

"A Tesla coil?" asked Justice.

"Dunno. I ain't exactly in orbit when it comes to scientific know-how. Point is, before I stuck my hand in to get the sand brick, this recorded voice starts with the crazy talk. 'Pink, green, blue, Xanadu.' On repeat then it cuts off and the coil burns out." Eight Ball moved with a squeak of leather. "You gotta admit, that ain't right."

"I don't know about right. Question is why didn't you tell Zar? If you've got no use for the information, why hold back?"

"I dunno. Guess I never came around to the idea that a guy can appear outta nowhere and get grafted onto a Ramrod team."

"Braxton said to trust Zar. He said to help him."

"Yeah, he did, and Braxton's the Big Daddy. But something don't sit right. What we got on Zar anyway 'cept he's fitting in some kind of mission in-between the Ramrod and we're the goofs playing bodyguard? I wanted to keep something back. In case you and me get in need of currency."

Zar was livid. He'd had a hunch the Fly was holding out on when it came to all that had occurred on top of the Trylon, and after he'd put his faith in him! Blood rushing to his face, he clanked down the metal steps and swung around to the side.

Justice stayed calm at the sight of him. Eight Ball got flinty-eyed and gave the matchstick in his mouth a savage chew.

"Any more secrets you'd like to spill?" It took all of Zar's self-control not to smash a fist into the Fly's face. "I thought you were okay," he spat. "Guess I figured if Justice thought you were decent...But now I'm not sure that's any sort of measure."

The girl's soft brown eyes flickered. Even in the heat of anger, Zar felt regret for his words. Hadn't Justice shown him kindness?

Eight Ball slung a thumb over his shoulder. "Cast an eyeball, Zar. We ain't in school now. We're in the Ramrod. Why'd I waste energy brawling with you?"

"Yeah, why waste energy on that, hey, when you can just get Justice to do your brawling for you?"

The Fly dipped his chin. "What happened earlier was my business. Even Justice pushed it by sticking her oar in. Except, Justice and me, we're tight while you, you're just the new kid."

Zar's rage cranked up a notch.

"At least I'm not a liar who can't kick it with the Pros anymore so plays dirty on the field to steal himself a ride."

Eight Ball had him by the neck of his t-shirt in seconds. Zar scrabbled to get free, but the Fly's hold on him just tightened.

"Don't be a germ," he breathed close to Zar's face.

"Let him go," said Justice sternly in the background.

Eight Ball broke out a grin. "Chill, Justice. I ain't about to shake it down with one of my own team." He released Zar and gave him a tap on one cheek – a display of affection which made Zar want to murder the Fly more than anything that had gone before.

"I'm sorry I kept a piece of the puzzle back, bro. But wrap your head around it from our position. Why should we help you? We've only Braxton's so say you're on the stick."

Justice put a hand on the Fly's forearm. Her gaze flowed to Zar.

"Even before you swept in like a fireball, Zar, I was going to insist that Eight Ball give you the full facts, my argument being you strike me as a fighter – and it takes one to know one." She inclined her head. "I've got a feeling about you, Zar. As I would have told Eight Ball, sometimes you have to go out on a limb for folk and hope they prove you right." Her gaze intensified. "You will prove me right, won't you, Zar?"

Their conversation was interrupted by wolf whistles coming from the parking lot.

Zar swallowed. He rubbed at his throat where the stranglehold had aggravated the skin. But his anger had softened and now there was this new interruption to give them all breathing space.

"Something tells me we're missing out," he muttered.

"This needs eyeballing." Eight Ball strode away from the steps. Justice and Zar followed him into the parking lot where the gang members and Ramrod crew had formed a crowd around a posse of cheerleaders shaking their pom poms and blowing kisses.

The girls stacked themselves into a human pyramid then executed a neat series of tumble downs. They jived, thrust, leapt, and somersaulted while chanting:

"Buckle down, touch down, Get ready to roll,

Who's gonna race, Risk their s-oh-oul,

Do the hula! Do the twirl!

Whether co-cool boy or a ho-hot girl,

Quad, trike or bike, she or he,

In sand, on land, at the place to be,

At X. and A. and N. and A. and D. and U.

At heaven on earth, at Xanadu!"

The cheerleaders dropped into the splits, shaking their pom poms.

Eight Ball took his matchstick out of his mouth.

"Well, ain't that the most."

§

# Chapter 24

Zar settled back into the driver seat, exhilarated by the rush of night air across his face. It was a relief to be away from the diner. His team and Fa's had shown mutual courtesy on exiting the parking lot; the same couldn't be said for Fabrienne's crew who had acted like possessed bumper cars. It was also great to be behind the wheel again. Increasingly he was realising just how impotent he felt in terms of the Ramrod Rally trials. Yes, he might have manoeuvred Persia into letting him drive her car, but she was refusing to single him out otherwise, which made him ask himself why he was even on the team? No reason as far as he could see, except to go on the wild goose chase his father had set up. And of course he'd move heaven and earth to solve the Paranascope trail and catch his father's killer in the process. But that didn't alter the fact that he was a fifteen year old motor sports enthusiast and, instead of taking part in the most exciting race of his life, he was being forced to sit things out on the sidelines!

"There! Xanadu Leisure Park," said Persia.

Zar slung the Roadrunner right and joined his team in turning in where a spot-lit billboard advertised the fact.

"You scooting off for a while?" the bodyguard asked, seemingly nonplussed.

Increasingly frustrated at having to constantly opt out of the rally, Zar dug his heels in. "I'll stick around and get my bearings first. Thanks anyway."

The team captain blew a bubble with her gum. "No sweat. I'm guessing you wanna know what freak show they got lined up next. Not that Justice is gonna to turn fooey on us. She's the bomb when it comes to bike trials."

"Any chance you'd give me a shot instead of Justice?" Zar physically pulled away from her in his seat, already anticipated rejection.

Persia lent over and rubbed his shoulder, setting off all sorts of fireworks inside Zar despite his anger.

"I've got to pick the right racer for each event. Eight Ball's cut so that's him out. The cheerleaders called quads, trikes and bikes for this gig and Justice is the bomb on her Tomahawk."

"Plus picking her is one way to get on her good side again," Zar snapped.

He immediately felt bad. He was so busy trying to live this new independent life of his that he was in danger of distancing anyone who tried to get close. Persia, Raina...

Glancing across at the bodyguard, he couldn't help feeling the couple of years age difference between them made all the difference. Persia was jaded if self-assured. In comparison, he was just a bag of broken pieces.

"Ignore me. I've stuff on my mind and this..." He gestured to the yellow brick road stretching out in front and flanked by more tripedial floodlighting. Signposts pointed off to Dixies Drive-in, Sugar Bowl Ice Cream Parlour, All Stars Bowling Alley and Hula Beach. "Its like the whole world's gone crazy."

Persia nodded. "What's real crazy is Justice thinking I hooked up with Ruby. I catch the stink of hate coming offa her. You dig?"

"And you didn't?" Zar tried to be adult about the idea. Persia snapped her taloned fingers an inch from his face. She gave his head a scrub, which didn't do much to teach him a lesson.

"Look honey, Justice ain't never gonna trip on our friendship. Far as she's concerned, I was bad news from the get go. But I know she'll be copasetic out on the track all the same."

They pulled in behind Valentine and Eight Ball, the Fly now riding shotgun in the Cadillac. The idling Road Runner purred.

Zar kept his eyes on the apple pie landscape. "You're wrong, you know. The real problem is you not checking in on her after Ruby's death." He felt obliged in his defence

273

of Justice. But the idea of trying to fix a squabble between girls did not sit well.

Persia stared over. "You two been jiving about me?"

"You're always going to provoke conversation, Persia."

The team captain sighed. She smiled weakly. "I'd have made a good cop, Zar. You wanna know the worse thing about looking like I do? I ain't a girl to lie back and be idolised. I've known there were jerks in this world who'd hurt or steal or whip up hate from the get go, and I've always wanted to be the one to take them down. Know who I idolised as a little girl growing up in Era 7.0? Not Barbie. That kinda sugar and spice and all things nice? No way. I wanted to hang with Wonder Woman, rustle me a villain or several with that freaky gold lasso of hers. A few more years on me and I just knew I had to find a way to play the super hero in real life. I hadda become a cop." She pursed her luscious lips. "When the cadet academy threw me out, I lost myself. Guess I didn't stop to think how others lost themselves too around that time."

"The Uniform threw you out?" Zar gasped.

"Yeah, but don't worry, honey. Its old news. You don't need to jive with me on that score."

Feeling scratchy inside his own skin, Zar didn't pursue the fact. Persia stared out the windshield at Justice on her Tomahawk then switched to the rear view where Valentine shouldered his way out of the Cadillac, a hand to his trilby.

"Funny how you neglect the ones who matter and waste heartbeats on those who don't." She popped the handle and slipped out before Zar could think of an answer.

He was distracted by a buzz at his wrist. Ripping off the spooling ticker tape, he scanned Tripster's latest message.

'Music note icon and an empty bubble tube. Location – Xanadu Leisure Park.'

Zar rubbed the heel of a palm into one eye. "That doesn't narrow it down much."

§

# Chapter 25

"To your marks!" called the head cheerleader, shaking her pom poms like a maniacal squirrel. She flick-flacked backwards, performing a triple somersault to land alongside the Start flag, which she pulled out the sand and twirled like a baton.

Justice finished letting air out of her tyres to aid grip. On the outside, she was all about staying calm. Inside though, her heartbeat had altered into quick bursts of energy. She'd forgotten how good it felt, this sense of tight-wound anticipation before the start of a race.

Starting the engine, she trickled the Tomahawk forward, its silver guts on fire under the floodlights. She heard generators adding their throaty rub to the lap of water at the shore. Hula Beach was a manmade creation. She felt like an astronaut stepping out onto a fabricated moon.

The beach was littered with scrap. Justice squinted at the metal bridge swaying between oil drums, a minefield of whirligigs, a craning mechanism, a section of track at the shoreline, and a giant sand hill. She and the two riders from the opposing teams faced an assault course. With the added complication of live cargo.

"Ladies and gentlemen. The Xanadu Tigers cheerleading squad are waving from their marks around the field," announced the head cheerleader. "Competitors, you must navigate the course and save the cheerleaders." She indicated a star-shaped platform in the centre of the field. "Deliver the squad to the Star of Safety where I'll award a red, purple or yellow ribbon. Time's up when the last girl is on the star. Victory belongs to whoever rescues the most cheerleaders."

"Damsels in distress?" Justice glanced at the junior hog trials' champ astride his Harley V-rod and the teen engineer on the Kettenkrad bike tank. They acknowledged her dry tone with a nod.

Uniform kept the crowd to the sidelines. The head cheerleader held up the Start flag.

"Ready, set...Go! Go! Go!" she shrieked, swiping the flag to and fro.

The V-rod banked right with a meaty rumble. It was a more measured departure for the Kettenkrad which sledged off in the direction of the metal bridge, caterpillar tracks whirring.

Justice knew that traversing the assault course on a Dodge Tomahawk was like riding a torpedo through grease. One wrong move and a rider was on the fast slide to suicide. But she wasn't just any rider, she told herself, working to calm the thud-thud of her heart up underneath her ribs. There was much for her to prove as a racer, and no time like the present to embark on with the task.

She put her heels to the thunderous ribcage, braced against the air pressure and punched the throttle.

On the far side of the star stage and about a quarter of a kilometre down the beach, four concentric discs branched off a giant iron trunk. Up top was a high kicking cheerleader.

Circling the iron trunk, Justice upped the revs and powered at the stalk of the thing. There was a tense vertical climb, in which she felt like a kid again leaning backwards on a swing before she flipped the bike forty-five degrees. The front wheels gripped and she powered up onto the first disc, which immediately started to rotate.

Her breath caught as she saw the danger in an instant; the first disc was heading around to pass below a second, smaller disc no more than a metre higher up the trunk. Both discs were saw-tooted around the perimeter, both revolving.

The only option was to trust her instincts; no different to when she judged the right moment to duck or level an opponent with a well-placed hook in the boxing ring.

Slipping a leg over, Justice tipped the bike onto its side and tucked on top of it just as the second disc passed overhead. She was in shadow momentarily, a great crunch of gears beating at her ears. Then the light shone in and she was back astride the revving monster and eying a kick-step attached to the trunk. Twisting up the gas, she drove at the trunk, hoisted the bike up under her, caught the front on the kick-step and soared to the second level.

"Yay!" The cheerleader shook her pom-poms at Justice, who threw the Tomahawk to the floor as the third, smaller disc sliced an arm's length above her. She tried to right the bike but the disc flew swiftly back around and, drawing a sharp breath, she was forced to flatten down again. On the third attempt, she made it up, juiced the bike and struck another kick-plate on the iron trunk.

Clawing up and out onto the third disc, she skidded to a halt, eyes bright with adrenaline. The final, smallest platform rotated like a fight star half a metre in.

"I'm going to need you to climb on behind," she hollered.

For an instant, she was afraid the cheerleader would wimp out. But then the girl launched head over heels and slammed down onto the back of the Tomahawk saddle.

Justice felt the girl's arms wrap around her waist, an alien sensation since Ruby's death. It charged her like a set of ignition leads.

"Hold on," she shot over a shoulder. "We're heading down."

She mashed the throttle and drove into space. The bike sliced through the air and seemed to fly for a few seconds. Gravity kicked in and they crashed down to earth in an explosion of sand. They sped back to the Star of Safety. Justice swept the bike around and in to the edge of the stage.

"This is where you get off," she said, feeling a rush of cold as the cheerleader released her waist and slid away.

Justice scouted out her opponents. The v-rod was heading back to the stage, a skinny redhead sat in the rider's lap. The hog champion was clearly enjoying the girl's attention and weaving a punch-drunk route. Meanwhile, the motorbike tank was manoeuvring between another set of obstacles. Whirling iron arms acted as scythes; every few seconds, one would slice the Kettenkrad's bodywork. Lucky for the driver, his vehicle was perfect to take on that minefield.

But what were the chances of her slipping past to bag more cheerleader cargo? Justice drove up to the whirligig minefield. At the far end was the cheerleader, a gold skinned dancer who pirouetted on a dais.

"Come and get me, boys!" teased the girl.

Justice didn't take offence. She'd been called worse. In front, the Kettenkrad took out four scythe mechanisms which attempted a strike. It would take a mighty blade to dent that military titanium body, Justice reasoned, enthralled by the toy-like design of the miniature tank with a driver's seat sunk into its front third. The slick motion of its caterpillar tracks ensured the vehicle looked indigenous to the beach, a serious opponent.

Justice threaded the Tomahawk between the upended drums of the first four whirligigs. The Kettenkrad maintained the lead, and it was then that Justice spotted the driver's error. The first few whirligigs had been hip level so that the lethal arms had struck the reinforced sides of the motorbike tank. But a few more metres in, the mechanisms started to rise on pneumatic stilts then rapidly descend in thin wisps of steam.

A lesser competitor might have called out to the Kettenkrad's rider in warning. To Justice's mind, an opponent would never thank her for the humiliation of having saved them. Instead, she trusted the engineer to notice the rise of the machines, even to have factored it into his game plan. Meanwhile, she acted on her own.

Blistering forward, she slid sideways and drove one side of the bike into the sand. The whooshing wheels kept her in motion; the bike slipped beneath the first whirligig, the scythe skimming millimetres from her face. Riding the bike like a surfboard, Justice banked in and out the variegated whirligigs.

"Watch out!" cried the cheerleader at the exact moment that Justice realised she was heading for a pair of rotating scythes aligned on popping pneumatics. One second, the scythes were near the ground, the next they were a couple of metres up, the change so rapid it was impossible to pre-calculate.

Leaping back into the saddle, Justice yanked up the Tomahawk to perform a wheelie and headed dead centre. Bike and rider slid between the slightest gap as the scythes drew apart. Electrified by the riskiness of the manoeuvre, she brought the Tomahawk's front wheels back down in a tremendous ricochet of suspension.

"Get on!" she told the cheerleader, who was staring over the edge of the dais.

"I'll wait for that one. It looks more stable." The cheerleader pointed back at the Kettenkrad, ploughing on through the series of pneumatic risers and seemingly without a driver. The soldier had a suspended bucket seat, a feature which allowed him to crane back inside the hold.

"Jump on. I'll look after you!"

"No thank..."

Justice hadn't time or inclination to stand there and argue. She grabbed the girl's ankle and yanked. "I said I'll look after you," she cried, raking up a tidal wave of sand as she circled on the spot to stop her passenger jumping ship.

She braked and saw the Kettenkrad hammer towards the last two whirligigs. It slowed suddenly, as if its rider realised it made sense to wait, just in case Justice failed to make it through but her cargo remained intact.

Justice squinted past the blur of arms between the two whirligigs. Could she time the return right given the additional load of the cheerleader? She hauled on the gas, kept with the momentum and tipped forward, lifting the bike's backend into a stoppie. The girl screamed but clung on, nails digging in at Justice's neck. They flew between the rotating drums, the blurring scythes giving off a high whistle.

The Tomahawk touched down. Justice powered past the bike tank, in and out the decapitated whirligigs and bombed it back to the stage.

"You can get off now," she shouted, bringing the bike to a halt. The cheerleader struggled onto the stage before rushing to the edge to throw up.

"Deliver the squad to the Star of Safety," Justice repeated to herself. The rules said nothing about what state the girls had to be in when they got there.

§

# Chapter 26

The miniature steam train pulled in at the station. Raina inclined her head. "Shall we?"

Zar shot her a look that said he would rather suck razorblades. But he got inside an empty carriage and sat on one of two benches facing each other.

Raina clambered in. She opted for the opposite bench.

With a blast of a whistle, the train pulled away.

Zar gripped the frames of the open windows either side. "You didn't need to come. What if Justice needs a second? Who's going to fill in? Jesse?"

"Jesse can handle most things." Raina had an inkling Zar saw Jesse as a threat both professionally and personally. The idea amused as much as it irritated. "Anyway, why shouldn't I take a break? You slink away any time you fancy."

"And treated like a sub as a result," Zar shot back. "The rest of you get a role in this thing but I've got to opt out at my dad's say so. Must be nice to know you can take time out to join me and still feel part of the Ramrod."

Raina went hot in the cheeks. She was angry at herself for tagging along. If Zar had wanted her help, he would have asked. But instead she had taken it on herself to want to help. Watching Zar glower as he stared out of the open carriage, she hadn't the first idea why.

"How'd you get off this thing?" she said quietly.

Zar nodded at a swag of velvet rope above the open doorway. He frowned.

"Leaving already?"

"Much as I'd love to offer my services as a punch bag for the evening, I think I'll keep my pride and split." Raina reached for the rope. Zar leant out of his seat and closed his hand around hers.

"Don't go." He sunk back down into his seat, still holding onto her hand.

Feeling a rush of blood to her face again, Raina pulled her hand away. But she regretted acting so coldly as Zar crushed a thumb and finger into his eyelids, rubbing them. He seemed immensely tired all of a sudden. And she kind of knew how he was feeling. Yes, she'd been young when her father died, and he had succumbed to illness – a quieter type of violence than murder. But she knew how it felt to be prematurely alone in the world.

The words wouldn't come though and she just stared out at the weird leisure park. To their right was the stretch of Hula Beach not set aside for the Ramrod trial, silvered sands patched with gangs of kids and bonfires. To their left was a large car park and the sprawling white igloo of an ice cream parlour. Buddy Holly's 'That'll Be The Day' blasted from inside. Hot rods roamed out front like Komodo Dragons.

Her gaze slid back to Zar. What kind of pressure must he been under, trying to solve some weird series of tasks set by his father while simultaneously taking part in the Ramrod Rally. It wasn't like they were back at school, racing bangers on the test tracks. The Ramrod was the real deal and Zar wasn't getting a moment to savour the experience.

"All this must be exhausting," she said.

"You mean the Ramrod?" Zar dropped his hand from his face.

"I mean this task you've got on top of everything else you're going through. I guess adrenaline's getting you through."

Zar curled up one side of his upper lip. In that environment, he'd the look of a young Elvis.

"A friend said I should accept help. Another went so far as to suggest my dad might've set me challenges that required it. So I'm glad to have you along, Raina." He stared over at her until she wanted to look away but refused to let herself, and he sighed. "I've not been very nice, have I?"

"We haven't been very nice to each other," she replied, not wanting to let him off the hook while unsure why she cared about his opinion. It wasn't like she'd ever sat home thinking about Zar Punkstar. Then there was the air he gave off that every girl was just dying to lock lips with him if he only cared to invite them to. But she couldn't help thinking the ego was all an act. He also had a way of looking at her, like he was now, eyes hooded, head at a tilt.

"Who'd've thought we'd spend an evening together the same week I swiped victory from under your nose?" he laughed, and aggravated her anew.

"It was a fluke you won."

He smiled. "I'll admit there was luck involved. But you're the one who tagged me Lucky 13."

Raina shook her head. "Don't you ever get tired of the bravado?" She looked at him questioningly. "Don't you ever want to let up?"

"You're right." He slid onto one knee and took her hand again. "Help me, Raina Jubilique. You're my only hope."

Suppressing a smile, she put a foot to his shoulder and pushed him over. "You're an idiot, Punkstar."

He eased back onto his seat, acquiring that young Elvis look to him again that made her want to punch and kiss him all in one. Rubbing a hand about the back of his neck, he looked serious suddenly.

"I need to solve a riddle that leads to a physical clue. It's to do with my dad's murder and it's somewhere in the Xanadu Leisure Park. 'Pink, green, blue, Xanadu.' That's another clue. And there's a music note icon. The icons are key to the location."

"Well, we're in the right era to be thinking in terms of music. The 1950s gave us rock 'n' roll and, with it, teenagers," she supplied.

Zar stared past her into the next carriage, occupied by Jocks in sweats and high tailed girls. "Sounds like you envy these wannabes."

"Are they?" She wondered how long it would be before Zar valued escapism. Perhaps he hadn't grieved for long enough yet to occasionally want to sink down into a land of 'lets pretend.' For her, there were times when she missed her father so much she would jump at the chance. And really, where did reality start and pretend end? In Era 5.0, all was sugar coated in nostalgia, and, yes, she guessed it was possible to get sick on the taste, but how much simpler life seemed, how much more colourful. Like a drug, it helped her forget.

She offered Zar a sad smile.

"We all need a little fantasy in our life, Zar."

The train ack-acked over the tracks. Voices rose and faded. Music bled in and out. Zar drew near. Raina tried to process the jumble of hurt, hate and liking, tried to smooth it all out before his lips met hers.

A flash of movement caught her eye. *Pink, green, blue...Pink, green, blue.*

"That's it!" She pointed out of the open window. They were passing a range of fountains lit with colourful gels and spilling either side of giant letters that spelt out 'Dixie Drive-In.'

"Now we need the music connection," she muttered awkwardly, unsure what, if anything, had been about to occur.

Zar switched his gaze to the fountains.

He sat back on the bench opposite.

"Fancy a date at the drive-in?"

§

The v-rod arrived at Justice's shoulder. Apparently the hog champ was bombing his way to the same craning apparatus she was aiming for. Justice tucked in her chin and punched the gas, powering away. She hit wet sand at the shoreline and eased in the break.

Large iron girders stuck up from the water like the foundations of a jetty. A length of track ran out from the sand and corkscrewed up and around the girders. Ten metres or so out into the water, the last upright was capped with a large metal bucket. Justice guessed that the hint of blonde hair poking out from inside was a giveaway as to the cheerleader's whereabouts.

Hitting the track, she kept steady on the gas and concentrated on the climb. Turning into the first bend, she felt the Tomahawk's wheels pass over a ridge in the track. Seconds later, she was startled by a jolt and a sense of peddling backwards. The track moved under her, a travelator in permanent descent. As she entered the second bend of the corkscrew, she glimpsed the v-rod at the start of the track.

Justice weighed her options. The v-rod would be handicapped by the same shunting motion. It wouldn't pay her to increase acceleration on that narrow track when one wrong twist of the handlebars could land her in Lady Luck Lough and out of the game. But she could opt for middle ground.

Teasing the revs, she settled into a confident pace for the next two bends. *Calmly does it*, she told herself. One loop behind, the v-rod had the advantage of a hefty wheel base. The Tomahawk was nimbler though.

Just as she got into a rhythm, the rules changed. With a pneumatic wheeze, the travelator slowed considerably. Justice felt the Tomahawk's conjoined back wheels revolve loosely, giving off the stench of burnout. The bike got its grip again in time for the track to dramatically speed up.

*Dirty tricksters*, thought Justice as she shot dangerously close to the edge, angling back in just as the travelator slowed again. A clatter from the geared mechanism below and the track was actually vibrating at the same time that its motion switched back and forth. Justice tucked into the supporting upright and circled around to face an s-bend of track that took her further out across the water.

Her nerve failed momentarily. Justice pictured Ruby, preserved in her mind as that young beautiful girl who dared to love her back. It was enough to steady her as she negotiated the s-bend to arrive at the last giant girder.

The v-rod started out on the s-bend in her wake. Justice seesawed between gas and brake as she climbed the spiralling track that ran around the girder. As she came around to face the beach a third time, she heard a great whir of free-spinning wheels as the v-rod mistimed its approach to the narrow, weaving track. It careered off the s-bend and plunged into the shallow waters below.

Justice wasn't one to gloat. She hooked around onto a plinth at the top of the girder and brought the Tomahawk to a sideways skid. The vehicle idled under her like a purring tyrannosaurus. One side of the huge iron bucket was lowered to form a ramp. Trickling the bike inside, she found the cheerleader inspecting her nails.

"Ooh, you're a girl!" The cheerleader looked terrified.

Justice saw a bike block at the far end of the bucket. She dismounted and steered her ride in, triggering an automatic clamp that adjusted to the size of the Tomahawk's wheels.

"Got something to hold onto?" she asked.

"These bands?" The cheerleader pointed to two pairs of leather hand grips hanging off the walls.

"Then I'd suggest you hang on," Justice called, securing her hands in the nearest set of grips as the ramp started to rise. Seconds later, the bucket lurched sideways, clamped down onto the narrow track and started a teeth-shattering descent.

§

They made their way in and out the lines of cars. Zar did his best not to look in any vehicles. He'd seen enough movies to guess at what went on behind those steamy windows.

In the distance, a huge screen showed intermission adverts. *Hot popcorn, so gold and good and fresh out of the popper...Sizzling hotdogs just bursting with juicy goodness...*Zar tuned out for the most until he became aware of a familiar voice.

"Braxton Earl here to tell you about the swell offer on reconditioned Cadillacs over at our showroom on Johnson Street. We're knocking 15% off advertised prices. We got boilers, smoke stacks, glass hose, hybrid engines and every kind of luxury import from Berlin, Sydney, Birmingham and Tokyo. So get yourselves down to Braxton MotorCity Dealership and say Braxton sent you. We're here to do a deal."

Zar stared across the lot at Braxton's tanned face and shark smile.

"Weird, isn't it?" said Raina, by his side.

"What's that?" He kept on walking.

"Braxton. The man gets everywhere. Its like he's always watching."

"Creeps me out." Zar dug his hands into his pockets, hooked up his shoulders and tried not to think about how close he had come to locking lips with Raina.

"He's okay. Got an empire in the Eras. Plus he seems to have your back."

"So far." Zar let the subject drop. Era 5.0 was full of visual candy. He needed to stay alert.

Soon they were below the giant screen and looking over a fence at a floodlit kids' playground.

"What's with a playground at a drive-in?"

"Drive-ins were meant to family friendly." Raina climbed up, hooked a leg over and sat on the top rung of the fence. "Explains why there's also a crazy golf course."

Zar stepped up onto the lowest rung and saw a second fenced area beyond the playground.

Suddenly her whole face lit up. He couldn't help thinking that she was extraordinary looking, eyes so very energetic and rimmed with long black lashes.

"You seen the sign?" she gasped excitedly.

He wanted to stay looking at her, but forced his gaze to the lettered arch over the gateway.

"'Beep Bop A Lula Crazy Golf?'" He glanced at her and grinned. "The last symbol was a music note and that name sounds like a song title. Raina Jubilique. You're not just a pretty face." Hopping over the fence, he held out a hand to Raina, who considered him a second before accepting the offer and jumping down. She pulled away though and started to stride across the playground. Zar shook his head, secretly impressed by her, and followed.

Just short of the golf course, Zar became aware of a familiar sense of being followed. He believed in instinct, had had his proven right many times out on the track. What were his instincts telling him now? He glanced back out the corner of his eye. Was that a figure at the far side of the playground? He whipped around. The playground was empty.

"You okay?" Raina shaded her eyes against the blaze of a floodlight overhead.

Zar concentrated on the sign at the entrance to the golf course. "Yeah. Let's take a look around."

They passed through a spring-hinged wooden gate. An elderly couple sat on a nearby bench. Two boys and a man, presumably their father, were engaged in a noisy bout of competitiveness at a helter skelter obstacle. Otherwise the area was deserted.

"Give me your hand," whispered Raina.

"Already did. You're the one who pulled away," Zar shot back churlishly.

"Shut up." Raina put her hand in his. "Look like we've a reason for being here." She nodded at the elderly couple and laid her head onto Zar's shoulder as they walked by.

The man and woman smiled.

As they moved away, Raina lifted her head and said quietly, "So what're we looking for?"

"Mechanical device triggered by a key – a beak off a Pro Leaguer Trophy."

"Which you just happened to bring with you?"

Zar retrieved the beak pendant from under his t-shirt then slid it back in.

Raina shook her head. "Didn't I say you were one Lucky 13?"

Zar liked the words from her lips. He hooked up his mouth in an awkward smile and shrugged. "Let's hope my luck holds out. Starting with deciding which apparatus would have appealed to my dad. Something mechanical and I guess music related given the clue." Forcing his mind begrudgingly off his companion, he scanned the golf course's weird architecture. In amongst the more traditional helter skelter, buckboard, wagon wheel and windmill was an outsized piano keyboard, a giant treble clef, a miniaturised dance hall, and a life-size Wurlitzer.

Raina stopped walking. "Gotta be the Wurlitzer."

Zar nodded. "Gotta be the Wurlitzer."

They approached the obstacle to find the dad and sons moving off from it and around the corner. No doubt its insides had been gutted to make way for the pipework for the golf balls, but it was a real Wurlitzer nonetheless. The cabinet featured two glass bubblers curving in around the main display glass and a stylised chrome grill and fittings.

Zar went around the back, where Elvis Presley's *Heartbreak Hotel* was being piped from a set of speakers.

"My dad was more of a *Jailhouse Rock* kind of a guy," he murmured.

"So why not try playing that instead?"

"Because this baby doesn't play selections anymore." He banged a fist on top of the jukebox. "It's just the carcass. A crazy golf obstacle."

"But the song tags are still in place, as are the number buttons. We could see if *Jailhouse Rock* is on there, dial it in, see what happens?"

Zar stared down at the ground and smiled. He couldn't fault Raina's logic.

Moving to the front of the Wurlitzer, he leant his hands on the glass and scanned the rows of song titles, scanned them again, and felt a sinking sensation.

With a sigh, he glanced sideways. "*Jailhouse Rock* isn't there."

Raina frowned. "Let's think about this. We know we're in the right general area thanks to whatever map you're following. We picked this spot because of the music note symbol. There were the fountains to indicate the way. Pink, green, blue, Xanadu."

Her eyes widened.

Zar stared at her quizzically. "What?"

The girl held up a finger to shush him. Zar caught his breath an instant as she moved in close by his shoulder. She peered in through the glass for a few moments, then shook back her shoulders and smiled quite brilliantly.

"New suggestion. Let's go with songs with those colours in the title. Look – you were along the right lines with Elvis. He's the only artist on this jukebox, and, luckily for you, he recorded tracks featuring all three colours. Start off, *Pink Cadillac*. 078. Punch it in."

Zar listened intently, welling up with fascination for this beautiful, intoxicating girl, and the hope she might be right. He leant in and pressed the 0, 7 and the 8. A stiff sound, like revolving metal, originated from inside the jukebox.

"Next?"

"Green..." Raina ran a fingertip down the glass. "*Green Green Grass Of Home*. 122."

Zar's hand trembled as he entered the new combination. This time the crackling from within sounded like piano wire.

"Last. Blue?"

Raina pressed her hand flat to the glass and scowled. "Looks like Elvis had a thing for blue. *Blue River, Blue Christmas, Blueberry Hill, Blue Suede Shoes...*"

An image flashed into Zar's mind: his father perched on a stool at one of the workshop benches, a greasemonkey in every aspect of his appearance bar those eclectic, colourful shoes of his. That was it, of course!

"What's the number code for *Blue Suede Shoes*?"

"164. Why?"

Zar couldn't stop grinning. "My dad always did have lousy taste in footwear."

He thumbed the 1, 6 and 4. There was a new grinding noise from inside the jukebox.

Raina pulled him aside as the chrome grid at the front of the Wurlitzer began to lower. Inside was a large rainbow coloured disc, the centre of which was hollow.

"I'm guessing that's got to be a keyhole." Zar stared back over either shoulder.

"I'll keep an eye out," said Raina.

Zar retrieved the beak pendant from around his neck. He fitted the base of the beak to the hollow inside the coloured disk and turned. Listening out for a release click, he kept on turning the beak round and round inside the lock. The two glass bubblers either side of the grid started to rise. He kept turning. Each bubbler tube moved up to reveal a small compartment.

Kneeling down, Zar retrieved the sand brick from the left hand compartment and a small brass heart from the right. He deposited the treasure in his rucksack along with the rest of his haul.

Slinging the bag up onto his shoulders, he pursed his lips and exhaled. He had all the pieces now and in spite of his sensing that someone had been following him the whole time. Yet he was also suspicious that he had been meant to do precisely that all along. Whoever this tail was, they had been on him since the start of the race, always a few calculated steps behind.

"What now?" Raina's voice came to him as from a distance.

Zar shook off his paranoia and refocused. "We find the team and pray Justice secured those much needed points. Then we get the hell out of the Eras and back home."

§

The Tomahawk flew out of the bucket like a shooting star. Ahead, the Kettenkrad was dropping off another cheerleader at the stage. Pulling in to the opposite side, Justice called up to a couple of girls to assist.

"Don't get your knickers in a twist. Your friend's just fainted." She nodded at the makeshift rollercoaster of the travelator and the giant bucket. "I take it she drew the short straw."

A quick headcount revealed the three girls she had rescued with their red tags, three more with the Kettenkrad's yellow, and two with the v-rod's purple. With no sign of the Harley on shore, it was a two horse race between her and the Kettenkrad – already on its way to the final hurdle.

Justice didn't hurry. She knew it paid to take the time to see a situation every which way. The Tomahawk was the faster vehicle. But the Kettenkrad had weight distribution and bulk on its side, things that would aid it considerably on the final obstacle, a huge sand bank with a cheerleader up top.

The bike tank started its assent. Justice blocked out the jeers from the crowd. *Look at every angle.* Her eyes absorbed the vista – the rippled beach, the apparatus making up the assault course, the gradient of the sand bank, the bucket she'd just exited...

She opened the Tomahawk up. The sound of the engine was a metalmorphised scream. Dual wheels bounced under her on deeply cushioned suspension. She might have been riding the waves in a speed boat.

Ten metres before she hit the bank, Justice carved right and headed back to the giant bucket. She struck the ramp at speed, ripped the bike sideways and up the inner wall, and rode around the inside of the bucket, the momentum carrying her past the open side and back around. Nine, ten, eleven times, she circled the enclosure before steering hard at the upper rim.

The Tomahawk cleared the top and flew through the air as a projectile. It struck the sand bank three quarters up, the momentum propelling Justice past the roaring Kettenkrad on a steeply rising diagonal. Just as she sensed the laws of physics stretched to the max, the Tomahawk crested the top of the sand bank and crashed down onto the plateau at the summit.

Justice sheared the bike around and to a halt, one foot on the floor.

"Get on!" she commanded between breaths. She could hear the rumble of the bike tank. They had four, five seconds at most before the platform got crowded.

The cheerleader stared uncertainly at the Tomahawk. Justice didn't give her the chance to argue her preference. With a roar of black noise, she charged forward and scooped the girl onto the bike. As the Kettenkrad grumbled up onto the platform, she dove over the drop-off, the cheerleader using the full force of her lungs to express her discontent.

Their descent was a rush of churning organs and wide-pinned eyes. Justice chose a zigzagging route in an effort to fight the gravitational force and stay upright. She guessed the Kettenkrad would opt for a more direct route down, presumably with the idea of cutting her off at the base.

"Hang tight," she shouted, and, hooking out from the cliff, re-entered air space. Below, the bike tank chugged down off the sand bank and onto the straight. The Tomahawk came back down to earth a few metres ahead, ricocheting off deep fairings before it sliced in alongside the stage. Justice's passenger staggered onto the platform, collapsed and took the red ribbon she was offered.

The head cheerleader performed a star jump while blowing hard on her whistle. "Victory to the reds! Victory to the reds!" she shrieked.

Justice glanced back at the Kettenkrad, idling back up the beach. The young Pro Leaguer rider batted a hand off his forehead in salute. Further away, she saw the hog rider drag his drenched v-rod in from the shore.

Hoisting her Tomahawk onto its stand, she dismounted and, accompanied by the cheers of the crowd, took to the star-shaped stage. The head cheerleader hung a garland around Justice's neck and held up her arm for her in a victory salute.

Justice stared at the crowd, searching for one face. She found it. Eight Ball put his fingers between his lips and whistled. He grinned at her, his expression softening into something more intuitive.

Eyes lifting to the night sky, she brought the garland to her lips and kissed it.

"For you, Ruby," she whispered.

§

# Chapter 27

A kilometre into the Sabkha, the light pollution off the Eras gave way to a darkness that was almost palpable while the humidity had drivers roll down windows and shift uncomfortably in their seats. Giant iron tongues, ramps, slider tubes and chain bridges wormed up from the shadows as if the belly of the Sabkha had been sliced and its guts spilt. Wisps of fog flew into the headlights. Low in the driver seat, Zar imagined he saw the glow of lightspeed Bi-Oculars in the middle-distance.

"Did you know they'd stagger the teams on the return?" he asked by way of conversation. The weird atmosphere unsettled him.

"Riflers are more active under cover of night. By staggering us, Riflers get a nudge that says, 'Give it a shot, man. You're only up against one team.' Its bogue to set us up like that, but ain't that the way of the Ramrod."

"You think we'll get attacked?" Zar remembered the Rifler punks he'd encountered at the Grand Dame Casino. It didn't pay to underestimate them.

"Freaky if they don't lay a hit on us," said Persia evenly. She inclined her head onto one shoulder then the other, easing out the knots.

Zar listened past their convoy's engines. The dark was a still, swollen heart. Anytime it could start beating.

"I'm guessing your side project in the Eras' turned out copacetic."

"Huh?"

"Forgot you speak Stupid," Persia teased, referring back to when they'd first met at the Death Pit. "Copacetic. Means all right. Safe," she appended.

Zar's cheeks coloured. He was glad of the dimmed illumination in the car. "I got what I came for. Now I've just got to put the pieces together." In the case of the sand bricks, quite literally he thought but kept the knowledge to himself. The sooner they were back abroad the ferry and he could slip off and contact Tripster for feedback, the better.

"Far out, dude." Persia glanced over. "There'll be other races, Zar," she added, as if easing her own guilt at excluding Zar from the trials as much as reassuring him.

As the team captain's gaze returned to the Cadillac in front, it occurred to Zar that she had been right to exclude him from the trials. With all the pieces of the puzzle in his possession, he had a fighting chance of unlocking the truth about Sol's murder – and that meant more than taking part in any race.

He cleared his throat. "Folk off this team have helped me a great deal. More than I'd ever have guessed they could."

Persia nodded. "I reckon we're all part of it, whatever you've got going on. This" – she gestured to the ghost world beyond the windscreen. "This is just fun and games. But your daddy's quest? I've a hunch it's gonna affect every freakin' last one of us. So we got your back, Zar."

She winked at him and Zar felt a surge of liking as well as sympathy for the team captain. It wasn't his style to play agony aunt, even less not match maker, but he owed Persia. She'd taken him under her wing, and despite having her own issues to shoulder.

He glanced over at her. "Persia. Can I ask you something?"

"Shoot." She flipped the glove compartment and retrieved a pack of gum. Slipping the cover off a strip, she folded it up into her mouth.

"I know two of your team mates died in the last Ramrod. I know Justice lost her girlfriend, Ruby, and Frank Oz lost his eldest son. I also know you were betrayed by the team mechanic who sabotaged your vehicles – it was reported everywhere. What I don't know is where Valentine comes in to the picture, as in why you talk and act like you despise him when anyone can see you're out to protect yourself."

The team captain blew a bubble with her gum. It popped. She kept on chewing and Zar stared out at the roiling dark. Had Persia taken offence?

"Eighteen months ago, I was a cadet with Era 7.0's Racer Riot division," she said suddenly, and with a sigh in her voice. "A good part of the training was about acing it in the classroom, but we also had to prove we could cut it for real. I loved being in the thick of the desert races and the Ramrods, the smell of cooked up tyres and engine rind. Really loved it, you dig?" She swallowed audibly, and then shook her head as if dispelling the reminder. "Anyhow, one night there's a throw down at the border between 3.0 and 7.0. Apple-pie stiffs living alongside mellow cats? Always a funky brew. This time it was a drug run gone sour. Mixed up in the middle was Valentine."

Zar's gaze flicked between the road and Persia. Her face twitched in an effort to keep her emotions masked.

"Fox that one, able to jive his way outta anything. Sold me a line about he'd got involved with a bad scene, how he'd tried to cut loose that night and how his ex-pals turned jive turkey before I moseyed onto the scene. I musta been tripping 'cause I bought his story and let him peel out that night with my phone number." Persia let slip a sad smile. "I thought Valentine was the bomb, especially when he asked me to come on board a team in the Ramrod. You don't need me to sell that trip to you. The Ramrod, man! Day of the race, we're jamming it. Set to win no sweat when bam!" She slapped a hand on the dash. "Two of our team get fire-balled in their vehicles. Uniform peel out the woodwork and whaddaya know, the team mechanic's gone and sabotaged us. At whose bribe? That remains the stickler. Meantime, I'm stitched up."

"They thought you'd sided with the mechanic?"

Persia cleared her throat and nodded slowly. "Uniform cranked the trunk of the VH Charger I drove and whadda they find but a bogue stash of Razzledazzle. Enough pills to set up my own drug store. Gotta hand it to Valentine. No better cover than a Ramrod if you wanna transport hot merchandise across the borders without the fuzz on your tail."

She took in a deep lungful and let the air seep out. "To lay it on you simple, they arrested Valentine and had me down as a suspect, which was enough to make my superiors jumpy. Didn't take long for them to break foul and keep me on pen pusher duties. While forensics failed to pinpoint Valentine, it was the end of the line for me. Too many sneers from my fellow cadets, too many trying it on 'cause they thought I'd make a bent cop."

Zar heard the team leader's voice crack. He glanced sideways, but Persia had already brought her emotions back under control. Her face was marble.

"You know what the real bummer was? Not Valentine lying or using me or getting off. Nah, the killer was he never came to look for me. So, tell me this much, Zar. If Valentine wasn't an operator, why'd he kick me to the curb?"

"I don't know, Persia." Zar shook his head. Valentine dealing drugs? It didn't sit right. "I've met enough punk dealers to know the type and Valentine isn't it. Plus, my mum has this saying. We hurt the ones we love the most." He stared over at her. "I've seen how Valentine looks at you."

Persia rolled her eyes. "Honey, I ain't saying I'm a stone fox or nothing, but I've had enough dudes give me the eye before."

"Not like Valentine. He looks at you like he's thinking about something more than most guys."

"Well, sugar, ain't you the love doctor!"

"Not really." Again, Zar was grateful for the shade inside the car.

Apparently Persia had had enough with the heart-to-heart for one evening. She backed off. "Yeah, well, it's gonna take more than a look for me to forgive Valentine

Heart. In the meantime, wanna offer an opinion as to why we're off-roading?"

§

Tripster leant back in his tank chair and scratched his head. He blew a raspberry. A sand brick hologram projected in midair over the VDU Mat. Parts of the thing appeared worn...no, deliberately hacked away. He sat forward and waved his fingers inward. The model rotated on a 45 degree axis. He flicked a sensor streak embedded in the VDU Mat. The brick reduced in size as two more appeared alongside.

"Gooey..." Tripster flowed his hands between the bricks and set them spinning. "Fooey..." He swiped both hands down. All three bricks froze mid-motion. "...Ooey."

There was a dark patch, tucked into a tiny crag in one brick. Tripster rubbed his nostrils. He pushed the other two bricks to the back, reducing them in size. A light tap to the sensor streak and the first brick swelled to the size of a football.

Perching on the edge of the sofa, he poked at the dark patch. A magnification grid appeared over the spot like a mesh bandage. Using tiny motions of a finger, he enlarged the anomaly. He let out a soft whistle. It was a barcode. Beneath it were the numbers 2, 3 and 1, the same sequence of bubbles in the first tube.

Pushing the brick away, he dragged in one of the others. It had its own dark patch – another barcode. 7, 3 and 1. The sequence related to the second sand brick.

He zoomed in on the third sand brick and its barcode of 0, 2 and 0. The number string corresponded to the two blue eyes of the brass skull trinket, Zar's third find. Which left one sand brick outstanding.

Tripster dragged a hand through his hair. He hoped all this effort was worth it. Sure, he and Zar had had a strained relationship ever since the accident. Once the sorries and tears over spilt milk were out of the way, there had never seemed much more to say on the matter. But he did genuinely want to help his friend. Alongside taking part in the Ramrod, the pressure of Zar solving clues for a dad whose respect he'd craved had to be immense.

But if anyone could come up smelling of roses, it was Zar, Tripster mused with a mix of pride and sourness. In the meantime, he was assigned the role of brain as per usual, his latest task being to step into Sol Punkstar's shoes and unlock the heart of the conundrum. Because that was what he guessed he was looking at here, a series of puzzle pieces to be slotted together...

*Slotted together*. Tripster rubbed his nostrils again. Reducing the third sand brick in size, he brought the other two into play, aligning each so their barcodes faced inwards. He inched the bricks in. They slotted together to form a sphere with a missing quarter.

Tripster pulled back his lips. "Freakin' A."

A rap to the door made him scoop out his arms over the VDU Mat. The brick holograms dissolved.

He dragged a cushion onto his knee and tried to decide what to do for the best. He was in Mindy Punkstar's apartment pod. Was he going to have to deal with Sol's grieving relatives? What if Mindy hadn't paid her dealer and heavies were ready to weigh in? Either way, there was a half tonne of steel between him and whoever stood outside.

Manipulating his fingers over the sensor pad, he advanced the tank chair to the front door and warily brought his eye to spy plate.

"Well, will you look at that?" Yanking out the copper funnel on its drag hose, he put his lips to the mouthpiece. "What can I do for you, Mister Earl?"

"You can let me in for starters," came the reply.

Tripster slid the spy plate shut. What now? Was he meant to welcome in this Braxton character simply because he'd put together a Ramrod team that included Zar and excluded him?

"I can guess what you're thinking, kid. Why should I let in the guy who stitched me up? And I gotta see your logic. Thing is, I was only trying to protect Zar."

Tripster revolved the brass wheel in the centre of the oval door. Steam flooded out as the titanium rods shot in. Taking a deep breath, he hit the gel pad in the middle of the wheel to activate the pneumatic door release. With his tank chair blocking the way in, Tripster stared hard at the visitor.

"Protect Zar from what?"

"Your run in with Uniform last year is exactly the kind of fuel a journalist needs to power a headline. Think about it. Does Zar need any added attention right now? Plus, he said you were the brain who could best interpret the Paranascope scroll and all accounts verify the fact. 3.9 grade point average, first kid in your year to win a scholarship for the Automotive Science and Engineering Academy."

"Yeah, yeah, I'm a bona fide Einstein."

"Nah, you're not just a science boffin. You're a hacker poster boy! When you wanted race stats, you just nipped inside that city's mainframe matrix thingamajig..."

Braxton shook his hands with the razzmatazz of a jazz

singer. "...and got them. Only thing to trip you up? Failure to grasp it was illegal and cover your tracks." He winked.

"So you've got me all figured out?" Tripster went to punch the gel pad and shut the man out. The last thing he needed right then was some fool come to rub salt into a far too recent wound.

But the promoter disarmed him. "I know why you and Zar have a complicated friendship. The two of you were ten when the accident happened. I know you were the smart kid, always goofing off to impress your friend, and I know Zar was the wise mouth street punk. I know you and he climbed the Ziplines one night when the track was closed. I know you tried to pull Zar up when he slipped and you both fell in the process. I know the Scooper only caught Zar." Braxton gestured to the tank chair and grimaced. "I know its gotta kill you to be stuck in that contraption while Zar's gallivanting off in the Ramrod."

"You know zip about Zar and me!" Tripster's hand made a fist above the gel pad. "Yeah, we've got a few glitches to iron out, but he's my best friend and I'm not about to let you or any other idiot stir things up between us."

"Glad to hear it because Zar's about to hit a whole load of bother and I'm gonna need you to help me work him free of it," cut in the promoter.

Tripster felt his insides squeeze. Zar was in trouble?

He'd two choices. Keep the man out in the cold and risk Zar's life, or let him in and risk Zar's anger?

He reversed begrudgingly.

Stepping over the threshold, the promoter showed his practised smile. It wavered.

"You're a whizz kid. You gotta help me warn him."

"About?" Tripster punched the gel pad. The front door sealed. He led the way back into the living room, chair treads whirring like a gutter bot.

Braxton waited until they were settled, Tripster in front of the bay window that gave out onto the colourless, industrial view while he paced back and forth.

"Okay, just like you and Zar have history, well, I guess I have my own. With Nikolay Obshina."

"Obshina!" Tripster's eyes shone. "The Super Leaguer?" He couldn't help but be impressed.

"Yeah, among other things." Braxton thrust his hands into his pants' pockets and kept on pacing. "Four years ago, I asked Nikolay to consider a merger between Braxton Motor Dealerships and Obshina Enterprises. Fool that I was, I'd got the thirst to keep on climbing

317

that corporate ladder and squeezing Frank out with a monopoly seemed a logical step. Only..." Braxton played with his tie. "Nikolay made it clear that a merger between our two businesses would be, well, to use his phrase *laughable*. And yeah, I see your face, kid. I ain't proud of our little tête à tête back then. I ain't proud of a few things."

The promoter looked older to Tripster. Life's heaviness hung about him.

"I'm a wheeler dealer, kid. Era folk don't embrace just any old hoodlum. No surrie. They buy from me because I'm the wiseguy salesman. And I've been trying to use those same tactics on Nikolay to protect Zar. I offered Nikolay a 50/50 stake in Sol's invention if he'd let Zar be for the duration of the race. Promised to deliver anything Zar discovered on a plate to Nikolay. It was my attempt to reel my old Super Leaguer friend in, you know. Except, Nikolay's got tired of waiting."

"So you're saying that Nikolay Obshina, as in the Super Leaguer, Nikolay Obshina, is going to put Zar in danger?" Tripster had a hysterical urge to laugh the promoter out the room.

Braxton pulled back his jacket sleeve to reveal a fancy Data Streamer watch. The face was covered in a layer of dried Goo.

"I guessed you'd make this hard, and, trust me kid, if I could've got the clear evidence against Nikolay before now, you think I'd come to talk to a juvenile felon? Fact of it is trying to record inside Obshina Enterprises is harder than a Tin Lizzie's sit-up-and-beg bench. But if you ain't gonna accept the story on my say so – and no reason why you should – then I gotta rely on you being the brain Zar said you were. I coated this thing in Goo and aimed it as close to Nikolay's direction as I dare. Now I know these new models don't use Goo and I'd no way to dial a number up to try it anyway in case the sticky stuff puffed up and Nikolay caught a glimpse, but you reckon there's anyway you can pull something offa it. I know Goo magnifies its own bulk to coat objects. Clever stuff. But d'you reckon it can remember what it's seen?"

"A kind of memofoam?" Tripster's chest got tight. His hacker methods were shared by a select few. He so didn't want to share them with the promoter with the shark's smile and twinkling eyes.

"Look, I'm gonna make this easy on you." Braxton took off his watch and handed it over. "I'm disappearing out into the corridor for a stretch. When you're done here, you can call me back in. Or leave me hanging. Up to you."

He strode over to the door, punched the gel pad and stepped out into the hallway. The door revolved back in.

Inside the minute Tripster had Braxton's watch hooked up to his VDU Mat. A half-moon of ornate platinum slid out from beneath the watch face – the keyboard. Tripster tapped codes into the device, manipulated the tiny crank at the edge and conjured a seemingly telepathic wormhole between the watch face and the Goo. A figure bubbled up. The image was poor quality and kept cutting out, presumably as Braxton's sleeve had rubbed back and forth over his wrist.

"Thanks for joining me this evening," said the figure.

Tripster recognised Nikolay Obshina's chocolate monotone, but it could just as easily been a passable impression of the very famous Super Leaguer. But while the recording was too shadowy to stand up in court, the way the figure moved with a distinctive grace struck Tripster as authentic.

"Vodka." The figure pushed a glass across the desk.

A hand stretched in and took the shot. An instant later, the emptied glass was returned to the table.

Nikolay went to offer a refill.

Braxton spoke. "We ain't exactly drinking buddies yet." His hand stretched over the glass. "First off we gotta get our hands on the blueprint. The Ramrod's still in progress, which means there's nothing to do except wait until Zar's done solving his dad's puzzle and crosses the finish line."

"Except, it seems a waste of time and opportunity to leave the puzzle pieces in the boy's possession."

"Well, ain't nothing we can do about that. We don't know how Sol Punkstar worked his puzzle, even if the kid's solved it yet. All we can do is wait for Zar to finish the Ramrod then your old buddy here'll acquire the blueprint."

"Except I don't feel inclined to do that. This whole arrangement? You, Braxton, would appear to have the upper hand."

"I'm just protecting my interests and ensuring folk don't get hurt."

"Indeed. You have a key, you say, which will unlock Sol's puzzle and that is the carrot dangled before me, the donkey." Nikolay's R'asian accent thickened. "Because you do think me a donkey, Braxton."

"Quite the reverse. I think you're a great judge of the right way and the wrong way to swing a business deal. In this case, you know I'm not about to hand over the key until I know that Zar is home safe and sound."

"That's the deal? The boy finishes in one piece?"

"One *alive* piece," Tripster heard Braxton clarify.

"Naturally." The figure of Nikolay poured a shot of liquor, drank it down and stared over. "Then I should tell you the boy will encounter a welcoming committee when his team cross the salt plains tonight. The Riflers will not harm him. Their job is to retrieve the puzzle pieces."

"Sheesh! Whaddaya wanna go and rock the boat for?" exclaimed Braxton, clearly exasperated. "We don't even know if the kid's found anything."

"I know that the boy has successfully located several puzzle pieces already. It has been in my interests to have him tailed."

"But if Zar's got the pieces, why not let him expend the energy bringing them back and working out what they trigger? It's not like I'm about to hand over the key if you're gonna play dirty with me."

Nikolay leant forward suddenly. "I hate it when bugs try to crawl up your coat tails. You understand what I am saying, Braxton? If I am the donkey then you are..."

"The bug."

There the replay fractured and cut out.

"No way!" Tripster knitted his fingers and slung his hands behind his head. It took him a moment to absorb the shock of Nikolay's threat. But then he remembered why Braxton had come to him in the first place.

The front door peeled open to reveal Braxton stood immediately behind it.

"Well?" asked the promoter. "Whaddya you think?"

Tripster backed up. "I think we'd better get word to Zar."

§

# Chapter 28

The ride got rockier as they headed into a graveyard of rusted obstacles left over from the desert races.

"Think your girlfriend's lost her bearings?" said Persia.

"Raina's not my girlfriend," Zar shot aside.

"She should be."

Before Zar could respond, Valentine's Cadillac screamed hard left, revealing a giant cactus of iron in the road ahead. On it too soon, Zar pumped the brake, shot the stick into second and clawed the Road Runner aside last second. They rattled over the cancered concrete of a side road. The fog was thick as mud.

He eased off the gas. "That's whack! What the hell's going on?"

"Shhh." Persia rested a finger against her lips and Zar listened. Engine noise came to him in waves. It was impossible to pinpoint from where.

"Now what?" He shivered in spite of the heat. The ever-remoulding atmosphere unsettled him.

Persia's eyes shone. "Now we hope there ain't too many of them."

"Riflers?" Zar glanced every which way. There was a glow of headlights to his right. "Hell," he whispered.

The burning amber bulbs belonged to one mammoth machine.

"If things turn sticky, reverse into the fog at speed and pray we don't rear-end on any steel remains."

"Hold on." Red paintwork, froths of steam escaping the tremendous fly wheel, corrugated hose draped like juicy entrails…"It's the fire truck!" Zar exclaimed.

"Dynamite!" Persia chewed her gum enthusiastically. "You gotta hand it to Jesse. He can navigate, for sure."

Couldn't he? Alongside elation at seeing the fire truck power through the fog, Zar got a sense of foreboding. He cut the gas and retrieved the rucksack from the backseat. He and Persia stepped out into the steaming dark.

As they approached the idling fire truck, thoughts tumbled through Zar's mind. How'd Jesse know where to look for them? Plus, the fire truck was meant to be heading up the convoy. So why couldn't they hear the rest of their team's engines?

"We should get Raina and floor it," Zar muttered.

"Whaddaya mean, honey?"

"How'd Jesse find us, Persia? Out here. In all this. Said yourself he knew these routes like he'd driven them before."

"You sure are suspicious of that dude, Zar. Is it 'cause Raina's riding shotgun with him?"

Zar nodded at the fire truck cab. "She isn't anymore. Where's Raina, Persia? Where the hell is Raina?"

"Let's ask," said Persia, stomping ahead.

"How's it hanging?" she called as the mechanic swung down from the cab. "Gimme some skin, man." She held out her hand to Jesse as Zar caught up. The mechanic gave a stiff smile and slipped his hand into the team captain's.

"Where's Raina at?" said Persia innocently. Zar noticed she didn't loosen her grip on Jesse's hand.

"Taking a nap, sweet lips." Jesse narrowed his eyes. "Guess our action across the wastelands musta tired her out." He winked at Zar, who wanted to break the mechanic's freckled face.

"Why'd we leave the main road?" Zar demanded. He struggled to keep his voice even. "On the way here, you seemed to have the best route sussed, or was that just a fluke?"

"You'll have to ask the team scout. Raina might be easy on the eye but she's a retard when it comes to reading maps." The twitch of Jesse's upper lip dared Zar into starting something – until he apparently remembered Persia's grip on him. "Wanna let go of my hand, sweet lips?"

Persia eyed the mechanic intently. "You ratted us out, Jesse?" She glanced over at Zar, her beauty hardened. "Check the cab. See if you can lay your hands on our scout?"

Fear washed over Zar, sickly, oscillating between heat and ice, and pinpricking his skin. Nothing felt right. He hurried across the peeling plates of the Sabkha, aware of green eyes in the darkness. Stepping up onto the truck's tread plate, he peered in at the open window and saw Raina lying across the bench seat in the cab, blanket hauled over her face, asleep to all intents and purposes. Except, what he had learnt about Raina over the week was enough to convince him she was a gearhead who'd sooner cut off her own hand than miss one second of that race. More than that, he knew she'd do her damndest to steer their team home. Sleeping on the job wasn't her style.

He cranked the door and levered it wide.

"Raina?"

"You got her?" called Persia.

"Yeah, she's just..." Zar grabbed hold of the blanket and pulled it down. The girl stared back at him with frightened eyes, hands bound, mouth gagged.

"Tied up back here!" He leapt into the cabin and tugged the knots loose at Raina's wrists, vaguely aware of Persia and Jesse struggling outside.

Hands freed, Raina reached up behind her head and tore off the gag. She spoke in rattling sobs. "The bastard knocked me out. My head!" She pressed a hand to the bruise at her temple. Glancing out the windscreen, her eyes grew wide with panic.

"They got Persia, Zar."

"They?" Zar forced himself to look out the front windscreen. He saw Jesse dabbing at his bloody mouth and Persia with her arms pinned by a couple of street punks. Five more circled the perimeter of light cast by the fire truck's headlights and the Road Runner's roof-mounted spots.

"Riflers," he breathed, hatred bubbling up inside of him like acid.

"Come out, come out, Mister Rat!" taunted a voice he'd heard before.

Zar's first instinct was to get him and Raina the hell away from there. He went to slam the door and shut them in. Raina who laid a hand on his arm.

"We've got to help Persia."

Zar wanted to cry out, 'No, we don't! We need to get shot of these punks before they destroy everything.' But he also knew he wasn't the sort to leave a team mate in the gutter.

He inhaled deeply and slung the door back open. Jumping from the cab, he held out a hand to Raina, which she took for once without argument. She stepped down and he tucked her in to his waist. She could object all she wanted later, but right then he needed to feel her near, both from a desire to protect her as well as take comfort from her.

"It's a surprise to see you so far from your nest, Lothaniel, but its quite the night for surprises," he muttered, rubbing Raina's side to reassure them both.

"Boys! You remember Mister Rat whom we flushed from our quarters recently." The gang leader hooked up his lip. "A sentimentalist, as I recall."

"So, is it happy coincidence us bumping into each other or would I be right in suspecting you're employed by the same scum who employed Jesse to stitch us up?"

Lothaniel looked pleased. "We had an arrangement with your Mister Snitch here via a mutual colleague."

"Vladimir." Jesse spat a mouthful of blood onto the ground. "Had his eye on you the whole race, Punkstar."

It was Raina who reacted. "So that's the way of things, huh, Jesse? You honourless skank!" She tried to prise herself out of Zar's grip, a lit firecracker.

Zar maintained his hold while equally incensed. He'd interrupted Jesse and Vlad talking earlier that evening at the diner. What he had allowed to pass as banter between rival teams mates now turned out to be the discussion of this very set up.

"There's too many of them," he told the girl in his arms. "Whatever they want isn't worth getting hurt over."

He couldn't tell himself the same. Knowing he had been tailed by Vlad throughout the race put a different spin on the situation, and he saw suddenly that this was no ordinary Riflers' heist. He had sidestepped his father's body only to lead their foe straight to whatever it was Sol had died to protect.

"Since your boss isn't here, can I ask what you want?" he glowered.

"Me, I'm all about the money, Zar," said Jesse matter-of-factly. He saluted Persia. "Quite the slug you gave me there, sugar lips."

The team captain bit her thumb at him. Jesse smiled.

"I made sure no harm was gonna come to you. Better than the last mechanic to rat on you, hey, Persia? But I got a life to build, not to mention a fiancé with expensive tastes. You've met my beau, haven't you, Zar? Isha Earl, daughter of Braxton Earl. Yeah, I see that look and I'll give it to ya. She's stiff at first. But warm her up and she's a goer!"

The Riflers joined in the mechanic's dirty laughter.

"And you, Lothaniel?" Zar glared at the chief pirate. "What's your loot?"

Lothaniel sauntered over, swinging a silver pocket watch by its chain. He leant in to Zar's ear. "The flesh from your bones," he whispered. He cocked his head over a shoulder. "Alley up, gentlemen. Alley up!"

The eyes in the dark materialised into silhouetted figures who cracked and wielded glow sticks.

"Road Runner here's a vision, but for me and my boys, it's all about the parts. The sticky green." Lothaniel rubbed a thumb off a forefinger.

Riflers descended on the muscle car in a swarm. Mirrors were torn free like limbs from sockets, nuts were driven anti-clockwise, wheels jacked and wrangled off, window trim peeled back, glass loosened and lifted. Zar was reminded of a wildlife documentary where the film accelerates and carrion is decimated by insects in seconds. His stomach turned and he looked at Persia, expecting to see a look of anguish for the destruction of her vehicle, not to mention a second betrayal by a Ramrod mechanic. But her face had a marble-like stillness.

Zar couldn't understand why their bodyguard was remaining peaceable at the sidelines. Sure, she'd a couple of punk kids on her, the mohawk and the club kid he recalled from the casino. But a fighter like Persia could crack their skulls in seconds...unless she wanted the Riflers fixed on the vehicles and not the passengers. Or the contents of his rucksack.

He felt fresh awe for Persia, alongside hurt to see the Road Runner stripped to its steel skeleton.

"Nothing left to pilfer, gents?" Lothaniel enquired of his crew. "Torch it, Jack 'en Dore," he instructed with a limp wave.

The teen vamp and the ponytailed warrior, both of whom Zar recognised from the casino, strode over to the car's remains. While the warrior tossed a lit Zippo onto the torn seat of the muscle car, the vamp helped the fire on its way with spurts of lighter fuel from a can.

"Keep the fire truck intact. Nice little operation, that one." Lothaniel rested his hands on his skinny hips and grinned at Zar. "I'll take your watch too. Pretty antique like that'll fetch a dime or two."

Zar's face warped with hatred. The watch was his link to Tripster. His rage quadrupled when Lothaniel added, "And the rucksack if you please, Mister Rat."

"You can go to Hell."

A flash of silver and Zar felt a blade at his throat. Out the corner of an eye, he saw Persia tear into her captors. Both were laid out cold in seconds. Her rescue attempt was cut short when Lothaniel spun Zar around to show the placement of the blade.

Unfastening the watch strap, Zar handed it over his shoulder. The Rifler was a flick of spit at his ear. "Now the rucksack, if you please Mister Rat. Therein lies the true gold."

"Still think no one'll get hurt because of you, Jesse?" Zar heard Persia aim at the mechanic.

"They want a rucksack, I say give it to him." There was alarm in Jesse's voice. "I ain't interested in any rucksack. I just know I was told where to bring you tonight and guaranteed safe passage with these boys."

Lothaniel let out a belly laugh.

"Oh lordy. Mister Snitch thinks he's bagging free board and lodgings aboard one of our perambulators!"

The gang offered up their nasty laughter again, except this time it was aimed at the mechanic.

"Hang on, you ghoul!" spat Jesse.

"That's Mister Ghoul to you," said Lothaniel coldly. "And here's the heads up on something' else." He lent in to Zar's ear. "After you exited our lair, the gent called Vladimir entered and in not so many words but with plenty of cash flashing, strikes a deal – one which sees Mister Snitch here played like a deck of cards. Now, Maw, avail me of your right hook and lay Mister Snitch out cold."

Jesse spun around only to aid the delivery of the club kid's fist to his jaw. He hit the ground and didn't get up.

Lothaniel dragged the rucksack straps off Zar's shoulders one handed so as not to relinquish the pressure of the blade and stepped away suddenly. He slung the bag over to the club kid who opened it and pulled out one of the sand bricks.

"Swap." Lothaniel tossed the blade to the club kid at the same time the brick was slung his way. The kid caught the blade by the handle. Lothaniel snatched the brick out of the air and held it up to the artificial light. Apparently he didn't care for what he saw. He propelled the brick back over to the club kid, who tucked it back inside the rucksack.

"Not to my taste, but ain't it folks' quirks which make the world go round? One pretty I do care for is that slung about Mister Rat's neck." Lothaniel snatched his blade from the air when it was tossed back and, in a swift flow of motion, pointed it at Raina's stomach.

"The Albatross beak!" he spat.

Zar dragged the leather thong from around his neck and handed it over. His whole body shook with rage.

Lothaniel eyed the beak pendant, pocketed it and tipped an imaginary hat. "Pleasure doin' business."

"I'll gut you with your own blade before you get one kilometre from here," growled Zar, unable to contain himself.

Walking away, the Rifler leader threw up his hands in mock alarm. Haloed by flames off the husk of the Road Runner, he turned and gestured about him. "You and whose army, Mister Rat?"

"Don't know about an army, but I'm one hell of a freedom fighter." Silhouetted on the far side of the burning iron carcass, her long limbs stretched either side the revving Tomahawk, Justice looked like a ghost rider.

"Waiting for me?" she shot at Persia, who ran forward and swung an elbow into Lothaniel's chest, following through to connect the flat of a hand with his windpipe.

The Rifler nest erupted. Justice powered into the thick of it, driving her iron fists into soft guts. She moulded down with the flow of her machine, flying at the Rifler braves with their skinny tattooed bodies, bone necklaces and painted faces. Persia, meanwhile, was a coast and rip of motion. A Rifler ducked; she got him tight under the chin. Another tore in with a barrage of hooks she blocked with a forearm.

Lothaniel brandished an air horn. A blast sent the Riflers skittering across the salt flats, abandoning glow sticks as they ran. The air filled with the roar of sand buggies receding into the dark.

"Start up the fire truck. We're going after them!" Zar shouted to Raina, who nodded and charged over to Jesse. She frisked the mechanic for the keys as he started to come around.

"Freakin' A, my head! Raina, babe, give me a hand up."

"Rot in your own juices, Jesse." Raina turned heel. She slung open the door of the fire truck. Moments later, the engine started up and settled into a coagulated pulse.

"Let's get after them. Persia, ride with us! Justice, you want to take the lead?" Zar called over a shoulder, jogging over to the passenger door. Glancing back, he realised neither women were moving. Instead, Persia had her hand on Justice's shoulder. The pair seemed deep in discussion.

He tightened his fists, digging the nails into his palms to channel the enormity of his frustration. Time was ticking. The desert felt empty.

Dashing back over, he caught the trail end of their conversation.

"...sisters don't slack on one another and I'm truly done in over it, honey."

"I guess we're both pig headed, Persia. But we're reconciled. I think Ruby's spirit will rest easier for the fact."

"Look, I know you got stuff to discuss, but the Riflers, they're getting away with the sand bricks, the beak I won...they're getting away with everything!" exclaimed Zar, tearing at the chains at his belt.

Persia released Justice's shoulder. She lent in and lightly kissed Zar on the cheek. "Hush, honey."

He stepped back abruptly. "What do you mean *hush*?"

"The Riflers are long gone to ground," said Justice quietly.

Zar glared at the Africonian. Her soft knowing eyes drained all the fight and energy and hate from him. Only hurt remained.

"I've lost it all," he said. His legs buckled and he crouched down, head tucked under his arms. His mind whirled with the agony of shame and heartbreak. This boss Lothaniel had talked about had stolen so much from him – a father and, consequently, a mother. Now, in taking the sand bricks, the leech had cut him free of all purpose. Zar couldn't imagine despising someone more. He breathed sporadically.

"Time to go, honey." Draping an arm around his shoulder, Persia encouraged him to stand. Zar scrubbed his fists into his eyes, keen to scuff away reality. His hands fell to his sides. When he blinked, he saw only fragments of light.

"The race isn't over yet, Zar." Justice's gaze stripped his emotions bare. At the same time, her assertiveness woke a semblance of hope in him. Then Jesse hacked and spat into the dark.

"Dirty stinking cockroaches." Jesse staggered to his feet. "Riflers stitched me up!" Sweeping out his arms, he grinned maniacally. "Guess you're gonna leave me to the ghosts too? Let me be picked apart by whatever scavengers find me first."

"Zar, keep Raina company in the fire truck," said Justice. She flexed her knuckles. "Persia and I have a little business with Jesse here."

"No you don't!" Jesse stumbled back a couple of steps and was forced to cradle his forehead in a palm. "My head's already on fire. Tell them, Zar. I told Vlad I wasn't into violence. See, I'm not the same as the mechanic who hurt your friends on the last Ramrod Run. I've got a conscience!"

"You were the one who backhanded Raina." Justice put her hands on her hips. "Betray your own and don't be surprised if they make you bleed. Persia and I, we've got to make you bleed, you see that, don't you?"

"Gonna act like the last gearhead to betray us on this circuit then think you can stay cool. That's fooey." Persia connected the toe of her boot with the mechanic's kneecap. He let out a squeal like a piglet, turned heel and tried to run for it. Justice was by his side in easy strides, scooping him back into the glow off the fire truck's headlights. Persia took out the mechanic's feet with a low roundhouse kick. Justice's right hook caught him on the way down.

"Wait! Wait! What if I've information to offer in exchange for letting a guy keep his looks?" Jesse blathered, hands raised against more blows.

"Not interested." Justice grasped Jesse's hair and yanked back his head, her fist readied.

"Stop!" cried Zar. He'd witnessed his fair share of vigilante justice at the Death Pit and long lost any sense of squeamishness. But right that instant, with the Riflers fled, the trail was cold. He needed names.

"Jesse, if I get these two to go gentle on you, you've got to tell me who you've been working for."

"I don't do gentle," said Persia.

Zar stared at her with pleading eyes. "Jesse didn't kill anyone. He's a douchebag, sure. But he's a douchebag with information I need."

His gaze flicked between the two girls. They gave each other a nod and stepped back.

The mechanic glared at Justice. "I think you cracked a rib, bitch." He honked in his throat and spat aside a mouthful of blood. "Give you this much. Ever think you know a guy only to find that underneath the suit, the suntan, the freakin' sunbeam of a smile, he's out to fleece you?"

"Braxton Earl," said Zar softly, recognising the description.

"Don't bad mouth Braxton while I'm in earshot," muttered Justice.

"You think Braxton won't look to darker methods to keep his empire ticking over?" sneered Jesse. "No one gets set up in Autodrome like Braxton without conducting a few dirty deals. Take you and Ruby."

Zar saw Justice physically stiffen.

"Isha told me how Braxton had lipstick marks planted on Ruby so you two would get juiced for the Ramrod. Said tension made a team more aggressive and want to win more. Only, how was he to know Ruby'd get killed while the two of you weren't speaking? Ever wonder why he played nursemaid so often after?"

Justice fell silent. She twisted a silver band on an index finger.

Jesse scrubbed at his hair, aggravating the red spikes. "I'll give you the low down on Braxton in return for a ride back home."

"What do you know?" said Zar tightly.

The mechanic flipped a thumb off a nostril as if confiding against listening ears. "Braxton got me a spot on this team so I could keep tabs on you. Said I wasn't to interfere, just watch and let him know if anything, if anybody, got in your way. Helped that I'd worked these salt flats as a kid. My dad was Shane Riot."

"Shane Riot?" Persia let out a low whistle. "Helluva desert rider. Yeah, I see it now. You got the same bug eyes. Your daddy know you're trading in folks' lives now?"

"Wasn't meant to be like that," sulked Jesse. "I got sold a line. This Vlad dude called me over at the diner. Said Braxton wanted me to arrange for Zar's vehicle to be separated off from the rest of the team in the wastelands. No problem, I said. Extra thousand in my pocket for my trouble, said Vlad. Definitely no problem, I said. Only, as soon as those Riflers turned up, things take a nasty turn and I'm duped."

"Braxton asked you to keep tabs on me but wasn't actually connected with what happened out here tonight?"

"Guess so."

"So we've got nothing on Braxton other than that he asked you to watch out for me?"

"Braxton's a sly old dog, but he ain't the type to sell out his own team," said Persia, mangling a stick of gum between her lips. "And Jesse's a duffus, sure, but he can't help his brains being stitched into his pants. As for his backhanding Raina, I think we've struck even on that score." She hauled Jesse up, who managed to get to his feet before concussion took effect and his legs collapsed under him.

Justice hoisted the mechanic across the back of her shoulders like a hunting prize. "I'll stick him on the Tomahawk. Persia, how's abouts you and Zar haul up in the fire truck with Raina?"

Justice slid Jesse onto the front of the Tomahawk's saddle, settled in behind and started up the engine. Zar squinted at Persia.

"Reckon Eight Ball and Valentine will have reached the ferry port by now. Shall we catch them up."

"Sure thing, honey," Persia answered as if dazed. Zar followed her gaze to the remains of the Road Runner, flaming in the night like a funeral pyre.

"Sorry about your ride, Persia."

"No drama. It was just a hunk of metal."

He placed his own chaste kiss on her cheek. "There's no such thing in Autodrome."

§

Tripster still didn't trust the promoter entirely even as he keyed the number into the first in a rig of antique Goo watches he had hooked up to the VDU Mat. He'd always trusted too easily, a shortcoming which had seen him used on more than one occasion. His social awkwardness made him too enthusiastic in public, too eager to please no matter the cost. As the ring tone ticked out, he remembered his pathetic attempt to glean race log information for Zar – the burn of the Uniforms' questioning, and the cold steel of the cell as he'd awaited sentence. Ironically, if the Uniform had looked hard enough they would have discovered a network of underground surveillance built around the legacy technology of Goo and rooting to the DVU Mat belonging to a certain Tripster Devon King. But they didn't look.

The line connected with a faint click. A gaunt face bubbled up from the centre of the VDU Mat. Tripster instinctually leant away.

"Good evening, gentlemen. Lothaniel Bartleby at your service." Playful eyes fastened on Tripster then Braxton.

Tripster rubbed at his nostrils. "I must've dialled wrong."

"The gent who handed over this timepiece would've loved to answer you good folk personally, except he's a little lost out in the Sabkha right now."

"A stinking Rifler!" Braxton lunged forward and splattered the leering hologram. The trace of nasty laughter hung in the air.

Tripster grabbed at his cropped dreads. "They got to him first."

"Okay, okay." Braxton started to pace, rubbing his chin as if to remould it. "You don't get into the promotions racket like me without the self-belief it'll all come right in the end. I came to you, whizz kid, because we gotta find a way to stitch up a guy as popular as Nikolay Obshina and so he can't squirm outta it." The promoter jabbed a finger at the extravagant watch around his wrist. "You gotta help me find a way to get the donkey to bray. You with me?"

Tripster cocked his head. "Not in the slightest."

"Ain't no way a guy like Nikolay Obshina is gonna act up for the cameras. But if he doesn't know they are there..."

"You're talking about using Goo."

"Exactly. No one sees Goo as a viable form of communication because it was only ever marketed as a gimmick. But you and your band of kid hackers worked out a new use for the stuff."

Tripster dragged a hand down over his face. He sighed. "I've got to be honest with you, Mister Earl. It's no good getting excited about me and the other geeks I hang out with over the Goo network. We use it to out-tech-talk each other, scan comedy shaped fruit, spy on girls. This hacker scenario you've dreamt up, it's super cool but it's not true."

"For most of your buddies, I'm sure that's the case. But you Tripster Devon King." Braxton put his hands on the arms of the tank chair and brought his shark smile closer. "You've already been arrested for wire fraud. All I'm asking you to do is take the skills you already have and use them for the greater good." He frowned and stood up straight, hands on hips. "Reckon you can stretch to saving Zar's life a second time?"

§

# Chapter 29

The Rifler chief handed over the rucksack with its broken biscuits of sand bricks and included an antique Data Streamer watch as a bonus. Vlad greased the thief's hand with his father's dollars, taking pleasure from the fact.

Half an hour later, Vlad was hauled up in the black whale of his hearse, the motion of the ferry giving the vehicle an unnatural sense of floating. With the driver window wound down, he could hear the voices of his team mates echoing through the hull. They were taunting the rich girl, Fabrienne Oz, like a pack of hyenas circling their prey. Just a short time ago, the girl had used her hips and lips as currency, luring that slobbering gang into forming a team for her. Now he sensed that as much as his team mates were growing tired of the tease, so Fabrienne was growing uncomfortable with her salacious role – scared of it even. Before the jibes got too heated, Fabrienne turned her back and stalked away. She made it to her steam coach, and, stepping onto a weight sensor platform, ascended to the carriage.

Vlad lost interest. Without the thrill of potential violence, his team mates' antics bored him. Instead he pulled a sand brick out of the rucksack and examined it. Just a hunk of brick. Nothing special.

As he slung the brick back inside the rucksack, his eye was drawn to the stolen Data Streamer watch resting on the dash, and it occurred to him the item was far more interesting. He didn't have any Vitreous Goo sticks; like most folk, he'd long since rejected Goo in preference for the traditional, less intrusive phone call. The ticker tape concentrate was three quarters full though.

Vlad played with the watch. Uniform would have extracted every possible shred of evidence from Sol Punkstar's workshop by now. For the duration of the Ramrod, no one had been able to touch him. But an hour would see him across the finish line. It wouldn't matter then which team triumphed – he'd be too busy stepping down into the Vaults while cuffed to a Uniform officer. Unless his father could be persuaded to intervene.

He pulled out the chrome half moon from beneath the watch face. Keys concertinaed out like a peacock tail. Vlad typed in his message and thumbed the tiny crank. His father had long since abandoned Vitreous Goo. But the Data Streamer communication would still feed through the central telecoms board at Obshina Enterprises. As Vlad knew acutely, for a man like Nikolay Obshina, absolute power over what information bled in and out those walls was paramount.

Waiting on an answer, Vlad stared out the windshield and watched his team mates move about the hull. He suspected most were in it for the prize money rather than the acclaim of winning the Ramrod. He also suspected their team captain had bitten off more than she could chew in recruiting her team from the darker circuits of Autodrome. Lucky for Fabrienne Oz, she paid well. Otherwise, he had a few ideas about how the motley crew would have spent their idle time aboard the ferry.

He sensed a faint vibration at his wrist. Ticker tape spooled off the watch. He tore off the strip and read its solitary statement: Без муки нет науки. *Adversity is a good teacher.*

Vlad crushed the strip inside a fist. So that was to be the way it was going to play out. His father would remain the superstar and he would take the fall for all that had occurred in Sol Punkstar's workshop. His comfort would be the gross injustice Nikolay would publically protest on his behalf and the costly lawyers who would find all manner of explanation as to why the workshop was plastered with his DNA. The case would collapse. But in the meantime, could it be that his father wanted to teach him a lesson?

A second vibration at his wrist took him by surprise. He snapped the new strip of ticker tape free and scanned it, a faint burst of hope inside his chest.

"Hide sand bricks in the trunk. One of my men will collect after your arrest."

Vlad tossed the second strip of tape aside and let out a guttural roar.

§

The ferry scuttled over the surface of the Lough like a giant crustacean. Zar felt buried alive in the guts of the thing. Voices came to him in waves from the far end of the hold. The colossal iron lung wheezed overhead.

A cold space opened up just below his ribs, threatening to paralyse his entire body with numbness. He had lost everything to the Riflers – the sand bricks, the Albatross beak, even his watch. The least of his troubles had been the humiliation of reaching the port only to find the rival teams' ferries long departed.

"How you doing, buddy?" It was Valentine. Moonlight streamed in above the wave guard, making a death mask of the young man's angular face.

Zar shrugged his shoulders. Where to begin explaining how badly he was doing? He stared back out at the star speckled sky.

Valentine moved alongside him, arms folded. Neither spoke for a while. Eventually Valentine shook his head and said, "I sure was sorry to sour things between us back in my era. I didn't mean to flimflam you with that cop, I was just trying to steer us clear of a sticky situation."

Zar kept staring over the wave guard. Tears pricked his eyes. He'd forgotten about the embarrassment Valentine had caused him even before the Riflers stole everything that mattered to him and sent his whole world to Hell. Yet here was Valentine, trying to make amends for what Zar could now see as a well intentioned intervention which probably saved his life. He grimaced; Valentine's apology only rubbed salt into the wound of his own failures. Failure to justify to his father's trust in him. Failure to bring a murderer to justice. Failure to know what to do or even think anymore.

"It doesn't matter anyway," he muttered, partly to Valentine, partly to himself. "None of it matters anymore."

There was a tense silence between them. Then, as easy as if he was discussing the weather, Valentine said, "I was gasing with an acquaintance of yours the other day. Detective Black."

"Sooty?" Zar felt his stomach 360. He tore his gaze away from the sky.

Valentine glanced over a shoulder. The rest of the team milled at the opposite end. He stared back over at Zar, eyes hardened.

"I'm the kind of guy that folk take one look at and mark down as a player. Truth of it is though, I ain't made that way. Could've made a fast buck, could've bedded a different show gal every night if I wanted to. But even a player's gonna wake up one day all alone with a whiskey-soured mouth and a cold spot in the bed. Sooner or later, he's gotta make his choice. To be that jerk in the clink, or to be Superman."

Valentine slid a hand into one pocket of his pants. He cleared his throat. "I've never been the sort to approve of using an innocent guy as a pawn so I'm gonna let you in on a truth or two." He produced a wallet from his pocket. Keeping it close by his hip, he flipped it open long enough for Zar to see the watermarked badge of N.A.R.P. – Autodrome's Narcotics Agency for Reprimand and Prosecution.

"You're N.A.R.P. now?" Zar felt a tremendous pitch in perspective. Persia had been right when she said he couldn't trust anyone, not even his own team. Jesse lay trussed up in the back of Valentine's Cadillac, but the gangster was as much of a double-crosser. Was anyone on his team who they said they were?

He lent back against a girder, livid at the deception. But a new, unexpected emotion filtered through – pure relief that he wasn't alone. Along the way, others had become involved in Sol's puzzle. Just maybe they were all part of the bigger picture.

His face freshened with understanding. "The night Persia met you..?"

"I was a N.A.R.P. cadet. My cover had been blown and a whole lotta lead squirted my way. Six months I'd spent infiltrating the Razzledazzle racket in Era 3.0 in an effort to pin down the source. I'd got in with a gang, but one night I made the mistake of pushing too hard for answers. Seems in my enthusiasm, I stepped outta character and gave my new buddies the jitters."

Valentine ran a thumb and finger around his hat rim as if taking comfort from the action. "Uniform was told to break up a street war between rival gangs. Persia Gold was tasked with retrieving me, a kid caught in the crossfire. One glance and I was gone on the gal." He smiled. "Seemed Persia had a tight spot in her heart for me too. Then I got assigned to the Ramrod." The hardness came back into his eyes. "I'd waved my right to tell Persia the truth the day I signed on to train with N.A.R.P., but I didn't see why she couldn't join me on the rally."

Tipping off his hat, Valentine rubbed his forehead. "And, hell, didn't we get stitched up every which way. I'd been set to traffic drugs to some major players in the Eras – no boundary checks meant plain sailing for a trunkful of them pretty pills. But then Ruby got dusted, Franklin Oz too. Uniform arrived on the scene and, before I know it, there's me and Persia in the firing line when they pop the trunk to our ride."

He settled his hat back on his head. "I was eighteen, streetwise but just a baby when it came to dealing with the law. I hadda go through with the arrest, at least until N.A.R.P. sent me outta town to let the heat cool. As for Persia, they were all set to let a Uniform grunt like her take the fall. Best deal I could wrangle for her was a trainee desk job." Valentine's eyes greased. He brushed a hand across his lips. "I hadda let the doll go. For her sake."

Zar rubbed a palm up into one eye. How was he meant to feel about all this? On the one hand, he felt intense sympathy for Valentine and Persia. Such a horrific set of circumstances, and such a brutal way to tear two kids apart. But on the other hand, he couldn't deny the reeling sense of discomfort which threatened to overwhelm him. Was anyone on his team a whole person? Or were they all frayed around the edges?

As if sensing Zar's need to sit with the information a while, Valentine shook back his shoulders and offered, "Anyhow, when it comes to Vladimir, don't sweat it on the grunt. Minute he crosses the finish line, Uniform will move in to arrest him, recovering your property in the process."

"Why don't they just arrest him now?" It turned Zar's stomach to think of Vlad pawing over the sand bricks, even making sense of them in time.

"Two reasons. First, why Jesse's tied up here rather than back on the salt flats. Ramrod registration dictates that Uniform cannot detain a team player for a suspected misdemeanour until the game is finished."

"Calling the Ramrod a game is right." Zar stared at the riveted floor. A buckle of pain tightened around his throat. His eyes burned with exhaustion.

"Second reason. Connections. You remember who tugged on the blast horn to start this race?"

Zar felt a fresh blow. Vladimir's father, Nikolay Obshina, was a god amongst the racing fraternity. "Why would Nikolay Obshina's son be interested in the puzzle pieces?" he said as much to himself as to the gangster.

Valentine's expression intensified. "Sorry, Zar, but in my official capacity, I gotta ask. What exactly is your father's legacy?"

They were interrupted by Justice, arrived a few metres away.

"We'll be docking soon. Persia wants a word."

She strode away.

"We'll talk more once we're home and dry." Valentine's voice was tight with frustration. As they started for the opposite end of the hull, he muttered, "Just steer clear of Vladimir. It's a helluva ask but I need him to cross that finish line before Uniform can legally arrest him."

Zar kept walking.

§

Persia's team gathered around her like militia on the cusp of war.

"Our return trip across the wastelands brought us in at third place. So that's one point to us, two points to Fa's team for coming second, and three points to Fabrienne's team for winning. Which means..."

"Everything rests on the final sprint." Valentine grimaced. "Okay, so the fire truck is the slowest vehicle we've got. I'd say Fabrienne's steam coach is more style over speed. And Fa's got to keep his monster truck grounded else the suspension'll flip him."

"It's any team's race," murmured Eight Ball, patting his shoulder where Justice had patched the stab wound with surgistrips.

Overhead, the concertinaing lung slowed to a soft rustle.

Persia crossed her arms. "With Jesse retired, I need a fresh handler for the fire truck. Dual-fuelled. Sixty thousand pounds of weight. Zar? You wanna wrestle our red lady here?"

Zar glanced at the fire truck. He felt a tremendous crush of pride; Persia was handing him a lifeline in terms of his direct involvement in the race, and at such a crucial stage. He could drive the last stretch of the Ramrod as an active participant and not just a kid brought along for the ride on a promoter's say so.

But then he glanced around him at the circle of team mates, and he saw hope, exhaustion, and the overwhelming need to win engraved on every face. It wasn't just about him anymore. They were a team. And just as they as individuals had helped him find the puzzle pieces, so he owed them a debt as a collective. It was time to do the right thing.

He shook his head. "Steam machines are shick, but I'm a gearhead. Thanks for the shout out though."

Everyone exchanged glances.

"I'll drive it." Raina slung her hands on her hips. She jutted her chin.

Zar met the girl's fierce gaze. She was the perfect choice.

Persia nodded slowly. "Alright then. Zar and me will ride with you."

The lung cut out overhead, its drone replaced with the shouts of the dockmen, the spool of greased chain and the grind of hefty cogs. The wave guard started to descend.

"Time to beat the drag!" announced Persia.

The team dispersed to their vehicles.

§

# Chapter 30

Raina yanked the pull chain of the air horn, unleashing its long dry toot.

"The freak better move or I'll splat him on the mudguard."

Hands braced against the dash with its bib of dials, plungers and every sort of instrument, Persia popped a candy bubble. "He's got you marked as sweet, sister. Not the type to do him in."

"Then its time to get a little less sweet." Raina slung the huge spoked steering wheel left and right, zigzagging into the path of the Glideslide. The teen scientist seemed to delight in their impromptu dance, winding his white bird of a machine back and forth – less opponent than irritation.

"Take the idiot out!" shouted Zar, sat the other side of Persia, nose pressed to the windshield.

"Not my style," Raina muttered. Even so, she tugged the throttle that protruded from the floor like an eye on a stalk. The truck shunted forward to knock elbows with the scientist and send the Glideslide into a tailspin.

"Sometimes you don't have to hurt folk to move them out your way." She weighted the comment towards Zar.

"Sometimes to move folk out of your way you have to hurt them," Zar shot back as the scientist scooped back in from the side.

"I'm climbing out back," said Persia. "Gonna stoke this dinosaur, sister, even if you don't need to haul on the extra gas." The team captain opened the small door to the rear of the cab and crawled through it on her elbows. A well-aimed stab of a heel punched the door back in.

Raina hooked the truck left, following the contour of the highway. She might be wielding an iron giant with a two metre high front fender for a jaw, but it was the smaller, fragile-looking Glideslide which had dictated the game so far.

"Want me to act as look out?" asked Zar as Raina caught a second drift of movement in a wing mirror.

"That's a well timed offer," she murmured, distracted by whatever had pinned itself into the fire truck's slipstream. A hand at her shoulder brought her back around.

"Keep this beast steady." Zar held her gaze a moment. Then he raised his hands to the ceiling crank, wound it anticlockwise and tipped back the hatch. Hands bracing the sides, he swung his legs up through the hatch and squeezed out.

Seconds later, Raina heard him shout down, "You got a bug on your tail!"

She cursed. But what damage could a bug do to an iron monster like the fire truck...Except it wasn't after them, she realised, staring past the Glideslide to Justice on the Tomahawk.

Distracted, she took a corner wide. The bug zipped out and around.

She heard the distinct creak of the truck's roof-mounted telescope.

"Bug's gonna try something," Zar called down, his voice accompanied by the ammonia scent of steam and the roar of bubbles off the boiler.

Raina saw a new skull marker a kilometre or so away.

"Hold tight!" she cried, reining in the throttle while pumping the break. The truck edged off the Artery onto the slip last second while the bug sped on. Raina allowed herself a tight smile. The other vehicles in her rear view managed the route switch. Maybe the SS bug elite recruits weren't so hot after all?

But as she hooked a left under the overpass and emerged the far side, she was suddenly aware of a shadow looming overhead. With a mix of fear and awe, she saw the undercarriage of the bug pass above her and sweep down to slot in ahead of the game and hard on the heels of the Glideslide. In that instant, she saw the flaw in the bioengineered machine. Yes, the Glideslide was hardwired into the rider's neural responses, but its design prevented the simplest of manoeuvres, namely a glance back over a shoulder. The bug whipped 180 degrees around, aiming twin exhausts at the Glideslide like a spraying skunk. Only luck kept the Glideslide's rider alive – a twist in the road meant the kid avoided a faceful of burnout but lost focus, careering sideways. The bug flipped back around and powered away. Raina didn't ease up any.

"Yowzer! You see how close that dude came to getting roasted?" Persia poured herself back through the small door and plonked down onto the bench seat. "Zar gone walkabout?" she asked. Her face was smudged with cinders.

Raina's gaze flicked to the ceiling hatch. "Up top."

"That'll help then for what I'm about to suggest. I see you got your eyeball on Justice. Way that bug is cooking in close to her, we gotta juice it for sure. I've banked us a bellyful of steam. I say we get Zar to scout an ideal spot to cut loose and you drive that bug back to whatever Hell it clawed out of."

"Bugs," Raina corrected. She nodded at the bug's twin which had shot out from an alley, the worst kind of doppelganger.

"Even more reason to help Justice out."

"Can't promise even this hunk of iron can withstand two sets of exhausts." Raina watched the filmy gulfstreams pouring off each bug's rear. She narrowed her gaze. The bugs were nippy next to a Goliath like the fire truck and the force off their dual jets was considerable. But they were built for the open spaces of the desert, and while she had no chance against them when it came to speed, she did have the advantage of body mass.

Ahead the road tapered to the width of one large vehicle.

She glanced across. "Can you tell Zar to crank the fire bell when we're ten metres off?"

Persia swept up her legs and stretched a hand to unhook the hatch while Raina checked the pressure gauge – a brass clock orbited by smaller macro-environmental dials. The needle flickered dangerously close to the red. Persia had obviously stoked the boiler with a vengeance, a ploy to help Raina lose her inhibitions and mow down any opposition who got in her way.

*Okay then.* Raina stared dead ahead. The Supra, the steam coach, the hearse, Valentine's Cadillac, and the sand buggy all raced through the gap. A revolution or two of the wheels separated Justice and the bugs.

Persia slammed the roof hatch shut and plonked back down onto the seat.

"Deed's done, honey. Zar's gonna ring that bell then tuck in behind the flame shield."

Raina just had time to absorb the information before the bell rattled overhead. Seconds stretched. *Dive now, Zar. Get in tight behind the flame shield.* Raina's hand went to the throttle. She yanked the lever towards her, unleashing a gush of steam that ran hot through the pipes, firmed up behind the pistons and ripped through the engine.

Justice's Tomahawk flew through the passage just as the fire truck roared up behind, knocking the twin bugs aside like skittles. In the rear view, Raina saw both flip their back ends towards her, sending out twin sheets of flame as she charged through the gap. The bugs pulled up short just in time. But she had gained enough distance to keep them at bay until the end of the race.

"We're on a straight," she gasped. Her heart crackled, producing its own kinetic energy. "Zar'll be okay. I'm sure he can extinguish any fire," she added.

"Or set one burning."

Raina squinted at the team captain, who rewarded her with a wink and blew a pink gum bubble.

§

Sweat blistering at his forehead, feet shaken from under him every few seconds, Zar wrestled the fire hose off its coil, aimed at the flames and squeezed the trigger. Water foamed from the mouth of the hose. The flames died out, leaving behind a bitumen stench and wisps of blue-black smoke.

The truck's speed was increasing. It had lightened considerably now that the water tank was almost drained, Zar realised. He restacked the hose and stumbled over to the coke trough. They were down to the last couple of shovels. At the same time, he noticed that Vlad's caddy hearse was catching up.

A projected skull blazed into view a few kilometres east. They were heading for Black Stacks; Zar's racer gut told him so. Which meant the fire truck was going to need refuelling.

He lifted the ceiling hatch and swung down into the cabin.

"Finish line is Black Stacks, I'm sure of it. Keep using steam at this rate and we'll be twiddling our thumbs at the roadside." He noticed the sheen of sweat at Raina's forehead and how she bit her bottom lip, determined to steer them home.

Persia hugged a long leg into her chest. "Chill 'n be cool, bro. I hadda get us some muscle back there else Justice would've got fried. Literally."

"I've been relying on steam to power us so far," said Raina. "Meant we've kept pace with the rest and used up the weightiest fuel first. Now, thanks to this truck's combo-engine, we've got a fistful of steam to keep us ticking over plus a tank of gas to give us wings. You guys just need to pray I'm capable of slinging this beast in and out Autodrome's dark corners."

"Ain't no other duo could handle this hunk of iron." Persia flashed her perfect smile. "You two make a good team."

Zar had a hunch she might be right. Raina appeared too intent on the road to comment.

§

# Chapter 31

Fabrienne Oz brushed a wisp of black hair behind an ear and returned both hands to the steering rod. Driving the rod forward, she manipulated a small rollerball under both thumbs to activate the hydraulic scaffold below. The glass carriage rotated on a 45 degree axis, allowing her to stare back at the opposition.

A short way behind, the brass dung beetle of a Cadillac had un-shuttered one of its wings and was in the process of folding out a gleaming feeler.

*Nasty little insect.* Fabrienne rotated back up. Her environment rippled on its flexible backbone. She stayed secure in her harness, perched on an ornate brass stool that ack-acked from one end of a small horseshoe track to the other.

"Not now, Fa," she muttered as her twin brother's monster truck lurched out in front, forcing her to yank on leather brake reins suspended from the ceiling. Steam enveloped the exterior of the carriage as its motion slowed; Fabrienne felt set afloat.

The cloud thinned to reveal Fa hauling on his brakes to aggravate her further. *Hadn't her brother eyes to see the Cadillac?* Yes, the Ramrod had only ever been about the two of them proving who was the best racer. But that didn't stop other drivers from fostering personal ambitions. Or outstaying their welcome.

Fabrienne waited for Fa to touch the brake again. Then she swept out into the other lane, powered the steam valve forward to accelerate and overtake, and hooked back in ahead of the monster truck. Scooting the rollerball 180 degrees, she hung upside down in her harness, hair fanning like an oil spill. Her stare pierced the truck's windshield to find the black pearls of her brother's eyes.

Fa nodded. *I see him now.*

Fabrienne righted herself as the caravan entered the cleared streets of Meat Market. She noticed the terrible road surface while unaffected, the iron wheels of the coach straddling every pothole. Nonetheless, she was unsettled. Blistered and peeling paintwork, boarded up storefronts, sidewalks strewn with garbage...these were the kind of streets where her fellow team mates scuttled between life's boards.

Her mind leapt between ways to shake off the Cadillac to how queer it was to compete outside the protective shell of Black Stacks. She had waited so long to race in the real world of the city, but now she felt disconcerted by that same reality. There was something blasé about life and death on Autodrome's highways and byways. In contrast, the sanitary environment of her home, Black Stacks, had allowed her and Fa to engage one another in safe, well-matched bouts. The decision to challenge Fa to enter the Ramrod Rally on an opposing team to her own and, most daringly of all, behind their father's back, seemed petty now.

Fabrienne's stomach rose and fell in nauseous waves, and it had nothing to do with the motion of the carriage. She felt strange and vulnerable around her team mates. For her, the fun had long since leaked out of the Ramrod.

Not that she was about to admit as much to Fa. A childlike frown appeared between her eyes. She could imagine her brother crowing if he'd an inkling how close her team had come to mutiny, or how much she wished they'd stayed at home.

Fabrienne hardened up. In spite of everything, she had successfully managed a team of felons who would soon as slit her throat if it hadn't been for the reminder of the prize money. The finish was just a matter of surviving a few more blocks.

She turned her attention to the rear view where Fa was powering in alongside the Cadillac despite the weaponry at its wing. It occurred to her that Fa relished the idea of taking on the armed Cadillac. Distanced from the action in the cab of his monster truck, he'd feel utterly invincible. Except, Fa was kidding himself if he thought there was no safer ride. As their father had emphasised when Fa purchased the vehicle, a monster truck could prove lethal if handled badly.

"Don't get cocky," she whispered out loud.

The sentiment fell on deaf ears. With a screeching gearshift and the burn of brakes, the monster truck reversed clean over the roof of the Cadillac.

Fabrienne gasped. The speed of the manoeuvre left the truck airborne an instant before it crashed back down onto the road behind the caddy, sparing his opponent the full weight of the truck.

They sped into a backstreet. The road surface looked like sloughed scales. As the Cadillac accelerated, Fabrienne decided it would be easiest to take the vehicle out herself. Fa was too much of a hothead when what was required was simple outmanoeuvring. Given the size of the coach, it would be impossible for the mobster to see what lay ahead while beautifully easy for her to choose the rockiest path.

Fabrienne sealed off the steam, decelerating tight in to the caddy's nose. She noticed a rift in the road a few metres away and held a steady course. The huge wheels of the coach sang in their iron throats beneath her and she passed smoothly over the anomaly. Behind, the Cadillac wailed on its brakes, cut a 360 drift and just cleared the edge of the rift.

The mobster had Lady Luck on his side! Or maybe not...the caddy kept sliding to ricochet off one of the coach wheels. Fabrienne felt the impact. Her carriage swung in its scaffold like a rocked cradle. She wrestled the steering rod in an effort to maintain course.

As the momentum settled, she saw the Cadillac draw away, the blade that usually protruded from its flank snapped clean off. She also noticed Fa swing in behind the caddy, apparently bored of taking a backseat. With fresh irritation, she realised it was impossible for her to continue blocking the Cadillac's line of sight when Fa's monster truck was directly behind it.

In that instant, Fabrienne lost interest. She had removed the threat in the form of the Cadillac's weaponry. Now she could opt out.

Easing off, she watched the Cadillac scoot past, followed closely by Fa, whose wave she returned with an air of nonchalance.

§

Fa glared at his rear view. Had his sister really conceded the fight? Her regal wave as he passed suggested as much.

He hunkered low in his seat. It was refreshing to engage an opponent without his sister wadding in. But that wasn't how they operated. Their father had engaged tutors from every racing discipline to help them hone skills they were never meant to use in the outside world – and, without exception, Fabrienne had always found a way to muscle in on his turn. Apparently though, when it came to taking on the mobster, his sister just wasn't feeling it.

Focusing on the Cadillac in front, Fa wondered if, like he, Fabrienne found the idea of the Ramrod Rally more fun than its reality. Together, they'd grown to despise their father's restrictions, likewise, his drawing comparisons with their dead brother, Franklyn, and always finding them lacking. But the game of racing in the outside world had soured over the last few hours, serving only as a reminder of how Franklin had died.

Fa brushed a hand back over his forehead. It was too late for regrets. All that remained now was the finish. He couldn't afford to let up.

A skull projection bloodied the sky and they left Meat Market behind, the terraces of upper eastside becoming visible over the rooftops. A few kilometres ahead was Black Stacks. Fa longed for his first glimpse of the factory, its scaffolded heights dominating the landscape like an automatron's fortress.

But the route siphoned off and they were directed into a residential wormhole. Housing pods piled high either side like fungus on the trunk of the city. Fa grew hot with annoyance. The Cadillac slid through the narrow streets like a well measured breath. He, on the other hand, was forced to ease off and nudge his dinosaur of a ride around endless corners. The truck bit back more than once, lurching sideways to ricochet down off its hydraulics while he wrestled the shift. Fabrienne remained a ghost of motion in the rear view.

*Light on the steering. Steady on the gas. And if you're gonna jump her, hit the ramp dead centre.* Straining against the confines of his harness, Fa was haunted by his father's words. But Frank had never owned a monster truck, just as he'd no patience with hover bugs or Glideslides. The man was a hotrodder. A play-it-safe kind of a guy. As for his son...Fa saw a low wall curve up from the sidewalk a few metres ahead and smirked. Frank was a traditionalist, Fabrienne was a strategist, and he was a chancer. All he had to do was line up a wheel with the wall, hit it just right, use his body weight to counteract the pendulum effect and leapfrog the Cadillac, or better still, crush it beneath him.

He mounted the sidewalk and lined up the right wheel with the low wall. Seconds later, the rim hit the makeshift ramp. The cab leapt skyward and, for an instant, Fa was flying. When the cab started to tip, he slung hard aside in his harness.

"Straighten up", he demanded. "Straighten up!"

His organs pitched on a foreign axis. The truck kept to its trajectory. There was a tremendous jarring sensation and a great splurge of engine noise. He ricocheted forward to strain against the harness, flew back like a ragdoll and was dragged forward on invisible hooks again.

*The truck's rolling. I shot it wrong*, he realised through a mess of nausea.

§

Fabrienne could recall the precise moment that her eldest brother, Franklyn Oz, died in the Ramrod one year before. 5.15pm, on a sweltering Sunday interrupted only by live coverage of the Ramrod in every home across Autodrome, including Black Stacks. One moment, she and Fa were listening jealously to their father's praise of Franklyn's manoeuvres. The next, Franklyn's rod had gone up in flames.

Watching Fa's truck spin off the road, imagining her twin's flesh mauled more with each rotation, Fabrienne felt the same fracturing of the self that she'd seen in her father's face a year before. The truck shattered a glass store front, bunny hopped off its hydraulics to smash a couple of first floor pod balconies, and seesawed back onto its roof in a side road.

Fabrienne didn't think twice. She steered up onto the sidewalk, hauled on the brake noose and revolved the brass reel at her waist to un-pinch the harness. A tug on a second noose released the exit hatch. She jumped onto a small circular platform, triggered the hydraulics and whooshed down to ground level.

In seconds, she was charging over the glass littered sidewalk and throwing herself around into the side street, where she was struck by blind panic. The truck was beached, its colossal wheels tearing at the air, smoke belching off its exhaust – a bad sign. Fa hadn't activated the red toggle located at arm's length on the dash and killed the engine.

Raising an arm to protect her face against the fumes, Fabrienne approached the rear of the vehicle. She'd studied enough vehicles to know that, by law, monster trucks were required to be fitted with an external kill switch. Locating the pull behind the license plate, she planted her feet firmly and tugged the handle. The engine cut, leaving behind an atmosphere thick with burnout and not knowing.

Fabrienne ran around to the driver side. She crouched and peered in.

"Fa?"

The harness was empty. Her gaze went to the makeshift floor of the roof and the human shape there.

"Fa."

An indelible hush conquered the noise of the city. Fabrienne reached a hand inside. She stroked the hair from Fa's forehead and became aware of a dark residue on her fingertips. Time stretched as she fell off sideways, legs crossed beneath her.

Just as a scream threatened to escape her throat, Fa stirred, the slightest movement but enough to have Fabrienne choke, "Wake up, Fa! Wake up!"

Eyes stirred behind closed lids.

She pressed a palm to his forehead. "It's Fabrienne. I insist you wake up."

Slowly, as if the idea of letting in life's light was unappealing, Fa opened his eyes.

"Fab?" He blinked. Shifting up onto an elbow with a groan, he stared at his sister in surprise. "What're you doing here, Fab? What about the Ramrod?"

Fabrienne swallowed. Pride caught in her throat, small discomfort next to the guttural ache she'd felt moments earlier. She glanced back at the empty road. The receding noise of engines hung like vapour in the air.

"It's just a game, Fa. We can play it again sometime. Opposing teams aren't meant to help each other out, but I suggest you and I get in my steam coach and cross the finish line together this one, and I assure you, only time."

§

"Frank!"

Nikolay Obshina held up his hands as if surprised to see Frank Oz. A team of bodyguards in military black stepped into the room ahead of him, wielding scanners like loaded rifles. They scoured the room – the bank of screens along one wall, the peculiar green marble statues at each corner. They even stepped out onto the balcony.

One bodyguard went to access the door that led off to Frank's office.

"You won't be going in there," said Frank firmly.

"That's okay, gentlemen." Nikolay entered the room. "You may leave." He waved a hand as if batting away a cloud of flies. The bodyguards exited, the silver shield door closing behind them.

Nikolay strode into the centre of the room. He wore navy riding pants, a shirt panelled with folk embroidery and a brocaded long coat pinned over one shoulder. On another, the clothes would have looked ostentatious. Nikolay wore them with flair.

"Hello Nikolay." Frank started to rise from his chair.

Nikolay waved him down. "Not necessary, Frank. I've come to keep you company, not exhaust you."

Frank settled back. He smiled tightly. "You received my invitation?"

"So it would appear." Nikolay rested his hands on the back of Frank's chair. "We're to see in the end of the Ramrod together. Autodrome's originator alongside its champion Super Leaguer. Now retired I should add."

"Speak for yourself."

"Ah, but its fresh blood that's taking control of the steering wheel these days."

Nikolay gestured beyond the tall French windows. "It isn't news to you that Fa and Fabrienne entered the Ramrod?"

Frank turned knowing eyes on his guest. "Terrestrial has broadcast as much ever since the names of the entrants were released."

"Forgive me, Frank, but how do you feel about that?"

"I try not to feel." Frank gestured to an apparatus on a nearby table that comprised of glass pipes housed in a miniature steel rig. "I concentrate all my energy on my rehabilitation. You see how the pipes are at angles to one another. The aim is to realign them."

"Yes, yes, you must keep the old mind busy," said Nikolay dismissively. He returned to his line of questioning. "Then why did you reinstate the rally? It's such a burden, so much paperwork, route mapping, allocation of Uniform security..." He intensified his gaze. "Did you seek to exorcise a ghost?"

Frank took his time in replying while aligning the first tube with the second. "I left the details of the rally to others. Just put my signature where they told me to." He aligned the second and third tubes. "As for ghosts, I've never been a spiritual man, Nikolay. Engines. They speak to me. But the dead? My hope is they were laid to rest a long time ago. The one spirit I do have use for is vengeance. I'd like to see that phantom strap on armour and send arrows into the hearts of men with murder on their conscience." His hand hovered near the fourth tube.

"Whaddaya reckon, Nikolay? Do you think men like that live in fear of the hell that awaits them?"

"I've no idea, Frank. I'm not as superstitious as my ancestors. But I do believe the sin lies with he who committed it. Like the mechanic who engineered the deaths a year ago and was dredged from Lady Luck Lough a day later. Given the circumstances, it was difficult for me to lead a team to victory that morning."

Linking his hands behind his back, Nikolay glanced out the French windows and exclaimed with fresh interest, "I can see vehicles emerging from the residential warren to the east. Come and see, Frank."

Frank left the fifth and last tube out of the synch with the rest of the apparatus and made his way across the room in bursts of heavy movement. He shuffled out onto the balcony and settled himself in a steel rocking chair. Beyond the gates of Black Stacks, the crowd gave off a constant buzz.

"Pass me the Bi-Oculars," he said gruffly as Nikolay joined him.

Nikolay retrieved a malachite-green case from a low table. He unsnapped the lid and shook out a set of lightweight tube bi-oculars.

"These?" He offered them.

"You should know. Your company invented them," Frank unravelled a rubberised strap from a side compartment, slipped it over his head and secured the dual sights at his eyes.

"Manufacture, yes. Invent, no. I leave the creative streak to others. My forte is identifying a need then dealing in the pieces necessary to satisfy that market."

"Ah, you do yourself an injustice there, Nikolay. Your ambitions to grow Obshina Enterprises as a company and help swell the ranks of the Rupine Group is common knowledge in the business world." Adjusting the scopes, Frank located a trail of creamy headlights.

"We all need ambitions, Frank. Take my eldest son, Vladimir, for example. He is out there racing now, I believe on Fabrienne's team," Nikolay relaxed into the seat opposite. "Strange how things turn out," he added.

"Strange indeed," said Frank. Through the bi-oculars, he saw an aura of disturbed dust above the city as night gave way to dawn. He focused in on one of the giant screens projecting the event down a skyscraper wall.

§

A vast window gave out onto the waking city. Tripster sat at the huge ammonite slab of a desk, surrounded by the tools of his trade. A couple of rucksacks burgeoned with steel wire, cabling, jacks, various pliers, soldering equipment and several boxes of Goo sticks. His VDU Mat was in the middle of the desk, surrounded by rigs of old Data Streamer watches. The watches gave off a faint copper scent and whirred in unison like a swarm of metal bees.

He was working like crazy, the kid who tripped and fell at ten years of age and who found himself resigned to a tank chair like something tossed onto life's scrap pile. But this was the environment in which he shone. All he had to do was reach out across the Goo network and link in.

Fingers weaving back and forth above the VDU Mat, he transformed into a technological spell maker. Codes fed out across the banks of watches; he pranged each tiny crank in turn and the dial tones erupted. He shushed at them instinctually, finger to his lips. What if the monster next door pricked up his ears?

But then the underground network across the city started to pick up. In bedrooms, in basements, in libraries, in comic stores, others took the call on their antenaed Goo watches and paid that data forward, hooking into the television screens that projected over high rises and inside every household as well as the metal obelisks that pumped out race stats on each street corner.

The Goo that was spread over the racks of antique Data Streamer watches started to puff up.

"We're coming to get you," Tripster whispered.

§

# Chapter 32

Watercolours bled across the sky. Where the streets broadened on the approach to Black Stacks, the gathered crowds were kept to the sidewalk by steel fencing and a large Uniform presence.

Hooking an arm out the open passenger window, Zar tried to soak it all in. Loss worried at him like a sore spot, more so now that he was back on home ground. But he also recognised it as one of those times in life when every minute should be savoured. It was difficult to know who was ranked where, but for that instant at least, he tried to pretend it didn't matter. This was what it was all about, the rush of cool air against his face, the cacophony from the sidewalk, the rumble of engines.

A hand closed around his shoulder. He pulled his head back in.

Persia flashed her extraordinary smile. "Either Frank Oz's kids are tryin' to fake us out or we've left them in the dirt."

"And their teams?" Raina's arms tensed either side the huge steering wheel. She glistened with sweat.

"Shoot up top and give us the lowdown, Zar, honey. I'll keep our tough little sister here company. She's doin' a helluva job." Persia fed her long limbs over Zar. She slipped by him in a brush of silky hair and sandalwood.

Zar grunted. It was impossible to deny Persia's smoky sweet appeal, but it was Raina who prayed on his mind. He wanted to stay. Let Raina know he'd never seen anyone handle a vehicle the size and mechanical complexity of the fire truck with that degree of grit. Admit how her prettiness complemented her skills as a driver. Thank her for persevering with him. Ask her to be by his side. But right then wasn't the time.

Raina glanced up as he craned the roof hatch.

"Thanks, Zar." Her wide mouth pinched at a corner.

"Just get us across the finish line," said Zar softly. He swung up and through.

Noise immediately assaulted him from all directions. The air was thick with fumes and smoke. Gripping the rim of the flame shield, he steadied himself and swept his gaze in all directions.

The scene was a race-junkie's heaven. Spectators waved their arms like rippling sand. A stampede of iron dinosaurs raged all around. Pack animals, they knocked elbows and snapped at each other's heels – the bike tank Kettenkrad, the elite bugs, the Harley V-rod, and materialising through the faint morning mist back at the start of the straight, the steam coach.

Zar gripped the flame shield, riding the rooftop like a surfboard. In Raina's hands, the fire truck was a weapon to smash aside any vehicle that tried to overtake. She zigzagged, produced wheel spins to kick up blinding dust, and never once did her speed vary.

"Just keep us steady!" he called to anyone listening. "We're nearly there!"

Out in front, Valentine's Cadillac was a war horse set on fire by the first rays of the sun. To the fore, Justice moulded around the brushed steel Tomahawk. Ahead loomed Black Stacks, a Chocolate Factory stained with soot and wreathed in pipework. The factory gates stood open. A huge neon arc proclaimed 'Finish' over the entrance.

Zar's pain gave way to glittering excitement. He was on the final stretch of the Ramrod Rally – the race he had dreamt of entering for what seemed an eternity. He'd witnessed some tremendous displays of mechanical prowess and driving skill – Persia manoeuvring the Road Runner through the flaming hell of Coddington Dock, Eight Ball's descent from the heights of the Trylon on his manmade batwings, Valentine outsmarting both the opposition and the robot army in the Hemisphere, Justice defying the laws of physics on her extraterrestrial Tomahawk, and now Raina, blocking the opposition behind the dual-fuelled fire truck and bombing it to the finish. He replayed those thrilling moments like Paranascope images taken with the lenses of his eyes. What a ride! What a race!

His elation was short-lived. He noticed the hearse pull ahead of the rest of the vehicles. As the hearse drew close to the fire truck's bumper, the grunt hauled up in the driver seat held something up. A rucksack, Zar realised with absolute hatred.

All they had to do was get across the finish line and Vlad would be arrested and the rucksack placed back into his hands. Except it seemed the thug had different ideas. Vlad cut an unexpected path through the steel barrier and between the crowds to disappear up the ramp of the local Ziplines station.

Zar didn't pause to think. His skateboard was fastened in a makeshift sling at his back; he pulled it free and ran to the back of the fire truck where vehicles thundered in pursuit. He ran at the edge, leapt and brought the board tight in beneath his heels.

The landing was brutal. Shock waves jarred his shins and anklebones. He forced himself to close off the pain while weaving in and out the speeding juggernauts. Horns blasted. Brakes squealed. Steel crushed off steel.

He reached the sidewalk in seconds. The crowd roared with fresh enthusiasm. Zar fuelled his leg muscles with rage and kicked off and up onto the ramp. The barrier had apparently been lowered when Uniform closed the station; the hearse had smashed it aside. Zar skidded sideways to a halt. At the far end of the platform, the hearse had been dumped at an angle. The winch of the iron elevator was singing with steam.

§

"Wait until they're back inside," hissed Braxton at Tripster's shoulder. The Goo sheathing the statues was doing an excellent job of transmitting events inside the next room, Tripster having embedded a wireless transmission sequence into the intelligent constituent. But the last thing they wanted was to spook Nikolay.

"Too many screens everywhere." Tripster swam his hands above the VDU. "The information is already filtering out."

"Ah, come on, Frank. Reel him in," said Braxton softly. He went over to the window and braced his hands against the glass. Beyond, the city was ablaze with newborn golden light.

"Relax," shot Tripster back over a shoulder. "A man like Frank Oz didn't come to head up Autodrome without enough smarts to catch a donkey."

§

A vein pulsed at Nikolay's forehead. He sucked the flesh in at his cheeks.

"What the hell is that boy doing? This is no time for detours."

The noise of the crowd lifted to an ecstatic crescendo as the first set of vehicles charged between the gates and over the finish line. A silver bullet of a quadricycle scuffed up the white pebbles of the courtyard followed by a bronzed, bruised Cadillac and a steam-belching fire truck.

"Maybe the burden of the stolen sand bricks he is carrying has proved too great. On the other hand, as a young man inclined towards murder, your son isn't going to think twice before adding theft, and now it would appear, sabotage, to the list. He takes after his father."

"What exactly are you getting at, Frank, old buddy, old man?" Nikolay's expression hardened. The noise of arriving vehicles broke around them like a storm.

Frank pressed forward in his chair. "I'm talking about an empire built on pain and addiction. I'm talking betrayal of peoples' lives. Of me the day you arranged for that son of a bitch mechanic to see to it that your opposition crumbled. Of Autodrome which you have tried to corrupt it into your own vile vision."

Frank got hooks in his eyes and buried them into the man opposite. "In co-operation with homicide and N.A.R.P., I reinstated the Ramrod in order to flush you out. Nothing would stop you trying to get your hands on Sol Punkstar's invention, and in the desperation to expand your empire, you got sloppy." Frank shook his head. "Riflers will always talk if you've got the green."

"You've nothing on me," spat Nikolay. He leapt from his chair and lent over Frank, his preserved looks corrupted. "You stupid, inefficient vegetable! Think you have any sway in this city anymore? Where are your bodyguards? Where's the Uniform ready to arrest me? You're just a sad lonely old man, Frank, who can't race anymore and begrudges the rest of the city its little piece of happiness."

"Happiness? You've created an underclass of drug addicts!" Frank pressed up out of his chair. He attempted to push Nikolay aside but the ex-Super Leaguer pinned him at both shoulders. Nikolay's face was livid.

"Not everyone can achieve the heady heights of Black Stacks, Frank. Most folk are born ordinary. The most they can hope to achieve is adoration of a select few who conquer the city's race tracks. So I've helped steer them to a dreamtime where they feel safe and loved, and where they can forget how messed up this city really is. We don't value life. We value gears, MPH, engine oil and pistons. The poorer residents, well, we dispose of them in the city's slums. But I give them an escape, a way to fuel their inner happiness. I give them Razzledazzle. And thanks to Sol Punkstar's invention, I'll soon achieve a monopoly over the global market to rival even the Rupine Group."

Frank got a slant to his mouth. "Only you don't have Sol Punkstar's invention, do you, Nikolay? You don't even have the puzzle pieces that lead to it."

Nikolay followed Frank's gaze past the gates of Black Stacks to two figures charging pell-mell over the Ziplines.

§

# Chapter 33

The Ziplines reflected in the early morning sunlight like mericulal ribbons. Below, the streets formed a vein-like mass around Black Stacks. Zar rode his board, the heating air in his face.

The tallest incline not to merit a lift hill rose up ahead. Zar made wings of his arms. The skateboard wheels chittered beneath his feet. He flew up the incline like a knife through silk. At the crest, his board skimmed clear of the track and he leapt into the air. For a few seconds, he felt free of all the weight he had been shouldering. He was just a kid in love with the race and with no greater responsibility than to soar in its element.

Then he landed, the board buckling slightly beneath him as it absorbed the impact, and he was suddenly aware of his flesh again. He was also filled with loathing at the sight of Vlad twenty metres or so out in front. The brute was on foot. There was nothing of grace in the guy's running style, but he drove on, the slabs of his arms bent to aid prolusion, his blockish head dipped to cut the headwind.

Seeing his rucksack slung over one of Vlad's shoulders intensified Zar's rage. There had been no real privacy over the course of the Ramrod. Vlad had been the invisible agent at his back every step. But now it was his turn to join in unexpectedly.

Ahead was a lift hill, the arc of which actually passed over the top of the rising sun to form a colossal metallic rainbow. It was motionless; no doubt Uniform had automatically shut down the anti-rollback ratchet when they closed the station. But Vlad seemed to have the measure of his obstacles. The 'Go' override lever stuck up from the sponged groove to the right of the track. Running past, he hooked out an arm and slammed the lever forward. The ribs of the lift hill crawled into motion. Levering himself into one of the giant grooves, Vlad glanced back. His eyes bore into Zar. He might have been a Minotaur escaped from the labyrinth.

Zar focused on the rising metal steps seconds away. He struck the assent accurately, the wheels of his board slotting into the correct gauge in the pre-grooved surface. The clockwork was a whip of ticktocking underfoot. The track had its own clunky heartbeat.

Several metres above, Vlad disappeared over the crest of the lift hill. Zar concentrated on the ebb and flow of his breath. The sand bricks were everything. If he could just distract the grunt for long enough, surely the Uniform would catch up?

Vlad, it seemed, had other ideas. As the incline peaked, Zar surfed forward and over, readying himself for the swift descent. Instead, a huge fist slugged him in the chest and drove the breath from his lungs. He floundered, dredging air into his lungs in great gulps. Forcing himself to recover, he hunkered down on his board and pulled away just as the fist flew in for a second blow. The meat pans of Vlad's feet sounded noisily on the track behind. Zar glanced back to see the thug revolve his arms through thin air, go to fall on the slippery descent and regain his balance last moment. In that instant, Zar saw that as much as Vlad might have the advantage of bulk, his size restricted the speed of his reactions.

Zar leant back. The nose of his board rose up, sparks showering off the truck grinds. Vlad had no such brake system; he careered past Zar, who limboed clear of the hand that grasped for him. Angling forwards, Zar used his body weight to increase momentum again and slide in behind Vlad, who craned his square head over one shoulder then the other as he ran, arms outstretched.

Could the grunt keep his balance and fight him off? There was a good ten metre descent left. Zar swallowed hard. He imagined his dad taking pride in him, his mother stretching free of the suffocating layers of Razzledazzle addiction, Raina thinking the very best of him instead of the very worst, and he decided to test the theory.

Slamming down on the front of his board, he kicked it up into his hand and felt the polished skim of the track underfoot. It was incredibly hard to maintain his footing, but he made for the side barrier, feeding the board into the makeshift harness at his back as he ran. At the last instant, he leapt, stepped up onto the barrier rail and propelled himself off it.

He landed astride Vlad's back. The Goliath tried to swing him off, but Zar gripped tight with his knees, freeing up a hand to tug the rucksack open. A fist crushed up into his kidneys; Zar yelped in pain but got a grip on a sand brick, which he pulled clear and rammed into one of his board shorts' pocket. The brute bucked his shoulders and rolled full circle at the hips. Zar caught up a second brick and slid it into the opposite pocket. But just as he was reaching for a third brick, Vlad hit the straight and pulled up sharply. Feet planted on the track, he shook Zar free with the power of a steel-built rhinoceros and sent him skating into the sponge barrier at force.

§

"You're boring me, old man."

Nikolay stormed off the balcony and Frank followed him back inside.

"What's the matter, Nikolay? Aren't I painting you in the best light? We both know how pristine you like to keep your public image."

Nikolay's expression was blade sharp. "Look around you, Frank. Autodrome has entered a new age where the rich are superstars and the poor are vermin who'll sacrifice their young to the racetrack for a fistful of dimes. You created that! Does that make you proud? Was that your brilliant vision? I say what right have you to criticise my business practices when your own create suffering?"

Frank lowered his eyes. "I've never stepped outside the law, Nikolay. And I've no say over the financial climate of this city."

"Owner of the largest automobile plant in the city has no say in how the wealth is split? Ridiculous," hissed Nikolay. He ran a hand down his crisp, intricately embroidered shirt. "I know what its like to have nothing. The Red Depression stripped my family of their estate and other assets. Inside two generations, my family fell from nouveaux rich to peasantry. So what then if I aspire to sit pretty in the Rupine Group? So what if I have fought tooth and nail to drag me and mine back up to the top of the pile."

"But what about the folk you trampled on the way?"

"Like Franklyn, you mean? He wasn't meant to die, you fool! The mechanic was just supposed to put those team mates' vehicles out of actions. You can't hold me to account for those deaths. The city needed a new Super Leaguer and didn't I deliver!"

The confession appeared to strike Frank like a fist. He rested back against the table on which the glass tubing apparatus stood.

"You know, Nikolay. I've been trying to crack this damned recuperation device for months now. Last night, I managed it. The control returned to my fingers, you see? Which is kind of symbolic since I'm thinking this big old juggernaut of a city needs its driver back."

Frank gestured to the bank of screens. "I've got something to show you." He hit the remote. Every screen flashed on to show the room in which they were stood. As Frank spoke, his words and reactions were echoed on screen.

"Our conversation today has been playing out over every communication network in the city. But this is not a spontaneous sting, Nikolay. We have your drug trade routes monitored and mapped. N.A.R.P. has infiltrated the dealer network to establish a solid chain of command that leads straight to Obshina Enterprises. The only link missing was the physical location of the production plant. But now we have that too. The icing on the cake is a full and complete confession to all charges."

He gestured to the green statues in every corner of the room and the two seemingly mildewed water spouts out on the balcony. "Vitreous Goo might be legacy technology but it still delivers a clear and accurate picture of real time events."

Nikolay's hand was at the door release patch in seconds. He didn't make it beyond. Frank got a solid grip on the glass tube apparatus and smashed it over the ex-Super Leaguer's head at full force. Nikolay collapsed to the floor.

Frank let his arm drop, the remains of the shattered apparatus hanging limply from his hand. He stared dead ahead into the lens of Goo coating one statue.

"I may be a weak fool." He swiped a hand across his lips. "But I'm getting stronger."

§

Out on the Ziplines, Vlad stood over Zar and broke out a jagged smile.

"Без муки нет науки. *Adversity is a good teacher.* It is my father's saying. He thinks he can scare me into being a better son. But I've played his games before. Now I play on my terms." He put out one of his giant hands. "Give me the sand bricks."

Zar shuffled backwards. His shoulder pulsed with pain, dislocated by the fall.

"They aren't yours!" he spat.

His gaze fell on the reaching hand and a large signet ring on Vlad's index finger. Sooty's words echoed in his mind: "Whoever slugged your dad wore a signet ring the size of a small moon." He remembered the curse Vlad had levied at him in the Death Pit. Zamochit. *The breaking of bones.* A new depth of cold seeped through Zar's flesh. When Vlad said those words a few days earlier, Sol was already dead. In other words, the thug had already delivered on his promise.

"Rot in hell, murderer!" Zar thundered. Grasping the skateboard out of its harness at his back, he smashed it into the thug's ribs. Vlad buckled forwards, the rucksack sliding off his shoulder to hit the deck with a thud. Zar made a grab for it, just as Vlad recovered his footing, lowered his head and rammed Zar hard in the stomach, the momentum carrying both of them over the edge of the track.

Time itself seemed to snag. Zar clawed at the air.

*Not this way, not now.*

His saviour came in the form of an iron handgrip which he grasped with every residual trace of strength. Vlad – a living dead boy – tumbled away below; Zar didn't listen for the impact of soft flesh on the sidewalk below. Every part of him was given over to self-preservation.

He hung suspended at the top of a sharp drop. Dangling by one arm, he looked up to see the thick steel cable that underpinned the track. In the terrifying seconds between life's preservation and plunging to his death, Zar jammed his skateboard underneath the cable with his free hand, sucked in a lungful of air, braced himself against the pain, rocked back and leapt. There was a ricochet of motion as the soft metal trucks of his board bounced off the pinioned wire, and he felt each jolt as a fresh knife to his shoulder. Every cell in his body flamed as he travelled down the drop at lightening speed. Gravity assaulted him like a second skin of lead, and he fought to cling on, fought hard even as the ligaments tore.

Zar screamed in agony. His ears filled with the sound of static, the sky turned the colour of blood, and suddenly he was falling.

§

"Zar! Zar!"

Raina ripped aside the concertinaed iron gate of the elevator and ran out. The upper platform was immersed in morning mist. She froze and tried to listen past the muffled noise of the city. The desert air crushed around her, and all of the blinding rage and heartache she had retained from when her father died came raining down upon her again.

*No, she would not give up hope!*

Eyes greased with tears, she charged to the edge of the platform, slammed her hips against the barrier and stared down into the ether.

"Zar?"

The city whispered below.

"Zar!"

Nothing. Her understanding of hope, of justice, fell apart and she stumbled away from the barrier. The Ramrod, the puzzle pieces, how Zar had come to light her up on the inside...all for nothing now. Crouching, she dropped her chin to her chest and wrapped her arms around her knees. Squeezing shut her eyes, she tried to blank out the world and slip away into the darkness.

Raina sensed the smooth greased motion nearby at the same instant she heard the swish of unfolding steel. Peeling open her eyelids, she looked up to see the steel jaw of a Scooper crane in over the platform. The bucket tipped and lowered. The rubberised seal of the capping net released.

Inside stood Zar, one Lucky 13, sand bricks cradled in his good arm, skateboard underfoot. He grinned and the sun burnt through the mist, filling their world with golden light.

§

# Chapter 34

The elevator rattled to a halt in a great burst of steam.

Zar winced against the pain in his shoulder. He glanced at Raina and shook his head. "I'm sorry about the Ramrod. You guys were there for me through the race and then I go and screw things up for you at the last."

"What do you mean?" Raina put her hand on the elevator gate.

"I didn't cross the finish line. Every team member has to finish, remember?"

The girl didn't reply, just stepped up close, slid a hand around the back of his head and brought his lips to hers. The kiss electrified his senses, spooling down into the pit of him where the sensation mellowed into a new, unexpected calm. All the heartache got wrapped up in it and for those few brief moments, he didn't feel alone.

He smiled, a little foolish, as she pulled away.

"That fall must've really messed with your head, Zar Punkstar."

He raised a quizzical eyebrow and Raina laughed.

"The Scooper dropped you at Black Stacks' private Zipline station. Granted, you chose an unorthodox approach but you crossed the finish line, Zar." Her smile was a radial. "We won, Zar! We won the Ramrod!"

She slung back the elevator door. The noise of the crowd hit him like a seismic wave. Hundreds of flashbulbs blinded him.

§

"Fabrienne."

"Hello, father." Fabrienne's poise faltered under Frank Oz's scrutiny, less R'asian princess than little-girl-lost-in-the-woods.

"Fa."

Frank shifted his attention to his son, who opened his mouth to speak then seemed to think better of it and stayed silent.

Watching from the sidelines with his winning team, Zar saw how the Oz children must look to their father. He had been fixed up by the Medics branch of the Uniform on his arrival, his dislocated arm popped back in and the glass cut from his Rifler run-in at the Casino stitched up. But the Oz twins were equally bruised and dishevelled. Did it hurt Frank to see them like that, or was it enough to have them returned to him? Unlike his eldest son, Franklyn.

Apparently Frank had no intention of sharing how he felt inside.

"Enjoyed your adventure?" he said in a measured tone.

Fabrienne jutted her chin. "Of course, father."

"You flipped your truck, Fa?"

Fa didn't reply, indication enough of his humiliation at the fact.

Frank maintained the same cool tone. "Monster trucks entertain the masses at the Death Pit. Find a driver's car for outside these walls. Something clunky you can really manoeuvre."

His focus switched back to Fabrienne. "Helping Fa meant you lost the rally. You allowed sentiment to rule your head." There was a pause, in which Fabrienne seemed to visibly sink. "Much as I have this past year since Franklyn died, an easy and, I hope, forgivable mistake," Frank added, an audible break in his voice.

There was a difficult silence before Fa said quietly, "Thank you for reinstating the Ramrod, father."

Fabrienne regained her regal air. "We thought we'd entered without your permission, but now I think you meant for us to take part all along."

Frank shook his head, smiling to himself. "Oh no, it took some persuasion for me to agree to either the

Ramrod's reinstatement or your taking part in it. But Braxton always did have the gift of the gab."

Yet again, Zar felt his world somersault. *Braxton* had arranged for Fa and Fabrienne to participate in the Ramrod Rally? Even more impressive, the promoter had persuaded Frank Oz to let his surviving children take part?

"Braxton Earl?" Fa stared at his sister. "The agent," he clarified, and Fabrienne arched one beautiful eyebrow. "He contacted me a couple of days before the Ramrod was officially reinstated. Offered to make us superstars. Said it'd be the ultimate way to show our father that we were capable of racing Pro League out on the city's circuits." He frowned at his father. "Said it'd satisfy you once and for all that we weren't going to end up like Franklyn."

"Said all that, did he?" Frank crossed his arms and nodded. "Braxton really did a number on you." His eyes went to the winning team. "Same as Zar Punkstar," he said at volume, and Zar visibly winced under the great man's scrutiny. "How'd you like Braxton, Zar? Slippery sort? Yeah, I see you agree. I bet your team's had you all mixed up with their defence of him. Wanna know why? Because Braxton didn't build an empire in the Eras without knowing who to butter up or how to dodge the punches. What your team mates know from the time he managed them as desert racers is that Braxton is a rock solid alibi. But it's that first impression of something darker that's kept Braxton in with the city's hoodlums *and* inside the law."

Zar's temper flashfired in spite of his awe at standing in the private quarters of Black Stacks and being addressed by Frank Oz himself. "Since when did Braxton Earl pull the shots?" he demanded. Why was everything so tied up in knots around him? He couldn't tell anymore where the truth began and the lies ended.

Frank narrowed his eyes. "Since Braxton persuaded me to work alongside Homicide and N.A.R.P. to lay a sting for this city's chief drug lord, Nikolay Obshina."

The atmosphere in the room crystallised.

Frank's gaze went to Justice. "The Ramrod was the one race that had always eluded Nikolay. A year ago he bought his way to the prize, and my son and your friend Ruby paid the ultimate price."

Justice's beautiful brown eyes misted.

Frank nodded at the girl in acknowledgement of her pain. He said firmly, "Many times since then I've been tempted to organise a one way trip to hell for my old pal, Nikolay. But there is a right way and a wrong way to exact revenge, and I suspect you know which side I come down on."

Try as he might, Zar couldn't share Frank's restraint. "Shame you didn't act sooner. My father was murdered this week by Nikolay's son!"

This time the emotion was too much to bear. Heart threatening to burst from his chest, Zar felt the hot flood of tears down his cheeks. He scrubbed them away with a fist, but the hurt was overwhelming and his breath caught as he tried to suffocate the sobs. He buried his face in his elbow.

Luckily no one tried to physically comfort him. Instead, he heard Frank say softly, "I know, buddy, I know. Life's a raw deal sometimes."

Bunching his t-shirt up at the waist and wiping his eyes, Zar saw that Frank had lowered his head and was pinching the bridge of his nose. The old man stayed silent a moment. Then he dropped his hand and stared over with such a look of strength that Zar felt simultaneously ashamed and in awe.

"Zar, I didn't become the main financier of Autodrome without setting myself a strict moral code. All evidence needed to point incontestably to Nikolay's guilt before I'd pin Franklyn's death on him, just as you need understand that Vlad might have killed your father but it was Nikolay who sent him to the workshop that day. Why? Well now. The key to that information lies...where, Detective Black?"

"With Sol's blueprints." Detective 'Sooty' Black stepped over the threshold into the room, a black VDU device tucked under an arm. "How are you, Frank?"

Zar felt the final strands of understanding slip from his fingers. What was Sooty doing inside Black Stacks? And why were he and Frank Oz behaving like old friends? "I thought we'd been invited in to shake the hand of Mister Frank and get a trophy. Since when have you and Mister Frank been pals, Sooty?" he said raggedly, his voice betraying the sluice of emotions inside of him.

"Since Detective Black headed up the Homicide investigation into the murders of Franklyn and Ruby a year ago." Frank's voice got an edge. "Folks, Zar and I have business with Detective Black. If you wouldn't mind stepping out a while."

Fa and Fabrienne looked confused, but alongside the others, started for the door.

"Not you, Special Agent Valentine Heart?" said Frank – and Zar's heart leapt. The secret was out.

Valentine adjusted his hat and squinted over. "Mister Frank."

"Sheesh, Valentine!" exploded Eight Ball. "You're a N.A.R.P. cop? Ya kidding me! Remind me never to rattle your cage."

"If I was interested in gang spats, I'd have hauled you to the clink way back, Eight Ball. As it stands, you're Mary Poppins next to the dirty rats I've been hanging with."

Valentine stared at Persia, who let out an abrupt, hysterical laugh.

"You always were a cheese weasel," she said. A sour smile corrupted her perfect features. Zar caught the shimmer of tears in her eyes. It stilled his own heightened emotions. She quickly glanced away.

Superficially at least, the N.A.R.P officer remained all about the job.

"You want me to stick around?" said Valentine to Frank, squaring his shoulders.

Frank inclined his head. "I've you to thank for this past year of N.A.R.P. investigation. If its okay with Zar, I reckon you're entitled to some answers too."

Zar was dumbfounded. The man seemed so free and easy with the information he had fought to uncover and protect!

"I didn't risk my neck out on the Ziplines just so I could hand over my dad's secrets," he spat. "No offence, Mister Frank, you're a racing god, but this week has been hell on earth and I can't tell who's the angel and who's the demon anymore. My team, they've had my back these last twenty four hours, but I've only just met you."

Frank smiled gently.

"Go on now Fa, Fabrienne," he said softly. Seemingly relieved to escape the formalities, the twins disappeared off down the corridor, already debating which out of the two had proven the better racer over the course of the Ramrod.

"Zar, you gotta trust Frank," Sooty shot aside, but Frank held up his hand.

"You don't have to do anything anymore, do you, Zar? Life's dealt you a bad hand and I doubt you're inclined to trust a living soul because you're told to. I knew another like you once. Franklyn, my eldest. He was sparky. But now my two youngest keep me on my toes."

Zar saw a bob of sentiment in the man's throat. Frank kept his gaze steady.

"So your team have earned your respect. I hope I can do the same. You may not be aware of the fact, but Nikolay Obshina was arrested this morning on suspicion of drug trafficking and three counts of solicitation to commit first degree murder."

Zar gasped, as if a tourniquet had released from around his guts. He tucked his hands under his armpits.

"Three counts? Ruby, Franklyn, and my father, Sol." His expression darkened.

"So, you say your trust your team?" Frank stared at Zar intently.

"I do." Zar glanced behind him. His gaze settled on Raina. The girl looked uncertain, as if trying to make her mind up whether to go to him. He held out his hand and she stepped up beside him. Her hand slid into his, firm and comforting.

Frank nodded. "Okay then." He gestured to Sooty. "I see you got my VDU Mat back from the investigation. Wanna set it up on this table?"

As Sooty set the machine down and started it up, Frank concentrated on Zar.

"I want to play you a message that was sent to me by your father a short time ago. I'm sorry to say my previous debilitation meant I didn't receive it until Detective Black traced it here yesterday. I think you and your team mates will find the contents of the message very interesting."

§

Seeing his father's face materialise above the VDU Mat unleashed a new, intense mess of pain in Zar. He crushed his hand around Raina's. His eyes ached with tears yet to fall.

The hologram showed professional restraint. His father had attempted to control his natural, erratic energy when delivering his message to Frank Oz, Zar realised. Which meant it had been of incalculable importance to Sol.

"Frank. It's been a few years but I'm hoping you remember me. Sol Punkstar, was architect now inventor." Sol nervously tugged out the band to loosen his hair then bunched it back into a ponytail. "I've got to tell you a story, Frank, and I'm sorry to say every word is true. I haven't broadcast these facts before now because I was scared for the safety of my wife and boy. But things have got to the point when I'm less and less certain I'll see in a new sunrise. As for my family, well, perhaps they'd be safer facing their enemies head on."

Clearly burdened by what he had to say, Sol still spoke with clarity. "Several years ago I worked as chief architect for Obshina Enterprises. In accordance with Nikolay Obshina's requirements, I drew up designs for an underground production plant in the desert south of the Eras." Sol shook his head, a little wild and looking more of the man Zar had come to know and tolerate as a father. "I confused Nikolay with a decent human being. There he was, creating such a vital additional to Autodrome's brilliant future, and I had an idea and needed someone to share it with."

Sol's eyes burnt out from the hologram. "An air engine, Frank. I was in the process of inventing an air engine. Just think of the freedom if the fuel to drive our automobiles was free. Just think of the economic consequences for the city, how it'd narrow the gap between east and west." He frowned. "Back then, my idea required nurturing. I still needed to find the spark of life to fuel the engine, but the blueprint was coming along very nicely. Nikolay was impressed. What a vision! What a future! I was put on retainer with the understanding we would jointly launch the technology on completion. Except, a man like Nikolay Obshina was never going to play fair. And then there was the underground production plant. I wasn't the most streetwise man in the world, but I got enough from Nikolay's requirements to know the plant had nothing to do with automobile design and everything to do with large scale pharmaceutical production."

Sol let out a sigh. He rubbed his eyes, blinked and refocused. "When I confronted Nikolay and told him I was rescinding the offer of a share in my air engine design, he threatened my wife and son. I countered that I retained the blueprint detailing the precise location of the Razzledazzle plant. We parted company on a stalemate, but not before Nikolay had already got his hooks into somebody close to me."

His Adam's apple bobbed. "Nikolay organised for my wife to be seduced by drugs. She was having a hard time of it with a young child and me working late more often than not, and she got this new friend. Susan Green — divorcee, employer of Obshina Enterprises, Razzledazzle dealer. Nikolay confessed to setting the whole thing up the day I took back my integrity but lost any rights to stick around my family." Sol tugged at his ponytail. "Figured I'd done enough damage by that point."

Zar felt himself mentally tuck up into a ball. He pictured his mother in the decaying bubble of their home, the demands of a child exaggerated by her husband's absence — and felt fresh guilt for the path she took. He forced himself to concentrate on his father's voice.

"For the longest time, it's been in Nikolay's interests to keep me alive. But recently I hit on the spark to ignite my air engine, and now it seems even the walls have eyes." Sol got back his maniacal look. "I am afraid for my wife and son. I keep my distance but..." His eyes moved side-to-side. He was edgy as a cat. "As I said earlier, it may be a case of my son facing his enemies head on. Which is why in the event of my death, he alone will have access to the blueprint." Sol fixed on the air in front of him. "If Zar succeeds in unlocking the blueprints, I trust you to do right by them, Frank. Use the air engine for good. As for Nikolay's drug pit, well, you know what to do there." He appeared to struggle for words before adding, "And, Frank. Please tell my boy, Zar, something from me. Wish him luck, love, a long life, and, if he can manage it, compassion."

The hologram cut out. Zar's stomach churned. It was like losing his father all over again.

He let Raina go. She pressed a palm to the small of his back. A brief smile crossed her beautiful lips and a secret pact passed between them, to do with support and care and mutual need. She returned to the others.

Zar became aware of a different hand on his shoulder.

"Enough bad things have happened in this city over recent years. Its time I got back on my feet and helped Autodrome do the same." Frank nodded towards the VDU Mat. "Starting with this air engine invention of your father's. Reckon you can solve his puzzle now you got all the pieces?"

Zar pulled a sand brick from each pocket and weighed the measure of them. "I just don't know," he said softly.

"Once I get hold of Tripster, we might be able to work something out."

"The kid in the tank chair?" Frank pointed at a second door and tucked up his lips. "In there, and I have to say I'll be grateful if you'd distract him. Only so many questions a fella can answer about himself before the enthusiasm starts to wane."

"Tripster's here?" Zar didn't know how to even begin to process that piece of information. All he knew was how overwhelmingly happy he was to know his friend was near.

"He is, and I have him to thank for the technology that enabled us to broadcast Nikolay's confession this morning. See for yourself." Frank walked steadily over to a bank of screens across one wall. He lit them up with a flash of a remote.

Zar saw Nikolay leaning over Frank, who was seated. The ex Super Leaguerer's words rang out. "...But I give them an escape, a way to fuel their inner happiness. I give them Razzledazzle. And thanks to Sol Punkstar's invention, I'll soon achieve a monopoly over the global market."

"They're playing reruns on every station," explained Frank.

Zar sensed his amazement mirrored by the rest of his team. Each screen showed some section of the same conversation between Frank and Nikolay inside the very room they were standing in now.

"Tripster helped you to do this," he said quietly. All he could think was what a talent, and what a friend!

§

Zar entered Frank's office to find Tripster hunched over his VDU Mat, busy with the holographic images of the sand bricks he'd rendered earlier and surrounded by racks of old Data Streamer watches. Braxton Earl sat at the large desk, pranging one of the parabolic mirror arms of the Paranascope.

"Kid!" Braxton raised a finger to his lips. "I mean, Zar. Come in, fella. Come in." He cocked his head towards Tripster. "Your buddy here's just about cracked the gist of it."

Tripster broke out a big friendly smile. "Zar, man. Are we glad to have you back or what? When that Rifler brat appeared on your watch, I was sure you were a gona."

"Hey, Braxton. Tripster." Zar bobbed his head in greeting, but then couldn't find a reason to suppress how he really felt and grinned broadly. "It's good to see you, bud. Thanks so much for having my back out there."

"Oh. Yeah. Sure, no problem." Tripster looked taken aback. He nervily rubbed a finger across his nostrils, but at last nodded gravely and seemed to understand how much Zar meant it.

"We tried to warn you, Zar. Braxton, he had a heads up on Jesse's double-crossing thanks to Nikolay's fat mouth." Tripster's eyes widened. "Braxton's one of the good guys, Zar. Sooty confirmed it."

"So I hear."

"It's a vicious rumour." Braxton winked. "Now don't you go spreading it."

The promoter tapped the Paranascope crank.

"Reckon its time to fire up this baby."

He twisted the crank. The scroll rotated around the spool and the extraordinary hologram of Autodrome flickered into view. Gasps came from the doorway; while his team were respectful enough to keep their distance, natural curiosity glued them to events inside the office.

Zar offloaded the sand bricks out of his pockets onto the desk. He emptied the other two out of his rucksack.

"Okay. Each sand brick has a barcode that corresponds to its number puzzle. We're talking tiny engravings. There. You see?" Tripster held up a sand brick to the light that came streaming in at the office's expansive windows. Zar squinted at the brick's surface. Like a magic eye picture, the barcode suddenly offered itself up.

"2, 3, 1."

"This brick aligns with the first number sequence. Get it? Now, here's the clever bit. We can slot the bricks together by lining up the number sequences with one another." Tripster squinted at another brick. "1, 6 and 4. This is the fourth piece you found? What about the trinket?"

Zar unloaded the brass icons from his back pocket – the 'zero' eight ball, the pin up, the skull, and the heart.

"If we just bring these babies together…" Tripster slotted the four bricks together to form a rough ball. He inspected it. His nose crinkled. "I may be tripping here, Zar, but I think that's a keyhole."

"The Albatross beak!" Zar exclaimed. Of course! The brick ball had the same lock mechanism as the secret compartment in Sol's garage pit and each section of the puzzle trail.

But his hope sank like a stone. "The Rifler chief stole it."

"Well, in this company, someone gotta have a spare. Mister Frank, Braxton?" Tripster held out his hands expectantly.

"I live my racing dreams through my kids. I might have built this city, but its professional racing circuit was always out of my league," said Frank with clear regret.

"Likewise," echoed Braxton.

"Valentine? Eight Ball? Justice?" Zar's gaze switched sharply between the team members at the doorway.

Eight Ball shook his head. "Sorry, bro. We were desert racers. Pro League was never our style."

"Great." Zar felt hollow. Without the brass beak, he was still locked out of the secrets Sol had died to protect.

"I know where you can get one."

Raina stepped past the rest of the team and into the office.

Zar thought she looked mesmerising in the pale gold light spilling in at the window. Her hair washed over her shoulders, its exuberant browns mixed in with reds and ambers. And that face – all cheekbones and almond eyes.

She stared at Zar. "Remember me saying that my father didn't believe in desecrating his winnings?"

"The fountain in your family's courtyard!" Zar's voice was light with possibility. He wanted to hold the girl and press his lips to hers again so that he could rescue her from the pain of her past, just as she was rescuing him.

"My dad believed in the perfect rider and the perfect race." Raina smiled. "Since it's you in need of the beak, I think he'd approve."

§

Raina returned inside the hour and presented Zar with the brass beak. Her face flushed as his fingers lingered around hers.

"I know what this means to you."

She met his gaze. "I know you do."

He released his grip and passed the beak to Tripster, who grasped it with enthusiasm, fitted it in the keyhole and turned it. There was a dull click.

Tripster stuck his tongue out a corner of his mouth. "Now that is something." He held the ball to the light. Then he twisted it apart to some degree, the upper half shifting anti-clockwise, the lower half clockwise. "Your dad certainly knew how to bury a secret." He offered the brick ball up to Zar. "Take a look."

Zar took the ball in his hands. It had twisted open to reveal a thin metal band around its radius. Text spiralled around the metal band. Zar revolved the ball and read out the words.

"Luck. Love. Long Life. Compassion." He glanced at Frank. "Same message my dad asked you to give me. Luck..." His hand lingered over the 'zero' eight ball trinket before moving to the brass pin-up girl. "Love." He resisted glancing in Raina's direction and moved onto the skull. "Long Life," he said with a sardonic smile. His gaze settled on the heart. "Compassion," he said softly.

Tripster fizzled over with energy. "The final trinket. The heart." He threw his arms out wide. "What's the heart of this city, Mister Frank?"

Resting against his desk as naturally as if he'd never been away from it, Frank Oz answered determinedly, "Black Stacks."

Tripster squinted back at Zar. "I'm guessing your dad needs an offering."

Carrying the brick ball, Zar entered the holographic map of Autodrome and strode over to where the representation of Black Stacks broke free of the surrounding buildings. He raised his arms and positioned the ball over the top of the factory like a guiding star. Instantly, lines of brilliant blue burst from its centre, streaking out in all directions, over and under one another until at last they resolved themselves into two projected sheets of information – one, an architectural blueprint, the other, a series of interlayered sketches and algorithms.

Valentine removed his hat and peered at the architectural blueprint. "The production plant," he marvelled.

Admiring the web of sketches and algorithms, Tripster whispered, "The air engine." He pointed up at a row of symbols and froze suddenly. "Your dad only went and redefined the thing he hated most, Zar. The true act of compassion."

Eyes like miniature supernovas, Tripster stared across at Zar who held the ball of intelligence over the iron heart of the city. "The air engine's creative genome is Razzledazzle, Zar. Razzledazzle is the life spark!"

§

# Chapter 35

Spectators crowded the terraces. Engines roared, cranks juddered, pistons wheezed, air horns blasted, and Zar breathed it all in. It felt ridiculously good to be back in the Death Pit.

"There's Braxton!" Raina pulled him after her down the wide terrace steps.

Braxton greeted them at the bottom. Sharp suited, skin the tone of umber, he held out his arms.

"How's my favourite pair of love birds?"

Zar scuffed at his hair. But when Raina squeezed his hand and curved her soft red lips, the embarrassment switched into a whole deal of liking. She was beautiful, this girl at his side. He fed his arm about her waist and drew her closer.

"It's great to be back." *Wasn't it just?* He listened to the latest batch of reengineered vehicles fighting it out in the arena. Every flash of steel and lick of revs combined into a dark lullaby. It rocked his sorrows to sleep.

Braxton flashed his shark smile. "How long you been signed to Braxton Earl Promotions, Zar? One week, two max, and already I got a big shooter wanting to make you an offer. Over here, kid...Ah, I'll call you kid if I want to.

I've earned that much," he shot in answer to Zar's glare. "Come on."

They followed Braxton to the far end of the terrace where a group of suits were holed up in a roped off VIP area.

"Business with Mister Raol," Braxton told the bodyguards on duty.

One of the suits broke free of the group, shouting, "Braxton! Good to see you. Yes, let him in. The others too."

The bodyguards unpinned the rope.

Mister Raol greeted them with back slaps and enthusiasm. He was an imposing man, broad shouldered, shrewd eyed, and seemingly settled into the spread of age and quietly pleased about it.

Braxton knocked Zar with an elbow. "Zar, meet Mister Raol, one of Autodrome's chief financial investors in all things race related."

"Although I must stress I'm not so much a business stiff as a race enthusiast. I'm about the grit and grime of the road, Zar. Right now, I'm looking to sign a bunch of Pro League racers alongside the best of the rest, and your name, well, it's got to be top of that list." The investor's cheeks coloured up. Zar recognised the reaction as awkwardness but couldn't understand why. But then

Mister Raol gave up on his restraint and Zar found himself locked in a generous embrace.

Mister Raol pulled away to clutch Zar's stiffened shoulders. "You saved my boy's life! Eugene Raol," he clarified, adding eagerly, "He was in the care of a bodyguard called Persia Gold. At least until the little punk decided to slug her one. As I hear it, the lucky critter only escaped the Death Pit alive because you muscled in with a dose of insulin that kept him out the grave. But, hell, I'd have noticed a Pro League newbie with the kind of skills you are offering anyway. Same goes for your girl here. Raina Jubilique." Mister Raol presented his hand to Raina. "Two weeks after the Ramrod and you're still the darling of the broadsheets. Way you handled that fire truck?" He shook his head in wonderment.

Leaning in, he shook both of their hands again. "Anyway, Braxton's got the details. You have a read of the terms I'm offering. Generous terms, I should add. I'll await your responses with eager anticipation."

Zar glanced across at Raina, who shrugged her shoulders.

"Mister Raol. I'm still not clear what exactly it is that you're asking Raina and me to sign up to?" he confessed.

Braxton and Mister Raol exchanged a look. Their excitement bubbled over.

"I'm bringing back the desert races," said Mister Raol, made young again by his obvious delight. "And I've got to tell you, Zar Punkstar, Raina Jubilique. I hope you've made peace with the devil that is the Sabkha because I want you both on board."

§

"It's a good offer." Braxton took a slurp from his snow cone. He nodded at the empty arena. "You're meant for more than this, Zar."

"Maybe." Zar tucked his arms around his waist. It all still felt like a dream – the best sort of dream – but it was impossible for him to move on when he still had questions needing answers.

"Braxton, I've got to ask you. All this stuff with my dad, how you worked alongside Homicide and N.A.R.P and Mister Frank to bring Nikolay in. How'd you know about Sol's invention in the first place?"

Braxton looked him straight in the eye. "Remember the first time we met over at your place. I told you Sol and I were buddies. Don't think you believed me. You're a fella got to see things with your own eyes, but Sol never was one to share his life's details easily. Over the years, he and I would share a beer now and then and remember

427

the good times when he was a mechanic over at the drag strips and I'd ambitions of my own. Over the course of those conversations, he told me about his invention, an air engine, also Nikolay's threats. I didn't take either seriously. I even went so far as try to buddy up with Nikolay once, so convinced was I Sol had a mind full of nonsense. Didn't take me long in Nikolay's company to see that I was the fool." Braxton shifted uneasily in his seat. The memories took their toll. "Anyway, Sol comes to me one night and gets the promise I'll help you race the Ramrod in the event of his death. You know the rest."

Zar stared back at Braxton. "Thanks for making good on that promise."

"No problem, kid."

"And you're right. You did give me an ice cream once. I remember now."

Braxton nodded slowly. He looked past Zar's shoulder and his mouth lit up.

"You find them, gal?"

"One of them, plus another couple of stragglers" said Raina with a smile.

"IHola!" Raina's flashy friend followed, encased in a tight red dress, and in company.

"Hey guys!" Tripster's tank chair descended the wide steps of the terraces, snorting merrily like a metal warthog.

As Tripster pulled in alongside the bench, Zar lent in. "So you and Katiana an item now?"

Tripster winked. "Well, you know." He tapped the arm of his tank chair. "Girls can't resist a set of wheels, man."

On cue, the crowds parted like a biblical sea and Persia Gold emerged.

"Howdy. Mind if I haul up a while, dudes?" Persia's luscious lips crept up.

"Persia! Wow, you look, well, like you always look." Zar caught Raina's eye but the two girls just shrugged at one another and laughed.

"Still cute, still got a smart mouth." Persia put a cowboy boot up on the bench, a pose that only exaggerated her long limbs and which had passersby literally tripping over each other. "So how's it hanging?"

Zar rubbed a hand around the back of his neck. "Day at a time kind of deal, you know?" he said honestly, and Persia nodded in acknowledgement.

"And your momma?"

"Sooty's taking care of her over at his pad. Whether she'll stay clean...well, her and Sooty, they got each other."

"And as long as Mister Frank delivers on his promise and gets the air engine up and running, Razzledazzle will have a whole new application. Maybe it'll dry up at street level." Raina's angular face darkened. "Or at least sky rocket in price because of its rarity."

Zar nodded. "Either way, Sooty'll work it out."

"Sounds like someone's ready to spread their wings." Persia's tone was somewhere between concern and acceptance.

"Parents. They're breakable. Best not to rely on them." Zar knew his words were harsh but, strangely, they comforted him. He turned 16 in a couple of months. It was time to free himself of ghosts, living or dead.

"So where's the rest of the gang?" interrupted Braxton with his air of a ringmaster. In answer, a roar of engines broke out and the studded roller pulled aside. A fresh barrage of metal monsters charged into the arena. Tearing up the dampened dust, they let loose the hells bells of their air horns.

"One guess," said Raina.

Zar studied the vehicles and there they were – three ex-desert racers unleashed. Encased in the glorious golden angles of his Cadillac, Valentine raised his hat in greeting. Matchstick in mouth, Eight Ball leant out the glassless window of a ghost-flamed black and yellow

Buick. He knocked a hand off his brow and crowed like a rooster. Slunk down in the open cock pit of a skeletal Superstox, Justice waved, seemed to notice Braxton and offered a less friendly salute.

Zar saw the promoter's face drop.

"Justice still hasn't forgiven you for the fight you arranged between her and Ruby, huh?" He almost felt sorry for Braxton. Almost.

"We got time to mend." Braxton shrugged, but it was clear he laboured under a weight of guilt. Having assisted in Vladimir's death, even if the brute deserved it, Zar knew what it felt like to carry that burden. There was no lightening it though for either of them.

He switched his attention to Persia. "What about you and Valentine?"

"We're talking." she replied tersely. She met his gaze and added more softly, "That's enough for now."

Before he could reply, Zar felt a tap on his shoulder.

"Punkstar."

He turned around to see Davey X grinning at him.

"Davey! Hey. How's it going?"

"Same old violence, different day. Look, your buddies down there asked me to give you a message. They said to tell you to eyeball number 9."

"What the..?"

Alongside his companions, Zar stood up and approached the barrier separating the crowd from the battlefield. He squinted across the arena at a beaten up old Chevy, the number 9 slapped lopsidedly across the wing. A grinning imp was in the driver's seat. An antique Data Streamer watch at his wrist, the Rifler chief, Lothaniel waved enthusiastically to the crowds. At least until he spotted Zar. The fire visibly drained from him.

Davey nodded towards the arena. "Gonna remind those freaks how to play hard ball?" He held out a set of keys. "I hear there's a reconditioned 1931 Ford roadster backstage. Goes by the name of Grey Rat?"

Zar beamed and snatched up the keys. "Thanks, dude."

Staring out at the steam and gas titans, he felt a thrill in the pit of his stomach.

Raina's soft hands pressed either side his face.

"Go get him, Lucky 13."